THE MIDNIGHT GUARDIAN
HOUR OF DARKNESS

by John C. Bruening

A Flinch Books Production

THE MIDNIGHT GUARDIAN: HOUR OF DARKNESS

Copyright © 2016 by John C. Bruening

All concepts and characters © 2016 John C. Bruening

Cover illustration: Thomas Gianni
Cover design and interior page formatting: Maggie Ryel

Editors: Jim Beard and Duane Spurlock

ISBN: 978-0-9977903-0-6

Flinch Books and the Flinch Books logo
© Jim Beard and John C. Bruening

Contact us at www.facebook.com/flinchbooks
and at flinchbooks@yahoo.com

For Mariah,
who had no doubt

PROLOGUE
1922

It was early August, and the summer had not been kind to Union City.

Jimmy stood in the stairway vestibule and glanced out the window at the street five stories below him. Outside, a heavy fog hung in the night air, diffusing the glow from the streetlamps into a murky haze and shutting out the moonlight entirely.

The damp and oppressive weather was nothing new. So far this season, there had been very little sun and far too much rain, and temperatures had remained cool. For what seemed like months, a persistent cloud had taken a permanent position over the beleaguered metropolis.

The vestibule was a small space, ten feet by eight feet, that separated the stairwell from the main hallway of the fifth floor. The building was the Union City Justice Center—the seat of judicial authority serving not just the city proper but the entire county surrounding it. The fifth floor of the Justice Center housed the offices of the district attorney and his staff.

By day, the forty-year-old building hummed with activity as lawyers, investigators, judges and other dedicated personnel picked up where the police left off—weighing evidence, hearing testimony, delivering sentences, waging the eternal battle to keep the scales balanced and keep the people safe. Most nights, though, with the late hours of one day giving way to the wee hours of the next, the halls were dark and silent. Most nights, the only security on hand would have been a single guard, someone to make the rounds throughout the building once every hour and inevitably watch the sun come up without incident.

But tonight was not like most nights. Tonight was different. Tonight, the stakes were much higher, and an uneventful night was anything but guaranteed.

Jimmy was a police lieutenant with nineteen-and-a-half years on the Union City force. He'd been put in charge of a six-man detail of officers—himself and Joe Dobbs at the top of the stairs, two more men at the building's main entrance at street level, and two more at the rear entrance leading out to the parking garage.

Dobbs glanced out the same window at the gloom and shook his head. "Nothing like the night shift, eh, Lieutenant?" The undercurrent of sarcasm was unmistakable. He was a young cop, less than two years out of the academy. As such, he had very little control over where he landed on the duty roster on any given week. For him and rookies like him, the overnight shift was as common as it was unpopular.

Jimmy shrugged. "Doesn't bother me," he said. "I've been doing it for years."

Dobbs' brow furrowed. "Yeah, I know. I don't get it. You've put in almost twenty years, and you still spend more time working this city in the dark than in the daylight."

Jimmy frowned. "That's just the way it worked for me. My wife's a schoolteacher. She went off to school every morning, and I got to be at home with my son during the day when he was growing up."

"With that kind of a schedule, it's a surprise you and she had a kid at all."

Jimmy grinned. He didn't say a word, but the twinkle in his eye suggested that he and his wife had managed to find enough time together along the way to do what needed to be done to start a family.

Dobbs responded with a sly grin of his own. "How old is your boy now?" he said.

"Hardly a boy anymore," said Jimmy. "Just turned eighteen. Starting college in just a few weeks."

"College? Hey, that's great. Guess that means no overnight police beat for him, huh?"

"Nah. He's got big plans. Always has. Ever since he was a kid. Science, engineering. Always building things."

Dobbs nodded. "Yeah? Hey, maybe he can come back and build us a baseball stadium, like the one they just finished a couple months ago in New York for the Yankees."

Just a few blocks away, the clock in the tower of St. Michael's Cathedral tolled the midnight hour. The ominous sound made its way through the quiet downtown streets and up the stairwell of the Justice Center. At the final stroke, Jimmy turned to Dobbs. Neither man bothered to check his watch. St. Michael was never wrong.

"You took the last round," said Jimmy. "I guess I'm up." He checked his flashlight and dug the keys out of his pocket. He turned and unlocked the heavy oak door leading into the hallway, a space of paneled walls and tiled floor that began with a waiting area furnished with a receptionist's desk and a few chairs, then opened up to a wider space with a series of secretarial desks arranged bullpen style. Along each wall of this open space were the offices of the district attorney, his assistants and other higher-ranking staff members.

He'd been up here a few times before—in the daytime hours, when the offices were humming with activity and energy. Tonight, the hallway was quiet, dimly lit by the eerie glow of a single low-watt bulb in an emergency ceiling fixture just above where he was standing, and by an identical fixture at the opposite end of the ceiling.

Jimmy flicked on the flashlight and began his sweep of the entire floor, stopping to poke his head into every room along the wall— offices, meeting rooms, even storage closets and restrooms. He did a thorough sweep of each space with the flashlight beam. The first few rooms, at least, looked just as dark and quiet as they had two hours earlier when he last checked the hallway.

The police department normally didn't assign an overnight detail to the Justice Center, but the circumstances of this night were unusual. The official explanation from above had been short and cryptic: They were there to guard some important files that were being stored temporarily in a safe in the district attorney's office.

But Jimmy had seen and heard enough to know that there was more to this assignment than just the official explanation. He'd been following the stories in the *Tribune* and on the *Chronicle* for more than a year now. He'd heard the talk in the precinct—some of it out in the open, some of it in hushed tones among his superiors behind half-closed doors. He'd heard the news out of Chicago—about Capone and the bootlegging and the gangland killings—and he knew that similar stories were playing out in other cities as well, including the one where he lived and worked.

Something dark had descended upon Union City, something sinister that preyed on people's worst fears and exploited their baser instincts at the same time. If there was something he could do to drive it away—even some small thing—he would do it without hesitating or flinching.

The assignment had come directly from the chief—as opposed to the chief's second in command, Captain Taggert, which would have been consistent with the usual protocol. That alone led Jimmy to believe that there was something pretty important behind this security detail. When the chief had first approached him, there was the implication that if all went well, there would be a promotion at the other end. Jimmy hoped so. A bump in rank would mean a bump in pay, which would come in handy with his son getting ready to start college in the fall.

College. It was an opportunity Jimmy himself had never had. But the police work had suited him well—well enough for him to stay on the force for nearly twenty years. He had done well, and he had no regrets. But his son would go to college, and Jimmy knew he would do well in his own way. He was a bright kid, full of energy and enthusiasm. Good grades, and athletic too. Smart as a whip. A natural at anything mechanical or electrical. Hell, there wasn't a single gadget that he couldn't...

Jimmy stopped.

The beam of his flashlight froze on the wall of the corridor as he tried to tune his ears to a momentary sound in the distance. It was brief, something faint, from well beyond the fifth floor. A pop-pop-pop, like firecrackers. Outside the building. Down on the street, most likely.

He turned, took a step back toward the vestibule. "Dobbs?"

A pause, then Dobbs' voice came back to him from the doorway dividing the vestibule from the main hallway: "Lieutenant? Did you hear that?"

"Yeah. Was that outside?" He started heading back toward Dobbs at a brisk pace, his hand unconsciously hovering around the service revolver at his right hip.

"I think so," said Dobbs. The younger officer stood backlit in the doorway, his face shadowed in the dim lighting, but as Jimmy retraced his steps toward the entrance to the hallway, he could hear the sudden tension in the younger cop's voice. "Not sure, but it sounded—"

Dobbs never finished the sentence.

The next moments passed through Jimmy's mind in agonizing slow motion as the entire doorway separating the vestibule from the rest of the fifth floor—and a large portion of the wall around the doorway—erupted in a deafening explosion. In a split second that could just as easily have been an eternity, his mind could register only confusion as the blast sent a barrage of plaster, mortar, wood and other debris in all directions, including his own.

Jimmy felt himself being thrown backward by the blast—back into the main office space—like some discarded rag doll. He slammed into something—a wall, maybe a column—and slid to the floor with a hard thud. His shoulders had taken most of the impact, but his head took enough of a bang to cloud his senses. The room spun crazily. He lost consciousness briefly. Thirty seconds? A couple minutes? There was no way to know.

When he came to, he was aware of a searing pain in his right leg, but the ringing in his ears was even more disorienting than any pain in his extremities.

He heard shouting from some other part of the building, at least three or four different voices. He couldn't make out specific words, but the voices themselves sounded hostile. Not police response, but something else entirely. Something adversarial. He was fairly certain the sound was coming from one of the lower floors. After a few seconds, the shouting grew louder, mixed with rapid footsteps, and he realized that whoever he was hearing was coming up the stairs. Quickly.

Coming for the files.

Jimmy tried to stand, only to be stopped suddenly by a knife of pain that shot from his leg to his hip and further upward. He winced, let out only a small grunt, and settled back onto the floor.

All the lights in the hallway were out. That and the haze of dust raised by the explosion made it hard for Jimmy to see his immediate surroundings. The nearest light source was the damaged ceiling fixture in the vestibule that hung limp from its mounting, flickering and sputtering, throwing an eerie, uneven glow into the main hallway where he lay. It was enough light for him to make out the jumble of overturned chairs, loose papers, toppled file cabinets, broken glass and other debris covering the floor all around him.

He reached down for his flashlight, but it wasn't in his belt. He realized that he'd been holding it at the time of the blast, and that it must have been knocked out of his hand. Squinting in the darkness and the haze, he saw it within arm's reach and grabbed it. He turned it on just long enough to examine his leg. It was mess. His pant leg was torn and bloody from mid-thigh all the way to his shoe.

He guessed that he'd taken a hit from a sizable chunk of debris, and the blood and the pain were enough to tell him that the wound was pretty severe. He stared at the tattered pant leg for a couple more seconds, just long enough to see the stain of blood spreading across what was left of the fabric.

More than severe, he thought.

He shut off the flashlight and forced himself to remain calm, to think clearly. He almost called for Dobbs, but with the sounds from the stairs getting closer, he kept quiet. Instead, he turned the flashlight back on and scanned the devastated space that had been an office just a few minutes earlier.

He swept once around the area with the beam, then a second time. The entire place was in a shambles, much like the space immediately around him, but he spotted Dobbs on the third sweep. He was lying on his side, about halfway between Jimmy's position on the floor and the blown-out doorway. Dobbs was facing away from Jimmy, his body unmoving and partly eclipsed by a large overturned desk. There was no way to tell at this distance or in this minimal light whether Dobbs was breathing. Whatever the case, he didn't look good.

Jimmy crawled toward him, trying not to jar his damaged leg but only having minimal luck in the process. He locked his jaw down hard, forcing himself not to cry out. Crossing a distance of only twelve feet seemed to take an eternity that was probably no more than twenty seconds, but he eventually reached Dobbs.

He edged around the overturned desk just enough to get a view of the back of the young officer's head. It was all he needed to see. Part of the skull had been blown open by the blast, and what was left was a mass of blood, shattered bone and gray matter. There was no need to look into his eyes or check for a pulse.

He could only assume that the four men of the security detail stationed at ground level had met a similar fate.

Jimmy slid back behind the desk, listening as the footsteps and the shouting grew louder. Whoever they were, they'd be at the fifth floor in another thirty seconds at the most.

Propped on one elbow, he reached down and unholstered his service revolver, quickly checking to make sure it was fully loaded. He turned slightly and glanced over his shoulder at the door to the DA's office some thirty feet behind him. The glass window on the door had shattered, but apparently the door itself had been far enough away from the source of the blast that it was still on its hinges—and presumably still locked.

The footsteps were coming up the last flight of steps. Jimmy heard an exchange of surly, barking voices.

"Fifth floor!"

"This is it, Duke!"

Jimmy peered around the side of the desk and squinted into the flickering light of the vestibule. He saw the first figure appear at the top of the stairs, and hesitated a half-second to make sure it wasn't a police officer. The figure wore a long black coat. His face was rat-like, with a pencil-thin mustache, and his greased-back hair caught the glimmer of the flickering light overhead. He held a Thompson semiautomatic machine gun in both hands, and he looked as though he was getting ready to aim it into the blown-out doorway and into the main office area.

Definitely not a police officer.

Jimmy took aim and fired. The bullet caught the gunman in the face, and he immediately went down.

There was a momentary silence, and Jimmy could only figure that it was taking a few seconds for the gunman's partners to realize what had just happened. And then there was shouting, and the frantic scuffle of feet as the men behind the first gunman—how many, he didn't know—scrambled for cover.

After a moment, a voice from the vestibule shouted into the main room: "Ya might as well give it up right now, copper! We got a lotta guns out here!"

"Yeah," Jimmy whispered to himself, "but one less shooter than you had a few seconds ago."

A second Tommy gun poked around the broken remains of the door frame—the shooter protected by what was left of the wall—and spat a stream of lead down the hallway. Whoever was shooting obviously had no idea that Jimmy was on the floor, because the hail of bullets sailed three feet over his head.

Jimmy took aim at the trigger hand, the only part of the gunman that was exposed, and squeezed off another shot. The spray of bullets stopped suddenly, and an anguished curse from behind the broken wall confirmed that his aim had been true.

Jimmy started feeling a little shaky. He glanced down at his pant leg and saw that it was now completely soaked. He was losing a lot of blood. Way too much. A couple more minutes—maybe less—and he'd slip into shock.

A head poked around the edge of the doorway. Jimmy fired, but the head ducked back behind the wall too quickly.

A voice said, "Floor! He's on the floor!"

A third gunman with a Tommy took a bold step into the open space and laid down a line of fire along the floor. The gunman had started his sweep about eight or ten feet to Jimmy's left, which gave Jimmy the second or two he needed to take aim at the gunman's chest and fire.

The gunman rocked back and dropped the weapon, but not before two rounds from the machine gun tore into Jimmy's left shoulder.

Jimmy swore. The dull pain in his leg was now eclipsed by the fire in his collarbone. What's more, the shaking grew worse by the second. In another minute he wouldn't be able to shoot at all.

He'd taken down two gunmen and wounded a third. But how many more were in the hallway? And how many more might be coming up the stairs?

And then he heard the sirens.

Okay, he thought. *Hold them off for just a couple more minutes. Just a couple more.*

He had three more rounds in his revolver, and more ammo in his belt. But were his hands even steady enough to reload at this point?

He heard more footsteps from below, coming up the stairs.

Dammit. How many more?

A voice from the vestibule. "Gino, get a move on! We got trouble up here!"

The sirens grew louder.

A voice from the stairwell. "Yeah, we're gonna have some trouble down below in a minute!"

Another figure—presumably the one named Gino—appeared at the top of the stairs with yet another Tommy gun. Fortunately for Jimmy, Gino made the same mistake the first gunman had made just minutes ago. Framed by the jagged remains of the doorway, Gino was an easy target, even for shaky hands. Jimmy fired a single round into his chest and dropped him where he stood.

The voice in the vestibule, the one who'd called for Gino, spat out a vicious curse.

The sirens were right outside now, at ground level—at least four cars, as near as Jimmy could tell. Amid the wail, he could hear the squeal of breaks, the slamming of doors, the shouts from police officers ordering hands in the air.

Behind it all was the sound of more sirens in the distance and fast approaching.

Peering from his half-sitting, half-reclining position behind the overturned desk, Jimmy tried to focus his eyes on the gaping hole in the doorway, tried to spot any sudden movements by additional gunmen lurking around the edges of the damaged walls. He heard moaning from more than one voice. He could only guess, but it could have been the gunman he'd just dropped, or the one he'd clipped on the hand a few moments ago—or maybe both.

But it was getting harder to see. After a few more seconds, his vision grew hazy, dark around the edges, and he struggled to hold onto his revolver as a deathly chill swept over him.

Not quite twenty years, he thought.

The last sound he heard was yet another wave of footsteps pounding up the stairs, the adrenaline-charged scuffle of armed law officers bursting into the rubble that littered the vestibule at the top of stairs. He heard gunfire, and shouts from his brothers in arms as they corralled the last of the intruders at gunpoint and manhandled them into submission.

He heard someone shout the words "Jimmy," and "hurt," and "ambulance."

But he knew it was too late for any of that.

Then the sounds and the voices faded to distant echoes.

He thought of his wife. His son. He felt a sadness for them, but only for a moment.

And then he slipped away, content in the knowledge that he had fought the good fight in the dark hour.

The evidence was secure.

He had protected the city.

1936

CHAPTER 1
DAY IN COURT

The man in the black robe and the high-backed chair said, "Sixty days," and brought the gavel down with a wooden smack that echoed throughout the courtroom.

Jack Hunter blinked, momentarily stunned, but recovered quickly. "Sixty days?" he said. He rose from his chair, knowing that his window of opportunity was short and the judge would move immediately to the next case on the docket.

"Your Honor," said Hunter, addressing the man seated at the raised bench at the front of the courtroom, "I must ask for a reconsideration of the sentence." He was vaguely aware, even in this spacious room, that his voice was perhaps a little louder and more strident than it needed to be. "The charge here is aggravated assault with a deadly weapon, and the circumstances of the case—combined with the defendant's lengthy prior record—clearly warrant a much stiffer sentence than sixty days. Frankly, I believe that six to eight months would be more appropriate."

"Mr. Hunter," said the judge, looking down and across the room at him over a pair of glasses sitting low on his nose, "if you are truly interested in what's appropriate, I recommend that you change your tone when addressing the bench."

Hunter took in a deep breath, fighting to take the edge out of his voice. He was, after all, an assistant district attorney. A professional. For the most part, he had a reputation for being cool and efficient in the courtroom. He'd learned a few years ago that this kind of aggravation just came with the territory. But the Honorable Anthony Reynolds was a notorious hardcase, and Hunter had been on edge from the moment he found out that Reynolds would be hearing the case.

And it didn't help that the defendant, Lorenzo Valentine, was a career criminal, a stubborn leftover from an era when organized crime held Union City in a deadly grip of fear.

Reynolds pushed his glasses back up his nose and glanced down at the paperwork on the bench in front of him. "Mr. Hunter, I'm looking at a long docket," he said with a frown, his eyes still averted, "just like I did yesterday and the day before that, and several days before that. And I suspect that the docket will be equally long tomorrow."

Hunter was silent, not sure where the judge was going with this. Reynolds shuffled a few papers and continued. "Now, all of this speaks very well of the efforts of our police force and you and the rest of your colleagues in the district attorney's office. However, the drawback here is that our county jail is getting rather crowded—even for short-term occupancy—and the two penitentiaries downstate are getting equally full. Consequently, I have to adjust my sentencing accordingly. Now, I am well aware of Mr. Valentine's rather, uh, distinguished record, but I'm also aware that the Glenwood neighborhood is badly in need of some cleanup. And given that that has been his primary area of activity in recent months, I'm going to have him assigned to neighborhood cleaning and restoration in that district."

Hunter looked away, biting back the anger that came from knowing that a second-rate thug from a long-defunct crime organization who two weeks earlier had put a nightclub waitress in the hospital by breaking her jaw with the butt of his revolver—a weapon that had been in his possession illegally—would serve a significant chunk of his sentence for the offense by picking up trash and planting flowers. Hardly a case of the punishment fitting the crime.

The DA's office had gotten involved in the case because of Valentine's prior record and past affiliations. The city had come a long way in its efforts to clean itself up since the reign of organized crime during Prohibition, but there was plenty of residue from the old days still lurking in the shadows and waiting for opportunities. Every small timer who might point the law toward something bigger and more significant was worth looking into.

But to Hunter's way of thinking, a few weeks in jail and a few more of community service didn't exactly amount to turning up the heat under Valentine or anyone of significance to whom Valentine might be connected.

Hunter shrugged off the irritation and turned to look back at the bench, where Reynolds was staring directly at him and apparently waiting for a response.

"Any problems with that, Mr. Hunter?"

Hunter heaved an exasperated sigh and shook his head. The shining star from the DA's office was apparently not quite at its usual brightness this morning. "None whatsoever, Your Honor," he said.

"Very well." Reynolds brought the gavel one more time. "Next case."

As the bailiff's voice launched into the details of the next item on the docket, Hunter turned and glanced across the center aisle to where Valentine and his lawyer, one Dominic LoCastro, were seated. LoCastro, a slippery looking reptile in an expensive suit, looked back at him and smirked.

Hunter held his gaze for a moment then looked away, gathering his papers and slipping them into his briefcase. He had a meeting back at his office in a half hour.

He hoped his next appointment would be more satisfying than the one he'd just wrapped up.

CHAPTER 2
DIAMOND'S PLAN

At a few minutes after eleven o'clock in the morning, Nicky Diamond sat alone at the desk in the upstairs office of the Paramount, a restaurant and nightclub located on West Tenth Street, in the southwest corner of Union City's entertainment district. Diamond was a wiry, fierce-looking individual with slick graying hair, a hawk nose, and a wide-eyed expression that suggested a perennial state of intense concentration—and possibly agitation—even at times when the prevailing circumstances were relatively calm and non-threatening.

He had been at the office since before dawn. He had arrived there early to await a phone call from one of his men. The call had come as expected, and he'd made a few calls to some of his other contacts in the hours that followed. Now, with the midday sun shining on the world outside, he sat in dim lighting controlled by carefully adjusted window shades and a single desk lamp—just enough for him to study the figures in a ledger laying open on the desk in front of him.

To his right on the broad desktop was a ceramic ashtray filled with the usual mound of ashes and crushed cigarette stubs, along with nearly a dozen small tin cylinders. Each cylinder measured about two-and-a-half inches in length by a half-inch in diameter, and each was broken at one end with nothing inside.

Diamond turned a page of the ledger. Save for the occasional street noises that made their way up from two stories below, the only sound in the room was the murmur of the radio along the wall behind him, just within his reach.

On paper, The Paramount Club belonged to David "Dutch" Markowitz, a small-time hustler whose prior experience in the restaurant and nightclub business consisted of running a security team—nothing more than four guys with guns, thick wallets and lengthy police records—at a short-lived burlesque club about five years earlier. But the man who was really in charge at the Paramount was Nicky Diamond.

His name didn't appear anywhere on the Paramount's lease, nor did it appear on any other paperwork relative to the nightclub's commercial permits, its liquor license or any other aspect of the business. He had nothing to do with booking the orchestras or planning the menu or staffing the kitchen. Nevertheless, he had bankrolled Markowitz with sufficient cash to open the place about four months earlier—just as he was starting to regain a foothold in Union City's gambling operations—and keep it humming four nights a week with music, food and liquor. In return, Diamond had commandeered about sixty percent of the office space in the upper room to serve as one of a few places around town from which he could manage his business affairs and still maintain a low profile at the same time.

Other than the plush gambling hall he'd set up in the basement since he took over the operation, Diamond had never fully explained to Markowitz the exact nature and extent of his business. And given his own checkered past, Markowitz knew better than to ask a lot of questions. He just ran the day-to-day operations, collected his money from Diamond's payroll and otherwise kept himself scarce.

The restaurant downstairs would be opening in less than a half hour to serve the lunch clientele, but that was actually the last thing on Diamond's mind. Indeed, The Paramount Club was actually just a small part of what made up the ledger in front of him. The book was a much more comprehensive accounting of all of his operations throughout Union City. The Paramount was one line item in a much larger operation.

A buzzer sounded on the desk. Diamond closed the ledger and flipped a switch on the box that had generated the noise.

"Yeah?"

A tinny voice belched from the box: "It's Louie. We're back."

Diamond didn't respond. He merely switched off the intercom and pressed another switch on the same box to unlock the back-door entrance downstairs. Within a few seconds, he could hear the stairwell doorway open down the hall from the office and several sets of footsteps in the hallway.

Diamond heard a soft knock at the door to the office. He said, "Come," and four men stepped inside.

First was Louie Simone, who had buzzed from downstairs. The same Louie Simone who had made the early morning call several hours ago. Simone was one of Diamond's primary lieutenants, an operative who had taken care of a lot of the advance work and logistics that enabled Diamond to re-establish operations in Union City several months earlier without drawing the attention of the police.

Diamond noted the European cut of Simone's suit and the expensive shoes, and he wondered if he was paying his operative too much. For a guy who'd been charged with keeping things on the quiet, Simone seemed to spend a lot of time and money on his appearance.

Behind Simone were Carl "Duke" Duchovny and Johnny Kowalski. Duke had been part of the Diamond operation from way back, all the way back to the Prohibition days, before Diamond did his time in the pen. Kowalski, thick-framed and beefy in the face, was a utility man—good with a gun and even better behind the wheel of any car. He usually handled the security and transport detail.

The last to come through the door was Sparks, a slight figure whose entrance prompted a double-take from Diamond. The mob boss looked squarely at him, glanced toward the window on the wall to his right, then looked back at him with a furrowed brow. "What the hell...?" he muttered. "Anybody see you come in?"

Sparks shook his head. "No," he said, glancing at the other three men. "I came in through the alley, with everyone else."

"You need to stay out of sight," Diamond warned. "You've been a secret for a long time, and we need to keep it that way."

Sparks shrugged. "Sorry, Nick," he said. "It was a long night, but it's okay. There was no one down in the alley. Nobody saw me."

Diamond looked skeptical, but he brushed it off and got down to business. "Okay, tell me everything," he said, glancing at all the men standing in front of his desk and eventually focusing on Simone. "You said the cops were there and you had a little trouble."

Simone shrugged. "Only a little," he said. Diamond glanced at Duke, who was watching Simone and doing a poor job of hiding the contemptuous scowl that was taking shape on his face. "There was some shooting from both sides, but all of our boys are fine. Kowalski tagged one of the cops. Grazed him in the arm. I'm hearing it was minimal and he'll be okay."

"And you got the stuff from the plant?"

"Got it."

Diamond felt something catch in his chest. "All of it? Everything we talked about?"

"Everything on his list," said Simone, tilting his head toward Sparks. "It's all still in the truck, and the truck is locked up at the warehouse."

Some part of Diamond wanted to ride to where the truck had been locked up and inspect the contents himself. Look at them. Touch them. Instead, he took a deep breath and focused his attention on the conversation at hand. "Fine," he said.

He turned his attention to Sparks. "You know what to do with it, right?"

Sparks nodded. "I already have two people working on it."

"Okay. I want to see it when it's ready. All of it."

Sparks nodded again.

Diamond paused for a moment to open a desk drawer and slip the ledger inside. "Alright," he said, closing the drawer, "the first order of business is going to be Stu Hirschfeld."

Simone took a seat in the chair on the other side of the desk, directly across from Diamond, and examined his fingernails absent-mindedly. Sparks and Kowalski leaned against a wall toward the back of the room. Duke stood by the door, hands in his pockets, with a wary eye on Simone.

Diamond looked at all of them and kept talking. "We all remember Hirschfeld, right?" he said. "He ran a little whiskey operation in town back in the old days until we shut him down. He tried to give us a little trouble, but we took care of it, and in the end he stayed out of the way."

Duke frowned. "Is he still even in town? He's been quiet for a long time. He never had much going on after we took the steam out of his operation."

"Oh, he's around," said Diamond. "He's got three clubs here in the Entertainment District. We've got people telling us he's running tables in the basement of every one of them. Bringing in some nice receipts, too."

"I hear he's been running them for a while," said Simone, "since before you've been back."

"Well, I'm back now," said Diamond, his voice suddenly going cold, "and it's getting a little crowded."

"You been in touch with him?" said Sparks.

Diamond frowned and nodded. "Of course I've been in touch with him," he said. "I'm a reasonable man. I met with him a couple weeks ago to discuss business in the way that gentlemen do. Unfortunately, I don't think he quite understands my feelings about the territory. I told him I'm planning to control the gambling operations in this city. He had some reservations about that, but I made it clear that this wasn't something that was on the table for negotiation. He was even less happy about that. By the time the meeting was over, I don't think we were seeing eye to eye."

Kowalski, still leaning against the wall, shuffled his a feet. "So what happens?" he said.

Diamond shrugged. "It's very simple," he said. "I'm going to send him a message that should clear up any confusion he might still have about my intentions. We're going to hit one of his three clubs tonight."

"Which one?" said Duke.

"The Blue Star, the one on West Twenty-First. We could level the place with the amount of stuff you took from the chemical plant last night and still have plenty left over, but we're not going to do that." He gestured at Sparks. "You all know about the little present that Sparks here has put together for Hirschfeld and his clientele. It should be enough to put a dent in the place and send a clear message at the same time."

All eyes, including Diamond's, turned toward Sparks, who returned the glances. Diamond pointed an index finger at him in a gesture of caution and addressed him directly. "I don't want too much damage. Understand? I want to send a message, and that's all. There's good money being made in that place, and I want it. So there's no reason to scare people away or completely destroy the joint altogether."

Sparks' mouth twisted into a self-assured grin. "Nick," he said, "I've been doing this kind of work for you for a long time. I've never failed you. Have a little faith, okay?"

Diamond held his gaze for a moment. He didn't like the grin. Something about it made him feel a little bit small, and he didn't like feeling small—not even a little bit—especially in front of his other men. But he let it go. Sparks was an important part of the operation. His expertise would be critical throughout the next several weeks and beyond.

Duke broke the silence. "Hirschfeld has a reputation from way back for being pretty stubborn," he said. "Suppose he doesn't give in?"

"If not, we hit another one of his clubs," Diamond said. "And if he doesn't get the message, we hit the third. And if we have to, we do what we have to do to get him out of the way permanently." He paused. "But this is business, and while Stu may be a little stubborn, he's also a smart businessman. I want to believe he's not going to let things go that far."

The room went silent. Diamond leaned back in his chair and scanned each of the four faces on the other side of his desk. "Alright," he said. "So everything's taken care of? Everything's ready?"

Simone leaned forward and made a reassuring gesture. "No worries,

Nick." He jerked a thumb over his shoulder in Sparks' direction. "Me and Sparks have this taken care of."

Duke's eyes darted back and forth between Simone and Diamond. He sucked in a blast of air through his nose and pushed himself away from the wall.

"No, Nick," he said, his voice taut. "Everything's not good. I don't like this."

Diamond looked at Duke without registering an expression. Then Diamond glanced at every face in the room and sensed the tension quickly escalating to a level that was almost palpable.

Duke was scowling, his face red and getting redder. His fists, one of them scarred from a long-ago wound, clenched and unclenched. Simone responded with a dismissive glance and a smirk.

Duke looked like he might blow up in a matter of moments.

And Diamond loved it when things blew up…

CHAPTER 3
GAMBLERS AND THIEVES

Back in the DA's office, Hunter was the first to step into the conference room. Square-jawed and solid of frame, he stood less than an inch shy of six feet tall, with light-brown hair and dark eyes. Despite his frustrating setback in the courtroom some thirty minutes earlier, he moved through the room with the confidence and grace of an athlete. At thirty-two, an age when many men of his generation were already growing soft, he had clearly maintained much of the physical prowess he'd demonstrated as a state champion in wrestling and track-and-field during his high school years more than a decade earlier.

These days, though, Hunter faced off against his adversaries in a much different arena, one where the stakes were much higher than high school sports championships. He went head to head with some of the most dangerous criminals and criminal organizations in the entire state.

After five years in the district attorney's office—the last two of which had been spent as an assistant DA—his record in the courtroom was as formidable as it had been during those high school years.

Hunter dropped his legal pad on the long wooden table and set his coffee cup down next to it. He glanced over his right shoulder and nodded to Ed Gallagher—his boss, the district attorney for Union City—who entered the room just a few seconds behind him.

Gallagher nodded back and moved to the chair at the head of the table. He had a head of silver hair that was receding at the temples, and a pipe clamped between his teeth. His load was similar to Hunter's—a notepad and a couple of manila folders in one hand and coffee in the other. He positioned it all on the table in front of the end chair, then crossed the room to grab an ashtray off the top of a file cabinet.

"Taggert and Dugan called about ten minutes ago," said Gallagher. "They're on their way." He settled into his chair and tapped dead ashes from the pipe into the ashtray.

Hunter sat down. "Any word on the raid last night?"

"They hit Frankie's last night. That place on Sheldon, near West Seventeenth. That's all I know. If they came up with anything worthwhile, I suspect we'll know when they get here." Gallagher glanced at the door. "Taggert's been playing it pretty close to the vest."

Hunter shrugged. "Not sure I blame him. The last thing he needs is his entire department, the DA's office and half of City Hall all the way up to the mayor talking about plans for a police raid. Surprise is the whole idea. If enough people know, there's not much of a surprise."

Gallagher glanced over his shoulder and dropped his voice a notch or two. "Yeah, and that's not even taking into account the very real possibility that someone in one of those places—the police department, City Hall, even this place—could be spreading information where it shouldn't be going."

It wasn't the first time Gallagher had suggested the possibility of confidential police information getting into the wrong hands intentionally. Hunter wanted to believe that the days of cops on the take and other police and legal corruption were behind them—a cancer that had been exorcised from the city in the previous decade—but he'd already been in the game long enough and seen enough along the way not to be naïve.

There was a gentle knock at the door, and both men looked up.

Betty Carlyle, the lead secretary in the DA's office, peered in at them. "Mr. Taggert and Mr. Dugan are here," she said.

Gallagher nodded and Hunter gave Betty a quick glance before she turned away and disappeared. Without further ceremony, the men entered the room moments later. Like the DA and his assistant, each of the two men from the police department carried his own share of paperwork.

Sam Taggert, the chief of police, was in his mid-fifties, with nearly white hair and a lined face. He was a little bit soft around the middle, but he looked as though he might have been in good shape once upon a time.

Right behind Taggert was Lieutenant Mike Dugan, the head of the detective bureau and Taggert's right-hand man. He was a couple years shy of forty, a little taller than Taggert and much more solid. His hair was thinning and showing a bit of gray, but not much. Hunter had once heard that Dugan had done some middleweight boxing when he was in his twenties. It showed.

Gallagher waved to two empty chairs. "Have a seat, gentlemen."

The men sat. There was little need for preamble. Gallagher locked eyes with Taggert and said, "Tell me."

"We went into Frankie's Lounge last night."

Gallagher nodded. "And?"

Taggert grunted. "Running tables. In the basement. Hell, we knew he was before we got there. We'd been watching the place for three weeks."

Gallagher shook his head. "That's two more since the beginning of this month."

Hunter leaned forward in his chair. "How many are we up to now?" he said. "Four?"

"Five," said Dugan. "Five in the last three months. Three nightclubs. The fourth was a restaurant—just food, no entertainment."

"And the fifth one was the bakery," said Gallagher.

"Yeah," said Taggert with a mirthless laugh and a shake of his head. "A bakery. Can you believe that? Selling cakes up front and rolling dice in the back."

Gallagher glanced from the chief to the detective and spread his hands in a speculative gesture. "So, are we seeing any patterns?"

Dugan shrugged. "Nothing other than the obvious one. Clearly, we're seeing a rise in illegal gambling and racketeering citywide."

"Well, sure," said Gallagher, "but the question is who. Any familiar names or faces showing up in these raids?"

"No. Just small-time club owners, and they're not talking," said Taggert. "They'll spend a few hours in jail, maybe a whole night at the most. But they always seem to make bail."

"Who's posting it?" said Hunter.

"Usually some hired hand from the club will show up—a bouncer, a waitress, whoever." Taggert glanced at his notes. "We even had a guy with a kitchen apron come in with a thick wad of bills. It was the cook from The Deuce, that place on Redwood Avenue."

"Mickey Flannery's place," said Gallagher.

"Probably safe to say it wasn't the cook's money," said Hunter.

Taggert snorted. "I highly doubt Flannery pays his kitchen staff that well."

"So, for now, at least," said Hunter, "there's nothing to tie it all together—nothing pointing to one person or one central operation."

Taggert shifted in his chair. "No," he said.

There was silence in the room for a moment. Hunter glanced from Taggert to Dugan—both of whom had averted their eyes— then exchanged a look with Gallagher. From the hallway came the usual sounds—a faraway typewriter, the murmur of voices, a ringing telephone, footsteps up and down the tiled corridor and past the door of the room where the four men were seated.

"But there's something else," the chief said finally.

Hunter and Gallagher leaned forward slightly and watched as Taggert turned to Dugan and nodded. The detective picked up the story, glancing at a sheet of notes from his folder.

"Seven hours ago, a little after three-thirty this morning, there was a break-in at Pharaoh Chemical. The place in the River District, over near the—"

"I know where it is," Hunter interrupted. He felt a tightness in his chest, and he took in a deep breath in an effort to suppress an anger that had been simmering for years. The break-in at the chemical plant suggested a possibility that no one wanted to consider—a possibility that suddenly raised the level of tension in the room.

Dugan paused for a moment to lock eyes with Hunter, then went on with his report of the break-in. "As far as we know, the suspects made off in an unmarked delivery truck with several barrels of different materials. Exactly what materials, we don't know yet."

"Anybody get a look at the plates?" said Hunter.

Dugan shook his head. "It was dark, and the truck was moving pretty fast. And on top of that, there happened to be shotguns blowing lead out of either side as it was driving away, which tends to be a little distracting when you're trying to pay attention to license plates."

"Anyone get hurt?" said Gallagher.

"One of our boys got grazed in the arm," said Dugan. "A few stitches and bandages and a couple days off. He'll live."

"Plenty of delivery trucks in this town," said Gallagher. "Be hard to narrow it down without knowing the plates."

"Well, there's this," said Dugan, pulling a sheet from the file. "It isn't much, but we know where the tires came from."

Hunter and Gallagher looked at the detective, waiting for more.

"Some solvents spilled on the access driveway during the holdup. The truck must've driven through the gunk, because the tires left some pretty clear tracks on the pavement. We got a clear enough outline of the tread that we were able to identify the brand and trace the tires back to the manufacturer."

Gallagher shrugged. "That's good detective work, but does it really tell us much?"

"Maybe not much," said Dugan, "but in this case, I think it tells us something."

Gallagher arched an eyebrow. "In this case?"

Dugan looked back at his sheet. "A company called Sherwood Tire and Rubber," he said, "located in Chicago."

The room was silent for a moment as Gallagher leveled his gaze at Dugan, then looked at everyone else around the conference table.

"Chicago," Gallagher said.

Dugan nodded. "Chicago." He slipped the sheet back onto the folder and continued. "And it's worth noting here that Sherwood's distribution is limited to the state of Illinois. So whoever bought these tires bought them in Illinois. Now, granted, they could have bought them in Rockford, or Springfield, or Peoria. They could have bought them anywhere in the state."

Hunter stroked his chin. "Or they could have bought them in Chicago."

"Or in Chicago, yeah."

Gallagher raised his hand in a speculative gesture. "So the truck is likely from out of state as well," he said. "Likely from Illinois."

Dugan nodded. "We have everyone on every shift on the lookout for a truck with Illinois plates," he said. "But we may not find much. Truth is, anybody who's going to go to the trouble of robbing a chemical plant is probably going to cover his tracks by fixing the getaway vehicle with local plates."

Hunter exhaled impatiently and leveled his gaze at Taggert. "Okay, let's cut to the chase," he said. "Could it be Diamond?"

The police chief leaned back in his chair, pausing as though he were gathering his thoughts for a long-winded answer. In the end, he apparently thought better of it. "Could be," he said.

Hunter nodded, his face a grim mask.

"Now, hold on," said Gallagher. "Connecting a break-in at a chemical plant with a rise in illegal gambling seems like a bit of a stretch. I don't think we should be jumping to—"

"Come on, Ed," Hunter interrupted, gesturing to the other two men across the table. "We've all been living and working in this town for a long time. We all have long memories. It's part of our job."

Gallagher returned his gaze and said nothing.

Hunter looked at Taggert. "Where's Diamond now? Is he out yet?"

Taggert thumbed through the papers in his file folder and reshuffled a single sheet to the top of the pile. He read directly from the rap sheet: "Nicholas Diamond, born in 1891 in Montevago, Sicily. Formerly known as Niccolo Diamante prior to his arrival in the United States in 1894. Also known among his associates as Nicky Dynamite." He paused and rolled his eyes. "And as I'm sure we all remember, the newspapers just took that alias and ran with it."

He scanned further down the page and kept reading: "Released from Stanton, a federal penitentiary about forty miles south of Chicago, in 1934 after serving a twelve-year sentence for a series of crimes committed in Union City and surrounding areas, including aggravated manslaughter, conspiracy to commit murder, armed robbery, illegal trafficking of alcohol and firearms…"

Without the aid of a file full of papers, Hunter added to the list from memory: "…Illegal use of explosives, destruction of municipal government property…"

Taggert cleared his throat. "Yeah, those too." His eyes continued to move down the page. "Last known whereabouts, Chicago, Illinois. Apparently, he has a cousin there."

"As of when?" said Gallagher.

"Illinois parole authorities say they have a record of him residing in an apartment there up until about four or five months ago," said Dugan.

Gallagher raised an eyebrow. "But?"

"He apparently vacated the premises in April," Dugan continued. "No forwarding address. Current whereabouts unknown."

"So he's been out of state prison for two years," Hunter summarized, "he relocated to Chicago for a year and a half, and now he could be anywhere."

Taggert looked at Dugan, and the detective nodded. "That's the picture we have right now," said the chief.

"Okay," said Gallagher. "No arrests in the Pharaoh break-in?"

"No," said Dugan. "A car responded to the call a little after midnight. Several shots were fired, as the chief mentioned a minute ago. Whoever broke into the place made off with the stuff before the responding officers' backup arrived."

"The plant manager at Pharaoh has shut down operations for the day," said Taggert. "That'll give some of the other detectives on Mike's crew a chance to look around and do a complete inventory of what's still there and what's missing. We should have a better picture by this afternoon."

All four men weighed the information in silence. The only sound in the room came from Gallagher striking a match and relighting his pipe with a few short puffs.

Gallagher dropped the dead match into an ashtray. "It's been, what, fifteen years since that place was robbed?"

"Exactly," said Hunter. "Nineteen-twenty-one."

Dugan looked back and forth between the police chief and the district attorney. "I was still a beat cop in those days," he said, "but I've read the file."

"Before my time, too," said Hunter. "But I know the story by heart."

"The break-in fifteen years ago was done by Diamond's crew," said Gallagher, taking a draw from his pipe. "The guy had a hell of

27

a bootleg operation in this whole corner of the state. The revenues were enormous, not just from the liquor itself, but from the protection money he was collecting from the gin joints that sold it."

"And he had an enforcement policy that wasn't very subtle," Taggert added. "Any establishments that didn't cooperate usually ended up with half their buildings blown wide open with explosives. We figured out that he was manufacturing the explosives with the chemicals he took from the plant."

The chief sat back in his chair and shook his head. "Christ, that guy had a screw loose," he said. "I'm not even sure it was about the liquor business after a while. I think he just liked to watch things blow up— storefronts, cars, a couple banks. It got to be like his calling card. Hell, there was that farmer out in Briggs Township who was doing a good trade out of his cellar. Diamond got wind of it and put some muscle on the old guy. When he wouldn't give Diamond a cut of the business, the whole place burned down—the house, the barn, everything." Taggert shook his head again. "And everyone."

"But anything that noisy and destructive gets to be sloppy business pretty quickly," said Gallagher, picking up the story again. "After a while, you start leaving a trail, especially when you get your supply of explosive materials from a place right here in town."

"Half the department was on Diamond's payroll at the time," said Taggert, "but the chief and the DA were still clean. They put together a small team, and kept a lid on it for months. It was slow work, and we never did figure out exactly who Diamond's connection was at Pharaoh, but we were able to build a case. We had a safe full of files and evidence tying Diamond to the production, shipment and sale of just about every ounce of liquor in this county and two others. And we also had plenty of evidence tying him to the stuff coming out of the Pharaoh plant."

Taggert poked a thumb toward the hallway outside the door of the briefing room. "It was all right here in this building—the files, the evidence, the depositions, all of it. Right here on this floor. And Diamond's crew almost got a hold of it one night, just a few days before the trial, but..."

His voice trailed off.

"Yeah, almost," said Hunter, his voice clipped and efficient. "Well, this trip down memory lane has been a pleasure, gentlemen, but unless we can establish some connections in the here and now, we're all just sitting around talking about the good old days. We need to be asking ourselves what this break-in at Pharaoh means, if anything."

He took a deep breath to gather his thoughts, then plowed ahead. "We're living in a different world now," he said. "It's not about liquor anymore. That's all on the up-and-up again, as of a few years ago with the repeal of Prohibition. If people are hiding in the basement or some secret back room of their favorite nightclub, they're not doing it to get a drink. They're doing it because somebody in that basement or back room is running tables, dealing cards or whatever else, because that's the stuff that isn't legal. Clearly not the most dangerous or destructive racket in the world, but still not legal."

Hunter focused his gaze on the police chief and the chief of detectives, forcing himself to remember that these two men were merely the messengers. "You gentlemen are the detectives," he said, "so you've probably already considered some of the assumptions that are running through my mind right now, but let me put them out on the table anyway. Based on the pattern we've seen so far, it's possible that somebody—we don't know who—is bankrolling these operations and keeping the club owners from staying locked up for too long. And if that's the case, we can assume that the person doing the bankrolling is probably controlling the entire operation. Sound reasonable so far?"

Taggert nodded. "And we don't know how large that operation may be," he said, "but we can assume that it's fairly well organized. And if it is, we can also assume that it's only going to get bigger and more entrenched as time goes on." Taggert paused to weigh what he was saying. "At least that's how it usually works, if history is any indication."

"Meanwhile," Hunter went on, "just this morning, somebody broke into Pharaoh Chemical in the river district. And the last time that happened, back in 1921, the job was connected to one Nicky Diamond, who had control over the liquor operation in this entire area at the time. And that same Nicky Diamond who robbed that same chemical plant once upon a time used the stuff from the plant to firebomb anyone who got in his way."

"And this is the same Nicky Diamond who was released from federal prison two years ago," said Dugan, "but whose whereabouts have been unknown for several months."

"So the question is," Gallagher interjected, "do either of these two situations—this surge in gambling and racketeering operations and a break-in at a chemical plant just this morning—have anything to do with each other? Or are we just jumping to conclusions because the last time that place got broken into, all hell broke loose in this town for the next several months?"

"Well, if you recall," said Taggert, "we were pretty certain at that time that someone inside that plant was connected to Diamond and his operation. We traced a lot of explosive material found at his various crime scenes back to Pharaoh—far more than what disappeared in the one heist. Truth be told, he was most likely tapping into a steady supply line of explosive material before the break-in."

Gallagher looked away from everyone else at the table and shook his head slowly. "But like Sam said, we were never able to pin down whoever that insider was."

Dugan interjected, "If any of the five club owners—well, four club owners and a baker—know anything about anything, they're not talking."

"Can you bring them back in and put a little more pressure on?" said Gallagher.

"We can't arrest them," said Dugan, "but we can exert a little pressure, so to speak, that might encourage them to come in and talk to us."

"They might get lawyers," said Taggert, "if they come at all."

Hunter shrugged. "Some might. Some maybe not. Let's face it, we've all seen some of the lawyers these guys work with. Are any of us really worried that they'd be tough customers?"

Dugan frowned, considering Hunter's suggestion. "It couldn't hurt," he said. "Meantime, the plant manager at Pharaoh might have more to tell us after he and the detectives finish going through the place."

"So maybe we have a clearer picture about the plant by the end of the day," said Gallagher.

"Maybe," said Dugan. "And as far as the nightclubs—and I'm not entirely ready to say that they're connected to the break-in—we keep following up on leads and poking our stick at some of the more questionable joints. And whoever we bring downtown as a result, we start turning up the heat under them a little more to see if we can get some sense of a central figure in all this."

Taggert shrugged. "It's a start anyway," he said. "Sometimes poking around makes things happen."

The room was silent for a moment. Gallagher looked at the other three men seated around the table. "Anything else?" he said.

The men shook their heads.

"Alright, then, gentlemen," said the DA, pushing his chair back and getting to his feet. The other men in the room responded in kind. "We all have things to do and a city to protect. Thanks for coming, and keep us posted about what you hear."

Dugan gathered up his paperwork and picked up his hat off the table. "I'll give one of you a call by the end of the day," he said. "Even if we don't know a damn thing more than we do now—which, unfortunately, is always a possibility."

Dugan and Taggert stepped back into the hallway with Gallagher and Hunter right behind them. After the ritual handshakes and parting noises, the two visitors from the police department headed toward the elevators.

Hunter watched them as they moved down the hall. Gallagher turned to him and started to say something, but Betty Carlyle appeared and told him he had a call. Gallagher tilted his head toward his office door as a signal for her to send the call to his desk, then headed for his office.

Hunter stepped back into his own office. He moved to the opposite wall and stood at the window for several minutes, hands in his pockets, eyes fixed on the street traffic on Liberty Avenue, five stories below. All the while, he felt vaguely uneasy, as though a demon that had been banished to the shadows was waiting for a chance to re-emerge.

CHAPTER 4
RESENTMENT EXPLODES

Duke tossed an angry glare at Simone as he took a couple steps toward Diamond's desk. Simone leaned back in his chair and watched with an arched eyebrow and a contemptuous smirk as Duke crossed the room.

"Look, Nicky, however you wanna handle Hirschfeld is up to you," said Duke. "You're the boss, and I'll do whatever you wanna do, 'cause I'm a loyal guy." He glanced one more time at Simone, then turned back to Diamond. "And that's what's buggin' me."

Diamond stared back at Duke, his face expressionless. Duke took in another deep breath and kept going. "I been your right-hand man for a lotta years," he said. "I been with you since the early days. I took a few bullets for you along the way, right up to that night when we tried to get the goods outta the Justice Center to keep you from going up the river. And we woulda done it, too, if it weren't for that one damn cop. And if nothin' else, we made sure he got his. And then all those years when you were doin' time, I took care of things. And that wasn't easy, because a lot of things happened while you were away. The police and the mayor and governor came down hard after Prohibition, and a lot of people either got put away or got the chair."

Duke had moved close enough to Diamond's desk to lean forward and put his hands on the edge that faced the room. He tilted his head over his right shoulder in Simone's direction. "And now along comes the boy wonder here," he said, his voice rising in volume and intensity, "with the smooth talk and the flashy clothes, actin' like he's your right-hand guy."

Simone made a chuckling noise that dripped with ridicule, which only seemed to make Duke angrier. Duke turned and glared at him over his shoulder, looking for a moment like he'd pull his piece and shoot the smirk off Simone's face. Instead, he glanced at Sparks and then turned back to face Diamond, leaning even farther over the desk.

"And then there's Sparks," Duke went on. Across the room, Sparks frowned, apparently bewildered by the diatribe that had suddenly turned in his direction. "He thinks he can move up to the front just because he knows all about the chemicals and the explosives, and he knows how much you like that stuff."

There was something in that last part that sounded to Diamond like an accusation or a judgment, and he'd had more than enough of both for one lifetime. His eyes narrowed slightly, but he remained silent, listening to what had now become a tirade.

And Duke kept going. "So where does that leave me, Nicky?" he said, poking his thumb at his own chest. "Huh? Where? That's what I wanna know. Hell, you and me been tight since before the war, but if this is how things are gonna go, I don't like it. If you're just gonna push your most loyal guy aside, I wanna know right now! I wanna know where I stand!"

And then he stopped. His jaw muscles flexed and his nostrils flared slightly. His breathing still came hard, but he'd apparently said his piece.

Diamond tilted his head to one side and looked at Duke for a long moment without saying a word, his face inert. Despite the silence, the room nearly crackled with an electric charge.

The tension broke when Diamond finally smiled at the man leaning over his desk.

"Duke..." said Diamond, opening his hands in a conciliatory gesture and speaking in a soothing voice in an effort to calm the nerves of an old and trusted friend. "Relax, pal. No need to worry. You know you've been one of my top guys for years. No need to get excited. Trust me, once we get this operation up and running, everyone'll get a piece of the action."

Duke let out a breath. Some of the hard lines in his face softened. He turned his head slightly and glanced at Simone, who sat with his legs crossed and casually studied his fingernails, seemingly oblivious to the harangue. Duke looked toward the back of the room at Sparks, who still wore the frown and stared at the floor.

Duke looked back at Diamond. "Yeah, well..." he muttered. "I took care of a lot of business while you were doin' time. I just don't wanna get pushed aside now that you're out."

Diamond rose from his chair just enough to reach cross the desk and give Duke a friendly chuck on the shoulder. "Come on, Duke," he said. "You know me better than that. We go way back, and you ought to know that you're an important part of this operation. Why would I want to leave you out?"

He opened the desk drawer. "Here," he said, reaching in with both hands. "I want you to have these."

"What's that?"

Diamond pulled out a pair of dice, one in each hand. He held up each dotted cube between the thumb and middle finger of each hand. They glinted in the overhead light, as though they'd been carefully polished.

"My lucky dice," said Diamond. "I had these with when I was in Stanton—the whole time."

Duke reached out and took the dice from Diamond's hands, holding each die in one hand, just as Diamond had held them a moment earlier. He frowned, examining both cubes as though they might bear some visible sign of magic power. "Yeah?"

"Sure," said Diamond, leaning back in his chair. "I tell you, me and the guys played a lot of games of craps with those when the warden wasn't around. They won me a lot of cigarettes and chocolate bars." He patted his stomach, glancing around the room at the other men. "A lot of chocolate bars," he said with a grin. "Had to take a few pounds off after I got out."

Everyone in the room made a small laughing noise, but the undercurrent of tension remained. Simone looked up from his fingernails and glanced back and forth between the man seated behind the desk and the man standing in front of it with a die in each hand. At the other end of the room, Sparks' eyes narrowed in a squint and his cheekbones tensed.

"Yeah, well, I didn't mean no disrespect, Nicky. I just—"

Diamond waved him off. "Ah, don't worry, Duke. Listen, you know me. I always take care of my boys, right?"

Duke shrugged. "Sure, Nicky. I know."

"Alright, then." He leaned back in his chair. "Now listen," he said. "Here's what you do with those dice. Next time you're at the tables— or maybe you're just playing a little poker, or whatever—and you feel like you need a little luck, you pull out those dice and tap 'em together three times. Like this here…"

Diamond propped his elbows on the desk and held the thumb and forefinger of each hand together as though he were still holding the dice. He tapped the fingers of each hand together three times to demonstrate.

Duke frowned at the dice. "Three times," he muttered. "Like this?"

Everybody in the room heard the first two taps of the dice in Duke's hands, but no one heard the third. It was obliterated by a sharp blast that filled the small room like the report from a 12-gauge shotgun. Diamond's eyes squeezed shut reflexively at the sound of the blast, but only for a split second. When he opened them, Simone and Kowalski both had their hands at either side of their heads covering their ears. Both were wincing. Simone, now doubled over in his chair, had assumed a similar protective stance as the other two men.

Sparks remained standing against the wall. He'd seen the blast coming and he'd avoided the pain by tucking his chin into his chest and pressing his index fingers to his ears.

But the most vivid image amid the nitrous haze that filled the room in the seconds after the explosion—the image that sent an intoxicating jolt through every inch of Diamond's body—was the sight of Duke, his face an ashen mask of pain and shock, his arms outstretched. Duke stared in wide-eyed in disbelief, his gaze shifting back and forth between his own arms and the man seated at the desk in front of him. A blood-chilling moan welled up from some dark chasm of his soul and reverberated throughout the room.

Duke might have been making a pleading gesture at Diamond, but there was no longer any way to be sure.

His hands had been blown off, leaving two mangled and bloody stumps at each wrist.

Time seemed to slow down for Diamond as he savored the moment, glancing back and forth between the gory mess where Duke's hands had once been, and looking deep into the horrified eyes of his longtime ally and confidant.

Duke, meanwhile, stared at the bloody mess at the end of each arm. "Oh, God. Oh my God, Nick…" His voice teetered on the edge of a hysterical shriek that was part shock, part revulsion and part physical pain. "The dice…They blew my…Jesus Christ, my hands…!"

Diamond seemed to snap back to reality at the sight of arterial spray dribbling onto the carpet in front of his desk. Small bits of ruined flesh and fragments of shattered bone smeared across Duke's jacket, pant legs and shoes. Not far from his right foot was a mangled chunk of something that might have been a finger. Diamond glanced down at his desktop and saw a few streaks of blood on his desk blotter. His gaze shifted to his lapels, where he found still more blood.

"Sonofabitch," he muttered, standing up from his chair and yanking off his jacket. "Get him out of here. Go!"

Simone got up from his chair. He and Kowalski moved awkwardly toward Duke, who was looking very pale and not too sure on his feet. "Nicky, for God's sake! How could—?"

Diamond wasn't listening. He was too busy barking at the two men standing at either side of Duke, both of them doing their best not to bloody themselves. He thrust his rumpled jacket at them. "Here, wrap this around him and get him out of here before this mess gets any worse."

Kowalski took the jacket and wrapped it around the two ruined limbs. Duke was still too much in shock to offer any resistance. A dark stain appeared on the wadded jacket almost immediately. Simone stepped behind Duke and steered him around to the door leading out of the office.

Kowalski said, "Where do you want us to—?"

"What the hell do I care? Take him downstairs and out the back! Just don't make a mess on the goddamn stairs."

Simone and Kowalski hustled Duke awkwardly out the door and toward the stairs. Sparks followed. The combination of pain, shock and blood loss was quickly getting the best of Duke, and his legs started to give out from under him.

"And then get back up here and clean all this up!" Diamond yelled after them.

The office door closed, and Diamond was alone in the room. He heard the uneven footsteps of three-and-a-half men shuffling down the stairs as he turned back to his desk. He lifted the stained blotter with his fingertips, taking care not to get any of the blood on his hands or his sleeves. He heard Duke's anguished moan echoing up the staircase, followed by the opening and then the slamming of the heavy metal door on the ground floor that led out to the alley behind the building.

He folded the blotter in half and shoved it into the wastebasket next to the desk. He thought about wiping his hands with a handkerchief, but cursed as he realized that the handkerchief was still in his jacket pocket, and the jacket was now a ruined mess in the alley, wrapped around the two bloody stumps at the end of Duke's arms.

He heard more moaning, followed by a single gunshot.

Then he heard nothing.

CHAPTER 5
A TIP TO THE PRESS

Hunter stepped off the elevator at twelve-thirty and moved through the main lobby of the Justice Center, still thinking about the meeting with Taggert and Dugan earlier that morning. Given the hour, he was also thinking about lunch. More specifically, he was thinking about something from Ottoman's, a sandwich shop on the plaza about four blocks to the west.

He was halfway to the revolving doors at the front entrance when a voice came at him from his right. "Whaddaya say, Jack?"

Hunter knew the voice before he even looked, but he turned anyway as a wiry figure in a fedora and a rumpled trench coat sidled up to him. A pair of intense brown eyes sparkled beneath the brim of the hat, and below that dangled an unlit Lucky from the hard line of a mouth.

"Hey, there, Maxie." Hunter kept moving as he spoke, and the energetic figure fell in step with him.

"What's new in the DA's office?"

"The usual. Protecting the good citizens of Union City."

"Sure. And what are you protecting them from on *this* particular day?"

Hunter weighed his next words carefully, as he always did when speaking to Bart "Max" Maxwell, one of the most widely read columnists for the *Union City Tribune*. Hunter had learned over the years that Max could be a pain in the ass, but he was also one of the most well-connected newspapermen in town. He had sources everywhere, from the highest levels of power to the shadowy, forgotten corners hit hard by tough economic times.

What's more, Hunter and Max had an understanding about the sharing of information. Shortly after Max first started hanging around the Justice Center a few years ago, Hunter had quickly learned that throwing him a few crumbs eventually paid off—usually with interest.

Hunter gave Max a sidelong glance. "I'm heading for the plaza to get a sandwich," he said to the reporter. "Walk with me." He pushed through the revolving door.

Max lit the cigarette and fell in step right behind him. "Great," he said. "I'm parked on the plaza anyway." He hopped into the section of the door immediately behind Hunter's and followed him through.

Once outside, both men squinted in the midday sunlight. Hunter turned right and headed west up Liberty Avenue. Max stayed abreast of him, taking a long drag on his cigarette. Hunter modulated his voice to compensate for the street sounds, but took care not to shout.

"Okay," he said, starting with the usual preamble. "We never had this conversation. Understand?"

The two men's eyes met in an unspoken agreement. "What conversation?" said Max. "I don't know what you're talking about. What'd you say your name was again?"

"Exactly. So, listen. You stay pretty cozy with some of the cops, right?" The question was rhetorical more than anything else.

Max shrugged. "I've got a few sources here and there," he said, but his eyes gave away what Hunter already knew. Max's connection to police activity went well beyond just a few sources.

"How about some of the restaurants and nightclubs?"

"That life can get a little expensive for a beat reporter, but there's a few places I like to go for a steak or a couple beers now and then. The Elliot Wilson Orchestra's at the Highlight Lounge two nights a month. I just saw them last week. Boy, they can fill that place up."

"Okay. You might want to ask around about a series of police raids over the past month or so."

There was a pause, and Max raised an eyebrow in a silent prompt for Hunter to keep talking.

"Taggert and his crew have been pretty quiet about it so far, but it looks like there are quite a few clubs in town that have been conducting some illegal back-room activity."

"Illegal like how?"

"Cards. Tables. Numbers. Pretty much any kind of gambling."

Max whistled. "Okay," he said. "Anybody in particular behind it."

"Don't know. But if you should get any ideas from anybody you talk to, I trust you'll be kind enough to pass that along."

Max's eyebrows went up and the corners of his mouth went down. "Sure, Jack."

They stopped at the corner of East Seventh—a short street that came off Liberty, near the courthouse—and waited for the traffic to clear before crossing. Hunter looked in Max's direction and started to speak when something in the distance, something thirty or forty yards beyond Max and up the narrow street, caught his attention. A black car pulled up to the curb on Seventh and came to a stop. The narrow street made the car seem even bigger and more out of place than it would have looked elsewhere.

A figure waiting at the curb stepped off, opened the back door of the car and disappeared into the back seat. Hunter only got a quick glimpse, but it was enough for him to recognize Anthony Reynolds, heading for lunch in style—no doubt to one of those upscale places where prominent judges and well-compensated lawyers with hopes of someday becoming prominent judges eat their lunches.

The car did a quick turnaround in an alley that came off of Seventh and drove away in the opposite direction.

The hard life of a district court judge, thought Hunter. *A nice new car and someone to drive you around in it.*

The traffic cleared at the intersection and both Hunter and Max stepped off the curb. Max noticed that Hunter had been distracted by something in the distance. The reporter glanced down the side street, then turned back to Hunter and said, "Hey, Jack, what gives?"

Hunter snorted and shook his head. "Ah, nothing. Just saw the Honorable Anthony Reynolds heading for lunch."

"Hardcase Reynolds?"

"The same. I just had the pleasure of spending a half-hour in his courtroom this morning."

Max shook his head. "Guy's an odd bird."

"I'll say."

Max was silent for a brief stretch of the sidewalk as more pedestrians and traffic noises swirled around them. He may have been waiting for Hunter to serve up some details about the court date, but Hunter went in a different direction.

"Max, you remember Nicky Diamond?"

Max grunted. "You kidding? How could I forget? How could *anybody* forget? Hell, Jack, he controlled this whole city during Prohibition."

"It was more than that. It was more like the whole county, and the two on either side of it."

"Sure. Jeez, he was one sick mug." Max shook his head at the grim memories. "Wiped out damn near every enemy in his path—other mobsters, cops, politicians, you name it. And the way he did it. Jeez, the fireworks! They didn't call him Nicky Dynamite for nothing. It wasn't just the shooting. He damn near blew up half the town." He jerked a thumb over his shoulder at the building they'd just left. "Hell, he even…"

Hunter's face hardened immediately, and Max's voice trailed off. His usually cynical expression gave way to a look of genuine compassion. "Sorry, Jack."

Hunter waved it off. "Forget it."

Max shrugged. "Anyway, the explosives were like his signature or something. Or some kind of crazy trademark. A big blast, a gaping hole in a wall or a doorway and a cloud of smoke was his way of saying 'Nicky Dynamite was here.' Boy, was he screwy."

The reporter took a drag on the cigarette. "Only twelve years," he said. "Guy should've got the chair."

"Well, that was the plan," said Hunter. "But two key witnesses never made it to the stand to testify. One committed suicide and the other just disappeared. For all anyone knows, he's in concrete at the bottom of Bright River."

Hunter felt the muscles in his neck tighten a little, the way they always did when he so much as thought about Diamond, let alone talked about him. "Remember where he used to get the goods to make the bombs?"

"Sure," said Max. "Pharaoh Chemical. That place in the River District."

"Well, here's where it gets interesting. The place was broken into last night."

Max stopped in mid-stride and turned completely in Hunter's direction. Hunter stopped, turned back and met the reporter's gaze.

Neither man spoke for a couple seconds as pedestrians moved around and past them in both directions.

"What are you saying, Jack?" Max's voice was almost hushed, despite the midday traffic noise.

Hunter shrugged, looked up and down the street, wondering whether he should have brought any of this up. "I don't know," he said. "I don't know what I'm saying. Taggert doesn't have enough to say anything conclusive."

Max started walking again, and Hunter fell in step. Max struggled to figure out what to ask first. "Who…What'd they make off with?"

"Don't know yet. Mike Dugan has some detectives there right now. The plant is temporarily shut down and the detectives are working with the plant crew to figure out exactly what's missing from the inventory and how much. They hope to have everything counted by the end of the day."

Max shook his head. "Easy heist?"

"No. They made off in an unmarked truck. Some cops were there,

40

and more were called in. Apparently the police put up a good fight, but whoever did the job had enough firepower to keep them at a distance. Far enough that no one could make the plates."

Max snorted. "Not like the old days."

"No. In the old days, back when half the force was on the take, the cops would have known about the break-in before the fact. And if they'd have shown up at all, they would have looked the other way when it happened."

Max said nothing for a moment—which was unusual for Max—then asked the inevitable. "You think it's Diamond?"

"I don't think anything yet." It wasn't entirely true. Hunter was starting to think something. He just didn't know what it was yet.

They slowed their pace and eventually stopped as they reached the curb at East Third. Max started to say something, but he was cut off by the low, ominous chug and rattle of a loaded dump truck obliterating the usual hum of midday traffic. The truck was pulling away from an equally noisy sandblasting operation on the other side of the intersection.

He stopped and turned away from Hunter to get a look at a towering stone structure on the other side of the street—a monolithic thing closed off to pedestrian traffic by temporary wooden barricades and surrounded on all sides by metal scaffolding.

Max shook his head. "Man, I wish they'd just finish that damned project already."

Hunter turned his eyes in the same direction. "It's been, what, six months now?"

"At least. It just seems like forever."

That damned project was the renovation of Union Arch, a fifty-foot-tall archway of granite and concrete, with stone stairs on either side that led up to a twenty-five-foot-long observation deck at the top. Union Arch towered over the sprawling Union Plaza, the geographic center of the city and the hub of no less than seven main avenues and streetcar lines that radiated in all directions toward the outer parts of the downtown and midtown districts.

Originally constructed at the beginning of the century and officially opened to the public in 1905 to commemorate the city's centennial, Union Arch had been closed since the winter months to repair the various spots of crumbling mortar and loose stones that had become a safety concern. The plan was to finish by the end of the summer, which was just three months off. A sense of anticipation had been brewing around town—especially among the downtown crowd—but Hunter could never determine how much of the excitement was about the rededication and reopening of the arch and how much was about putting an end to the noise, the traffic snarls and other inconveniences that the project had caused since the beginning of the year.

Nearly obscured by the scaffolding, the inscription in the stone panel at the top of the arch read:

UNION CITY

LIBERTY AND JUSTICE FOR ALL

Some two-hundred-fifty feet beyond the arch, a fountain stood in the center of the red-brick plaza, while the perimeter was defined by a series of newsstands, small shops, a diner, a cigar store, a florist and other storefronts and kiosks. The plaza was a twenty-four-hour hive of activity for pedestrians, office workers, street vendors, cabbies, newsboys, panhandlers, beat cops and just about every other segment of humanity.

Beyond the fountain, at the opposite end of the plaza from the arch, was the fifty-story Union Tower, by far the tallest structure in the county at seven-hundred-fifty feet, and the fifth-tallest building in the entire world. The basement of the skyscraper was a bustling rail station where inbound and outbound trains stopped throughout the day and most of the night. The ground floor included administrative offices, a restaurant, a couple newsstands, a post office, a visitor's center and other miscellaneous vendors. Everything from the second floor to the top was office space for law firms, accounting firms and various other businesses.

Along the front wall of the building facing the plaza, a row of canvas awnings hooded the windows on the first four floors and swayed in the breeze. The rest was a monolithic column of brick, mortar, steel and glass—all of it piercing the summer sky.

The combination of Union Tower and Union Arch—architectural bookends to the bustling downtown plaza—never failed to grab Hunter's attention. He stood at the curb and stared at the inscription over the arch for a moment, blocking out the street noise. He took a deep breath and let it out slowly.

"Where you headed?" said Max.

Hunter looked away from the arch and back at the reporter, who was eyeing him quizzically.

"Ottoman's," he said, jerking a thumb toward the plaza. "That new place. The corned beef is good."

"It is," said Max. "I've had it." He held his cigarette between two fingers and put it to his lips for a long drag. He blew a cloud of smoke and pointed to a parking space along the curb. "I'm here," he said.

He was referring to a 1917 Ford Model T Roadster parked twenty feet from where they were standing. Max stepped toward it and unlocked the metal storage box mounted on the back. Hunter followed, surveying the vehicle and shaking his head slowly. "Good Lord, Maxie, you're still driving this flivver?"

"You know it. My dad bought it just before the war, when I was twelve. Gave it to me before he died. Still runs like a top." He reached into the storage box and pulled out his briefcase.

Hunter eyed the battered toolbox and the generous coil of rope that were also tucked into the storage box. "And just how often do you have to get under the hood to keep this thing running like a top?" he said.

"Once a day," he said. "If I'm lucky."

"With all due respect to your late father, I'm betting the fact that you still drive this thing doesn't have a whole lot to do with any sentimentality toward him," said Hunter. "I'm thinking it's more about your salary."

Max slammed the lid down on the storage box. "Well, there's that too." He stepped around to the side of the car, opened the door and tossed the brief case onto the passenger seat. He turned back toward Hunter and tipped his hat. "Gotta run, Jack. You just keep protecting those good citizens, y'hear?"

Hunter's mouth twisted into a wry grin. "We do our best."

Max's expression sobered. He took a step toward Hunter and lowered his voice slightly, as though trying to protect a secret on a busy street. "And if you hear anything more from your cronies about that heist at the chemical plant—and who might've been behind it—the next sandwich is on me."

"Your cronies may know just as much as mine," said Hunter.

"Maybe more. You hear anything on the street, be sure to do your civic duty and pass it long."

Max nodded and flicked his cigarette butt into the street. "Always eager to help the law."

He climbed into the Model T and coaxed the engine to life.

Hunter shook his head as he watched the car chug and sputter away from the curb and into the distance.

CHAPTER 6
CHINATOWN ENCOUNTER

Lotus Street, the central artery running through Union City's Chinatown district, was still a busy place in the late afternoon hours. Johnny Kowalski maneuvered the Buick Roadmaster—an imposing beast of a car—down the congested stretch of road at a slow and uneven pace. He was frequently forced to yield to various obstacles along the way—chattering black-haired youngsters playing in the street, sidewalk vendors taking their business off the curb and onto the road, drivers unloading delivery trucks, even the occasional rickshaw runner with a passenger in tow. The eclectic swirl was typical of the bustling Asian neighborhood on any given day.

On either side of the street, storefront signs announced their wares in a combination of English and Chinese characters. Underneath some of the signs, shop owners with wizened faces peered through doors and windows, their eyes knowing but their expressions inscrutable.

This was Union City's small but authentic jewel of the Orient, an exotic world hidden deep within a more conventional one.

Nicky Diamond, however, saw it as anything but a jewel. He watched it all through the backseat window of the car with a bored, contemptuous stare. It wasn't enough that the streets of Union City were crawling with countless masses still scrambling to survive in the aftermath of a market crash seven years earlier. The streets had to be further crowded by the Orientals with their suspicious faces and even stranger customs. Worse yet, he was forced to do business with them as a means to rebuild his power base within the city.

But it would be a temporary means, and nothing more. He would make sure of it.

Louie Simone sat up front next to Kowalski, silently watching the street and everything on it. Even from his position in the back seat, Diamond noticed the bulk of Simone's shoulder holster underneath his open jacket. Simone was ready for any contingency that might come up as part of their scheduled meeting in Chinatown.

Next to Diamond in the back sat Vinnie Marshall, his primary advisor—his *consigliere*, as they would say in the old country. Marshall was the one he trusted more than any other, and for good reason. They had been like brothers since childhood—long before Duke or the alcohol operation during Prohibition or Simone or the prison sentence or any of the rest.

The Marsala family and the Diamante family had been close friends in Sicily, before either came to America. The Diamantes came over first, and the Marsalas came less than two years later. For a short time, the two families lived together in the same crowded tenement until the Marsalas could find housing of their own.

The Marsala family had an eighteen-year-old daughter, an astonishing beauty named Francesca. Within months after their arrival, Francesca Marsala became the mistress of Dale Kensington, one of Union City's most celebrated millionaires and a high-profile member of the society elite. Kensington's numerous lucrative ventures in industry and real estate in the late eighteen-hundreds had helped transform Union City from a modest nineteenth-century township into a thriving metropolis.

Less than a year after taking up with Kensington, Francesca became pregnant with his child. Nicky Diamond—then Niccolo Diamante—was only six when Vincenzo Marsala came into the world in 1897.

In a surprising turn of events, Kensington took full responsibility for the well-being of the boy and his mother within days after his arrival and for the remainder of his upbringing. Kensington had enough influence with the local and national press to keep any hint of scandal out of the papers. Francesca lived a quiet and very comfortable life until her death at age forty-one during the influenza epidemic of 1918.

Speculation about the motives behind Kensington's charity persisted through the years. Some said he took care of his illegitimate son and her mother out of a genuine sense of moral responsibility for their well-being. Others said he did it at gunpoint, with Francesca's

45

father at the trigger. Diamond never knew for sure.

What he did know was that Kensington arranged for Vincenzo Marsala's name to be legally changed at an early age to Vincent Marshall. Young Vincent, who turned out to be a remarkably bright and studious boy, attended the finest boarding schools in the state, and eventually enrolled at Harvard Law School, where he graduated near the top of his class.

Marshall's keen understanding of the law—along with a personal relationship that was familial long before it was professional—enabled him to unofficially and informally advise Diamond in his efforts to re-establish himself in Union City, yet keep his own professional reputation untarnished at the same time. Diamond, after all, had become nothing more than a bad memory in Union City's collective consciousness when he boarded the bus headed for state prison fourteen years earlier. Marshall's job was to keep things that way until Diamond was ready to reemerge.

Diamond broke the long silence in the car, muttering softly to Marshall. "That business with Valentine finished?"

"Yes. LoCastro took care of it. Valentine will spend two months in jail, with some community service, and it'll be done."

Diamond nodded. "He needs to know he can't make any more stupid mistakes like that." He paused and shook his head. "Beating up a waitress. That's cheap. And when he has to do time for it, it's costly to the operation. Things can be fixed, but only to a point."

Diamond continued to watch the street in silence. After the car covered another block, he spoke again. "Tell me again what Sun Lu wants to meet about."

Marshall folded his hands in his lap. "I'm told he wants to clarify the terms of the arrangement," he said. "Now that he's provided us with the initial shipment a few weeks ago, and with a second one coming tomorrow, he wants to know how long we'll be doing business."

Diamond's eyebrows furrowed. "As long as we need to," he said, with an edge of impatience creeping into his voice. "When we don't need to anymore, we stop."

"I'm not sure if that will be the answer he wants to hear. Up until now, we've conducted an exchange of money for services, but it seems that he's interested in something more. I think he's looking for something more like a partnership rather than merely a series of business transactions."

Diamond didn't answer.

Kowalski turned down a side street and drove another three- or four-hundred feet before pulling into a small lot behind a free-standing import shop. He cut the engine.

Before anyone in the car made a move, Diamond turned to Marshall. "I want you to do most of the talking," he said. He shook his head, his face a mask of contempt. "I don't understand these people, even when they do speak English."

Marshall nodded. Kowalski and Simone opened their doors and stepped out of the car, then opened the rear doors for Diamond and Marshall.

A hard-looking Asian with an expressionless face emerged from the rear entrance to the shop and stood under the small canvas awning over the door, arms folded and feet shoulder-width apart. He wore a gray mandarin jacket buttoned all the way up to the collar, with wide sleeves ending in equally wide cuffs. He stood no more than five-and-a-half feet tall, but there was no mistaking the power coiled up in his compact frame. He was clearly on hand for security purposes. Diamond suspected he was one of those who could do deadly things with his bare hands, but his trained eye noticed the sudden break in the otherwise smooth line of the bodyguard's jacket, near the waist. He immediately surmised that the Asian had a gun tucked underneath, either in a holster or a belt around the narrow black pants that ended with a pair of sandals. Diamond also speculated as to what kind of blade might be sheathed to the man's forearm in the ample hiding spaces created by the wide sleeves.

A second figure came through the back door as Diamond and his entourage approached the entrance. He was slightly taller than the first, but very similar in every other way—expression, demeanor, attire and hidden weaponry that wasn't all that hidden. Diamond wondered how many more like this they might encounter between the entrance to the shop and Sun Lu himself.

Diamond and his crew stopped at the door. The two Asians looked at all four of them with cold eyes. The shorter one pointed at Kowalski's chest and said, "Jacket." Diamond was fairly certain it was one of the few English words the man knew.

Kowalski looked back at the Asian with equally cold eyes and opened his jacket, revealing the Colt .38 Army Special in his belt. "It stays with me," he said in a tone that left little room for negotiation.

The Asian glared at him, then turned his attention to Simone to conduct the same ritual. Simone opened his jacket, revealing the shoulder holster holding his Remington 51. He tilted his head toward Kowalski. "You heard what the man said," Simone muttered. "The gat's mine, and it stays mine."

The taller Asian turned to Diamond and Marshall and gestured at their chests.

"Mr. Diamond and I are not carrying weapons," said Marshall.

The Asian held his gaze for a moment, then gestured again.

Diamond glared back at him, then rolled his eyes. "For crissake," he snarled under his breath, opening his jacket. Marshall did the same, but without expression or imprecation.

The taller Asian gave them both the once-over with his eyes, apparently speculating about their pants pockets or even their shoes, but he made no move to initiate a more thorough search.

The bodyguards glanced at each other, then turned toward the door. The shorter one opened it and Diamond, Marshall and Simone walked through. When Kowalski said he'd stay outside near the car, both bodyguards eyed him suspiciously but didn't argue.

The interior of the shop was nearly silent, save for the murmur of traffic from the street outside and the tick of a clock somewhere in the room. Diamond immediately noticed an herbal smell from some sort of burning incense.

The place was shelved from wall to wall and from floor to ceiling, and every inch of horizontal space was filled with a vast and diverse assortment of hand-crafted and exquisite Oriental items—clothing, furniture, figurines, clocks, wall hangings, toys, candles and candle holders, picture frames, serving sets, and countless other pieces, many of which Diamond couldn't recognize. All of it suggested a world too foreign for Diamond to even begin to comprehend.

The bodyguards ushered them silently down a short aisle that led to a room separated from the main area of the store by a wooden door with ornate brass fixtures. Hanging from the door was a wooden sign with Chinese characters painted on it. Diamond assumed the characters prohibited customer traffic.

The taller bodyguard opened the door and ushered the three men inside. Simone immediately took a position to the left of the door, while Diamond and Marshall moved further into the room.

Near the center of the room was a round table of intricately carved wood, with four similarly carved chairs surrounding it. A tea set, each porcelain piece hand-painted and delicate, had been carefully arranged there.

The shorter bodyguard gestured for Diamond and Marshall to wait, then disappeared into a room on the other side of the table, while the taller one went back out to the main area of the store, closing the door behind him. Diamond guessed he was heading back out to the parking lot to keep an eye on Kowalski.

Less than a minute later, the shorter bodyguard reemerged from the side room. Sun Lu, the proprietor of the shop, followed immediately behind him. After a few steps, the younger Oriental broke away, crossing the room and taking a position by the door leading to the customer area of the store.

Sun Lu was somewhere around eighty. His head and face were completely shaved, and despite his advanced years, his dark eyes were clear and the lines on his face were few.

He wore traditional Chinese garb—a blue satin robe with gold trim at the collar and cuffs, and a gold sash at the waist. The image of a swirling red dragon was embroidered on the front panels of the robe, which extended a few inches below his knees. Like his two bodyguards, Sun Lu wore straight black pants and sandals on his feet.

The merchant came to a stop several feet shy of where Diamond and Marshall were standing. "Gentlemen," he said with a slight bow. "Good afternoon. I am pleased that you were able to pay me a visit in my humble place of business."

Marshall bowed in return. Diamond nodded begrudgingly.

"I hope you will excuse my grandsons," said the old merchant. "The young sometimes fail to remember politeness, especially when they are feeling protective toward the elders of their family."

Although he maintained the accent of his native country, he spoke excellent English, in a cadence that was slow and thoughtful. There was something centered and elegant about his movements—even the smallest gestures—which suggested some deep inner wisdom that transcended his time and place. His facial expression was devoid of subterfuge, his serenity in the midst of tension disarming.

And all of this only made Diamond feel even more suspicious than he had been before he got out of the car.

Sun Lu gestured toward the table. "May I offer you some tea?"

Marshall responded with another small bow. "No, thank you," he said. "We wouldn't want to take much of your time."

"Please sit," said Sun Lu. All three men approached the table and settled into chairs. Sun Lu's movements were slower and more deliberate than those of the two younger men on the other side of the table.

"If you will permit," said Sun Lu, "I will have some tea for myself. It helps to keep my mind clear. A man of many years, such as I am, puts a high value on a clear mind."

Marshall nodded. "Of course."

Sun Lu poured tea into his cup and carefully set the pot back on the table. "I trust the product in our initial transaction was to your satisfaction."

"Yes," said Diamond. "It was acceptable."

Sun Lu closed his eyes and bowed his head slightly. "Very good," he said. "If it were anything less, I would want to be made aware. It would be most troubling, but I would want to be made aware. An unsatisfied customer is rarely a customer more than once."

Diamond did his best to suppress his irritation. *Hell*, he thought, *this is fortune cookie talk.*

"And what of our other services? Have the gentlemen been satisfied?"

Diamond nodded. "Yes, the other services have been acceptable as well."

Sun Lu lowered his eyelids and bowed his head again. "I am very pleased."

He took a sip of tea and put the cup down carefully. He paused for a long moment before speaking again. "My associates and I regard this initial transaction as an introduction to the services that are available to you," he said. "It would be helpful to know the extent of the business arrangement. There are certain costs associated with providing the products and services in which you have expressed an interest. If we can come to an agreement about how long we will do business and how frequently, we can make arrangements that would be financially and strategically beneficial to all."

"Unfortunately," said Marshall, "I don't believe we're ready to make a commitment like that at this time."

Sun Lu's head tilted slightly as he seemed to weigh the response. "That is unfortunate indeed," he said after a moment. "I had hoped that we could discuss a partnership. Associations based on trust are always preferable to those based on rivalry. There was a time, many years ago, when I was a younger man and you gentlemen were still very much in your youth, when this humble community engaged in fierce rivalries."

"The tong wars," said Diamond.

"Yes. That is how they were commonly known, especially outside of our community. Families were divided, people were hurt. Some were even killed. The deaths were often unfortunate, sometimes even needless. It was not a time of harmony for our people, and there was much trouble with the local authorities."

He looked down at his cup, his eyes faraway, as though he were contemplating Chinatown's violent past. After a moment, he looked up and waved a hand at the surrounding room. "Now, as then, I make my living as a simple merchant," he said. "I sell my wares to this community—and sometimes to those who come to our community from the city."

"But your life was never that simple."

"I had certain affiliations that were little known among the local authorities. I had a certain leadership responsibility."

"The Ho Sheng," said Marshall.

Sun Lu bowed yet again. Diamond noticed that the merchant would not refer to the Chinese tong by name himself. The Ho Sheng Brotherhood—although a mere shadow of what it had been years ago in terms of power and influence—was still a deeply revered entity, even if only in the memories of those still living in Chinatown who had been affiliated with it. The tong's presence in Union City dated all the way back to the late eighteen-hundreds. Many of those who had been lucky enough to survive those violent days had since died of natural causes and old age.

Diamond considered Sun Lu's comment about an arrangement that would be "strategically beneficial to all." The old merchant had been one of the most influential figures in the city's underworld due to his high-ranking status in a powerful Chinese tong. But those days had come and gone. Diamond suspected the old man saw a long-term business association as a last chance at reestablishing a foothold in the city's reconfigured power structure—for himself maybe, but perhaps more so for Chinatown's next generations.

Marshall paused. He appeared to gather his thoughts before speaking. "Sir, we have the utmost respect for your position in this community, and for the community's long and troubled history," he said, speaking in the deliberate cadence of a seasoned lawyer. "Indeed, we hold all of your associates in high regard, not just the ones here but in your homeland as well. We certainly want to maintain good relations with the Chinatown neighborhood in Union City. But Mr. Diamond is still in the early stages of re-establishing his operations in the city. It would be difficult for him to define the exact nature and extent of his long-term plans. I'm afraid we're not ready to commit to a long-term business arrangement at this time."

Sun Lu nodded slowly, and his expression grew more pensive. He rested his elbows on the table and folded his hands in front of his chin. His eyes looked far away, over the heads of Diamond and Marshall. The room was silent, so much so that Diamond could hear his own breathing and the breathing of the other two men seated at the table.

Nearly a minute passed before Sun Lu unlaced his fingers and placed his palms on the table.

"There are unique goods and services that you need to maintain your operation," he said, "and we have established that we alone are able to provide them—not just with the first shipment, but very soon with a second. We can continue to provide these things for you for a while longer, but like you, there are things we desire for the good of our community. There will come a time when we must have an understanding about our coexistence over time."

"I don't think there's any question that we can coexistent," said Marshall. "We're doing so now. Is there any feeling among you or your associates that the compensation for the goods and services that have been provided so far has been less than appropriate?"

"Your compensation has been most agreeable," said Sun Lu.

"We have absolutely no quarrel with the people of Chinatown," Marshall went on. "Mr. Diamond has no interest in extending his operations into this area."

Sun Lu paused again. "None that he has expressed," he said.

Diamond stared directly at Sun Lu, and the Chinese merchant—

who had been primarily addressing Marshall until now—turned his gaze back at Diamond and held it. The room was silent for a long moment, but this time with an undercurrent of tension that spread to every corner. Diamond finally broke the stare by arching an eyebrow and giving Marshall a sidelong glance.

"Gentlemen," said Sun Lu, "many of my people, and I among them, believe in the yin and the yang. It is the understanding that all things in nature—even those which may be opposites—are in fact connected, and for everything that is taken, something must be given in return. Indeed, you and I must ask ourselves and each other if we are willing to establish a relationship that will meet both of our needs."

He finished the tea in his cup and put it back down on the table without refilling it. "If there will be changes in the way business is conducted in Union City, they will likely have an effect on our community. I would be less than prudent if I did not expect to maintain some influence over the direction of the changes. I am a man of business, yes. But I am also a man who thinks carefully about the future of his business and his community."

More silence. Diamond sensed that Sun Lu had come to the end of the conversation. Apparently, Marshall had come to the same conclusion.

"You've given us much to think about," said the consigliere, "and we will certainly consider your words very carefully."

Sun Lu bowed his head slightly. "I trust that you will," he said. If he was experiencing any frustration or disappointment over the outcome of their meeting, his face betrayed nothing. "I am honored by your visit."

Sun Lu gripped the arms of his chair and rose slowly—and a little unsteadily. Marshall stood more quickly and stepped around the table toward the elderly merchant with his hand outstretched in a gesture of assistance. But it took less than an instant for the short, stocky bodyguard at the door to cross the room and insinuate himself between Marshall and Sun Lu. The Asian took the old man's arm and gently helped him straighten himself.

Sun Lu stood straight and took a step away from the chair. He turned to the bodyguard and muttered something in Chinese, gesturing to the door where the bodyguard had been standing and Simone was still standing.

The bodyguard looked at Diamond and Marshall and made a brusque gesture toward the door.

Marshall turned to Sun Lu one last time and bowed slightly. "We are grateful for your hospitality and your time."

Sun Lu bowed back to him, then turned to look at Diamond, who offered nothing more than a perfunctory nod and turned away.

Simone fell in step as the bodyguard ushered Diamond and Marshall through the doorway and back into the shop. The Asian walked behind them as they moved through the same warren of aisles by which they'd accessed the meeting room twenty minutes earlier. No words were spoken, nor was there any semblance of friendliness in the short walk to the back door.

Diamond squinted into the late afternoon sun when they pushed through the back door. Outside, they found Kowalski and the taller bodyguard in the parking lot, standing several yards apart, each acutely aware of the other without making eye contact, neither uttering a word, both coiled and ready to strike if needed.

All six men stood facing each other outside the building. Diamond turned and glared at the two Orientals for several seconds, and they glared back. No words were exchanged, but the expressions on the faces of the two Asians and the American crime boss spoke reams.

Marshall apparently sensed the tension and took Diamond's arm. "Nick," he muttered, gently steering Diamond away from the two Asians and toward the car. Diamond reluctantly broke off his stare.

Marshall caught Kowalski's eye, and Kowalski responded by moving across the lot to the car and opening the back door.

All four men got in and Kowalski immediately started the engine. They were back up the side street and back on the main drag through the neighborhood in less than thirty seconds.

"It's pretty clear to me," said Diamond without preamble. "We're using his supply channels to develop the operation, and he wants something more than straight payment. He wants a piece of the action."

Marshall nodded. "He knows you're still getting your footing and the operation is not fully established yet. He senses an opening, a temporary opportunity, and he wants to capitalize on it."

"He's not going to."

Kowalski slowed the car to a crawl at an intersection to maneuver his way through a cluster of pedestrians and street vendors. Simone watched the street scene through the windshield with a detached eye. Both men in the front seat remained silent.

"He could be a worthwhile ally, Nick," said Marshall. "At the height of their influence, the Ho Sheng had sufficient contacts and operations at either coast to bring a steady supply of opium and women into the country. And they've demonstrated an expertise in running gambling operations as well. It stands to reason that at least some of those connections still exist."

"He's not going to push his way in," Diamond insisted. "He can't. He may have connections, but he doesn't have the resources or the leverage he used to have. It would take him years to build the manpower the tongs used to have. Did you get a good look at him? He doesn't have that kind of time. Hell, the tongs were a thing of the past in this town by the end of the war. They had to get out of the way."

He paused and jutted his chin slightly. "They had to get out of the way to make room for me."

"Whatever the case," said Marshall, "we'll need to be judicious with the goods and services he's provided so far—including the shipment we're expecting in the next couple days. We can't expect the supply to be unlimited unless we're willing to negotiate a long-term deal with him."

Diamond didn't answer. His mind was already shifting to other more immediate matters. He checked his watch and glanced at the sky through the car window. It would be dark in a few hours, and there was still business to take care of at Stu Hirschfeld's place.

CHAPTER 7
BUZZ

Hunter was still thinking about all the pieces when he pulled into the parking lot behind The Republic Building at seven o'clock that evening. The nightclubs, the gambling, the break-ins at Pharaoh Chemical. And of course, the spectre of Nicky Diamond, lurking around the edges of the picture. Was there something connecting it all, or was he just jumping to conclusions? He cut the engine and sat behind the wheel for a moment with the window down, taking in a few deep breaths of June air.

He and Gallagher and the rest of the DA's office didn't know anything more about the break-in than they had at the beginning of the day. Gallagher had tried to reach Dugan late in the afternoon, but the sergeant on duty at the UCPD detective bureau told him that Dugan and his team of two other plainclothes detectives and two officers were still at Pharaoh, assessing the damage and waiting for the company's maintenance crew to clean up the mess in the warehouse and get some kind of definitive inventory of what had been taken and what was intact.

The best that Hunter and everyone could hope was that the investigation of the crime scene would wrap up before too late in the evening and they'd all have a clearer picture to look at in the morning.

Hunter rubbed his eyes for a moment. When he reopened them, he focused on the back wall of The Republic Building, the place he called home. It was a two-story brick structure that fronted on the corner of East Forty-Second and Whitney Avenue. It had been built in the 1880s, as the original headquarters of the *Union Tribune*, when the newspaper was still a small operation with a staff of only four or five people. By the start of the war, the paper had outgrown the location and moved to a larger building closer to downtown. Hunter's uncle, Frank Hunter, bought the building in 1919, right after the war ended, and converted it to an appliance repair shop on the ground floor. It had been a smart move on Uncle Frank's part. Forty-Second and Whitney was a high-traffic corner, a little more than four miles from downtown. And after the war, more and more houses around town were being wired for electricity, and with that came lamps, radios and other appliances—all of which needed repairs sooner or later.

Uncle Frank had run the shop until he passed away. Then Frank, Jr., Jack's cousin, took over the business. The younger Frank was a decorated war veteran who had answered to the nickname of "Buzz" ever since he was six years old.

When Jack and Buzz were still teenagers, they helped their fathers build two apartments into the top floor of the building, one at either end of a connecting hallway. After a few renters came and went, the units eventually became the living quarters of Jack and Buzz. This arrangement was especially convenient for Buzz, whose commute to the shop was nothing more than a short flight of stairs or a small elevator that he and Jack had built into a space behind one of the walls.

Jack emerged from the car and checked his watch. It was six-twenty. Buzz would have closed the shop at six. He walked across the alley to the back entrance and disarmed the electric alarm system before unlocking the door with his key. Inside, he passed through a small vestibule with an opposite door that led to a short hallway.

Two stairways came off the hallway. The one to the right led up to the two apartments on the second floor, and the other to the left led down to the basement. Between the two was a door that led to the store at ground level.

The stairway leading to the basement was slightly ajar, enough to cast a glow from the light fixture at the bottom of the steps.

Hunter called down the stairs but got no answer. He headed down to the basement, which was a large and well-organized storage room lined with shelving that was fully stocked with a vast inventory of electrical equipment. He moved through the room, a seemingly endless array of light bulbs, light fixtures, switches, electrical outlets, numerous spools of wire in a variety of gauges, fuses, replacement cords, vacuum tubes and other parts for just about any radio ever made, and probably a few other things even Hunter couldn't identify.

At the opposite end of the room was a second door that led to another staircase. This door was also ajar, and Hunter heard the murmur of *The Green Hornet* from a radio below.

He opened the door wider and leaned over the threshold. "Buzz? You down there?"

Hunter waited a moment. He heard the volume drop on the radio, then an adult voice brimming with boyish enthusiasm: "Hiya, Jack! Come on down!"

Hunter descended. At the bottom step, he scanned the cinderblock and concrete space and immediately burst out laughing.

Some twenty feet away, sitting on a wooden stool at a worn workbench, was Buzz, surrounded by a hodge-podge of tools and wire scraps and wearing a contraption on his head that defied description. The thing was a convoluted nest of induction coils, resistors, tubes, and a few things Hunter—even with his considerable knowledge of electrical circuits—couldn't recognize. What's more, the entire

57

apparatus was wired together in a confusing network that Hunter couldn't begin to understand.

The mass of components was mounted on a leather aviator's cap—a leftover that Buzz had brought home from the war. A few of the wires ran from circuits around Buzz's headpiece and fed directly into a pair of goggles secured to his face by a leather strap running over his ears and around the back of his head.

The assembly just about tripled the size of Buzz's head. In some places, the tubes and coils poked out even further—so much so that he had to be careful when turning to face left or right, so as not to tip over the workbench lamp or knock any tools or parts off the shelf immediately next to him.

Buzz looked back at him, speechless, his eyes obscured by the dark lenses of the goggles.

"What?" he said finally, apparently bewildered by Hunter's outburst.

After a mighty struggle to get the laughter under control, Hunter caught just enough breath to say, "Buzz, what the hell is that?" But it was just enough and no more. He was sputtering again before Buzz could even answer.

"It's the thing I was telling you about."

"What thing? You're always working on a thing, Buzz. I can never keep track."

"That article I told you about," said Buzz, turning slowly and carefully to avoid knocking anything off the shelf over his workbench. He reached for a copy of *Popular Science* at the top of a stack of other periodicals. The magazine was opened and folded back to the first page of an article. He passed it to Hunter.

"Oh, right," said Hunter. "I remember this. 'Improving the Mind with the Science of Cranial Stimulation.'" His brow furrowed. "Sounds like mad scientist stuff."

"Come on, Jack, I'm not sewing body parts together down here."

"Maybe not," Hunter said with a grin, "but your head looks a lot bigger now than it did when I left for work this morning."

Buzz flashed a sheepish grin of his own. "Seriously, Jack, it's pretty interesting. The idea is, you can improve mental capacity by exposing different areas of the brain to a magnetic field generated by an electric circuit."

Hunter raised an eyebrow. "Is it safe?"

"Sure it is. There's nothing invasive about it. It's not like sticking pins in people's heads or anything. It's really just like a scalp massage with an electric current. There was a guy in London who had some early success with it about twenty-five years ago, and there've been advancements since then."

Buzz leaned over and pointed to the magazine in Hunter's hand, taking care not to bang into him with the apparatus strapped to his head. "There's a diagram on the second page that explains the different areas of the brain and what they control," he said, "and there's some stuff in there about what other researchers have done and what kinds of results they've had. They use it to help people who've had strokes, or suffer from severe depression, stuff like that."

Hunter frowned as he scanned a few lines of the magazine article. "So they position induction coils in specific areas to stimulate brain activity," he said.

"Exactly."

"Direct current?"

"Yep." He waved at an elaborate dry cell assembly on his workbench that looked almost as convoluted as his headgear. "This power setup is pretty big and clumsy, but I bet I could come up with something less bulky. You know, maybe something you could carry around with you."

"You just cobbled all this together from what you saw in this article?"

Buzz shrugged. "Well, yeah. I've been working on it for about a week. Heck, people come into the shop with radios and lamps and toasters, and I can usually fix that stuff in a half-hour. That leaves me plenty of time to monkey around with something like this."

Hunter shook his head. "You amaze me, Buzz."

"It wasn't hard. I used all the information in the article as a start, but I made some adjustments to the coils. And I tried some different positions, too. I tell you, Jack, when you have this thing on, everything feels—I don't know—different, I guess. Clearer. Sharper. It's hard to explain. It's like you can think faster and better with this thing."

Hunter looked up from the magazine and examined some of the circuitry wrapped around Buzz's head. "Huh," he said. "Interesting."

"Wanna try it?"

Hunter laughed skeptically, closing the magazine and tossing it on the workbench. "You kidding me? It'd take you at least a half-hour to get that thing off your head and another half-hour to get it on mine."

"No, it'll just take a minute. Come on, try it."

Hunter shrugged. He couldn't deny that he was curious. Anytime Buzz built a gadget of any kind for any purpose, he was curious. It had been that way since they were kids.

He slipped out of his jacket and pulled off his tie.

Ten minutes later, with a lot of help from Buzz and a little bit of grumbling, Hunter had the contraption positioned on his head and the goggles strapped to his face. The whole thing made his head wobble, which made him feel silly. He was glad there were no mirrors in the room.

"Buzz, this is—"

"Hold on. I'm almost finished." Buzz made the final connections between the headgear and the goggles. He adjusted a couple coils, then slid his fingertips under the edges of the leather cap and smoothed it into position along the surface of Hunter's scalp.

He leaned back slightly and looked into the smoky brown lenses of the goggles positioned over Hunter's eyes. "Okay, you comfortable?"

"Hardly."

"Okay. Just relax and take a deep breath. I'm going to throw the switch."

Hunter arched an eyebrow. "This going to hurt?"

"No, but you're going to feel something. Trust me." Buzz put his index finger on the switch. "Ready?"

Hunter nodded, and Buzz threw the switch. The two men locked eyes for a moment, then Hunter glanced back at Buzz's finger still resting on the switch. He glanced around the room, waiting.

After four or five seconds, he shrugged. "I don't know, Buzz. I'm not really feeling any—"

Buzz raised an index finger. "Hold on."

"Whoa!" It came at Hunter in a rush. The entire room and everything in it suddenly looked brighter, every object in razor-sharp focus. The world nearly vibrated with clarity and intensity. His ears tuned themselves to the tiny tick of the clock hanging on the wall some twenty feet away, followed the hum of cars moving along the street eighteen feet above them at ground level. Eyes wide, mouth agape, he looked back at Buzz.

"See what I mean?"

"Wow. Everything is just…" Hunter stopped for a moment and listened. He could hear the air moving in and out of Buzz's lungs. *He could hear his heartbeat!* "My God, that's…Wow!"

Buzz kept his eyes on Hunter's face as he shifted his feet slightly and positioned himself between Hunter and the workbench. He reached around behind his back…

Hunter sensed the movement with an awareness that was almost prescient.

Buzz's right forearm jerked upward, releasing a handful of golf balls in the air over Hunter's head.

Hunter's eyes tracked all five balls at once—each one following an arc completely divergent from the other. No pattern, no order, no rhyme or reason. Five different spheres moving randomly through free space.

In less than a second, Hunter was holding all five balls—three in one hand and two in the other. He stared into his hands for a moment, shaking his head and stammering. "I…I don't…I can barely remember catching them!"

Buzz smiled. "Something, huh? If it's calibrated right, this thing can heighten your reflexes by a factor of ten. Shorten your response time by a similar measure. I had it on for about a half-hour before you came home, and I swear I could see and hear things coming almost before they happened." He reached around to the workbench again, and Hunter felt the same internal alarm go off in his head—just as it had before the balls went into the air.

Buzz smiled at the sudden wariness in Hunter's expression. "It's okay," he said. "No surprises this time." He held up a piece of paper torn out of a notebook. "Here, look at this. Just a column of random numbers. Look at them and tell me what—"

"Twelve-hundred-and-forty-seven."

Buzz responded with a grin. "Exactly," he said. "That's the other part. Enhanced cognitive power, just like the senses and the reflexes."

Hunter took the slip of paper from Buzz's hand and gave it a second glance. "Buzz, this column has almost twenty numbers. Most of them have three digits. But I just—"

"I know," said Buzz. He held up a hand. "Now. Stay right there." He moved across the room and reached for the light switch at the bottom of the stairs. "Get this."

Hunter waited. Five seconds later, Buzz was still standing at the bottom of the stairs, staring back at him without a word. "Get what, Buzz?"

"How many fingers am I holding up?"

"Four. Why?"

"How about now?"

"One."

"Now?"

"None. Your hands are down at your sides. Buzz, what're you—?"

"Jack, I killed the lights. We're eighteen feet below ground with no windows. We're in complete darkness."

"What? No, we're not. I can—"

"You can see in the dark," said Buzz. "Infrared goggles. I wired them directly to the helmet."

Hunter said nothing for a moment. He took a deep breath and let it out slowly, scanning the room and absorbing every minute detail of the shimmering reality that vibrated around him. He felt…more than human. And it was almost intoxicating.

"Wow," he said, almost in a whisper. "This is…I can barely…"

"You okay, Jack?"

"Yeah." He let out a short, nervous laugh. "Turn the lights back on. I need to get this thing off."

CHAPTER 8
DINNER AT HOME

A half-hour later, Hunter and Buzz were sitting across from each other at a table in the kitchen of Buzz's apartment, eating a dinner that consisted of deli sandwiches and root beer. The kitchen window was open, and the sounds of the evening—kids in the street, the faraway bark of a dog, an occasional car horn—wafted in from below and mixed with the sounds of a music program from the radio in the living room.

Buzz worked on a mouthful of corned beef. "I picked up razor blades at the drugstore today," he said. He looked a lot more recognizable now than he had when Hunter found him in full headgear in the sub-basement less than an hour earlier. He wore round glasses on a boyish face. His brown hair—in need of a comb, as usual—was peppered with gray and getting a little thin on top.

"Good thing," said Hunter. "Another week and I'd be cutting my face to ribbons."

"Doc Kendall said something kind of funny when I was there."

Dan "Doc" Kendall wasn't really a doctor, but he was close. He was the pharmacist and proprietor at Kendall Drug, about three blocks west of the Republic Building. It was a frequent stop for the Hunter boys whenever they needed aspirin, shoe polish, chewing gum, bicarbonate of soda or just about any other incidental item associated with everyday bachelor life—including razor blades.

"Yeah?" said Hunter. "What's that?"

Buzz took a swig of root beer. "Well, I went in and told him I needed razor blades. He shakes his head, all exasperated, and he says, 'Sure, razor blades I've got. But if you've got asthma, I can't help you.'"

Hunter's brow furrowed. "Asthma? I don't get it."

"Neither did I. I says to him, 'What's that got to do with razor blades?' But then he tells me he's had a run on those cylinders."

"What cylinders?"

"I mean those little tin inhalers that asthma patients use. Know what I'm talking about?"

"Oh, yeah," said Hunter. "The Benzedrine inhalers, with the powder inside. You inhale, and it shoots the powder into your lungs."

"Yeah, that's it. Doc says he's been sold out of the things for nearly two weeks, and every time he gets more, they get bought up just as fast."

"Huh. Well, it's summertime. Maybe it's the pollen in the air."

Buzz shrugged. "Maybe. Anyway, how was work?" he said.

Hunter did his best to hide his expression behind a swig of his own root beer. He responded with a shrug and nothing more. Buzz looked back at him and his eyes grew wary. "Uh-oh."

"Nothing, really. Just some chemicals stolen from a warehouse in the River District."

"Yeah?"

"Yeah. Some shooting, too."

"No kidding. They catch anybody?"

"No. The police were still investigating when I left the office.

Hopefully we'll know more tomorrow."

"Huh."

Buzz looked thoughtful for a moment, and Hunter could practically hear the wheels turning.

"What about you?" said Hunter, pivoting quickly to change the subject. "How was the store today?"

"Well, there wasn't any shooting," said Buzz. "I did close for about an hour around lunchtime to go and install an alarm on the side door of Mrs. Dooley's garage."

"Yeah?" Hunter suppressed a mischievous smile, but not entirely.

Buzz stopped chewing "What?"

"Nothing."

"Oh, here we go…"

Hunter cocked his head and raised an eyebrow. "I think she likes you, Buzz."

"Oh, come on. She's got that Plymouth that her husband bought a few years before he died, and she just wants to be sure it's safe."

"So she had you come right over."

Buzz rolled his eyes. "Yeah. So?"

"Just saying, Buzz."

"Well, it was pretty simple," said Buzz, obviously trying to steer the conversation back into a more technical direction. "She says she never uses that side door to her garage, so I set up a trip wire along with the hot wire. The hot wire is part of the alarm circuit, and it's tucked away where no one can get at it. The trip wire doesn't carry a current like the hot wire does, but it's set to a specific tension that holds the circuit open. Any change in that tension will close the circuit. So if an intruder or a car thief cuts the trip wire, or bumps into it, the circuit will close and the alarm will go off."

"And when it does, what happens? Does she call the police? Or does she call you?"

"Ah, nuts to you," Buzz growled, tossing a wadded napkin across the table. Hunter ducked and swatted it away in the nick of time.

"Hey, I'm just saying—"

"Uh-huh. And what about you, Mister Matchmaker? I don't see you going on any big dates lately. Successful young lawyer, high-falutin' assistant DA."

Hunter shrugged. "I've got plans."

Buzz's eyebrows went up. "Yeah?"

"Sure. She's down in the spare garage."

"Huh?"

"The Henderson."

"The Henderson? What, that heap you bought at the police department auction?"

"That heap was a police motorcycle until it was decommissioned."

"Gosh, Jack, that thing's been sitting down there for, what, almost two years now? I gave up on the idea that you'd ever get it out on the road. I just figured you'd eventually just get rid of it. Maybe sell it for scrap."

Hunter frowned. "You kidding me? I just had it out a couple weekends ago."

"Running okay?"

Hunter's eyes narrowed and his mouth twisted into a sly grin. "Better than okay," he said, "Gave it a good cleaning, for starters. The old filter was dirty, and there was a lot of grime in the air box. I just wasn't getting good combustion. So I cleaned out the box and put in a new filter."

"Yeah?"

"Yeah, and then there's the sprockets. Changed those too. More teeth in the back now and fewer in the front."

"Right. So the better gear ratio means a faster top speed. Maybe a lot faster if the ratio is right."

"Exactly."

Buzz put his hand up in a gesture of caution. "Better go easy, though," he said. "Drive that thing around town too fast and you're likely to get in trouble with the law."

Hunter's mouth turned up at one corner. "No," he said, shaking his head. "Wouldn't want to get in trouble with the law."

"Seriously, though, if you're going to boost the top speed, you'd better make sure the brakes are in good shape too."

"Already have. I'm taking it out on Saturday to test them."

Buzz took a bite of his sandwich and stared at Hunter for nearly half a minute as he chewed. From the other room, the sound of a siren and the staccato rat-a-tat of a machine gun came over the radio. The opening sound effects of *Gangbusters*.

Hunter looked back at him. "What?"

"So that's your weekend," said Buzz. It was more of statement than a question.

"Yeah. Why?"

Buzz finished the last of his root beer and shook his head.

"I'm starting to think maybe *you* should call Mrs. Dooley."

CHAPTER 9
DIAMOND STRIKES

At eleven-thirty, Nicky Diamond sat in the back seat of the Buick parked at the curb along Taylor Street, hidden in the shadows beyond the glow of a nearby streetlamp. Diamond sat behind the driver's seat, where Johnny Kowalski kept the headlights off but the engine idling at a quiet purr. Next to Diamond in the back seat sat Wireless, the other half—along with Sparks—of the two-man team that Diamond called his "technical crew."

Wireless was brown-haired and lanky, barely thirty years old. He'd been brought into the organization just a couple months earlier, shortly after Diamond returned to Union City. Diamond didn't even know his real name. He'd put the word out to his crew to recruit a specialist, someone with electrical expertise who could work with Sparks to develop equipment that would make it possible to trigger Sparks' explosives from remote locations. They came up with this boyish electrical wizard and shortwave hobbyist who fit the bill.

In a very short time, Wireless had made himself extremely useful to the organization. Diamond had left it all to Marshall and the rest of his crew to handle the details of his background, his occupation, his identity. As long as Wireless delivered what Diamond wanted, Diamond didn't ask questions.

Diamond turned to Wireless in the dimly lit back seat. "After tonight, I want you to start casing some of the public buildings downtown," he said. "I'm talking about City Hall, the Justice Center, the Courthouse. I want you to be familiar with the floor plan in each one. I want to be ready if we ever decide to plan a strike of some kind."

Wireless shrugged. "None of those places should be hard," he said. "The buildings themselves are easy. There's all kinds of places inside to wire stuff up and keep it hidden. It's the security you gotta watch out for. You gotta be careful about how to get the materials through the door."

Diamond nodded. "Be thinking about how you'd do that if you had to."

He turned away and looked out the car window at Taylor Street. It was a backstreet—not much more than a wide alley—whose only traffic was generated by delivery trucks, municipal garbage haulers and other service-related vehicles. At this late hour, the stretch of red brick pavement was completely deserted. As such, it provided the ideal vantage point for the three men in the car to watch The Blue Star Club, the brick building at the corner that fronted on West Twenty-First Street. The side wall of the Blue Star was no more than forty yards from where they were parked.

The inside of the car had been quiet for several minutes, save for the steady hum of the engine and the occasional sigh of Kowalski dragging on his cigarette and blowing smoke through the two-inch crack between the edge of his window and the door frame. The murmur of live music from a swing orchestra playing inside the building wafted toward the car and through the partially opened window, although no one inside the vehicle seemed remotely interested in the melody or the rhythm.

Diamond was more focused on the rectangular device in Wireless' hand—an oblong metal box similar in size and shape to a cigarette carton. A six-inch antenna protruded from the end of the box and a small red light on the housing cast a tiny glow in the otherwise dark interior of the car.

Diamond kept his eyes riveted on Wireless' hands as the electrical expert absently fingered the small toggle switch mounted just below the red light. Every other piece of his immediate surroundings— the leather upholstery underneath him, the purr of the engine, the breathing of the man seated in front of him, the murmur of far-off music—hovered at the farthest edges of his consciousness as his attention remained laser-focused on the metal box and the tiny red glow.

"You sure that thing's gonna work?" Diamond said.

Wireless gestured at the box. "What, this?" he said. "Yeah, this is easy. We don't need much of an antenna because we're in good range.

The building's not even two-hundred feet away."

"Let me see it," said Diamond, his breath catching.

Wireless handed the device to Diamond, who accepted it like a fragile item of great value. He felt the hairs on the back of his neck stand up as he measured the heft and balance of the thing. After only a few seconds, he had to shift it from one hand to the other to wipe the sweat of his palms on his pant leg. He ran a finger along the edge of the smooth metal housing, touched the small red light on the front panel and the switch just below it.

All this power, he thought. *The trigger for so much destruction, right here in my hand. One flip of this switch and the whole corner of the—*

"Uh oh..." It was Kowalski's voice.

Diamond looked up and saw the glow of headlights at the far end of Taylor Street, moving slowly toward them. He squinted for a moment, then recognized the vehicle as a police cruiser, rolling down the street from the opposite direction.

"Not sure I like the looks of this," muttered Kowalski.

Diamond glanced sideways at Wireless, who kept his gaze fixed out the front window at the cruiser as it came to a stop at the curb on the opposite side of the street from where Kowalski had parked, another twenty yards beyond the building. The lights on the front of the cruiser went out.

Diamond momentarily forgot the device in his hands. "Cut the engine, and keep the interior lights off," he told Kowalski. "And put out that damn cigarette. If that cop gets out of the car, I don't want anything to draw his attention to us."

The cruiser door opened, and the cop did get out. He shut the door behind him and strolled across the street toward the building.

"That's right officer, keep walking," Diamond murmured, his eyes following the figure as it crossed the street and stepped onto the curb. "We're just another empty car parked along the side of an empty street."

"I don't get it," said Kowalski. "What's he doing? Did somebody in there call the cops?"

"No, I'd call this a little quiet pressure," Diamond murmured, his eyes tracking the officer as he followed a narrow walkway along the side of the building that led to a service entrance in the rear. "Taggert's been watching the nightclubs for weeks now. Just a little visit to send a message."

A low-watt bulb illuminated the space over and around the back entrance well enough that the three men in the car could watch what was happening from a distance. The cop tapped on the door with his night stick. A moment later, the door opened and a burly looking man with dark hair and a white apron steeped out. *Kitchen staff,* Diamond thought.

The cop and the man in the apron exchanged a few words, then the man in the apron turned back toward the open door and a stepped aside to let a second man step out from inside the building. The second man wore a dark suit, and looked more like management. He spoke briefly with the officer, then gestured for him to step inside. The door closed behind them, and the alley was empty and still.

From Diamond's curbside vantage point forty yards away, it all looked cordial—maybe not exactly friendly, but not confrontational either.

The inside of the car fell silent as Diamond, Wireless and Kowalski trained their eyes on the door for a full minute. All three waited for someone to emerge or for something to happen, but the door didn't open again.

Kowalski glanced at Diamond in the rearview mirror and then back out the window at the building. He shifted uneasily in the front seat. He and Wireless both spoke at the same time.

"Hey, Nick, I don't know if this is such a—"

"If something happens when that cop's inside, there's gonna be—"

Diamond turned away from the window and glanced at both men as they spoke. He watched their lips move in the shadowy interior of the car, but their words—and the cautionary tone in their voices—just didn't register. His mind was somewhere entirely different. He turned and looked back out the window at the building.

Without preamble, without warning, he flexed his right thumb, throwing the switch on the box. In the same instant, the building erupted in a flash of light and a thundering roar.

Kowalski and Wireless, both caught completely off guard, jerked in their seats as the concussion of the blast slammed into the passenger side of the car and rocked the entire vehicle. Kowalski ducked instinctively, as though he expected something—some airborne chunk of debris— to sail across the open space and blast through a car window.

Diamond, unlike the other two occupants of the car, absorbed the sensation without even flinching.

The swirl of lights. The ominous wall of sound. The raw beauty. The exhilarating rush that bordered on ecstasy.

His thumb absent-mindedly flexed on the switch a second time—then a third and fourth—as though he might somehow make it happen again.

The brick and mortar of the building's south wall—toward the rear, not far from where the cop had stepped inside moments before—was now marked by a jagged and gaping hole that was eight feet high, six feet wide, littered with debris at its base and clouded by billows of dust.

The shouts and screams and sounds of confusion from inside the building made it even more alive, more visceral.

The pandemonium unfolded within fifteen seconds. A fire alarm blared from within the damaged structure, and scores of Blue Star patrons and staff spilled out of the front and rear entrances like rats from a burning sewer. Barely a minute after the explosion, the alley behind the building and the stretch of the street in front were filled with people screaming, shouting for help, or just meandering in a daze. Traffic on West Twenty-First Street ground to a halt, and pedestrians gaped in confusion and fear as a popular corner nightclub fell into chaos.

Kowalski looked at Diamond in the rearview mirror again, this time with a mix of agitation and apprehension. "Jesus, Nick, we have to go. There'll be more cops here any—"

"No!" Diamond barked, putting a hand up without looking away from the spectacle. His jaw flexed. His nostrils flared.

God. The raw, seductive beauty.

After a moment, he turned to Kowalski and waved toward the stretch of street ahead of them. "Alright," he said. "Go. Go!"

Kowalski started the car, put it in gear and hit the gas. As they sped away from the smoke and debris, the only sound inside the car—save for the roar of the engine and wail of far-off sirens responding to the carnage—was the voice of Nicky Diamond cackling in the darkness.

CHAPTER 10
THE GRIM TRUTH

Hunter arrived at the Justice Center at eight-twenty a.m. He wasn't in his office more than sixty seconds when Gallagher walked in, looking like he was ready to head out.

"Don't get too comfortable, Jack. Bentley wants to see us in his office before nine."

Hunter glanced at his watch and frowned. "The mayor? Now? What's going on?"

"I don't know. I just got a call from his secretary about ten minutes ago. Says it's urgent." He tilted his head toward the hallway outside the door. "Come on, we'll take my car. I had the garage attendant bring it around to the front of the building."

Hunter put his hat and jacket back on, and both men headed back down the hall toward the elevator.

Less than three minutes later, they were climbing into Gallagher's car parked at the curb directly in front of the main entrance to the Justice Center. City Hall was only four blocks to the west—close enough for a brisk, ten-minute walk—but Hunter sensed from Gallagher that the mayor's request was urgent enough to warrant a faster commute.

Gallagher pulled away from the curb and merged with the traffic. Hunter watched the mix of vehicles and pedestrians along Liberty Avenue.

"Any ideas?" said Hunter.

"Officially, no," said Gallagher. "But unofficially, I heard there was an explosion last night at the Blue Star on West Twenty-First.

Hunter stared out the window. There was plenty he could have asked, but he said nothing.

Four minutes later, Gallagher pulled up to the curb in front of City Hall. Both men climbed out of the car and up the steps leading to the main entrance to the stone building. Once inside the lobby, a nod from the desk guard was all they needed for access to the main hallway of the first floor.

Hunter and Gallagher both knew the layout well, and they headed up the stairs to the offices of Mayor Stephen Bentley. One of Bentley's assistants, a grim-faced older woman in a dark suit, met them in the third-floor hallway. She said, "This way, gentlemen," and ushered them the rest of the way to a conference room a couple doors down from the mayor's office.

Something about her voice, her body language—the very air inside the building—gave Hunter a bad feeling.

Bentley was already there, along with Taggert and Dugan—all of them standing, despite the long rectangular table centered in the room with eight chairs around it. Hunter was aware of some unspoken tension the minute he walked into the room. Taggert looked tired and gaunt, which seemed odd for him—or anyone—at eight-thirty-five in the morning.

All eyes were averted, save for the occasional quick and nervous glances in Hunter's direction. It was all so surreptitious, so awkward, as though everyone wanted to get a glimpse of Hunter's face, but no one wanted to be caught getting a glimpse of his face.

"Alright, everyone's here," said Bentley, stepping behind Gallagher to close the door behind the last two arrivals. His delivery was clipped, strictly business. He invited everyone to sit, and they did. He took a seat of his own at the head of the table and gestured toward Taggert, keeping his preamble to a minimum. "Sam has new information about some things that have been happening in the last couple days—and last night—and it's not good. I wanted to get everyone in on it as quickly as possible." He exchanged a glance with the police chief and said, "Go ahead, Sam."

Taggert pulled a small notebook out of his jacket and slapped it down on the table. "Alright," he said. "I'll cut to the chase. It's not pretty, but here it is. Last night a police officer was killed. A beat cop making the rounds at The Blue Star Supper Club, Stu Hirschfeld's place on West Twenty-First. He was one of three deaths. The others were a cook and a patron. Five others ended up at the hospital and they're still there."

"What happened?" prompted Gallagher.

"Someone tore the place open just before midnight."

"Tore it open," said Hunter. "Exactly what do you mean?"

Taggert glanced around the room. He locked eyes with Hunter for a moment, then looked back down at his sheet. "There was an explosion."

Hunter felt the hair on the back of his neck stand up. He looked back and forth between Taggert and Dugan and kept listening.

Dugan glanced at some notes of his own and cleared his throat. "Apparently it wasn't an accident," he said. "We brought in an inspector from the fire department, and he found traces of amatol—"

A barely perceptible murmur of tension made its way through the room. Gallagher dropped his pen on his legal pad and exhaled. Bentley shifted his chair. Taggert rubbed his chin.

Hunter stared back at Dugan without a word or even a movement. Dugan kept talking. "That's a combination of—"

"A combination of ammonium nitrate and trinitrotoluene, or TNT," Hunter interrupted. His voice was even, and cold as a stone. He'd learned the chemistry long ago, in a painful lesson. "A highly explosive material developed almost twenty years ago, during the war." He paused for a moment, flexing his jaw and feeling the blood pounding in his temples. "The stuff Nicky Diamond's gang used to use when they wanted to blow their way into a building." He paused one more time, then brought his statement to its inevitable conclusion. "A building like the Justice Center, for example."

Dugan and Hunter locked eyes across the table. Both men knew the final piece of the puzzle and where it fell.

Hunter kept his eyes on Dugan and tilted his head toward Gallagher, who was seated next to him. "And for the benefit of those of us who arrived a couple minutes late," he said, "can we assume that these were the very same chemicals that were stolen from the Pharaoh plant a little more than twenty-four hours ago?"

The detective's only response was a curt nod.

No one spoke for a moment, until Gallagher broke the silence. "So, he's here," he said. "Diamond's in Union City." He looked at everyone in the room. His words seemed to be a question as much as a statement.

Taggert nodded. "The evidence so far would certainly suggest that, yes. The M.O., the raw materials, the source of the raw materials—it all points to him."

The police chief shuffled a few sheets of paper. "And we have something else, too," he said. "Testimony from one of our officers at the scene, and probably the most definitive evidence yet to connect all this to Diamond."

Hunter leaned forward in his chair.

"Hirschfeld was at the club last night," Taggert went on, "and the officer heard him go off on a tear a few minutes after the explosion. The officer says in his report that Hirschfeld was in quite a state, screaming about Nicky Diamond being behind it all because Hirschfeld refused to play ball."

Hunter locked eyes with Gallagher and took in a deep breath of air. "Well, that's it, then," he said. "This is where the speculation ends. Diamond's connected to all this. Somehow."

"Not a big surprise at this point, based on all the other circumstances," said Gallagher. "Where's Hirschfeld now?"

"He's in custody," said Taggert. "He wasted no time getting a lawyer, and that lawyer is already going on and on about his client's financial hardship because his place of business will have to remain closed indefinitely. I can't tell you how much that just breaks my heart, but the fact is, Hirschfeld was running an illegal gambling operation, and that illegal activity is now connected to the death of three people—including a cop—and injury to five others."

"And it put a lot of other people at risk," said Gallagher.

Taggert shrugged. "Now, as you might guess," he said, "the lawyer has instructed him to keep his mouth shut, but I intend to hold him as long as we can, on the chance that we might get more out of him before we have to let him out."

Gallagher took the pipe from his mouth. His eyes narrowed slightly, and for a brief second, Hunter saw something feral in his eyes. "I'd be more than happy to have a chat with the lawyer myself," said Gallagher.

The chief nodded. "Might be a good idea."

Gallagher put the pipe back in his mouth and took a draw. "So this bombing was because of what," he said, "some kind of rivalry?"

"Sounds like it, yeah," said Taggert. "Sounds like Diamond may have issued some kind of threat or ultimatum to Hirschfeld previously, but Hirschfeld didn't comply. So Diamond sent Hirschfeld a message in his own unique way."

The police chief paused for a moment, rubbing his chin thoughtfully. His next words were tentative. "We've, uh…" he stopped short and glanced at Bentley, who nodded back at him.

"We've brought in a consultant," said Bentley, rising from his chair and moving to the door of the conference room. He opened the door and spoke to someone just outside, apparently the woman who'd met Hunter and Gallagher in the hallway a few minutes earlier. "Send him in," he murmured.

The mayor left the door ajar and kept talking as he walked back to his chair at the table. "We have an explosives expert who might be able to help us before this gets any further out of hand."

Before he had a chance to say anymore, the woman appeared at the door and ushered in a smallish, bespectacled man who looked vaguely familiar to Hunter. The man had brown hair turning gray, with very little on top of his head, and a bow tie at his collar. His gray suit appeared to be a half-size too small.

Bentley was still standing. "Ed, Jack, this is Oliver Pruett," he said. Pruett stepped into the room and shook hands with Gallagher and Hunter. "Dr. Pruett, you've already met Sam and Mike. This is Ed Gallagher, our district attorney, and Jack Hunter, our assistant DA."

Bentley kept talking as Pruett took a seat opposite Hunter. "Dr. Pruett has a Ph.D. in chemical engineering, and he currently works as a technical advisor for a mining company in Colorado. Some of you may remember that he also happens to be a former plant manager at Pharaoh Chemical, a position he left several years ago."

It all came back to Hunter as he listened to Bentley's introduction and stole a few glances at the new face across the table. He remembered the newspaper photos of Pruett during Diamond's prior reign in Union City, after the press got wind of the fact that Diamond's crew had been stealing from Pharaoh's inventory to supply raw materials for their boss' twisted coercion tactics. At the time, Pruett had given full cooperation to the police and the DA's office. He'd even suspended operations at the plant until Diamond was apprehended. He left Pharaoh and Union City just a month or two after Diamond had been put away. Pruett was more than a decade older now, and a little grayer to show for it, but Hunter remembered it all.

"Dr. Pruett," said Bentley, wrapping up the introduction, "I want to thank you for getting on a train at a moment's notice very late last night to come back here and lend a hand."

Pruett frowned. "I appreciate the vote of confidence," he said. His voice was measured, soft-spoken—what one might expect from a scientist. "I want to say I'm glad to help, but 'glad' seems like the wrong word in circumstances like these. I have some bad memories of what happened when I was at Pharaoh. I know we all do. I still consider it an unpleasant chapter in my career. I'm hoping this might be my chance to help get some resolution."

Gallagher leaned forward in his chair. "Dr. Pruett, based on what you know, based on what you remember from years ago, does anything about this event last night look like Nicky Diamond to you?"

Pruett paused to consider. "Well, I'm no detective," he said, "and I've only been back in Union City for less than three hours, but based on what the police chief and Detective Dugan have told me so far, it's hard to deny the similarities. It might be helpful to examine some of the debris from last night's explosion and compare it to the evidence from Diamond's work from years back. Most people who build explosive devices—even people who do it for legitimate purposes, like mining engineers or demolition experts—develop a certain signature, if you will."

"A personal style," suggested Gallagher. "Almost like a craftsman or an artist."

"Yes, exactly. I know it's hard to think of someone like this as an artist, but yes. I'm inclined to think Diamond himself doesn't have any expertise in the construction of chemically-based explosive devices. That was my thinking all along, even years ago. But whoever was doing it for him had a style. I'd be curious to know whether the signature from last night's explosion is similar to what we were seeing in Union City fourteen years ago."

Bentley turned to Taggert. "Sam, any trouble getting him access to the site and whatever's been collected so far?"

Taggert turned to Dugan and posed the same question with a raised eyebrow.

Dugan frowned. "If he can help us put the puzzle together and keep this from happening again, we'll get him anything he wants."

"I want you to escort him personally to the site," said Taggert. "Full access. As much time as he needs."

Dugan nodded. "Will do."

Taggert turned to the scientist who had just become a pivotal member of the investigative team. "Dr. Pruett, you said you're no detective. We may just turn you into one before this is all over."

Pruett shook his head and forced a wistful smile. "If I can help put a stop to this before it goes any further," he said, "it's a job I would gladly take on."

The police chief redirected his attention to Gallagher and Hunter. "We're planning another raid tonight," he said. "We've been gathering solid evidence pointing to illegal cards and tables at the Emerald Lounge, Marty McShane's place on Parkwood, near West Eighth." Taggert glanced at Bentley and then continued. "We thought about postponing it, given last night's events, but we're moving ahead. If the gambling activity city-wide is connected, we think this could turn out to be an important piece of the operation."

Hunter could have guessed at the private conversation between the chief and the mayor leading up to the decision. Taggert likely wanted to hold off and regroup in the aftermath of the Blue Star explosion, but Bentley would now be on a mission to get to the bottom of what's happening with the gambling at the clubs, especially if the explosion strengthened any suspected connection to Diamond.

Gallagher had been scribbling some lines on his notepad. He stopped and looked up at Taggert. "Sam, maybe this is related and maybe it's not," he said, "but we talked yesterday about further questioning of the club owners who'd been arrested in previous raids."

"That's still the plan," said Taggert. "The events of last night would be a perfect reason to turn up the heat under some of these characters."

"And a perfect defense," said Gallagher, "if any of their shady lawyers should ask about cause."

Before the conversation could veer any farther into strategy and tactics, Bentley tucked his pen into his jacket pocket and folded up his portfolio. "Gentlemen, I'm not going to bother with impassioned speeches, but let me be clear," he said. "I want every possible resource on this. Sam, I want reports every afternoon. And if there are developments earlier in the day, I want to know about them as they happen. If this is Diamond, we're talking about a madman and a murderer who nearly crippled this city several years ago. I remember it more clearly than I care to. I helped put this guy away fourteen years ago. I will not have him coming back to pick up where he left off. Not on my watch."

He stood up from his chair. "That's all for now," he said curtly. "Right now I need to make a phone call and pay my respects to a police officer's young widow. Thank you all for coming. Now let's get this under control."

He cleared out of the room, leaving the door open behind him.

The room fell silent in his wake.

Hunter stared out the window at the cloudless sky. "Tell me about the cop," he said finally.

"Patrolman Leonard Duffy," said Dugan. "Twenty-eight years old. Seven years on the force. Married, with a three-year-old daughter." He hesitated for a moment, then delivered the payoff punch. "Another baby on the way."

Hunter clenched his jaw. He took in a deep breath of air and held it, keeping his eyes fixed on the window for several more seconds before looking away to glance at Taggert. The chief sat motionless in his chair, arms crossed, staring into some distant place. His face was a mask of frustration.

Hunter had seen and heard more than enough, and he was fairly certain he could match whatever Taggert had roiling inside of him. He got up from his chair without a word and headed toward the door.

He heard Gallagher push his own chair back and stand up. "Jack, wait," he said. "We'll ride back together."

Hunter didn't stop. He barely turned his head when he reached the doorway and crossed the threshold. "I'll walk."

◆ ◆ ◆ ◆

Less than a half-hour later, Hunter was back in his office in the Justice Center, staring out his window with his back to the room. He'd lost track of how long he'd been standing there, looking down at Liberty Avenue five floors below but not paying any attention to the hustle of east-west traffic that filled the street.

He heard a knock at his door, but didn't turn. He heard the sounds of the door opening a few inches and the momentary escalation in the murmur of the outer hallway. He still didn't turn.

"Jack, we need to talk." It was Gallagher's voice.

Hunter didn't answer. He heard his boss step inside the office and close the door behind him.

Gallagher was silent at first, and Hunter could practically hear him rehearsing the opening line in his mind. "I'm thinking maybe you ought to stay away from this case," he said finally.

Hunter paused to consider the suggestion, but only briefly. "Well, with all due respect, Ed, you can think that all you want, but it's not going to happen."

He expected an argument, but didn't get one. He stuffed his hands into his pockets, but didn't take his eyes off the street below. Neither man spoke for a long moment. The only sound in the room was the rumble of a streetcar and the blare of a car horn from the avenue.

"I can still see the marks on the front door," Hunter said finally.

"Say again?"

"Downstairs. The main entrance to this building," he said, tilting his chin toward the window. "The one facing the street. It was rebuilt after the explosion—the one fourteen years ago, I mean. But if you look closely, you can still see the scars on the some of the bricks and mortar."

"Jack…"

"I have to look at it every day when I come to work."

"Jack, if this is—"

"And then you come upstairs, and it's more of the same. The second explosion that night was at the entrance to this department, just down the hall. They rebuilt that too. New plaster, new door frame, new doors. But those scars are still there, too."

He heard Gallagher let out a frustrated sigh behind him.

"It's all still there, Ed," said Hunter, finally turning to face his boss. "Every day. It never goes away."

"Look, Jack, there isn't much doubt that it's Diamond. Everything we know so far points to it. The break-in, the shootings, definitely the explosives, all of it. And the testimony of that cop at Hirschfeld's place right after the blast, well that pretty much clinches it. He got twelve years for what he did to…for what he did. If we can tie him to this, and I know we can, then we can put him away for at least twelve more. Probably a lot more."

"Tell it to that cop's three-year-old daughter," said Hunter. "Or his wife. Or worst of all, the kid who'll never know him at all. Sounds to me like that first twelve years wasn't enough."

Gallagher was silent for a moment, as though searching for the right words. "Jack, I understand what this is about," he said slowly. "You lost a great deal to Diamond, more than a lot of people in this city. But it's a new day—for everybody, including guys like Diamond—and the world's a different place. Prohibition's been over for four years now. Gangsters can't get powerful on the alcohol trade anymore because the brewer down the block can make beer and sell it legally, and you and

I and everybody else can walk into a bar on any given day or night and drink it without breaking the law. So now he's looking for something new. He's—"

Hunter shook his head. "A new day? Maybe you don't remember, Ed, but I—"

Gallagher cut him off with a voice that was suddenly sharp. "That's enough, Jack! You know damn well I—"

"I remember it very clearly. Like yesterday. He came up out of the sewer and held this city in a death grip for three years." Hunter's voice had risen to match Gallagher's. Somewhere in the back of his mind, he wondered what kind of disciplinary action he might face for speaking to his superior this way, but he couldn't stop himself. "He was a disease, Ed, a dark cloud that hung over this city and damn near choked the life out of it. He had half the police department and at least a dozen judges and politicians in his pocket. Do you know how many civilians lost their lives, how many good cops died because of...?"

He stopped quickly and turned away, muttering a curse. He felt the old anger and sadness rise up in his chest, high enough that he thought his voice might crack if he kept on.

There was a long silence, not just in the office but outside the door, where the usual hum of activity had grown subdued and tense. Apparently the argument between the two men had spilled out to the hallway.

Gallagher finally broke the silence. "You finished?"

Hunter took a deep breath and let it out slowly. His mouth twisted into a frown, but he gave no answer one way or another.

After a moment, he grabbed his hat and his jacket, brushed past Gallagher and headed for the door. He stopped at the threshold and turned back toward the room. "You want to take me off this case, Ed? Go ahead." His voice was quieter now, more controlled, but no less taut. "But I'm going after this son of a bitch one way or another."

He turned and headed for the elevator, ignoring the awkward glances from the office staff along the length of the hallway.

CHAPTER 11
GRAVE ENCOUNTER

It was dark when Hunter drove up to the cemetery. The temperature had dropped at least ten degrees during the late afternoon, and a stiff breeze had kicked up. A storm was coming.

He'd meant to go home, but somehow the car had come here instead. He'd worked a long day that went well into the evening—all of it a coffee-fueled, anger-driven blur. He had skipped lunch because he'd had no appetite, and the thought of losing focus on the developing case—even for an hour—was unacceptable.

Hunter had smoothed things over with Gallagher after the argument in his office in the morning, but for the rest of the day, the remainder of the staff—secretaries, clerks, other attorneys, even the elevator man—knew enough to do what he asked and otherwise stay out of his way.

Gallagher's office and the police department had spent the day in constant communication while the incident was still fresh, sifting through what was left of the Blue Star, questioning witnesses and running down leads. Two of the five people who'd been hospitalized after the blast were in no shape to talk to the police or anyone else about the events of the night before. The three who could talk chose not to, presumably for fear of being directly or indirectly implicated in an illegal gambling operation. "I was just there to have dinner and hear some music" was the standard line.

Hunter had spoken with Taggert later in the afternoon. The chief was in a sour mood that Hunter could only attribute to feelings of remorse, guilt, frustration—or more likely some combination of all three. He'd sent Len Duffy to the Blue Star as a way of sending a subtle message—nothing heavy-handed, just a gesture to let Stu Hirschfeld know the police were keeping an eye on the place and everything that was going on inside. No one, least of all Taggert, expected the social call to turn deadly.

It all felt painfully familiar to Hunter as he got out of the car and headed up the small hill, watching the elm branches sway in silhouette against the starless night sky. Wounds that had been festering for years were suddenly reopened, and the anger that spilled out included a measure of sadness as well. In some small corner of his soul, he was eighteen again, college-bound and full of optimism one minute, grief-stricken and adrift the next.

He knew the way, even in the dark. He'd climbed this hill so many times in the past fourteen years. And yet, for all of his natural athleticism, for all his strength and stamina, there was always something about the climb that winded him a little.

He passed two gravestones, then a third, tugging at the brim of his fedora to keep it from blowing off in the wind. His pace slowed as he covered another fifteen feet and then stopped at the next stone. Taking in a deep breath, he put his hands in the pockets of his trench coat and looked down at the thick, rectangular slab of granite standing straight up from the ground, its face shrouded in darkness.

He stared at the stone for a long time, replaying decades of memories, suppressing years of anger, trying as he always did when he visited this place to make sense of the senseless.

This time, for the first time, he had figured out a way to do it.

A flash of lightning illuminated the stone for just a moment, just long enough for Hunter to read the words engraved on its surface:

LT. JAMES M. "JIMMY" HUNTER
1880 - 1922
LOVING HUSBAND AND FATHER
DEVOTED PUBLIC SERVANT
PROTECTOR OF THE CITY IN THE HOUR OF DARKNESS

The sky darkened again, but Hunter kept his eyes fixed on the stone. "I'll get him, Pop," he said aloud. "I'll bring him down."

The hills answered with a gust of wind and a low roll of thunder. He stood for a moment longer, then turned away and headed toward his car.

CHAPTER 12
BUSINESS PLANS

Nicky Diamond stood at the window of his office on the second floor of The Paramount Club, watching the ominous-looking sky through the narrow spaces between the slats in the blinds. The wind had been gusting for the past twenty minutes, and the rain was just starting. There was no way to know how long it might last, but he could already tell it would be heavy.

After a few minutes, he turned away from the window and directed his gaze at Vinnie Marshall, who sat in an armchair near Diamond's desk.

"This weather," Diamond said. "Is it going to cause any problems at McShane's?"

"No," said Marshall. "I just heard from Louie about twenty minutes ago. He says everything's on schedule. The place is just about cleared out. The tables, the cards, the furniture, everything related to the back room operation has been swept. The dealers and the extra waitresses have been sent home and told to lay low until they're told otherwise. Another half-hour and there'll be nothing there but a big storage room—spare tables and chairs, linens, dinnerware, the usual items you'd find in the back room of a restaurant. Nothing more."

Outside, the rain intensified quickly. Diamond glanced at the window as the spray slashed against the glass, then looked back at Marshall. "We know the cops are planning to go in at around eleven tonight," he said. "I don't want them finding anything but dinner and music and dancing when they get there."

Marshall nodded in a gesture of reassurance. "I'm sure Louie will take care of it."

Diamond crossed the room to his desk. Just to the right of the brand new felt blotter was an ashtray piled high with a mix of stale-smelling cigarette ash and broken tin cylinders. A light dusting of ashes and white powder covered the smooth oak desktop in the area surrounding the ashtray.

A banker's lamp hooded in green glass threw a soft glow on the blotter and a random assortment of other items on the desk: a telephone, a decorative pen holder and inkwell, the intercom box wired to the rear entrance to the building one floor below, a set of car keys, his gun, the same leather-bound ledger he'd been studying the day before, and four unbroken cylinders identical to the empty ones in the ashtray.

He picked up one of the four cylinders and broke it open, then proceeded with the usual ritual—pulling out the powder-coated paper strip, rolling it into a tiny ball and popping it into his mouth like a pill.

It was his second hit in less than an hour. Within a few seconds, he felt the usual surge of energy and clarity. But he noticed that the kick was getting harder to maintain over time than it had been before. It took more hits than it used to. What's more, the kick was making him more jittery than before.

"I need more of these," he said, dropping the spent cylinder in the ashtray and flexing a fist to control the tremor in his hand.

"Louie says they're getting harder to find," said Marshall. "There are only so many drugstores in town."

Diamond glared back at him. "Then tell him to go to another town." Marshall didn't answer.

After a moment, Diamond picked up the ledger. "What about the shipment?" he said. "Is it here?"

"Louie said Kowalski stopped into Chinatown this afternoon to pick it up from Sun Lu," said Marshall. "Assuming everything is as it should be, it'll be five boxes," he said. "Three-hundred packets per box."

"Fifteen-hundred packets," said Diamond.

"Right," said Marshall, glancing at his watch. "Louie said Kowalski would bring it after he's finished at McShane's."

"He needs to get it here without any detours or problems. The cops find that stuff on him and this whole thing falls apart."

Marshall nodded. "He'll be here."

He dropped the ledger on the desk. "What about the girls?"

"We're fine for now," said Marshall, "but if we expand our business, we'll need to do some recruiting. I know how you feel about Sun Lu, but we can't deny that his assistance has been helpful in that regard."

Diamond frowned and shook his head. "We need to keep him at a distance," he said. "I meant what I said yesterday. I don't want him too involved. Our relationship with him is supposed to be temporary—long enough to get what we need and get the inside track on his business at the same time so we can build an operation of our own."

He sat on the edge of the desk and leaned forward, ticking off items on his fingers. "Make sure we know where and how he's getting the goods—the shipping line, the intermediaries, any customs agents who've been paid off, everything and everyone in the chain. Follow it all the way to the West Coast, and then all the way back to China. He's useful to us now, but eventually I want to control all the shipping coming up and down that river. Once that happens, he won't be necessary anymore."

He leaned back and shrugged. "As for the girls," he said, "we need to do more of our own recruiting."

Marshall nodded. "The heyday of the Ho Sheng brotherhood may be long past, but we need to be careful. Sun Lu obviously still has connections back in China. And there may in fact be some surviving skeleton of an organization right here in the city. The cultural loyalties among the Chinese are strong, so it would be in our best interests not to foster any resentments. The consequences could be hard to predict."

Marshall deliberated for a moment, absently tapping two fingers of his right hand on the armrest of the chair. "It may take a little time to get ourselves better established, but eventually we won't need him."

Diamond shook his head. "The less time the better,' he said. "I don't want him getting—"

The buzz of the intercom cut him off. Diamond leaned across the desk and threw the switch. "Yeah?"

"It's Louie. We're finished at McShane's, and Kowalski's with us."

Diamond didn't respond. He cut the intercom connection and buzzed the downstairs door to let them in.

He slid off the edge of the desk and moved around it to take a seat in the desk chair. He glanced at Marshall and tapped an index finger on the front cover of the ledger. "When Kowalski gets up here with the boxes," he said, "make sure the accountant goes in here and makes everything current," he said.

Marshall nodded.

Diamond picked up another cylinder and broke it open. He repeated the ritual with the powder-coated paper and swallowed hard.

He dropped the spent capsule shell into the ashtray and waited for the kick.

He glanced at the two remaining cylinders on the desk and muttered quietly to himself.

"I need more of these."

CHAPTER 13
HARSH WORDS

It was raining hard by the time Hunter pulled in behind the Republic Building and eased the car into the garage. He killed the lights and turned off the engine, but sat in the darkness for a few moments before stepping out of the car.

The streets had been slick, and the storm had brought lightning and a driving rain. All of it, coming on the heels of the day's developments, had done little to loosen the knot that had formed in his shoulders during the ride home.

He could stand at his father's grave and make promises, but in the end, could he keep them? Serving justice, he had learned, was a slow process. Sometimes too slow. Right now, the mere thought of all the necessary protocols—the methodical gathering of evidence, the warrants, the building of the case—jangled his nerves and ignited the cold hard pit in his stomach. There was a demon on the loose—again—and barely twelve hours after making that determination, Hunter could already feel his patience wearing thin.

He stepped out of the car and punched the button on the wall-mounted electric garage door control. By the time the steel door had reached the concrete floor, he was inside the building.

In the vestibule between the two staircases, the door to the basement stairs was ajar, and a dim glow emanated from the lower level. Hunter checked his watch. It was almost nine, which meant that Buzz had closed the shop nearly three hours ago.

Hunter headed down the stairs to the basement, and found the storeroom empty as he knew he would. He crossed the room to the far wall, where the doorway leading down to the sub-basement was also ajar. He was halfway down the second flight of stairs when he felt a growing sense of irritation.

"That you, Jack?" Buzz's voice, from the bottom of the stairs.

"Yeah."

"Late night, huh?"

Hunter didn't answer. He hadn't even hit the bottom step when Buzz launched into an excited chatter.

"Jack, you really gotta take a look at this. I connected some small batteries to this thing so I could make the circuits a little bit smaller."

Hunter stopped at the bottom of the stairs and looked across the room at his cousin and the mask on the bench in front of him, surrounded by a jumble of tools and hardware. The mask was, in fact, much smaller and more streamlined than what Buzz had shown him just a day earlier. Beyond that, Hunter was only paying partial attention to what Buzz was saying.

He was more aware of the knot in his shoulders, growing tighter and more persistent.

"Now, get this," said Buzz. "The batteries are photoelectric cells. All they need is a good dose of light, maybe an hour or two, to charge them up. At a full charge, they'll be good for about twelve hours. Now, I think the cells are small enough that I might actually be able to weave them into the leather, and if I can reconfigure the circuits a little bit, I think I can make those smaller too. I'm betting I could get the whole thing down to a size where it would all fit into—"

"Buzz, stop," Hunter interrupted. "Just stop it, okay? What are you doing? You come down here and you play around with all this junk. For what? What purpose is that thing going to serve, really?"

Buzz's brow furrowed. He looked back at his cousin for a moment. "What's eating you?"

Hunter ignored the question, waving a hand at the long room and everything in it. "Look at this place," he snapped, his voice growing louder and more taut. "All these wires and tubes and parts and tools and bits and pieces of…of what? Buzz, we're not kids anymore, fixing all the neighborhood bicycles and building radios. We're grownups, and we're living in a grownup world. At least I am."

Part of him tried to stop the head of steam that was building, but some other part of him couldn't, and he just kept going. "What's the point of all this?" he said. "How much time do you spend down here, twenty feet under the ground? You call this a workshop? It's a dungeon. Is this all you're ever going to do? Run the shop during the day and then come down here every night like some kind of a mole and tinker with this crap and build silly little gadgets after hours? Do you have any idea what's going on in the world right now? In this city, even?"

Buzz put the screwdriver down slowly. His face had grown long, his shoulders sagged by the unexpected tirade. He shrugged at the question. "Well, yeah," he said quietly. "I read the papers. I watch the newsreels." He turned away and wiped his hands on a rag. "I listen to the radio."

His face darkened momentarily, as though he were suddenly transported nearly two decades back in time, to a place much less safe and familiar than his underground workshop. "Sometimes," he muttered, more to himself than to anyone else, "I think I've seen more than enough of the world, thank you very much."

"Well, you can read and watch and listen all you want," said Hunter, "but some of us have to actually live in this world and try to make sense of it. And it's not easy." He waved his hand around the room again. "And no amount of secret alarm circuits and automatic door openers and homemade generators and fifty-foot-high shortwave antennas and motorized gadgets are going to make it any better. And some goofy electrical hat sure as hell isn't going to do it either."

The room fell silent. Buzz frowned and scratched his head, his expression more wounded than angry. He put the rag down, and absently rearranged some of the tools on the bench in front of him.

"I'm sorry, Jack," he said after a moment, his voice subdued. "It's what I do. I build stuff. I fix stuff. We used to do it together. We used to have fun."

Hunter felt the worst of the storm pass. "Yeah, well," he said, his voice still irritated, but softer now, "fun is a luxury that I don't have a whole lot of time for these days."

Both men were silent. Buzz straightened a few more items on the workbench, his eyes distant. "You done?" His voice was hushed now, not at all confrontational.

Hunter heaved a sigh. "Yeah."

Buzz turned off the lamp over the workbench and rose from his chair. He turned toward the stairs, avoiding eye contact with Hunter as he walked past him "There's coffee on upstairs," he said quietly, "and I bought some stuff for sandwiches at the deli. You hungry?"

"No."

"Okay," he said, heading up the stairs. "I'm going to turn in."

Hunter said nothing, turning his back to the stairs as Buzz ascended. He took in a deep breath of air and pressed his thumb and forefinger to his eyes, trying to push back at the dull ache that was developing in his head. He didn't exhale until he heard the door close at the top of the stairs.

After a few moments, he turned and headed up the three flights that led first to the basement, then the main floor and then the second floor. He stood for a moment in the hallway that separated the two apartments, noticing the dim glow beneath the crack under the door to Buzz's apartment. He hesitated, then turned away.

He stepped into his own apartment and closed the door gently behind him, dropping his briefcase and car keys on a chair in the small living room. Without turning on any lights, he shuffled out of his trench coat and tossed it over the back of the sofa, then headed past the kitchen and down the hallway to the bedroom.

Inside, he turned on a lamp on the nightstand, then sat down at the edge of the bed and kicked off his shoes. His eyes absently scanned the room before coming to rest on a wall with two shelves mounted on it and a chest of drawers standing against it. He stood slowly, removing his tie and unbuttoning his cuffs, and took a couple steps to the oak chest—a finely crafted piece from the 1870s that had belonged to his grandfather.

Stuffing his hands into his pockets, he gazed at the sepia-toned black-and-white photographs on top of the chest. One was a picture of Hunter at seventeen, holding up two medals—one gold, one silver—at the 1921 state track and field championship. The gold had been for the hundred-yard dash, and the silver was for the two-mile.

The second photo was taken a year later—his last year of high school. It was a group picture of the Union City High School wrestling team. In the three years he'd spent on the team, he'd been one of their top wrestlers in his weight class.

Hunter sidestepped the chest of drawers and drifted toward the pair of shelves mounted on the wall. On the top shelf was a photograph of him in boxing trunks and shoes, leaning toward the camera in the classic stance—slightly crouched, feet shoulder-length apart, bare fists raised to his face in a defensive position. In addition to wrestling, he'd briefly taken up boxing in a community league during his last year of high school, but gave it up after only five fights—three wins, one loss and a split decision. More than ten years later, he still got down to the gym a couple days a week to work the bags, but whatever interest he'd had in being any kind of contender in the ring had vanished after his father died. Next to the boxing photo were two trophies— one for track and field and one for wrestling—with a couple medals draped over each.

On the second shelf was a photo of himself and Buzz, taken more than fifteen years ago in the workshop run by his uncle Frank—Buzz's father—before he moved his operation to its current location in the Republic Building. A blue ribbon draped over the frame, and Hunter pushed it aside to get a better view of the picture mounted inside. The two boys—one fourteen and the other eighteen, both clad in overalls and clutching hand tools—stood in front of an array of turning machines, sheet metal, and a hodgepodge of random materials and tools. With chins held high and faces smudged with grime, they mugged for the camera—a light-proof box that they themselves had built. They were the young wizards of Union City, masters of all things mechanical and scientific, self-made explorers in a new century of technological mysteries.

His gaze drifted to a photograph of his father, Lieutenant James Hunter of the Union City Police Department. It was a formal portrait of the officer in full uniform, taken in 1913 by the department in honor of his tenth anniversary on the force. The backdrop was an American flag and the Union City seal mounted on wood paneling.

Hunter remembered the day clearly. He was nine years old. Before the photograph was taken, there had been a brief presentation in City Council chambers. The police chief and the mayor made short speeches and presented his father with a service award. Afterward, the family had gone to dinner at a nice restaurant. In the course of the meal, at least a half-dozen people came to the table to shake his father's hand. His father had seemed a little embarrassed, as though he couldn't understand the fuss.

After a long moment, Hunter took in a deep breath and turned away from the images and artifacts of his past. Unbuttoning his shirt, he sat back on the bed, contemplating the years that had come and gone and the losses he'd incurred since the photos were taken. He silently cursed Nicky Diamond and the rest of the foul scum that lurked in the dim shadows of the city and preyed on its innocents.

He finished undressing and turned off the lamp as he slipped under the covers. In the silence, he lay on his back and stared at the ceiling for nearly a half-hour before finally dropping off to sleep.

CHAPTER 14
THE BEST DEFENSE

The next morning, Hunter showered and dressed and came down the flight of stairs that landed in the back room of the shop. Through the doorway, he saw Buzz at the front of the store, unlocking the front entrance and turning the OPEN sign to face the street. Hunter tentatively stepped out of the back room and into the space behind the sales counter. Buzz glanced at him nervously, then looked away. There was no resentment in his eyes, no bitterness. Just shame—like a child whose misbehavior had disappointed his parent, or a puppy that'd been swatted on the nose for chewing up a slipper.

He's seen so much in his time, and a lot of it hasn't been pleasant, Hunter thought. *The last thing he needs is approval from me, the younger cousin who was always hanging around.*

Hunter cleared his throat. "Buzz," he stammered. "Listen, I—"

His clumsy overture was cut short by the tinkling of the bell over the front door. A small-looking man—the first customer of the day—pushed the door open with his back, struggling with a Philco console radio that looked about as big as the man himself and maybe a little heavier.

Both Hunter and Buzz rushed from behind the counter to help the man get inside and set down his load. Hunter recognized the customer after a moment. He'd bought the same radio at the shop almost a year earlier, and he'd stopped in a few times since for smaller items—a desk lamp, some light bulbs, a couple fuses for his electrical box. His name was Walter, but that was all Hunter knew of him.

Walter spoke to Buzz in a hushed tone for a few minutes, like an anxious patient consulting with his doctor. Something about a persistent hum and some static. There was talk of a bad tube or a short in the wiring. Maybe an improper ground. Walter appeared concerned, but Buzz was the portrait of self-assurance. In the end, as always, his prognosis was upbeat.

Walter held his hat in his hand, fidgeting with the brim. "Think you can fix it before the weekend?" he said. "*The Lone Ranger* comes on at seven on Sunday night. I'd hate to miss it."

Buzz frowned and nodded. "Oh, yeah," he said with a shrug and a wave. "This one's a cinch." He moved back to the counter to write up a work order, and Walter suddenly looked years younger.

Hunter lingered for a moment to listen to the two men chat about the weather. He checked his watch and reluctantly headed back through the back room. He made his way through the rear entrance to the garage and climbed into his car, feeling a twinge of shame on top of the regret that still lingered from the night before.

He wasn't so special. The city was filled with good people fighting the good fight every day—including good people like Buzz, a quiet warrior who did his part in his own way to make Union City a safe place for the little guy.

◆　◆　◆　◆

Less than an hour later, Hunter was at his desk when Betty Carlyle knocked softly at his door and then poked her head through the doorway.

"Excuse me, Mr. Hunter," she said. "Mr. Gallagher would like to see you in his office right away."

Hunter stood up and stepped into the hallway. When he reached Gallagher's door, he found the district attorney on the phone. Gallagher looked up at him and waved him in, signaling him to close the door behind him. He put a hand over the mouthpiece of the headset and pointed his chin at a second phone on a small table at the opposite end of the room. "It's Taggert," he said in a low voice. "Pick it up."

Gallagher uncovered the mouthpiece and spoke into it. "Sam, Jack just walked in. I'm putting him on the extension."

Hunter picked up. "Morning, Chief. What's going on?"

Taggert sighed into his phone, which made a sound like a quick gust of wind on Hunter's end of the line. "I was just telling Ed. I've got some news."

"Okay," said Hunter. "Why do I get the feeling it's not good news?"

"Some of it's not," said Taggert. "We had a raid scheduled for last night at The Emerald Lounge, Marty McShane's place on Parkwood. You remember we talked about it at City Hall yesterday?"

"Right, I remember," said Hunter. "And?"

"It went sour."

"Sour how?"

"The place was completely clean when our men got there."

"Anything blow up?" said Hunter.

"No," said Taggert. "We put together a team of explosives experts from the fire department and sent them in with full armor, in case something were to go really bad. But nothing happened. They scoured the place from top to bottom and found nothing."

The line was silent for a moment, then Taggert spoke again, more to himself than anyone else. "I sure would like to know how they knew enough to clean up before we got there."

Hunter chose his next words carefully. "Well, is it possible that you—?"

"We had good information," said Taggert. "We've been watching this place for weeks. We even sent an undercover man in there a couple weeks ago, so we knew exactly what was going on." There was a pause, and Hunter could practically feel the frustration through the phone line. "This one should have been easy."

"Somebody's tipping these people off," Gallagher chimed in.

The line was silent for a moment. Hunter glanced at the closed office door, as though someone suspicious might be lurking on the other side of it.

"I agree," he said finally. "But somebody who?"

There was no answer, at least none that any of these three men knew.

Hunter heard Taggert clear his throat. "Listen," said the chief, shifting gears. "There's some business we need to take care of as soon as possible. Today. This is from the top, from Bentley. And given this latest development, I think it may be a good idea."

Hunter and Gallagher exchanged a silent glance across the room. "What is it?" said the district attorney.

"If someone wants to put this investigation out in the open, then fine, we do just that," said Taggert. "We beat them to it."

"What are you saying, Sam?" said Gallagher.

"We go on the offensive. Beginning with a press conference this afternoon. We tell everybody what we're doing. The whole damn city, including whoever's behind this. Let's face it, this town hates Nicky Diamond. They remember his story very clearly, and it was a nightmare in this city's history."

"Bentley sounds like he wants to declare war," said Hunter.

"His exact words," said Taggert. "And from where I sit, I think it's a good idea. It was one thing when a guy like Capone tried to improve his public image in Chicago by opening up soup kitchens to feed the poor. But Diamond? Hell, this guy has nothing redeeming on his record. So if we make it clear to everybody in this city what's going on, we could make him even more unpopular than he already is."

"So we tell the papers," said Hunter.

"And then some. Not just the *Tribune* and the *Chronicle* here in town, but any other newspaper in this part of the state. If that new outfit they call the Associated Press or any of the other wire services want a piece of it too, all the better. Hell, we even get it on some of the radio broadcasts if we can. If we can make it clear that the police have no tolerance for illegal gambling, we accomplish two things: we scare people away from these places, and we also start isolating Diamond and his operation."

"You realize," said Hunter, "that if you bring the press into this and start drawing a lot of attention, the feds will come sniffing around in a matter of days."

Gallagher snorted. "Knowing J. Edgar, he already has agents following this."

"Well, if he does," said Taggert, "he and his people need to just relax for a few minutes and give us some room to breathe."

All three men were silent for a moment. Gallagher looked across the room at Hunter, and both men nodded to each other. "I like it, Sam," Gallagher said finally. "I think if we go public with this and start naming names, we could get ourselves back into a better position. The more we let the people know about what's going on, the more we have them in our corner—and hopefully the less time they'll spend in the gambling joints if we can make them realize that there are far worse dangers there than just losing your money. If we can manage all that, then Diamond eventually loses some leverage."

"I like it too," said Hunter, "but let's be careful not to get too optimistic. Vice is vice. A few years ago it was the alcohol trade, now it's the gambling. They're the same in a lot of respects. Whether it's legal or not, the people who want to do it will find a way to do it. The only way you're going to completely empty those gambling joints and keep them empty is to shut them down and get rid of the guy who's running them."

"But in the end, it really isn't about the gambling," said Gallagher. "It's about a lunatic who wants to reinsert himself into the city's underworld and re-establish control of it."

"So we slow him down, hopefully, before he gains any more ground," said Hunter.

"Okay, so a press conference," said Gallagher. "When and where?"

"Twelve-thirty," said Taggert. "City Hall."

Hunter and Gallagher both looked at their watches and then glanced at each other.

"He's not wasting any time," said Hunter.

"He already has people making arrangements," said Taggert. "He's called in a few favors with Foley at the *Tribune* and Higgins at the *Chronicle*. They're both holding page one of their afternoon editions."

Gallagher paused for a moment and there was silence on the phone line. He glanced across the room at Hunter, and both men nodded to each other.

"Okay," said the DA. "Twelve-thirty. We'll both be there."

"Good," said Taggert, "Bentley wants all of us—himself, the police, the DA's office, City Council, everybody—to be back on the offensive with this in the next forty-eight hours. I feel the same way. We may not know exactly where Diamond is just yet, or the full extent of what he's doing, but we're taking the fight to him."

CHAPTER 15
CITY HALL ASSEMBLY

Despite the short notice, the press turnout at City Hall just a few hours later was impressive. Just one whiff of Nicky Dynamite—even the suggestion, without even mentioning him by name—and they came like moths to a flame.

By twenty minutes after noon, a handful of city officials and a much larger press corps had assembled in the main lobby of City Hall, an ornate, high-ceilinged space with marble-tiled floors that stretched for six-hundred square feet. A life-size bronze statue of Horace Ballard, Union City's first mayor, stood near the large glass doors at the main entrance to the building, greeting all visitors and bidding good day to those departing.

Bentley had chosen the location in an effort to maximize exposure. On any given day, the lobby was a bustling hub of high-volume and diverse midday traffic consisting of government employees, elected officials and their staff, police and firemen, lawyers and judges, and scores of citizens moving through the city's primary administrative building to address any number of random matters. The traffic on this day was no different.

An oak podium had been brought down from City Council chambers and positioned directly in front of the security guard's desk, slightly toward the back of the lobby and not far from the elevators.

Hunter scanned the lobby as members of the press continued to assemble in a loose cluster no more than twelve feet from the podium. Some scribbled in notebooks, others fiddled with photographic equipment, still others chattered with each other over cigarettes and the occasional coffee in a paper cup.

He recognized most of them, but there were several more whom he'd never seen before. Joe Cranley was there from the *Tribune*, along with a photographer named Hodges, whom Hunter had seen around town shooting everything from crime scenes to black-tie fundraisers to college football games.

Ken Tyler from the *Chronicle* was there as well, keeping up with the competition. He'd been a crime reporter for the better part of ten years, and he was generally pretty good with the facts. But like many of his colleagues at the *Chronicle*, Tyler had a habit of embellishing them a bit for the sake of drama. Tyler also had a photographer in tow—a guy named Darnell, who was rarely seen without a wad of gum between a pair of jaws that were constantly moving.

There was a reporter from the Norwood *Register*, a daily paper in a smaller town about thirty miles southwest of Union City, and another one from the Ashton County *Examiner*, based in the next county over. Ashton County was mostly farm country, but not so backwoods that their residents and their newspapermen didn't know about Nicky Diamond. Years earlier, he had shaken their quiet rural existence when he used their county roads as transport lines for alcohol headed for Lake City. More than a half-dozen state police and innocent civilians in Ashton County had lost their lives before Diamond's Prohibition-era reign of terror had come to an end.

And just as Taggert had suggested, even the local radio stations were on hand to get the story. Hunter noticed Jeff McCullough from WRUC, the ten-thousand-watt operation located just a few blocks from City Hall. George Freeman was also there from WKDY, another Union City station whose signal may not have been as powerful as its primary competitor's, but that minor shortcoming never stopped its staff from staying on top of the local news.

There were others Hunter didn't recognize, but he took note of their affiliations by glancing at their press badges. Two of them were from the wire services—one from United Press, the other from the Associated Press. The AP reporter had a photographer with him. Just a year earlier, AP had developed a process called wire photo, the transmission of photographs over telephone and telegraph lines. Hunter had read about the process in *Popular Science*, and somewhere in the back of his mind, some part of him that had nothing to do with the law and the Diamond case wanted to take the AP photographer aside and ask him a couple dozen questions about how it worked.

Hunter wandered over to a lean figure crouching near the main entrance and examining the frame around the door. The door itself had been propped open to the midday sunlight and traffic. On the cool marble floor, just a few inches from the man's bent knees, lay a bundle of cables that started at the podium in the center of the lobby and snaked their way out the door and onto the sidewalk.

"Lose something?" said Hunter.

The man noticed Hunter and stood up. "Hi," he said, putting his hand out. "Jack Hunter, right?"

Hunter took the hand and shook it. "Yes."

"Willis Gray," he said. "I'm the radio engineer at WRUC. I set up all the equipment for broadcasts like this."

"Pleasure," said Hunter.

"Yeah, I've seen your picture in the paper now and then. I recognized you right away."

"The curse of celebrity," said Hunter. "These lines go out to a truck or something?"

"Yeah, right at the curb. Transmitter in the back sends the signal to the station right up the street."

Hunter nodded. "I used to play around with shortwave a little," he said. "Just a hobby."

"Yeah? Me too," said Gray. "Ever since I was a kid. That's how I got into this racket in the first place." He turned and gestured to the door frame. "I was setting up the cables and I noticed the carving on this door frame."

"Part of the original building. Almost seventy years, I think."

Gray ran his hand along a short stretch of the smooth, dark oak. "Yeah, my father was a carpenter," he said. "Did stuff like this all the time. Always fascinated me when I was a kid. It was like art. I never got tired of looking at it."

Hunter was suddenly distracted by the sight of Bentley approaching the podium. "Excuse me," he said. "Looks like we're going to get started." He put his hand out. "Nice to meet you, William. Give us a good broadcast, okay?"

"Sure thing," said Gray. "And actually it's, uh, it's Willis."

Hunter had started to walk away, but he stopped and tilted his head in a sheepish gesture. "Sorry," he said tipping his hat. "Willis it is."

Gray shrugged. "It's okay," he said. "My friends call me Wireless."

CHAPTER 16
DECLARATION OF WAR

Bentley stood just a few feet from the podium, adjusting his tie as the clock ticked down the last two minutes before the scheduled start of the press gathering. To his right were Gallagher and Hunter, representing the district attorney's office. To the mayor's left were Taggert, Dugan and Pruett, representing the police department.

They were accompanied by two uniformed police officers, one standing on either side but slightly apart from the group, faces inert, watching everything.

Cameras flashed as Bentley stepped up to the podium and cleared his throat. Hunter continued to scan the lobby, noting at least another twenty people standing around the fringes of the press corps—curiosity-seekers who had stopped momentarily to catch a few minutes of the unusual gathering that was taking shape.

Bentley pulled a sheaf of papers from inside his jacket and unfolded it on the podium. He pulled his pocket watch from his vest and gave it a quick glance, then returned it to his vest pocket and looked up at the assembly of newsmen. "Alright, we'd best get started," he said. He straightened his notes on the podium and cleared his throat one last time.

The idle muttering fell to a hush, but the occasional flashbulb still popped as Bentley started to speak.

"Gentlemen, good afternoon," he said. "Thank you all very much for making arrangements to come here on such short notice." He pulled a pair of glasses from inside of his jacket and positioned them on his face. "We're all aware of some unfortunate and tragic events that have taken place in Union City over the last few days. We've been able to establish some connections between these events that we want all of you—and everyone in this city—to be aware of."

His eyes settled on the page unfolded in front of him. Among the press corps, about twenty in all, pens hovered over notepads. A couple more flashbulbs fired.

"In recent weeks, the police department and the district attorney's office have been aware of an increase in criminal activity relating to gambling and racketeering in several of the city's nightclubs and entertainment establishments. As we all know, the situation took a violent turn in the past forty-eight hours, following the explosion at The Blue Star Supper Club on West Twenty-First Street in the city's Entertainment District two nights ago. This terrible act of premeditated violence resulted in the death of one police officer, Patrolman Leonard Duffy, and two civilians. Five other citizens have been hospitalized as a result of the explosion."

Bentley tilted his head toward Taggert and Dugan while still keeping his eye on the press crew standing directly in front of him. "Police Chief Taggert and his detective bureau, under the direction of Lieutenant Mike Dugan, have been following the situation closely for the past few weeks leading up to the events at the Blue Star. Based on the evidence to date—including evidence that's still being gathered from the explosion the other night—they have reason to believe that the explosion at the nightclub was the result of a rivalry between opposing factions of organized crime that are trying to establish and maintain control over every aspect of the gambling activity in this city."

He's not going to come out and say it, thought Hunter. *He's going to leave it to one of the news hawks to bring it up.*

"Needless to say we are very concerned about these events, and we are deeply saddened by the loss of a fine young police officer," Bentley went on. "And most importantly, we are fiercely committed to apprehending the person or persons who committed these acts and bringing them to swift justice under the law."

With each sentence, each phrase, the mayor's voice grew more determined, more forceful. Hunter, who'd been watching the room, noted that a much larger crowd had assembled around the edges of the press corps—and more were still coming, from adjacent hallways and stairways, as though drawn by some kind of gravity. Every pair of eyes had locked onto Bentley.

The mayor looked up from the papers on the podium and met the collective gaze with a fiery conviction in his eyes that matched the one in his voice. "As of today," he continued, "the police department, the District Attorney's office, the mayor's office and all of City Hall is at war with any party who chooses to engage in or promote illegal gambling in this city."

Hunter glanced sideways and momentarily locked eyes with Gallagher. Both acknowledged an unspoken thought that was mutually understood: *This guy means business.*

"I have a clear message for the people of Union City, regardless of what side of the law they may choose to stand on," Bentley continued. "Any person or persons determined to be running one or any number of these establishments will be prosecuted to the fullest extent of the law."

Bentley raised an index finger in a gesture of emphasis. "And the message doesn't stop there," he said. "These gambling operations are successful only to the degree that they are able to draw a steady clientele. Any citizens who are found engaging in the illegal gambling activities hosted by these establishments will also be prosecuted to the fullest extent of the law."

He removed his glasses and leaned forward against the podium, sending the piercing gaze around the room one more time. "And finally, and perhaps most importantly," he said, "anyone found to be involved in any way with the illegal manufacture of explosive materials for purposes of breaking and entering—or any other violent criminal intent—will be prosecuted to the fullest extent of the law."

The press team was no longer looking down at their notebooks and scribbling quotes. Almost to a man, they had stopped and looked up, scrutinizing the intensity of Bentley's expression and hanging on his every word.

"Some may say that gambling is not a violent crime," he said, "but the tragic events of recent days have shown us that it can be. Violence and lawlessness of this nature have no place in Union City. We have stared into the face of evil before. We have proven in the past that we can rise up against it and overcome it. We will not allow it to take root again."

For a moment, Hunter half expected to hear applause. Instead, Bentley opened up the gathering to questions from the press. An urgent flurry of questions erupted from more than a dozen reporters.

Cranley, from the *Tribune*, was the first to cut through the chatter: "Chief Taggert, is this incident connected in any way with the break-in at Pharaoh Chemical a few nights ago?"

Taggert took a step forward and cleared his throat. "The best I can say at this time is that it may be," he said. "A preliminary investigation suggests that the chemical composition of the explosives used in the Blue Star incident is similar to the materials that were stolen from Pharaoh Chemical three nights ago. However, we can't be certain that the chemicals used at the Blue Star were in fact the same as those taken from the Pharaoh facility."

Taggert gestured in Pruett's direction. "Oliver Pruett, a chemical engineer, is working with the police department as a technical advisor," he said. "Some of you may recall that Dr. Pruett had been the plant manager at the Pharaoh facility several years ago. He is currently conducting some tests to make a more clear determination as to whether the materials from the Blue Star explosions and the stolen Pharaoh inventory are an exact match. But your question is certainly valid. It seems highly coincidental to us that explosives of this nature would be used less than twenty-four hours after the same kinds of materials were stolen from a location in the same city."

Again the voices bubbled up with questions. Tyler, from the *Chronicle*, cut through the chatter. "Mayor Bentley, let's cut to the chase," he said, sounding more than a little cocky. "Frankly, this all sounds a lot like Nicky Diamond. Is there evidence to suggest that he might be involved in any of this?"

Tyler had clearly expected to catch the mayor off guard and gain the upper hand by speaking the unspeakable. It didn't work.

"Yes," said Bentley, his unflinching gaze leveled directly at Tyler. The reporter shuffled his feet and averted his eyes. The bravado he'd displayed a moment earlier had vanished.

The one-word answer sent a jolt of electricity through the entire room. A new round of flashbulbs popped, and the chatter of questions from the press escalated to an unprecedented level. A murmur of tension and speculation passed among the onlookers who'd gathered around and behind the crowd of reporters.

And there it is, thought Hunter. A master stroke. In less than ten minutes punctuated by a one-word answer, Bentley had managed to bring Nicky Diamond back under the front-and-center scrutiny of the press and opened him up to the condemnation of the general public. His opening remarks were mostly generalities—even a few platitudes—but he'd put the city on the offensive, and he'd done it without even mentioning Diamond's name.

Tyler tried to shout over the noise, asking Bentley to elaborate, but the mayor shrugged him off and moved on to the next question.

It was the reporter from the Ashton County *Examiner:* "If this is the work of Nicky Diamond, do the police know his exact whereabouts? Is he currently operating somewhere in the city? And if so, where?"

"We don't have conclusive evidence to answer that question at this time," said Taggert. "We base our theory about Diamond on the evidence we've gathered from incidents that have taken place over the last few days, in comparison with methods and patterns connected to Diamond when he was previously operating in this city nearly fifteen years ago. The similarities are growing increasingly hard to ignore, but if we are correct that he is in Union City—and we believe that we are—we can't say at this time exactly where."

The answer triggered another wave of rapid-fire questions from all corners, but by this time, Hunter was watching more than listening, scanning the group of correspondents gathered in the lobby. The few who weren't all talking at once were scribbling in their notebooks, reloading their flashbulbs, or jockeying to make eye contact with the mayor or the police chief in preparation for the next question.

All except one.

Bart Maxwell. He was doing none of those things. He was looking directly back at Hunter, with an eyebrow arched.

Hunter had seen the look before. Max had information.

CHAPTER 17
SOMETHING LURKING

Ten minutes later it was over. Bentley had taken a few more questions, then brought the press conference to a close.

The correspondents dispersed, taking with them the sense of urgency that had escalated in the course of the twenty-minute gathering. Some scrambled for telephone booths to call in their stories, others hustled for their cars to get back to their desks and bang out copy on their own. Photographers dismantled their gear and packed it into bulky leather satchels and either climbed into their own cars or rode shotgun with their reporter colleagues. Typewriters and darkrooms were waiting. The afternoon editions were waiting, and the evening news broadcasts were not far behind.

Bentley turned to Hunter and the rest of the men standing at the podium. "I think it went well," the mayor said.

The rest nodded in agreement. "Well, like it or not," said Taggert, "we all know how this works. Anything that smells remotely like Nicky Diamond makes good copy and sells a lot of papers."

"And frankly," said Bentley, "that's what we wanted."

A few of the onlookers who'd gathered at the press conference lingered in the main lobby in clusters of two or three, muttering nervously amongst themselves about what it all might mean. For the most part, though, the electric energy that had filled the room earlier had subsided, and the flow of traffic through the main lobby was returning to normal.

Off to one side, Bentley's assistant spoke in hushed tones with the building manager about breaking down the podium and clearing the way for regularly scheduled City Hall business. The assistant also mentioned something to the manager about a maintenance project going on upstairs. Hunter stood in a cluster with the mayor and the rest of the press conference attendees. Taggert was talking to Gallagher about business he wanted to address before the end of the day.

But most of Hunter's attention was elsewhere. He'd been watching Max from the corner of his eye since the press conference broke up. Max had cleared out more slowly than the rest, slipping his notebook into a pocket of his trench coat and wandering through the revolving door of the main entrance to the stairway beyond.

Hunter tuned back into the conversation among the small group just as it was winding down. Bentley and his assistant were heading back upstairs to their offices. Pruett was catching a ride back to the police station with Taggert and Dugan, all three of them moving through the lobby toward the same revolving doors that Max had just stepped through.

Outside the building, at the top of the stairs, Gallagher started to say something to Hunter about heading back to the office together, but Hunter stopped him. "You go on ahead," he said. "I'll walk back. I need to make a stop. I'll be about five or ten minutes behind you."

Everyone made their way down the stairs and headed in different directions. Hunter walked casually up the street toward Maxwell, who was leaning against his Roadster at the curb. A Lucky dangled from his lips as he absently flipped through the pages of his notebook.

Max looked up from his notes as Hunter approached. The reporter tilted his chin at the doorway at the top of the steps from which they'd all just emerged. "Sounds like Bentley's on a crusade," he said.

Hunter glanced back the steps, then further down the street at nothing in particular. "He is," he said. "He should be." After a moment, he leveled his gaze at Max and lowered his voice slightly. "Anything new?"

"As a matter of fact, yeah."

"I'm listening."

Max took a deep breath. "You know The Paramount Club, the place on West Tenth?"

"Sure. Dutch Markowitz's place."

"Well, maybe not so much anymore."

Hunter frowned. "I don't follow you."

"I'm hearing Markowitz has taken on a partner. Let's just call him a silent partner. I say 'silent' because people either don't know who he is, or they just don't want to tell me. I do know this, though: whoever he is, he apparently has some muscle—enough to take over a sizable portion of Markowitz's business."

Max paused for a moment and chuckled. "Actually, based on what I'm hearing, I'm fairly certain this arrangement wasn't really Markowitz's idea at all," he said. "But Dutch has a pretty shady record, so he's not the kind of guy who's in a position to put up a fight when a guy with some muscle wants to move in and take a piece of his action."

Hunter frowned, staring into the traffic and weighing the information. "Gambling?" he said.

"And then some," said Max. "We all know about the restaurant and nightclub. Markowitz has been running that for years. But this other guy, whoever he is, apparently turned it into something much more than that. Had a crew in there on the down-low. You know, carpenters and painters and the like. Turned the basement into a pretty ritzy place—cards, roulette, over-under, bar, nice furniture, the works."

Max took out a lighter and lit the cigarette. "And here's the thing," he said. "Sure, this is a fancy gambling joint, but I'm hearing something else as well. I'm hearing that this guy, whoever he is, has turned The Paramount Club into his primary base of operations."

"And you have no idea who this person is," said Hunter.

Max shook his head, his mouth twisting into a frown. "If I did, Jack, I'd tell you. Listen, you know I've got good sources. The people I talk to are usually pretty willing to give me the low-down on what's happening around town. But when I ask about this stuff? The tune changes. Actually, the music stops altogether. Everybody seems a little nervous when I bring up the gambling operations."

Max hesitated, looking as though he were choosing his next words carefully. Hunter waited. "Now, I know the law's the law, Jack, and I'm not saying some laws are more okay to break than others. I sure wouldn't say that to someone from the DA's office. But let's face it, gambling may not be legit, but in the big scheme of illegal activity, it isn't exactly the kind of thing where the judge'll throw the book at you and give you the chair—especially if you're just a small timer looking to make a few extra bucks. But even still, no one wants to talk about this. It's like they're scared or something."

"More scared than you'd expect about something like a gambling operation."

Max nodded. "I think the gambling's a part of it, sure."

"But?"

"I think there's more going on."

"Such as?"

Max shook his head. "Don't know."

"A guess?"

"Can't even guess," said Max. "Like I said, the minute I start asking questions, people just shut up."

Hunter took a deep breath, processing the information. "So the nightclubs are a front for the gambling," he said, "and the gambling may be a front for something else."

"Yeah, that's what it feels like."

Hunter nodded. "You think this silent partner is Diamond?"

"Kinda hard to think otherwise," said Max. "I mean, he may be keeping a low profile, but there isn't much question at this point that he's somewhere in this picture." He gestured in a vague direction up the street, toward City Hall. "Hell, I'm sure you know more than I do, but we just heard the mayor himself add it all up for the whole city to hear, didn't we?"

Max opened up his palm and counted off the facts on his fingers. "Explosive materials stolen from a chemical factory, just like the old days," he said. "Nightclub blows up a couple nights later, just like the old days, and it looks like some kind of rivalry. You've got a chemistry professor working with the police who says the break-in and the explosion are connected. The mayor holds a press conference to announce a war on crime, and he makes some pretty direct references to a past that we all remember all too well. Then that peacock Tyler takes the bait and asks the mayor at point-blank range if he thinks it's Diamond, and the mayor says yes without even stopping to take a breath."

Max paused to take another drag on the Lucky. "Meanwhile, I'm getting word that some kind of mystery man has taken over a nightclub downtown and set up a big gambling operation," he said. "But whoever the guy is, whatever he's really up to, it's all scary enough that no one wants to talk about him. Hell, Jack, why *wouldn't* I think it's Diamond?"

Hunter paused, weighing Max's logic. A cab drove by. A newspaper truck drove by. "I know," he said finally. "I just needed to hear it from someone outside the loop."

More traffic passed. Max took another drag. "You going to tell Gallagher about the Paramount?" he said.

Hunter shook his head. "Don't know yet."

"It's good information."

"I don't doubt it."

Max arched an eyebrow. "But?"

"Gallagher and the police," said Hunter, "they like hard evidence. Especially in a case like this one."

Max shrugged. "Yeah, I know how this works," he said. "Not much faith in the fourth estate."

Hunter cracked a smile. "Don't take it hard," he said. "Mine's always been unshakable. And I'm a fan of your singing voice, too."

Max smirked. "Good to know," he said. "If you do pass it along, and if any cops take you up on it and go into the Paramount for a raid, you'll give me the inside track, right?"

"You'll be the first to know."

Max nodded. "I'll be around," he said. He took one last drag on his cigarette, then dropped it on the pavement and stomped it with his shoe. He turned and climbed into his car.

Seconds later, Hunter watched the back end of Max's car disappear into the midday traffic.

The Paramount, he thought. *Could be a lead. If I could just figure out what to do with it.*

CHAPTER 18
SCIENCE, LIES AND MAYHEM

Later that afternoon, Hunter stood in a makeshift laboratory at the end of a hallway in the police department. The space had actually been a maintenance room just days earlier, but the wash tub with hot and cold running water and the rectangular table adjacent to the tub was all Oliver Pruett needed to set up shop. He'd constructed a network of beakers, tubes, burners and other equipment on the table top to run tests on a variety of materials gathered just the day before from the site of The Blue Star Supper Club explosion. A neatly organized array of carefully tagged and catalogued debris—chunks of charred wood, plaster, brick and mortar—lined the floor along one wall. Nearly every piece had been subjected to a variety of procedures to test for certain chemical residues and combustive properties.

Pruett was standing just a couple feet away from the table, holding a chunk of scorched cinderblock that had been part of the west wall of the Blue Star. He was delivering a dissertation on the nature of chemical explosions in general and the specifics of the Blue Star explosion in particular. His narrative encompassed a variety of topics: high-volatility chemical reactions, the principles of chemical combustion, the residues frequently resulting from said combustion, high-velocity disbursement patterns.

There was more, but Hunter had trouble keeping up.

When Pruett got to the end of it all, he slipped his pen into the breast pocket of his lab coat and regarded Hunter with a worried frown. "I had hoped to enlighten you about the implications of the evidence, but I'm concerned that I may have confused you more than anything else."

"Well, I have to admit," said Hunter, "I may be fairly knowledgeable about the principals of mechanics and electricity, but this level of chemistry is a little bit over my head."

Pruett put up a hand in a reassuring gesture. "I understand," he said. "And you needn't worry if this doesn't make sense to you. That's why I'm here." He adjusted his glasses. "Let me boil it down to some very simple but unfortunate conclusions. The suspicions and concerns expressed by you and Mr. Gallagher, along with Chief Taggert and Detective Dugan in the police department, are not unwarranted. Based on what I'm seeing in these test samples, compared to the evidence and the documents from fourteen years ago, the explosives in both cases are of a very similar composition and nature. And if I were to make a guess based on many years of experience in this kind of analysis, they were likely developed by the same individual."

Hunter weighed the information for a moment. "So not only does this evidence point to Diamond," he said, "but it also suggests that the guy who's making bombs for him now is the same guy who was doing it for him several years ago?"

Pruett shrugged. "Well, as I've said before, I'm no detective. But the scientific evidence would certainly suggest that, yes."

Hunter felt a wave of frustration welling up, and he did his best to push it back down. "And we never determined who that person was several years ago."

Pruett sighed, signaling some frustration of his own. "No," he said. "Despite the best efforts of the police and even federal investigators at the time, we did not. Very few people outside of the police department knew this, but I even hired a private detective to monitor personnel at the plant, just to see if he might turn up any information that might be useful, but there was no suspicious activity on the part of anyone on any production shift that could be documented."

Hunter nodded. "Okay," he said after a moment. "So maybe this information isn't good news, but any information is helpful. I take it you've shared all this with Dugan and the chief?"

"Oh, yes, of course," said Pruett, returning the chunk of cinderblock to its proper place in the row of test samples along the floor. "I briefed both of them earlier today, just after I completed the tests." He stood back up and reached for a towel on the table to wipe his hands. "I asked you to meet me here because they wanted to make sure I went over the information with you."

"That's fine. I appreciate you keeping me informed. If nothing else, believe it or not, I always enjoy a good science lesson."

Pruett's face broke into a small smile that cut some of the earlier tension Hunter had been feeling. "Well," he said, dropping the towel back on the table, "I've been a chemist for many years, but never a chemistry teacher."

"I have to admit I've wondered about that," said Hunter. "How'd you get involved in chemistry in the first place?"

"I guess you'd say it's a family business," said Pruett. "Literally."

Hunter frowned. "I don't follow you."

"My father wasn't a chemist in the strictest sense of the word. He had no degree as such. But he ran a cleaning supply business—detergents, solvents, things of that nature—and he did hold a number of patents on household and industrial cleaning products."

"Wait a minute. This is the same company that made Pruett All-Purpose Cleaner?"

"The very same."

"That's *your* family?"

"It is."

"Huh. I had no idea the stuff was made right here in town. I remember the newspaper ads: 'Got a big cleaning job? You can do it with Pruett.'"

Pruett smiled. "My mother came up with that."

"And *my* mother used the stuff all the time. All over the house."

"Obviously two very smart women."

"Without a doubt," said Hunter. "But come to think of it, I haven't seen any of those ads in years."

"The business is not what it was," said Pruett. "We lost several big industrial customers right after the crash, so we've been forced to scale back quite a bit in the last five years or so. The inventory we do have is stored in a building at the end of Warehouse Row."

Hunter shook his head. "Same story with a lot of companies since the crash."

"Indeed. I had partial ownership when my father was still alive, and I inherited the entire operation after he passed away. But I've hired a management group to take care of the day-to-day operations so I could pursue other interests. It's a much more modest operation now, but we still have a processing facility in the Manufacturing District and offices right downtown." He tilted his head toward the west wall of the room. "In Union Tower, as a matter of fact. Up on the thirtieth floor."

"A lot of businesses have taken it hard in the last few years, or folded altogether," said Hunter. "Think yours can hang on through all this?

Pruett sighed. "I don't know," he said. "Sometimes I'm not even sure it's worth the effort. I've considered liquidating. Then again, if I wait a few years and the market improves, we can rebuild our customer base and I'll be glad I held on."

"Well, you won't get any good advice from me. I'm just a law man. I don't know much about the stock market."

"But you seem to know about much more than just the law. I don't know many lawyers and assistant district attorneys who know as much about mechanical and electrical engineering as you seem to. How did that come about?"

"Well, you were around for Diamond's last big show, so I'm sure you remember some of the story."

"I'm afraid I do, and it's tragic."

"My father was killed the summer before I was supposed to start college. I had planned to study engineering—mechanical and electrical engineering, to be exact. But I took a year off to help settle his affairs after he was gone. I guess I changed course somewhere in that year off, because when I did get to school I studied criminal justice instead. Then I went on to law school. Seven years after finishing law school, here I am."

"Perhaps you felt there was some unfinished business you could resolve."

Hunter shrugged. "I don't know," he said. "It just seemed like the thing to do."

"Well, even if it wasn't part of your original plan, do you derive some sense of satisfaction from the work?"

Hunter was about to answer when Taggert leaned his head in the doorway.

"Jack," he said. "I thought I heard your voice from down the hall. I'm glad you're here." He glanced at Pruett and then back at Hunter. "Do you have a minute?"

Hunter shook hands with Pruett and excused himself. The chemist sent him on his way with an assurance that he'd keep him and Gallagher informed about the results of any further tests.

Hunter joined Taggert in the hallway. "What's up, Chief?"

Taggert tilted his head down the hallway. "Follow me," he said, setting a brisk pace. Hunter fell into step alongside him.

"Something wrong?"

"No, but I thought you might want to see this."

Halfway up the corridor, they reached a door on the right-hand wall and Taggert grabbed the doorknob. "In here," he said. He opened the door and ushered Hunter into the room.

The lighting inside was dim, with a large, rectangular pane of glass along the left hand wall. On the other side of the glass, a questionable looking character—no more than twenty-one years old—sat in a chair at a table in a sparsely furnished cinderblock room. Standing over him was Mike Dugan. The murmur of Dugan's voice came through a small intercom box mounted the wall below the glass panel.

"Two-way mirror," said Taggert. "They can't see us, but obviously we can see them."

The chief gestured at the scene playing out on the other side of the glass. "Kid's name is Wally Flynn," he said. "Mike just sat him down a couple minutes ago. We picked him up for shoplifting at Bergman's, the drugstore on Harwell. Turns out he's a busboy at The Black Tie, the place on Nineteenth. He wasn't smart enough to ask for a lawyer—at least he hasn't yet—so we're making the most of his lack of good sense and taking the opportunity to ask him a few questions."

Hunter turned away from Taggert and watched through the glass as Dugan leaned in close to Flynn and turned up the heat.

"Know anything about Nicky Diamond?" he said. His voice was even, but the intensity was unmistakable, even through the small, tinny intercom box.

Flynn's eyes flickered for a split second. He looked down at his hands, and his face darkened. "Only what I used to read about him in the papers when I was a kid."

"You sure about that?"

"Me? You kiddin'? I'm just a cook in a nightclub. What would I know about a guy like Nicky Diamond?"

"You know Diamond's been out of jail for almost two years? Funny thing is, no one's really sure where he is now. Some people think he's right back here, building a new operation. Right here in Union City. You wouldn't know anything about that, would you?"

Flynn hunched forward, turning his head away from the intensity of Dugan's questions. "Me? Naw, I don't know nothin' about Nicky Diamond."

Hunter stared at the exchange from the other side of the glass. "He's lying."

"Sure he is," said Taggert, his arms folded and his eyes fixed on the same scene trough the two-way mirror. "But as long as he keeps saying no, and we have no hard evidence to the contrary, there are limits to what we can do or how long we can keep him here."

They stood at the window for another minute or so, watching Dugan work Flynn over. "This could take a while," Taggert said finally, "and it may not amount to much." He turned away from the window and steered Hunter down the hallway. "Here, come on in my office for a minute. I want to show you something."

They left the room and moved through a warren of hallways back to Taggert's office. Inside, the chief closed the door behind them. Without the formality of offering Hunter a seat, Taggert got right to the point by crossing the room to his desk and picking up a manila folder.

"We're keeping this under wraps for the time being, and I'm asking you to do the same." He handed the folder to Hunter. "I'm going to tell you right now they're not pretty."

Hunter took the folder, arching an eyebrow at the chief. Inside was a stack of twelve crime-scene photographs of a very dead body—male, late thirties, maybe early forties. Hunter thumbed through the stack, stopping at each image for a few seconds. Each picture had been taken from a different angle. Some were wide, showing the body crumpled into a garbage dumpster. Others were close-up on the head and face, front and back. Still others focused on his extremities, two of which appeared to be in very bad shape.

The victim had a wide-eyed but vacant expression of agony and terror, frozen in place not only by the instantaneous act of the camera but also by the hole in his right temple that was obviously a bullet wound.

The victim also had no hands.

"Do we know who he is?" said Hunter.

"We do. And you might too. Name's Carl Duchovny."

"Duke," said Hunter. "One of Diamond's crew in the old days. He was one of the thugs who shot at my father when he was guarding the doorway on the fifth floor of the Justice Center."

"That's the one. A couple trash collectors found him when they were doing their usual rounds this morning. Said the smell was really bad as soon as they brought their truck down the alley—worse than the usual rotten food you'll find in a dumpster on any given day. They took one look in the dumpster and called us."

Hunter flipped through the grisly collection a second time, stopping at one in particular. He looked up at Taggert. "Where the hell are his hands?"

"Obviously severed," said the chief.

"Yeah, obviously. But how? This looks pretty ragged."

"As of now, we're pretty sure they were blown off," said Taggert. "Livingston, the medical examiner, took a look at the body right after it was brought in. He says there are severe burn marks on both stumps, most likely from some sort of explosive. He needs to do a full examination of the residue on the tissue before he can get a definitive answer about what kinds of chemicals. I told him to ask Pruett for some assistance if he needs it."

"I assume the hands blew up first," said Hunter, "then the bullet in the head?"

"That's what Livingston says."

"So what does this tell us?"

"Good question," said Taggert. He tilted his head in the direction

113

of the interrogation room they'd just left. "Mike and I were talking about this earlier. Something seems, I don't know, unstable."

Hunter snorted. "Well, yeah," he said. "But if we're talking about Nicky Diamond, unstable isn't really anything new, is it?"

"No, but this tells me something's wrong internally." Taggert stepped behind his desk and settled into his chair. "In the old days, Diamond ran a tight ship. For all the chaos he caused in this city, there was never any indication of any internal fighting within his organization."

Hunter nodded, getting a handle on Taggert's line of thinking. "But now this guy," he said, tapping the stack of photos in his hand, "one of the earliest and most loyal members of Diamond's organization, gets killed in a way that looks like something Diamond himself might have done."

Taggert nodded.

"Dissent among the ranks," Hunter suggested.

"Maybe. Or maybe he's getting—how should I say it—less discerning in his ruthlessness."

Hunter thought for a moment, glancing absently through the stack of photos. "So, why now?" he said finally, looking up at the police chief. "What's different this time?"

"Hard to say," said Taggert. "He spent twelve years in prison. I'm sure that didn't help. And he's older. I'm no psychiatrist, but I have to believe that people as unbalanced as him don't get better over time if they don't get any help. They get worse."

Hunter looked back at the photos in his hand and shook his head. "Crazier than before," he said. "I wouldn't have thought that was possible."

"It's Nicky Diamond," said Taggert. "Anything's possible."

CHAPTER 19
A PLAN FOR DESTRUCTION

Diamond glared at the headline across the front page of the afternoon edition of the *Tribune*. He scanned the story above the fold and nearly spat at the photo of the mayor standing at a podium in the atrium of City Hall. He tore open the front section and scanned the remainder of the story on page three before tossing the whole wad of newsprint to the floor.

He grabbed the late edition of the *Chronicle* from his desk and followed the same ritual, but this time he threw the paper across the room when he was finished.

Marshall and Simone sat silently in chairs at the opposite end of the room, each in a separate corner.

"It's on the radio too," said Simone, keeping his voice even and devoid of emotion. He got up from his chair and moved toward the radio near Diamond's desk. "You want me to turn—?"

"No!" Diamond barked. "Leave it off, dammit!"

Marshall shifted in his chair. "Look, Nick, you can't let this rattle you," he said. "It's not like this is really a big surprise anyway, is it? We knew this morning when we got word from—"

"This Bentley," Diamond growled, as though he hadn't heard a word his consigliere had been saying. He stabbed a finger toward the heap of newsprint on the floor. "He thinks he's some kind of tough guy."

"He was a trial lawyer before he ran for mayor," said Marshall. "Most people considered him the best in the county. He was part of the prosecuting team that—"

"Oh, I know," said Diamond, redirecting his index finger from the papers on the floor to a place directly between Marshall's eyes. "I know exactly who he is. Part of that group of shysters who put me away for twelve years."

Marshall shrugged. "I'm just saying," he said. "He knows the system, and if he knew how to steer a courtroom full of jurors fourteen years ago, you can bet he's learned how to steer a city full of people in the years since then."

Diamond turned away and dismissed him with an irritated wave. He turned to Simone. "What about McShane's place? The cops go in last night?"

"They did. Just like we were told."

"And?"

Simone frowned and shook his head. "They didn't find a thing. Nothing was left behind."

"I don't want to find out later about anything that's going to give us away. No chips, no tickets, no receipts, none of it. Because once they start finding that stuff, it's just a matter of time before they start connecting it to our other operations."

"The place was cleared."

Diamond paced silently in front of his desk for a moment. "Alright," he said, changing gears in his mind. "What about tonight? The Stor-All place, I mean."

"Our information is good," said Simone. "We got a confirmation from a second source. The police have a warrant to go into the storage unit tonight."

Diamond stopped pacing and turned his gaze at Simone with a look of frustration. "Right," he said, an edge of annoyance in his voice. "And we have goods there, too. And I'm not just talking about the kind of gambling stuff we had at McShane's. We've got a few barrels of stuff from the Pharaoh heist in there. And there's the safe, with some leftover product from Sun Lu's last shipment a few weeks ago. We need to clear that place, too."

"We'll clear it out, said Simone. "I have Kowalski and four of our boys on it, just like last night at McShane's."

And then it hit Diamond, the same way it always did. A slow-moving wave through his gut that he'd known so well for most of his life—an urge that could only be satisfied one way. "No," he said. "I don't just want to clear it out." His voice had suddenly turned hoarse and husky, and his words came slowly as the idea took shape in his head. "I want to wire it up, too."

Marshall's expression darkened suddenly. "Wait," he said, leaning forward on his chair. "You mean blast it? Nick, I don't think—"

"No. I want to do it," said Diamond. The surge that had started in his gut was moving quickly to his head, mixing with the jolt from the last capsule he'd emptied onto his tongue just a few minutes earlier—just before Simone had brought the newspapers into his office. He felt his jaw flex involuntarily. He took in a deep breath of air and ran his tongue along the corner of his upper lip.

"Nick, I don't...Look, a cop got killed when we hit the Hirschfeld place the other night." He gestured at the papers on the floor. "That's exactly why the mayor and the cops and DA are turning up the heat."

Diamond shook his head. "I need you to wire it up," he said to Simone. "The cops want to send me a message? I can send one right back to them."

The room was silent for a moment. Marshall's expression suggested an uncertainty about how far to press his position. Simone, however, looked less conflicted. He had, after all, essentially positioned himself as the underboss—the primary lieutenant in Diamond's operation. And being a lieutenant meant doing what you were told to do.

"We can wire it, Nick," Simone said finally.

"Do you have enough time? After the others clear the place out, I mean?"

Simone glanced at Marshall, who was no longer making eye contact with the other two men in the room. The consigliere, who was supposed to be Diamond's primary advisor, had lost this particular battle and he knew it.

Simone appeared emboldened by Marshall's deferential posture. "Yeah," he said with a shrug. "I'll get Sparks and Wireless. We'll get it done."

Diamond looked at Simone, nodding his head slowly and somehow forming a smile on his face by turning the corners of his mouth downward rather than upward. "Alright," he said. "Make sure it gets wired up."

He was silent for a moment, his eyes drifting away to some faraway place. "I want to be there," he said, more to himself than anyone else in the room. Then his eyes refocused on Simone. "I want to see it when it happens."

Simone shrugged and nodded again. "Sure, boss," he said. "We can do that."

Diamond turned to Marshall and pointed at the scatter of newsprint at their feet.

"They want a war?" he said. "We'll give them a war."

CHAPTER 20
PLAYING WITH DYNAMITE

At nine o'clock that evening, Hunter found himself on West Tenth Street in the Entertainment District, standing at the curb about twenty yards from the entrance to The Paramount Club, leaning against a lamp post. As predicted, the late editions of the *Tribune* and the *Chronicle* had splashed the mayor's war on gambling—and the less than subtle suggestion of Nicky Diamond's involvement—all over their respective front pages. The newsstands had sold out of both papers in less than two hours, but Hunter had a copy of each folded under his left arm. What's more, the story had been at the top of the seven-o'clock news broadcasts on the local radio stations.

Hunter stepped away from the lamp post and made his way to the entrance to the Paramount. He pushed through the glass doors and stepped inside. The lobby, at least, was tastefully decorated without looking ritzy, but he couldn't help sensing an undercurrent of something else in the room—something cold and menacing. The thick, dark-haired bouncer standing in a corner of the lobby and eyeing everyone who came through the entrance didn't exactly put him at ease, but Hunter sensed that there was more to his gut feeling than just this goon.

A young woman in a flattering dress approached the hostess stand from somewhere deeper inside the room and welcomed Hunter to the club. He nodded thanks and glanced past her, into the dining room, where a fourteen-piece orchestra on the bandstand was just finishing a number and preparing for another.

The hostess offered to check Hunter's hat, but he declined. "Will anyone be joining you tonight, sir?" she said.

"No," said Hunter. "Just me."

The woman put on a smile that looked like part of the routine and not at all genuine. She took a menu from the stand and ushered him to a booth, where she indicated that a waitress would stop by the table shortly. She turned and walked away briskly, back toward her post in the lobby.

The comfortable upholstery in the booth and the dim lighting created an environment that would have prompted most patrons to sit back, relax, light up a cigarette and spend some money. But Hunter wasn't interested in any of that. He really wasn't sure why he was here.

No trouble, he reassured himself. *Just getting the lay of the land. Nothing more.*

But some other voice—something quiet but persistent, from some distant and undefined place—was saying something different.

He leaned forward, one elbow on the table, his hand stroking his chin while his eyes swept the spacious room. Hunter had no way to compare, because he'd never set foot in the place before, but tonight's crowd looked pretty well heeled. Plenty of suits, even a tuxedo or two. Fairly good-sized stage for the orchestra, which was well into a rendition of "Night and Day," and a dance floor that took up about a third of the room. These days, anyone who had the luxury of dining out on a weeknight—or any night, for that matter—was doing well. An assistant DA and most other members of the criminal justice system, on the other hand, rarely had the time or the resources on a Wednesday night for anything more than a deli sandwich.

A young woman in a short black waitress uniform approached the table. She was about twenty-five and pretty, but in a way that also seemed a little bit hard-edged. "Good evening, hon," she said. "Can I get you a drink?" She was doing a fair job of sounding pleasant, but there was a weariness in her voice that probably was the result of more than just physical fatigue.

Hunter looked at her for a moment, holding her gaze for a little longer than she was probably used to, then said, "I'll have a Manhattan."

"A Manhattan? Very good, sir." She glanced at the menu on the table in front of him. "Will you be having dinner tonight as well?"

Hunter frowned. "Haven't decided yet."

She nodded. "That's fine," she said. "I'll be right back with your drink."

Hunter nodded curtly, and the waitress moved away.

He continued to scan the room, this time glancing over his shoulder and seeing a wall that opened up to two sets of staircases—one heading up and the other heading down. There was a velvet rope blocking each staircase, and a big-looking goon standing at each rope. The message was clear. Whatever was upstairs or downstairs was off limits.

The band finished "Night and Day" and started into "April in Paris." The dance floor was a little thin, only three couples. One pair drifted back to their seats after the last song ended, while another stepped onto the floor as the next one started.

The waitress returned and set the drink in front of him. She started to ask again about whether he was interested in dinner, but Hunter held up a finger as he picked up the glass and put it to his lips. He took a short sip and made the OK sign with his thumb and forefinger. "Great," he said.

"Joey at the bar is one of the best in town."

"You may be right." He glanced around the room. "Busy tonight?"

"Seems that way."

"How long have you been working here?"

"Just started at seven."

"No, I mean how long since you first started working at this club?"

"Oh," she said, smiling a little at the misunderstanding. The smile actually looked genuine this time. "It's been a few months now."

"Business must be good if they're hiring."

She shrugged. "I guess so. Are you interested in dinner?"

"How good is business?" he said. And suddenly, he could feel the tone of the conversation shifting—almost as though someone else had begun speaking for him.

"I beg your pardon?" she said. Wary.

"Lot of action here?"

She looked away. "I'm not sure what you mean. We serve drinks and dinner, we have a band, and we have a dance floor."

"What else you got?"

"Mister, are you getting fresh with me?"

"Not really. What I'm curious about, though, is what's at the other end of those staircases," he said, gesturing over his shoulder. "The ones where those two happy looking fellas are standing. Maybe there's somebody important at the top of one staircase who can tell me about what happens at the bottom of the other."

The waitress stared at him for a moment with a gaze that had turned cold. "You gonna be smart with me or you gonna order?" Hunter knew he'd set her off when he heard her diction shift to something that sounded a little on the cheap side.

"So tell me who runs this place," he said, keeping his voice pleasant and conversational—which only seemed to rattle her even more.

Her nostrils flared. "Davey Markowitz," she said curtly. "You wanna talk to a manager? Believe me, I'd be glad to bring somebody over right now."

"How about Nicky Diamond?" he said, feigning idle curiosity. "Know anybody by that name? I'll talk to him if he's around."

"I...I don't...Listen, are you gonna order dinner?"

Hunter smiled. "Still deciding. I'll just work on my drink for a while."

She moved off in a huff.

In less than two minutes, the big ape from the lobby marched over to Hunter's table with the waitress at his heels. He'd pasted a flinty look on his face and made no effort to conceal the hardware in his jacket. He was still several feet away from the table and already talking tough. "There a problem, pal?"

Hunter stood up and squared his shoulders to the thug, who was now just a few feet away. "Pal?" said Hunter, cocking his head to one side. "That's funny, because I don't believe we've met." The thug came to a stop no more than two feet away from Hunter. He stood about two inches shorter than Hunter, but carried himself like a concrete block. The two men stared at each other for a moment, and the gorilla's eyes suddenly went hard and cold as Hunter started reaching into his jacket. The bouncer's thick paw quickly went into his own jacket. The waitress let out a small gasp.

"Relax, both of you," said Hunter, who stopped in mid-motion and glanced back and forth between the goon and the waitress standing behind the goon's left shoulder. He realized that something in his own voice had grown just as hard and just as cold as the thug's glare. "I'd have a hard time making trouble with a wallet."

He finished pulling out his black leather wallet and took out a card, his eyes holding the thug's stare all the while. He held the card in front of the thug's face, just two inches from his nose, intentionally crowding his space. "That's assuming you can read," he said. "Can you read, tough guy?"

The thug snatched the card out of Hunter's hand, glaring at Hunter for a few more seconds before glancing at the card.

"If you're planning to get tough," said Hunter, "or use either end of that heater inside your jacket, you might want to remember that these aren't the old days. You manhandle somebody from the DA's office, it doesn't get swept under the rug like it used to. You're likely to create a lot of trouble for yourself downtown."

"Listen, pal, I think you better—"

"Again with the pal," said Hunter, shaking his head. "Honestly, have we met before? Anyway, you be sure to show that card to anybody upstairs who might be interested in seeing it. Even if you can't read, maybe he can." Then, almost as an afterthought, he reached over to the table and picked up the folded newspapers. "And while you're at it," he said, smacking the papers at the thug's fat chest, "give him these too. Tell him to read all about it."

The thug held the papers to his chest at first, then let them drop to the floor as his eyes turned to angry, dark slits underneath a prominent brow. His nostrils flared, but he didn't say a word.

Hunter pulled a five dollar bill from his wallet and dropped it on the table. He looked past the thug's massive shoulder and locked eyes with the waitress. "Keep the change, miss," he said. "And by the way, you might give some thought to finding a better job in a more respectable place."

Without another word, he brushed past the goon, purposely bumping his elbow hard as he passed, and headed for the lobby and the exit. He could feel eyes on him from all directions as he moved through the room—waiters, busboys, other patrons, bouncers, the hostess—and he half expected someone to come up from behind and manhandle him on the way out. He was almost disappointed when it didn't happen. It'd been a few days since he'd spent any time on the bag in the gym, and he would have welcomed the opportunity to work off some steam.

From the corner of his eye, and from the hair standing up on the back of his neck, Hunter was aware of the thug following him, about five steps behind, all the way to the door leading out to the street. He reached the door and pushed through. The thug followed him all the way out to the sidewalk, where Hunter stopped, turned and looked directly at him.

The two men stood about no more than two feet apart, staring at each other under the glow from the lights over the club entrance. Hunter tilted his chin at the door that they'd just walked through. "I'd go back in if I were you," he said. "There's no telling what kind of riff-raff might be in there."

Both men stood still for a moment, holding each other's gaze. Finally, the thug curled his upper lip into a sneer, turned away and headed back inside.

Hunter watched the door close behind him. He took a deep breath and let it out slowly. After a moment, he turned into the night, flexed his shoulders and headed for his car.

CHAPTER 21
STOR-ALL STRIKE

At just a few minutes after midnight, Nicky Diamond stood on the flat, tar-covered roof of a vacant three-story building that faced Avery Road, one of two parallel east-west avenues that stretched for a half-mile directly through the River District. The corridor created by Avery and the adjacent Keller Road—each street a continuous string of warehouses and storage centers, punctuated at the very end by an electrical power station that spanned both blocks—had come to be known over the decades as Warehouse Row among dock workers, manufacturers, rail workers and the general citizenry of Union City.

Louie Simone also stood on the roof, just a few feet away from Diamond. They both kept themselves out of sight in the shadows created by a large air duct protruding from the roof. The building hadn't been used in years, and none of the ducts were functional, but they provided good cover—especially at night—for anyone trying to watch the street below and stay out of sight at the same time.

They'd climbed to the top of the building about a half-hour earlier by way of the fire escape built along the back wall. It had been a precarious ascent up the rusted, rickety structure, but Diamond had barely noticed. He'd been far more preoccupied with finding a place on the roof with the best possible view of the Stor-All facility immediately next door.

Stor-All was a company with three locations around town, the largest being in Warehouse Row. The business rented units of various sizes to companies, community organizations, schools, churches or any group or individual willing to pay a fee to stash their goods. The Stor-All complex that Diamond and Simone had been watching for the last thirty minutes consisted of more than a dozen units, all of them connected by a wide access drive that stretched all the way to an iron gate that fronted on Avery Road. A steel chain, wrapped around the rungs of the gate and secured with a padlock, secured the facility after hours.

Just inside the gate was a small administrative office—a spare wooden box with one door, one window, a desk, a chair, a file cabinet and not much else. The office was unoccupied at this late hour.

Diamond and Simone had left Johnny Kowalski in the car with the engine off in an alley back on the ground, along the wall on the opposite side of the building from the storage facility. Kowalski had parked the car in a patch of complete darkness, with immediate access to the alley's entrance and a clear view of the fire escape stairs Diamond and Simone had used to get to the roof.

Up above, Simone held a pair of binoculars in his hand and raised them to his face every couple minutes. There really wasn't much to see. There was virtually no traffic in this part of town at this hour, and the glow from the few intermittent street lights along the main strip barely cut through the inky blackness that hung over the district. The lights from Union Plaza at the heart of downtown were about a mile to the southwest. From where Diamond and Simone stood, they created a mild glow in the distant sky over their right shoulders and nothing more.

Diamond checked his watch. Ten minutes after twelve. They'd been told the police had planned the raid for midnight. But cops were cops, and they were never on time when it came to operations like this. Still, Diamond felt more edgy with each passing minute. What was the holdup?

His hand tremored slightly as he reached into his pocket and touched the two small cylinders inside. He pulled one out, bit off one end and spat the nub onto the roof beneath his feet. He pulled out the powder-coated strip of paper and stuck it to his tongue. He swallowed, then tossed the empty cylinder and looked down to examine the metal box in his left hand.

So sleek. So shiny.

With the small red indicator light staring back at him in the night like a ruby eye. And the switch just below the light.

God, so much power. Right here in my...

"Here they come," murmured Simone. Diamond looked up from the remote control device and saw him looking to the east through the binoculars. He tracked the direction of the field glasses and realized Simone was right. In the distance, more than a quarter mile off, a line of headlights had just turned from the south and was moving in their direction down Avery.

They came quietly and deliberately. No sirens and no flashing red and blue roof lights. Although they were still some distance away, their top speed appeared to be no more than twenty-five or thirty miles an hour.

"Looks like five cars," said Simone, watching the caravan and counting headlights through the binoculars. "No, six. I see five patrol cars and one that isn't marked."

Diamond felt the surge from the powder he'd just swallowed. His left thumb tapped involuntarily on the surface of the metal box. "Five patrol cars," he said. "That's gonna be at least ten cops, along with whoever's in the unmarked car. Maybe twelve altogether." A grin spread across his face slowly. "Good crowd for a fireworks show."

They watched the procession in silence. Simone took the binoculars away from his face and held them at his side as the cars approached. In less than five minutes, the five vehicles were lining up at the curb in front of the small Stor-All office building.

Simone leaned toward Diamond but kept his eyes on the cars gathered on the street below them. "Listen, Nick," he said, his voice barely more than a whisper, "I'm thinking when we're done here, we can't be hanging around too long. I mean, we need to get back down to the car and get out of here as fast as we can."

Diamond didn't answer. He too kept his eyes fixed on the cars, their headlights turned off but their engines still humming in the darkness.

The first door to open was on the passenger side of the unmarked car. A tall figure in a trench coat and hat stepped out. A uniformed officer emerged from the driver's side a couple seconds later. The tall man held a flashlight in his right hand and swept the beam across the front gate, scanning the office building just beyond.

Simone put the binoculars up one more time. "Dugan," he murmured after a moment.

"The chief of detectives," Diamond said with a smirk. "Nice to know they sent the top brass."

Dugan's driver walked around the back of the car and stood alongside the detective. More doors opened, and in a matter of seconds, four other officers were out of their cars. Each had a hand on the holster at his hip, and one carried a pair of long-handled steel cutters.

The group milled around at the curb. The murmur of voices— mostly Dugan's—made its way up to the roof. Diamond strained to hear, and from the corner of his eye he could see Simone tilt his head in the same effort. Judging from just his tone of voice, Dugan seemed to be outlining some kind of strategy for entering the facility, but neither Diamond nor Simone could make out any exact words.

After a few minutes, Dugan gestured to the cop with the steel cutters and issued the command. "Alright, Hobart," he said, waving the cop toward the gate.

With cops standing on either side of him, Hobart cut the chain. Two others stepped forward and pushed the gate open, forcing a squeal from rusty hinges.

Dugan and the rest of the crew climbed back into their respective vehicles and the caravan advanced slowly through the gate and down the access drive.

In less than thirty seconds, the group of cars came to a stop in front of one of the larger storage units. It was a twenty-five-hundred-square-foot structure with a sliding metal door that allowed enough clearance and parking space for a car or even a small truck. Like the front gate, the sliding door was secured with a lock and chain.

"Well, they're good detectives," said Simone, watching the operation through the binoculars. "They found the right unit."

After a minute or two, the officers—all of them this time—emerged from their cars. Diamond counted twelve, just as he'd guessed earlier.

The one named Hobart had the cutters in his hands again. All the others, including Dugan, had their guns drawn. They fanned out in a semicircle around the sliding door. Two cops, one at either end of the door, crouched low. They each held their revolvers in one hand while getting a firm handle on the bottom edge of the metal panel with the other.

"Okay," said Dugan. His voice was louder now, more taut. Diamond could easily make out the words from his position on the roof next door. He watched as Dugan nodded to Hobart. "Cut it."

Hobart nodded back and approached the chained door with cautious steps. Dugan quickly turned to other seven cops and waved them in the same direction as Hobart. "Cover him."

The surrounding cops drew down on the door, and Dugan said, "Go," setting in motion a carefully choreographed maneuver. Hobart broke the chain in a single stroke of the cutters, and the two cops on either side of the entrance immediately slid the door upward on its metal track.

A barrage of flashlight beams instantly filled the dark, cavernous space beyond the truck-sized entrance. Twelve guns went up—Dugan's and eleven others—all of them trained on the inside of the yawning space.

Dugan yelled, "Police!" and marched through the opening—his gun still up—flanked by cops who swept every corner of the room as they entered.

Once inside, they were no longer visible from where Diamond and Simone were standing on the rooftop next door.

Simone glanced at Diamond. Even in the darkness, Diamond could see the question in his lieutenant's eyes.

"We'll wait a couple minutes," said Diamond, absent-mindedly stroking his thumb along the metal housing of the detonator box in his left hand. His right index finger hovered over the switch, and he took in a deep burst of air through his nostrils.

Diamond saw something else in Simone's eyes. He knew what it was before he even asked. "What?" he snapped. His voice was still in a whisper, but he made no effort to mask the irritation.

Simone shrugged. "Nothing, Nick, I just...I'm just not sure if this is..." his voice trailed off, and he shuffled his feet on the tarred surface of the roof.

"Speak up!"

"It's just...I mean, there's a bunch of cops in there. You blow that charge now and somebody could..."

Diamond's face suddenly spread into a wide grin, and a cackle started up from someplace deep in his chest. He suppressed it just long enough to say, "You mean like this...?"

With no further fanfare, he threw the switch.

The concussion was instantaneous. It rang in their ears and thudded in their chests. Simone winced and doubled over, slapping his hands to his ears. Diamond, however, was oblivious to any physical discomfort. His cackle was full-throated now, and he squared his shoulders to the western property line of the storage facility and focused his gaze on the cavernous, smoking hole that had appeared there as a result of the blast.

Like a portal into hell itself, the opening threw an eerie, flickering glow into the night as the fire from the blast raged within. Even more chilling was the mix of shouts and moans from the police officers as they scrambled to regain control of their fouled mission.

Diamond took it all in with a a perverse sense of glee. He tore his eyes away just long enough to notice the faint reflection of uneven light from below him on the metal box in his hand, then he quickly looked back at the gaping hole in the wall and listened to the chaos from inside. He was vaguely aware of an involuntary twitch in his thumb as it continued to tap the detonator switch on the box.

The exhilarating tableau was suddenly interrupted by the sensation of something around his shoulder, something turning him away from his own handiwork.

Simone's arm, steering him away from the edge of the roof and toward the opposite end of the building.

"Nick, come on…"

Diamond resisted, planting his feet and craning his neck to maintain his view of the adjacent building. "No," he insisted, struggling to say in his place. "I need to—"

"No, we gotta go. We gotta meet Johnny and get outta here. There's gonna be more cops here real soon. And the fire department, too."

Diamond took one final look and reluctantly turned away, allowing Simone to hustle him toward the opposite end of the roof and the fire escape leading back to the ground.

Diamond went down first, eyeing the car below. Simone followed right behind him. Halfway down, Diamond heard the car engine come to life.

In less than ten seconds, they were both back on the ground and darting across the short stretch of the alley for the car. Simone jumped into the passenger side of the front seat. Diamond put his hand on the handle of the back seat door but hesitated. He turned to listen. Even here, with an entire three-story building now standing between him and the storage facility, he could still hear the sound of the chaos.

The car engine revved. "Nick, we gotta go!" It was Kowalski's voice through Simone's open window.

Diamond opened the door and jumped into the back seat. The car was already moving as he closed the door behind him and threw his head back, laughing uncontrollably—almost hysterically—as the car sped away into the night.

CHAPTER 22
THE QUIET HERO

Hunter awoke the next morning feeling uneasy. Even before he'd gone to bed the night before, he'd realized that his act at the Paramount had been brash and foolhardy—and would probably provide Gallagher with ammunition to make good on his threat to take him off the Diamond case. He had driven his car back to the Republic Building after leaving the club, then walked up the street to Angie's Diner, where he spent more than an hour drinking coffee in a booth and staring out the window at Forty-Second Street until the muscles in his neck and shoulders finally relaxed. He didn't get home until after eleven o'clock. He didn't get to sleep until almost one a.m.

He sat up and swung his legs onto the bedroom floor, doing his best to suppress the vague sense of irritation that was already brewing within him. The thought that the only thing between him and Nicky Diamond the night before had been a slow-witted thug and a short flight of stairs still put a knot in his stomach the morning after.

He rubbed his eyes, stood up and headed for the bathroom.

Less than a half-hour later, he was showered, shaved and dressed. He stepped out of his apartment and moved down the short hallway that led to Buzz's door. He took a deep breath and tapped lightly, but got no answer. After listening for a minute and hearing no sounds from inside, he headed for the stairs.

Downstairs, the shop was empty and the sign hanging in the front window was still turned to the CLOSED side. It was ten minutes after eight, and Buzz wouldn't open up for at least another twenty minutes.

Hunter turned and noticed that the basement door was ajar and the lights below were on. He descended the stairs and saw that the door to the sub-basement was open as well.

He crossed the room and quietly made his way down the second set of stairs, feeling heavy with remorse and trying to rehearse something conciliatory in his head before he got to the bottom.

Buzz was sitting at his workbench, his shoulders hunched and his back to the stairs, when Hunter reached the last step. Hunter couldn't say for sure from where he was standing, but Buzz appeared to be soldering a connection in the network of wires surrounding the headgear he'd shown Hunter a couple nights before.

Hunter waited a moment. He figured Buzz was either too submerged in his work to notice him, or he was still harboring enough resentment to just not speak to him at all.

He cleared his throat. "Hey, good morning, Buzz." He tried to sound casual, but his throat felt constricted and the greeting sounded clumsy.

Buzz looked up and turned to see Jack looking at him. His expression looked like that of a woodland creature staring into a pair of oncoming headlights. He dropped the soldering iron on the bench and stood up so quickly that his chair rocked backward and clattered to the floor.

"Oh, hey," he stammered. "Sorry, Jack. I just had a few more ideas about how…" He picked up the soldering iron and set it back in its metal tray. "Listen, I'm not…I won't waste any more time on this. Really, I won't. I just thought maybe I could adjust the sensors a little and—"

"Buzz, it's okay. You don't have to—"

"No, no, you were right. What you said the other night, I mean. I need to stop goofing around with this stuff and pay attention to more important things." He unplugged the soldering iron, then rearranged a few tools on his bench "Listen, I'll go upstairs and open up. I'll clean all this up later."

Hunter stepped aside as Buzz nervously brushed past him and headed up the stairs. Within seconds, he had disappeared into the upper part of the building.

Hunter stood silently at the bottom of the sub-basement steps. After a moment, he took in a deep breath of air and let it out slowly. He eyed the workbench and wandered over to it.

Sure enough, Buzz had continued his work on the headgear. It sat mounted on a wooden post, positioned directly under the glow of a high intensity desk lamp. It was the centerpiece amid a random assortment of tools scattered about the workbench. The thing stared blankly back at him through goggles that appeared to be smaller and more streamlined than the ones on the previous version he'd seen.

In fact, everything about it seemed smaller, more compact, with far less exposed circuitry. Just as Buzz had proposed the other night, he'd woven a row of some kind of photoelectric cells into the fabric of the leather cap along the center seam, which eliminated the need for any bulky wiring to a separate array of batteries. The crazy hodgepodge of coils and other circuitry on the earlier version had been reduced to a much tighter network of smaller components mounted on the back side. The smaller goggles were permanently secured to the leather cap with even rows of careful stitching on either side.

All in all, this new version looked less like a crazy bug-eyed hat and more like a mask. Hunter surveyed the entire assembly of leather and circuitry from various angles and shook his head in wonder. *How the hell does he do this?*

He hesitated, glancing at his watch and then over his shoulder at the staircase several feet behind him.

Just for a few seconds, he thought.

He carefully removed the mask from its pedestal and lifted it up to eye level. With much less effort and contortion than his previous test, he slipped it over his head and eyes and carefully smoothed it all into place.

Just as before, it came at him in a powerful wave. He felt a sudden heightening of his senses—sight, sound, even smell—that was almost dizzying in its intensity. His perception sharpened to a razor edge, and every detail of the room revealed itself to him in crystal clarity.

The light from the ceiling fixtures, the tick of the clock on the wall, the hum of traffic at street level nearly twenty feet above him and outside the building—it all seemed to amplify and vibrate around him at an uncharted frequency that somehow afforded him a glimpse of reality a split second before reality happened.

But somewhere in the heady experience, he realized it was time to go. In the short time since he'd put on the mask, he'd heard every tick of his wristwatch, and some previously untapped channel of his cognitive faculties had registered every second and computed the minutes that had passed. He knew before he even looked at his watch that it was four minutes after eight o'clock—four minutes and twelve seconds, to be exact. Time to head for the office.

Hunter slipped off the mask and took a deep breath, blinking a couple times to allow his eyes to adjust to the light on the room without the aid of cortical stimulation. He scanned his surroundings and realized that reality seemed dimmer without the mask—

131

somehow sluggish and less focused. The once crystalline sounds of his spring-wound wristwatch and even the hum if the incandescent bulb in the desk lamp had slipped away from him and into the stillness of the room.

He put the mask back on its pedestal on the workbench and looked at it one more time, shaking his head. After a moment, he picked up his briefcase and headed up the stairs, once again rehearsing some kind of peace overture in his mind.

When he reached the back room of the shop on the ground floor, the opportunity had already passed. Buzz had just unlocked the front door and opened the shop, and two customers were already at the counter. One was a heavy-set, gray-haired woman pointing to a toaster she'd brought in and conveying her dismay about its unacceptable performance at the breakfast table in recent days. The other customer—a tall, bespectacled man with a Tiffany table lamp in his hand—stood off to the side of the woman with the toaster and waited his turn.

Buzz took it all in like some kind of medicine man who offered the last glimmer of hope to the tribe when all seemed lost.

Hunter hesitated in the doorway behind the shop counter. Mostly hidden from view by the half-closed door, he looked at the appliances and their owners. He glanced over his shoulder at the door leading to the basement stairs and then back at the two customers.

You people have no idea, he thought.

He turned away reluctantly and left through the back door of the building.

CHAPTER 23
SAL'S REPORT

Diamond sat at his desk in his office above The Paramount Club. His eyes were bloodshot and underscored by dark circles, and he fidgeted with shaky fingers at the letter opener, the ashtray and other random objects on the desk—including his gun. It was eight-thirty in the morning, but aside from slumping in an easy chair in his adjacent private quarters for a little more than an hour, he'd barely slept at all the night before. By the time he'd come down from the mental and emotional rush of the fireworks at the Stor-All facility, the eastern sky outside his window was glowing and the usual delivery trucks were rumbling along the alley below him.

He popped open the last cylinder on his desk and swallowed the coated paper inside. He dropped the spent cylinder onto his desk, where it rolled to the edge and fell to the floor.

Vince Marshall sat in his usual armchair on a few feet from Diamond's desk. Louie Simone leaned against a bookshelf along the left-hand wall.

Diamond leaned across the desk and grabbed the morning edition of the *Tribune*. He rubbed his eyes and scanned the front page. For the second day in a row, the *Tribune* was trumpeting the police department's war on crime on its front page.

Diamond clamped down his jaw and grimaced, then opened to the inside pages.

"There's no mention of the Stor-All hit," said Simone, as though reading Diamond's thoughts. "It was almost one by the time you detonated the bomb and we high-tailed it out of there. None of the reporters would have got the story from the police or the fire department until two at the earliest. That would have been too late for the morning editions."

Diamond merely grunted. He'd closed up the paper and was now scanning the *Chronicle*, whose front-page content was consistent with that of the other paper. "I don't see the mayor having any trouble getting into the papers," he said.

Simone started to answer, but he was interrupted by a knock at the door. Diamond looked up from the paper at Simone and tilted his head toward the door. Simone crossed the room and opened it just a few inches—just enough to speak in a hushed tone to the visitor on the other side.

After a few seconds, Diamond furrowed his brow and turned toward the sound of the muttering.

Simone glanced over his shoulder at Diamond. "It's Dutch."

Diamond looked past Simone through the narrow opening of the door frame and saw Dutch Markowitz's timid expression. Diamond nodded to Simone, who opened the door wider. Markowitz hesitated on the other side of the threshold until Diamond waved him into the office. He did a double-take as a burly figure walked in behind him.

The two men stepped in front of Diamond's desk, looking like a pair of troublesome schoolboys who'd been called before the principal. Markowitz spoke first.

"Sorry to bother you, Nick," he said, obviously struggling to gather his thoughts. He folded his hands in front of himself, then put them at his sides, then made a nervous gesture toward the barrel-chested man standing next to him. "Anyway, this is Sal. He works in the lobby downstairs. He keeps things orderly. Makes sure nobody makes any trouble, you know…" his voice trailed off with a shrug.

Diamond looked back at him but didn't say a word. If Markowitz was waiting for a response, he was going to be waiting for a long time.

"So, anyway," Markowitz continued, "Sal says someone came into the club last night and…well, we thought you should know about it." He turned to Sal and tapped him on the arm. "Tell him."

Sal cleared his throat. "So, yeah," he said. "So this guy comes in last night at about nine. Loretta, the hostess, showed him to a table. Then Margie, the waitress, says he ordered a drink. She brings him the drink a couple minutes later and they start talking. No big deal. Just kinda friendly, you know."

Diamond stared back at him.

"She asks him if he wants to order dinner, and that's when he starts gettin' kinda funny."

Diamond frowned. "Funny how?"

"Starts askin' her questions," said Sal. "Says he's curious about what goes on upstairs and what goes on in the basement.

Diamond sat up in his chair. He glanced at Marshall and then back at Sal. "Go on."

"She says he, uh…he asked for you by name."

Diamond's eyes were suddenly laser focused. "Who was he? Did he say?"

Markowitz re-inserted himself into the conversation. "You bet he did," he said, reaching into his jacket. "He gave this to Sal before Sal told him to leave." He pulled a business card out of his jacket and glanced down at it, his face suddenly more nervous than it had been already. Markowitz clearly did not enjoy being the bearer of bad news to a guy like Nicky Diamond. "He's, uh…he's from the DA's office."

Marshall stood up suddenly and stepped forward. "Let me see that," he said, snatching the card from Markowitz's hand. He looked at the type and read the name aloud: "John J. Hunter, Assistant District Attorney."

Diamond blinked. He looked away—into some distant place—and the room fell silent. "Hunter," he said, digging deep into his memory. "There was that cop. On the night we blew open the Justice Center."

Marshall nodded. "This is his son."

Diamond looked back at Marshall and arched an eyebrow. "His son."

"Yes. He's been with the DA's office for five years now. He's been the assistant DA for the last two."

Diamond leaned back in his chair, contemplating this new piece of information. "His son," he said again. He nodded slowly, taking it in, until something like a smile crept across his face. "Oh, that's rich."

Diamond turned to Sal. "Tell me the rest," he said. "This guy got fresh with the waitress, so she came and found you?"

Sal nodded. "Yes, sir, that's right."

"Then what."

Sal shrugged. "He tried to give me the tough talk," he said. "He got pretty smart-alecky, too. Gave me that card and told me to give it to anybody upstairs who might be interested. Shoves a couple newspapers at me with the stories on the front page about that big announcement from the mayor yesterday afternoon, the one about—"

Diamond waved him off impatiently. "Yeah, I know all about it."

"Well, then he pays for his drink and walks out. I followed him all the way out to the sidewalk." He shrugged again. "I didn't want to do anything rough. I mean, hell, he's from the DA's office and all."

"That it?"

"Yeah. I came back inside after that."

Diamond nodded. "Alright," he said. He thought for a moment, reading the type on Hunter's card. "Alright," he said again. He looked up from the card at Sal and Markowitz. "Either one of you two see this guy in here again—or any cops, or any other law—I want to know. Right away. Don't wait to tell me. Understand?"

Markowitz and Sal nodded, their expressions sober.

"Tell the waitress and the hostess too. Understand?"

Both men nodded again.

"Alright," said Diamond, tilting his head toward the door. "Go on back downstairs."

Markowitz nodded, and he and Sal shuffled out of the room without a word. Simone held the door, then closed it behind them.

The room was silent, save for the tick of a clock on a corner table, but a palpable tension hung heavy in the hair. Diamond and Marshall looked at each other for a long moment.

"The police, the DA," Diamond said finally. "Can they touch us?"

Marshall shook his head. "Not without a warrant."

"And we have people to keep that from happening."

"Right."

"And what do we know about this guy?" said Diamond, holding up Hunter's calling card. "I mean, other than his old man is a dead cop."

Marshall frowned. "A lot of people see him as the up-and-comer," he said. "Next in line after Gallagher retires."

The room turned quiet again as the clock ticked out a few more seconds.

"You know where he lives?" said Diamond.

Marshall eyed him suspiciously. "Now, hold on, Nick…"

Diamond put his hand up in a placating gesture. "It's alright," he said. "It's alright, I just want to know what we know about him."

Marshall sighed. "You know the appliance repair shop at the corner of East Forty-Second and Whitney?"

"Uh-huh."

"His cousin owns the place. There's a couple apartments above the shop. They both live up there."

"He's got no wife? No kids?"

"No. Nothing like that."

"He lives there with his cousin."

"Yes," said Marshall.

Diamond nodded.

Marshall leaned forward in his chair and spoke slowly, obviously choosing his words carefully. "Listen, Nick," he said. "If the DA's office already has some idea of where you've established your base of operations, I think you really ought to stop and consider what—"

Diamond slammed a fist on the table. The ashtray, telephone and desk lamp all rattled from the impact. Marshall closed his mouth and leaned back in his chair.

Diamond looked across his desk at his consigliere with a dagger stare. He pointed an index finger directly at him and said in a carefully measured voice, "I did twelve years because one dumb, stubborn cop stayed alive just long enough to keep me from beating the rap." He picked up Hunter's card and tossed it across the desk. "And now his little boy thinks he can play tough-guy with me?"

"Nick, I'm just saying, if we start getting rough with an assistant DA, we could really—"

Diamond looked away and put his hand up to stop him, shaking his head vigorously. "I didn't say anything about getting rough with an assistant DA."

Marshall cocked his had slightly, his expression puzzled.

Diamond ignored the question in the other man's eyes. He glanced at Simone, still standing at the door, then back at Marshall.

"Okay," he said. His voice was less menacing now, but still businesslike. "Here's what we're gonna do..."

CHAPTER 24
A LEAK IN THE PIPELINE

Hunter made it to the top of the fifth-floor staircase of the Justice Center at eight-twenty and pushed through the hallway doors leading to the legal department. He moved down the hallway and took off his hat when he saw Betty Carlyle, who was up from her desk and standing at a tall metal filing cabinet with the middle drawer open. Focusing intently on the inside of the packed drawer, she held one file folder in her left hand and she was pulling out a second one with her right.

Hunter said, "Good morning, Miss Carlyle," just as Betty was closing the cabinet drawer and turning in his direction. She stopped suddenly, eyes wide, just in time to avoid colliding with him.

She let out a small gasp. "Mr. Hunter!" she said. "I'm sorry. I didn't see you standing here."

"No, that's alright. I didn't mean to startle you. And it's okay for you to call me Jack."

"Oh, no, that's..." she stopped and tapped her forehead, as though suddenly remembering something. "Oh, um...Mr. Gallagher is already here. He said he wanted to see you as soon as you get in."

Hunter glanced up the hallway and then back at Betty. "He in his office?"

"Yes," she said. "With Chief Taggert and Lieutenant Dugan from the police department."

Hunter had already started down the hall, but he stopped suddenly and turned back toward Betty. He looked at his watch, then looked back at her and frowned. "Taggert and Dugan are here?"

"Yes, sir. I think..." She glanced from side to side and took a step toward him, lowering her voice slightly. "I think something may have happened last night."

Hunter felt the hair on his neck stand up. "Something like what?" he said, noticing that he'd instinctively lowered his own voice.

She bit her lower lip. "I don't know, but I think it may not be good," she said. "They didn't have an appointment. They just called from the lobby and came up, and they didn't look happy when they got here. And the lieutenant has some kind of bandage on his head. He was wearing his hat when they came up, but I could see it."

Hunter frowned and looked in the direction of Gallagher's office.

"They've been in there for more than a half-hour," Betty added, "with the door closed."

Hunter nodded thanks and moved briskly down the hallway. He ducked into his own office just long enough to hang his hat and stow his briefcase on the floor next to his desk, then headed further down the hallway.

He stopped at Gallaher's office, knocked on the door and walked in without waiting for a response. The three men inside turned to look at him. Gallagher was seated at his desk, and Taggert was leaning against a cabinet. Dugan was in a chair with his elbow propped on an armrest and his hand at his right temple, where a rectangular bandage covered a four-inch stretch of real estate.

Gallagher said, "Morning, Jack," but there was nothing cheerful in his greeting.

Hunter nodded and scanned the three grim faces in the room, stopping at Dugan. "What the hell happened?"

"Diamond," said the chief.

Hunter glanced at Taggert, then back at Dugan. "What happened to your head?"

"We went into the Stor-All facility on Warehouse Row last night," said Dugan, "based on some solid information we'd been gathering for weeks. We know he had gambling paraphernalia in there."

"And?"

Dugan shook his head. "Well, in the short time we were there, we didn't find anything."

Hunter brow furrowed. "Short time?"

"He knew we were coming. Place was booby trapped."

"How bad?"

"Explosion and fire," said Taggert. "Two officers in the hospital, one with second degree burns, the other with a concussion. They'll be alright. One of them will have a few permanent scars, but they'll both survive."

"And you?"

Dugan waved it off. "I'm alright. A few cuts from some flying debris, and my ears are still ringing from the blast, but I'll live."

"What time?" said Hunter.

"Very early this morning," said Dugan, "not long after midnight."

Hunter nodded. "How bad was the fire?"

"Fire Station Three had a couple trucks there pretty quick," said Taggert. "It didn't get too far along."

Taggert paused. He squeezed his eyes shut and rubbed them with his thumb and forefinger. Hunter guessed he'd been up since sometime shortly after the call came in about the explosion.

"Ferguson had a fire inspector out there a couple hours ago, as soon as it was safe to go in," Taggert continued, "Pruett was with them."

"Do I even need to ask what they found?" said Hunter.

"Explosive chemicals, accelerant," said Dugan, "and some electrical wiring."

Hunter frowned at that last bit of information. "Probably a timer of some kind."

"Maybe. Osborne, the fire inspector, suggested the wiring could also have been part of some kind of remote control setup."

"Someone triggering the bomb from another location."

"Right," said Dugan. "But he couldn't be completely certain. It's a little out of his area of expertise. And the explosion and fire destroyed most of the evidence anyway."

Hunter moved to an empty chair in the room and sat down. It wasn't even nine o'clock, and he felt a tension starting in his neck and shoulders.

"We were just speculating before you walked in," said Gallagher.

Hunter arched an eyebrow. "About?"

Still leaning against the cabinet, Taggert folded his arms. "About who the hell is tipping Diamond off," he said. His frustration was palpable. "This is two times just this week—first McShane's, now this—that he seems to have known we were coming. And there have been other times before that. Somebody's telling him."

The room was silent for a moment.

"How many other detectives do you have on this?" said Hunter.

"Myself and three others," said Dugan. "Davis, Grant and Weller. They've been pounding the pavement, talking to people who we know were patrons at Hirschfeld's place the night it got hit. They've been sniffing around McShane's place too. They do good work, but there aren't a lot of leads."

"You sure they're clean?"

Dugan rubbed his chin. "They're both long-timers," he said. "We were at the academy at the same time, and we came up through the ranks together. They both made detective just a few years after I did. I trust them."

"Okay. So who else?"

Dugan shook his head.

"Pruett?" said Hunter.

Dugan looked back at Hunter, his face a sudden mix of incredulity and amusement. "That guy?" he said. "With the bow tie and glasses and the chemistry books? Does he look like someone who'd run with a boss like Diamond?"

Taggert shook his head. "No," he said, "the guy spends most of his time in that laboratory we set up for him at headquarters. You know what I'm talking about, Jack. You were just there yesterday." Hunter nodded as Taggert finished the thought: "He's spent most of this past week in there, examining fifty or sixty chunks of brick and wood just to help us figure out where the explosives are coming from."

Hunter recalled his conversation with Pruett the day before. He remembered the dry subject matter about combustion, dispersion and a few other concepts he couldn't understand.

No, he thought. *Not Pruett.*

"Okay," said Hunter, putting his palms up. "Then...?"

Dugan gestured toward the closed office door. "Somebody here?"

Gallagher snorted. "Don't see how," he said, shaking his head. "The only people in this department who are privy to police and detective operations are sitting in this room. I've been here for twenty-three years—the first ten as an assistant DA and the last thirteen as the DA. I had a hand in bringing Diamond down the last time."

He shifted in his chair and tilted his head toward Hunter. "That leaves Jack," he said, "and given Jack's personal history, anyone who believes that he'd have any desire to help Nicky Diamond is just as crazy as Diamond himself."

"Well, I don't know," said Dugan, "but there's a leak somewhere, and information about police operations is getting to the wrong places somehow."

Taggert turned toward Gallagher and leaned back in his chair slightly. He had no official authority over the district attorney, his assistant or anyone on his staff, but he knew Gallagher well enough and long enough to speak frankly about policy. "Ed, we need to tighten up our communications," he said. "From here on out, meetings about this case between the police department and the DA's office should be taking place at the highest level of security."

Gallagher nodded. "Agreed," he said.

"Doesn't matter how brief or inconsequential it may seem," Taggert went on. "We seal it up, no matter what. We bring in other personnel as needed, but only as needed. Otherwise it's just the four of us. Our staff, yours, everyone in between—everyone is informed about only what they need to know. Hell, I even think we need to consider what our secretaries and our switchboard operators are privy to."

Gallagher sat motionless in his chair, his elbow on an armrest and his hand at his chin. He stared silently out the window for a moment, then turned his gaze toward Dugan.

"I agree with Sam," said the DA. "I think it's safe to say that we all need to keep our eyes open—not just with regard to Diamond, but also to what's going on right in front of us and around us. If there's some pipeline of information from somewhere in law enforcement to somewhere in Diamond's operation, we need to figure out where it is and shut it off."

The room fell silent. After a moment, Dugan rose from his chair. "Alright," he said, wincing slightly from the obvious pain caused by the wound at his temple, "I have to get back. Pruett's in his lab right now, taking a closer look at some of the debris from the Stor-All center. I'm hoping he can tell us something new after he's looked at it, although I don't know what that might be."

Gallagher rose from his own chair. "Alright, keep us posted," he said to Dugan, "and take care of that business on your head."

Taggert was at the door with his hand on the knob. "One of us will be in touch this afternoon, regardless of what we hear or don't hear."

"And until then," said Hunter, "let's all try to keep our mouths shut."

◆　◆　◆　◆

In the midst of his other work, Hunter spent the remainder of the morning deliberating over information he'd been sitting on for the last twenty-four hours now. Somewhere around eleven-thirty, he knocked on Ed Gallagher's door.

The DA looked up and waved him in. "What's on your mind?"

Hunter stepped into the room and leaned against a bookshelf. "Something I've heard. A tip, I guess."

Gallagher lit his pipe. He took a draw and looked at Hunter for a moment through a billow of aromatic smoke. He took the pipe from between his teeth and pointed it at the chair on the other side of his desk.

Hunter took a seat. "I think we need to be taking a look at The Paramount Club," he said.

"Markowitz's place," said Gallagher. "On Tenth."

"Right."

"What makes you say that?"

Hunter shrugged. "Nothing solid," he said. "A tip, like I said."

Realization dawned on Gallagher's face. He leaned back in his chair and rolled his eyes. "You been talking to that newspaper clown again?"

"He's only a clown if his information isn't any good. His usually is."

"I don't care. What are you suggesting? We build a legal case against the most dangerous criminal in the history of this city by following up on tips from a gossip columnist? Hell, why don't we just call Walter Winchell? I'm sure he'd have some great advice."

"What if I told you I went there myself? What if I told you his information was good?"

"What?"

"I was there last night. I checked the place out myself."

Gallagher eyed him suspiciously. He said nothing for a moment, but when he did speak again, his voice was lower, more wary. "When you say you 'checked the place out,' what exactly do you mean?"

"I don't mean anything," said Hunter. "I paid a visit. I went in and had a drink."

"Right. You just happened to wander over there. The same day that a newspaper columnist told you it might be a hot spot in the biggest case the police are working on right now."

Hunter didn't answer.

"Seems like a hell of a coincidence." Gallagher leaned forward and rested his pipe in his ashtray, then put his palms down on the desk top and looked directly at Hunter with one eyebrow in a skeptical arch. "And what happened during the time you 'checked the place out'?" he said.

"Had a few words with the waitress."

"Yeah?"

"And then a few more with the bouncer."

Gallagher was glaring across the desk now. "Any punches thrown?" His voice was growing more stern by the minute. Hunter sensed the question wasn't entirely facetious.

"No."

Gallagher put a hand up in a yielding gesture. "Don't tell me the rest," he said, shaking his head. "Jack, I thought we already had this conversation. An assistant DA can't walk into a public establishment and pick a fight with the management because he thinks he has some personal score to settle. It's not how we do it. It's not how the law works, and you know it. Or you ought to."

Hunter thought he might be hearing the hint of a disciplinary threat. He started to protest, but Gallagher kept talking. "If we have probable cause, based on some kind of evidence from a police investigation, then we take the next appropriate step," said the DA. "But a tip from a reporter isn't enough to justify going to Reynolds or any other judge to request a search warrant. And even if it is a good tip—and I'm not saying it is—it sure as hell doesn't justify going into a place and poking a bear."

"Who said anything about a warrant? What about just having

an officer stop by the place, just to maintain a presence in the neighborhood? You know, just like the one who…" Hunter's voice trailed off. He realized immediately that he was taking the wrong tack.

Gallagher pounced. "Just like who?" he said. "The one who stopped by Hirschfeld's place?"

Hunter didn't answer, which gave Gallagher an opening to keep going. "Because if you'll recall, the one who stopped by Hirschfeld's place never went home again. Ever. So I think Sam Taggert and Mike Dugan are going to think good and hard before they send any more cops to pay any more friendly visits to suspicious nightclubs and restaurants. I can't speak for them, but I'm betting their strategy from here on out will be strictly business, backed by hard evidence, court orders and extra manpower."

Gallagher picked up his pipe and stuck it between his teeth as he leaned back his chair. He was silent for a moment as he took a big draw from the pipe and blew a puff of smoke. The ritual seemed to ease some of the tension on his face—and some in the room as well.

"Now," he said, his voice calmer, "if you think your information is worth pursuing—and again, I'm not saying I think it is—I suggest you start at the right place this time and take it to Dugan before you take it anywhere else."

Hunter nodded, suppressing a feeling of skepticism but keeping it to himself.

At the end of the day, Gallagher was still the boss.

◆　◆　◆　◆

Bart Maxwell was already sitting in a booth at Ottoman's, the sandwich shop at Union Plaza, when Hunter walked in. Hunter had called the newspaperman just a few minutes after finishing his early-morning meeting with Gallagher, Taggert and Dugan. He wasn't happy with the pace of the police investigation, and he'd asked Max to meet him for lunch. Hunter wondered if he might have dug up any information that could help move it along.

Hunter slid into the booth and noticed the half-eaten sandwich on Max's plate.

"Nice of you to wait," he said.

Max feigned wide-eyed innocence and gestured at the plate. "Hey,

I saved some for when you got here, see? That way, you'll feel better about picking up the check."

A waitress approached the table. Hunter ordered corned beef and coffee. He felt a pang of guilt as she turned away and headed for the kitchen. He and Buzz often had corned beef sandwiches together for dinner, but they'd barely spoken in nearly two days.

"Which one of us is going to go first?" said Max.

"I don't have much," said Hunter. "That's the problem."

"Hey, I told you about the Paramount, didn't I?"

"Yeah," said Hunter. "And like I said, they want something more solid than a tip from a newspaper columnist."

"A prophet is never recognized in his own land."

"And isn't that a damn shame. Actually, I just told Gallagher this morning. I haven't mentioned it to the police yet."

"You remember the agreement we have about anything that comes out of that information."

"I do."

"So what did Gallagher say?"

Hunter shook his head and snorted. "He wasn't terribly happy."

"How come?"

"Don't worry," said Hunter. "His dissatisfaction had more to do with me than with you."

Max frowned, his eyes questioning.

"I went to the Paramount myself."

Max blinked, then stared back at Hunter. "And?"

Hunter gave him the full account of his captivating meeting with the Paramount staff the night before.

"Playing with fire," said Max when Hunter had finished.

"Or as Gallagher put it, poking a bear."

"Every good writer sees the world in metaphors."

"Have you heard anything more?" said Hunter. "Anything more than the Paramount, I mean?"

"The DA's office gonna put me on the payroll?"

"We can't afford you."

Max picked up the remaining half of his sandwich and took a large bite. He chewed slowly. Hunter suspected that he was taking his time on purpose.

Max kept working his jaws, then stopped to sip some coffee. He put the cup down and shrugged. "I'm hearing things," he said, reaching into is jacket. "A couple people have loosened up a little since the big talk from the mayor yesterday. I guess some people just need to decide who they'd rather be in bigger trouble with."

"Hearing things like what?"

Max's hand reappeared with a rectangular notebook and a pen. He pushed his plate aside and opened the notebook to a clean page. "From the sounds of things, Diamond's all over the place."

Hunter frowned. "How do you mean?"

Max shrugged as he opened the pen and started writing. "Every joint's a revenue source," he said. "Doesn't matter what size."

"Okay," said Hunter. His voice went up like a question. Max wasn't telling him much that he or the police didn't already know.

Max closed the pen and tore out the page. "So here's small, medium and large," he said, pushing the paper across the table.

Hunter picked it up and looked at it. Three names. Three different establishments in the Entertainment District. A small tavern, a mid-level restaurant and a high-end nightclub.

He looked up at Max, who was tucking the pen and notebook back into his jacket. The reporter was looking away, distracted. His brow knotted slightly.

"What is it?" said Hunter.

Max shook his head. "There's more," he said. "More than just the gambling and the racketeering. But I still can't figure it out."

Hunter looked at the paper again, wondering if three leads would give him any more leverage than just the one if he were to take the information to Dugan.

"What're you gonna do with those?" said Max, as though he were reading Hunter's mind.

Hunter paused for a moment. Then for lack of a better answer, he said, "Try to make something happen."

CHAPTER 25
A MESSAGE IN STEAM

Hunter knew something was wrong the minute he turned down Forty-Second Street.

He came up Whitney Avenue at about eight-thirty. When he reached the corner, he noticed that the lights inside the shop in the Republic Building were still on and the OPEN sign was still hanging in the window—more than two hours after Buzz would have typically closed up for the evening. From his limited vantage point at the intersection, he saw no movement inside the shop.

He took a right on Whitney, then a left down the alley and headed for the garage behind the building.

He'd tried to call Buzz at six to let him know he'd be working late, but there was no answer. He hadn't thought much of it at the time. Buzz may have had his hands full at six—taking care of a last-minute customer at closing time, maybe sorting through some of the day's work orders, moving some appliances into the back room, or any number of other end-of-day tasks.

Three minutes later, Hunter was inside the back hallway of the building through the garage entrance. He moved through the back room behind the shop, and then into the shop itself. It was indeed empty. Music was playing on the cathedral radio on a shelf behind the counter. He switched it off, which left the shop in an eerie silence. He crossed the shop to the front door and found it unlocked.

He locked the door and turned the sign in the window to the CLOSED side, then headed back through the shop to the back room.

The stairway to the basement was dark, and there was no light from below. He threw a light on and went halfway down, calling for Buzz as he descended. There was no answer.

At the bottom of the stairs, he peered across the basement to the doorway leading to the sub-basement. There was no light there either.

He turned back and climbed the stairs at a quick pace, trying to ignore the knot of apprehension that was forming in his stomach. He turned at the ground floor and headed up the stairs leading up to the apartments on the second floor.

He called again. No answer.

He got to the top and checked the door to Buzz's apartment. It was unlocked. He started to open it, but stopped himself. The apprehension was suddenly a sickening fear. He took a deep breath and pushed open the door.

He called again, but the only answer was silence. He threw a light on and moved quickly through the apartment—kitchen, hallway, living room, bedroom, bathroom, even the closets. Everything appeared to be in order.

He left Buzz's apartment and moved quickly down the hall to his own, hoping to find a note on the door or some other clear sign that all was well.

Less than two minutes later, after a full sweep of his own apartment, there was no such sign.

He stood in his living room, trying hard to keep the growing sense of dread under control, forcing himself to think clearly.

Maybe he'd just intended to step out briefly—the deli or something—and was somehow delayed. But he would have locked the shop and put the sign up in the door that he'd be back in twenty minutes, a half-hour, whatever. And what kind of a delay would keep him away for two-and-a-half hours past closing time?

The ring of the telephone interrupted his thoughts, and his entire body literally jerked at the sound.

He grabbed the receiver. "Hello!"

"Hunter." It was just one word, but the voice on the other end sounded filthy, like a lifetime of cigarettes and alcohol, violence and depravity.

Hunter started to ask who it was but he already knew. He'd only heard the voice a few times before, in a courtroom many years earlier, but he remembered it like yesterday.

A low, guttural laugh came from the other end of the line. It lasted only a couple seconds, but it was long enough to turn Hunter's blood to ice.

"Diamond," he rasped. "You son of a—"

"Cool it, counselor," said Diamond. "Let's talk."

Hunter remained silent for a moment, then said, "Okay. Talk."

"I wanted to meet you in person," he said, feigning a conversational tone. "I sent some of my boys to stop by your place this morning—"

Hunter knew where this was going. "I swear to God, Diamond, I'll—"

"But your cousin, Mister Fixit, told them you weren't around."

Hunter's heart went to his throat. "And?"

"So they took him for a ride instead."

Hunter realized that "took him for a ride" could mean a lot of things. He feared the worst. "Where is he?"

"What, you wanna talk to him?"

"*Where is he!*"

There was silence on the line for a moment. Some muffled voices. Words that Hunter couldn't make out.

Then he heard a second voice on the line: "Hiya, Jack."

Hunter exhaled. He put a hand against the wall to steady himself.

"Hiya, Buzz." Hunter could hear the tremor in his own voice but he hoped Buzz couldn't. "You okay?"

"Yeah, I'm okay." He paused. "Listen, Jack, I hope you're not still sore at me."

Hunter shut his eyes tightly and clenched the fist that wasn't holding the phone. He silently cursed himself for not knocking on Buzz's door and making amends after tearing into him the other night.

"Buzz," he said, "forget about all that, okay? It's all in the past. And it was my fault, anyway." There was silence on the line for a moment as Hunter struggled for something to say to put his cousin at ease and also keep the line open as long as possible. "Buzz, you sure you're alright?"

"Yeah, I'm okay." He let out a nervous laugh. "This whole thing reminds me of that steam engine we built when we were kids. Remember that?"

"I sure do."

"The thing blew up and we were in water up to our ankles. Boy, I sure feel like I'm in some deep water now."

Hunter's brow furrowed. "I understand, Buzz," he said after a moment, although he wasn't sure if he really did. "But don't worry, okay? This isn't your fight. You just got caught in the middle of something that doesn't have anything to do with you. I'm going to get you some help. I'm going to get you out of—"

"Jack, they're telling me I have to get off the line now."

"No. Buzz, wait..."

More silence on the line. More muffled voices. Then the first voice returned:

"Hunter."

"Diamond, you son of a—"

"Spare me the tough talk, counselor. You did more than your share of that last night. Besides, I have a guest here, and I wouldn't want the conversation to get unpleasant."

"What the hell do you want?"

"Immunity."

Hunter snorted. "What?"

"You heard me. I want to be sure that there's no more nonsense like that visit you paid last night. When all is said and done, I'm a businessman. I provide certain entertainment services to my clientele. It's really no different than the old days."

"It's very different."

"Don't be so certain. The police and the district attorney may have cleaned up this city, but you'd be naïve to think that I no longer have a few well-placed connections."

"So you're saying you want everyone to just step back and give you all the room you think you need to reestablish yourself in this city."

"Yes."

"You're crazy. We don't make deals with thugs and murderers. Especially deals that involve handing them the keys to the city. You don't have a leg to stand on."

"I have your cousin," Diamond snapped. "And if I'm not mistaken, he's the last family you have in the world."

Hunter knew exactly what Diamond was doing. He was playing to his worst fears. And it was working.

"So you might want to talk to your boss," Diamond went on. "Maybe some of your cop friends, too. I'll give all of you some time to think about how you want this to go. We had a nice arrangement back in the old days. I'm sure we can work something out now and for the future. I'll call back in an hour."

Hunter started to speak, but he stopped when he heard the unmistakable click of the line disconnecting.

Hunter barked into what he knew was a dead telephone. "Hello! Diamond!" He slammed the phone down and swore.

He picked the receiver up again, brought it halfway to his ear. *Call Dugan*, he thought. *Tell him what he'd just…*

He put the telephone down.

He stared at some distant point in the dimly lit room.

"The Watt Building," he said aloud, to no one but himself. The words sounded odd in the grim silence of his living room.

Sure. The Watt Building, in the River District. Buzz had sent him a message in the short time he had on the phone.

He was talking about something they'd done once when they were kids. They'd built a half-scale working model of James Watt's original patented steam engine, the one from the late 1700s. But their model didn't blow up. There was never any ankle-deep water. They'd built it exactly to Watt's original specs, only by half, and it worked like a charm from the get-go. The thing took second-place in a state-wide scholastic science and industry competition when Hunter was in the seventh grade.

Buzz said he was in deep water. The Watt Building was right along the river at the deepest point—at Bright Bend, the place where the river turned northward. That's what he was talking about.

Other than sharing the same name, The Watt Building had nothing to do with the eighteenth-century inventor, but it didn't matter. Hunter would bet his life that Buzz was sending him a message in plain sight.

He picked the phone up again. He started to dial and then stopped after the second digit.

He felt a wave of hopelessness and tried to push away the sense of panic that was creeping around the edges of his consciousness.

How long would it take him to get hold of Dugan? And when he did, how many precious minutes would he waste explaining exactly what was happening, exactly where Buzz was being held, and exactly how he knew?

And if he did all that, then what?

How long would it take to get a detail of officers out to the River District?

And once they did get there, then what?

The building was old and vacant, but it was a fortress, and it would be crawling with Diamond's gunmen, inside and out. Any cops who showed up would be picked off before they even got out of their cars. Unless they could dodge bullets and move faster than any of those trigger-happy thugs could think, they'd be easy targets for anybody with a…

Hunter's runaway thought process came to a sudden, grinding halt. He jerked his head to one side, almost as though he'd heard someone or something call him from a distance.

Wait a minute…

Four seconds ticked by. More than enough time to make the decision.

He turned and bolted out of his apartment and down the hallway to the stairs.

Into the basement.

CHAPTER 26
A SURPRISE ENTRANCE

Eight minutes later, Hunter was on his motorcycle, working his way in a northwesterly direction at top speed through a zig-zag of main avenues and side streets—a less-traveled route that would circumvent heavy traffic and draw less attention from the police and the general citizenry to his excessive speed. He banked hard at the turns and took the straightaways at something close to seventy miles an hour.

He rocketed through the darkness with Buzz's mask strapped securely to his face and head. The sun was down now, but he kept his headlight out. He didn't need it. He had the night-vision goggles on the mask to give him a crystalline view of the road and everything ahead. Between the visual enhancement from the goggles and his ability to sense the vibrations coming up through the frame of the motorcycle itself, he sensed every imperfection in the pavement, every random stone in his path.

None of it slowed him down. Aided by the circuitry of the mask, his mind vibrated in harmony with the energy of the city. Every streetlamp, every bleat of a random car horn, every whiff of exhaust, every molecule of air rushing against the exposed half of his face—all of it, every tiny detail of the world around him—opened a momentary window into infinity. The situation may have been critical, but in Hunter's heightened state of perception and clarity, anything felt possible.

He gunned the engine. His destination was still a few miles ahead, but no more than two or three minutes, given his current speed.

The River District was a shipping and warehousing sector of town whose origins could be traced all the way back to the city's earliest years. Since the late seventeen-hundreds, when Union City was still known as Union Territory, the River District had been a critical destination for freighters and barges along Bright River. It was the port through which lumber, steel, coal, textiles and countless other commodities moved into and out of the region, which later became known as Union Village, and eventually Union City.

The Watt Building was one of the oldest structures in the district, built in 1828. The building had changed owners a couple times throughout the decades, until an industrialist named Edmund Winfield bought it in the late 1860s, shortly after the Civil War. Winfield owned a medium-sized company that made farming equipment for customers in more than a half-dozen Midwestern states. It was a booming business in the agrarian nineteenth century, but less so in the industrialized twentieth. The business eventually folded, and Winfield's sons—notorious for their financial ineptitude—foreclosed on the warehouse property. The building had been shuttered and unused since 1920.

Hunter revved the engine again and boosted his speed. He did his best to ignore any lingering second thoughts about whether he should have called Dugan and brought the police into this. And the truth was, they might come yet. Dugan might get wind of trouble and send some men anyway.

And that would be a mess. An encounter with the police at the scene of a kidnapping would put a masked assistant DA in a very awkward position, and would require a lot of explaining. It would likely mean the end of his career in the DA's office, the end of his law career, and maybe even an arrest.

And for as bad as all that sounded, the next few minutes could unfold into something far worse. If the police blustered their way into the situation without considering Diamond's characteristically erratic behavior, Diamond or any of his crew could get twitchy and Buzz could get hurt—or worse.

Hunter rounded the turn onto River Road, which was a half-mile stretch of warehouses that ran parallel to the south bank of the river, the city's northern border. The Watt Building was a little more than halfway down the strip. He gave the engine one last rev to propel himself along the road, then throttled back. After a few seconds, he cut the engine entirely and coasted the rest of the way on the bike's own momentum. He wanted his final approach to be as quiet as possible.

He was still two buildings shy of his destination when he made a quick turn to the right and cruised into a back alley. He coasted toward a veil of dense shadows near a concrete loading dock protruding from the back of the building and facing the river. In a single motion, he grabbed the brakes, jerked to a stop and hopped off the bike. He wheeled the vehicle into the shadows and parked it well out of sight.

There were lights mounted at regular intervals along the river, about every sixty feet for the entire stretch of buildings along River Road. They'd been installed years ago for the benefit of night-shift dock workers and freighter pilots moving up and down the waterway after sunset. The lights threw a little more illumination on the back of the buildings than Hunter would have preferred, but he'd still find enough cover to make his way to his destination.

He cut across the back lot of the building at a brisk jog and made his way into the similar loading zone of the next building over, taking in the briny smells coming off the river no more than a hundred feet away.

After a few more seconds he slowed his advance and came to a stop in the shadows at the back corner of the Watt Building. He leaned close to the outer wall and concentrated. Despite the building's steel and concrete construction, he heard voices from inside—too muffled for even his heightened senses to make out any specific details, but voices nonetheless.

He scanned the layout and noted a loading dock similar to those at the rear of the two buildings he'd just crossed. The dock was about fifty feet from where he was standing. A wood and metal awning covered the dock, and an unlit light fixture was mounted on the underside of the awning. The dock itself was deserted.

But Hunter had already determined from the sounds through the walls that there was activity inside. He stepped away from the corner of the building—not too far out of the shadows, but enough to get a better view of the entire back wall. The sliding metal door separating the loading dock from the rear section of the building was almost completely closed, save for a five-inch gap between the bottom edge of the door and the slab. Through the gap, even at this distance, Hunter could hear the murmur of voices and see a soft, uneven glow that was likely generated by some kind of lanterns.

It made sense. The building had been vacant for more than fifteen years. The electric power had likely been shut off long ago. Hunter figured the darkness could work in his favor.

At least he hoped so.

He stepped away from the corner of the building and moved along the back wall, crouching low and darting quickly from one patch of darkness to another. In a matter of seconds, he reached a pile of wooden crates stacked alongside the loading dock. He was now no more than eight feet from the sliding metal door. He stayed crouched, keeping himself well within the shadows.

He closed his eyes and focused his mind, tuning in to the sounds drifting out from the small space under the door.

"I'm out," said a voice. "I got garbage."

A second voice said, "I got jacks. Three."

Hunter heard the sound of playing cards slapping a hard surface, then a third voice, full of bravado: "Ha! Full house! That's all mine."

The jangle of loose change and paper money sliding along the same hard surface. A murmur of profanities. The scooping of random cards and the reshuffling of the deck.

Then a crackling sound. Paper of some kind. The *clink* of a cigarette lighter.

"Hey, don't light that thing in here. Take it outside."

"Yeah, I don't wanna be smellin' that damn thing in here all night."

"Awright, awright." A metal chair scraping against concrete. "Jeez, a couple a crybabies you guys are." Footsteps approaching the sliding door. "I'm s'posed to be takin' a look out back anyway."

Hunter seized the opportunity. He hoisted himself up the four-foot rise onto the dock and flattened himself against the back wall, just to the left of the door frame.

"Couple a crybabies," the voice muttered again. The scuffle of feet was right at the door now. Hunter watched the shaft of light from the other side of the door along the floor of the dock, caught the twitch of shadows from two feet shuffling just beyond the door.

A grunt of exertion and the door rattled upward.

A stubby figure stepped out onto the dock—fat cigar in one hand, lighter in the other. He was no more than five feet way from Hunter, but with his back turned to him and his attention solely on the cigar.

Stubby put the cigar between his teeth, raised the lighter and lit the opposite end. The flame rose and fell as he puffed steadily.

Hunter stepped forward. In a single, lightning-fast motion, he slapped the cigar away from Stubby's face, clamped his right hand over the man's gaping mouth and dealt a clubbing blow to the back of his neck with his left.

Stubby went limp, but Hunter eased him down to the concrete before he could make a noisy fall on his own.

Crouching next to the limp form, he stopped to listen.

"You got any money left?" The winner of the last hand. Smug, cocky.

"Yeah, don't you worry about my money. You just deal those cards when Artie gets back in here."

A self-satisfied chuckle from the first voice.

They hadn't heard a thing.

Hunter stepped away from Artie and slipped silently inside the door, immediately ducking behind a column of metal utility shelves stacked high with dusty ceramic tiles.

He peered between the stacks and got a look at the remaining men in the large back room. There were two of them, just as he had heard, off to the left and about fifteen feet from the door. They sat in battered metal chairs at a square table. The glow from two kerosene lanterns—positioned a couple feet apart on a stack of crates, just beyond where the two men sat—was the only light in the otherwise shadowy space.

Both men looked big and dumb. One wore suspenders over a shirt with an open collar. The other wore a loose tie, with his shirtsleeves rolled up to the elbows. They focused on their conversation and the assortment of items on the table in front of them—a deck of cards, some crumpled bills and coins, three bottles of beer, an ashtray and a gun.

Hunter figured the gun belonged to Suspenders, because Necktie carried his own in a shoulder holster strapped across his chest.

Suspenders shuffled the cards absently. "So what's Nicky planning to do with that guy?" he said.

Necktie took a swig from his beer bottle and shrugged. "I dunno. I just helped Kowalski get him here. They've had him up front for a couple hours now. I don't ask too many questions."

"He runs that repair shop on Forty-Second, right?"

Necktie nodded. "Uh-huh."

"So what the hell does he have to do with Nicky's plans?"

Necktie snorted. "Hey, I don't know," he said. "Like I said, I don't ask questions." He glanced away for a moment—into the darkness, toward the front of the building—then looked back at Suspenders, leaning forward and lowering his voice slightly. "Sometimes I think…" he raised a forefinger to the side of his head and made a winding motion. "Know what I'm sayin'?"

Suspenders stopped shuffling. He raised an eyebrow and nodded slowly. "Yeah," he said, lowering his own voice. "I know. You see the way he gobbles down them capsules?"

Necktie shook his head. "Two or three in an hour's time. Gets him pretty hopped up. You never know what he's gonna do next when he gets like that. I just try to do what he says and stay away from his bad side."

Hunter had heard enough. Without moving his head, he shifted his eyes toward the metal shelving directly in front of him.

Ceramic tiles, the decorative kind you'd find in some of the mansions out in Union Heights, well outside of downtown. They were eight inches square and about a half-inch thick, and they covered four shelves in stacks of thirty or more.

He held his breath and reached up, carefully taking two tiles off the top of the nearest stack. With every fraction of an inch he moved them, he made sure not to scrape them or tap them against each other. Any sound, however small, would give him away.

In a matter of seconds, he had one in each hand. He hefted both. They were a perfect weight in relation to their size.

He eyed the lanterns across the room. In a fleeting thought that was more intuition than calculation, he assessed the trajectory, allowing for the strength of his own throwing arm in relation to the distance between himself and the lanterns and their elevation off the floor.

He almost smiled. So simple.

He took a small step backward, just far enough from the shelf to give himself a clear shot. With a sharp snap of each wrist, he fired—first one and then the other, barely a second apart. They both spun across the room through open space in a straight line and found their marks, and the back room of the warehouse was suddenly plunged into an inky darkness.

Both men ducked instinctively and swore into the crippling blackness, their voices laced with panic in the face of what they couldn't see.

But Hunter could see it all. Suspenders fumbled around the tabletop for his gun. Necktie sprang from his chair and reached into his shoulder holster for his own weapon. The chair clattered to the floor, and Suspenders fired at the sound. The muzzle flash illuminated the room for a split second, and Necktie yelped when he realized he'd almost been hit by his partner's panicked shot.

"Hey, watchit, ya crazy sonofa—"

Suspenders ignored the warning, sweeping the room blindly with his gun. "What the hell...?" he growled, turning his head left and right, left and right, trying to make out something—anything, however fleeting—in the blanket of darkness. "Who's there!"

He fired again, apparently hoping to get off a lucky shot at a completely invisible target, but it was so far of the mark that Hunter actually coughed out a short, involuntary chuckle.

Necktie focused on the brief sound just enough to be dangerous. He raised his gun in Hunter's direction.

Hunter saw it all unfold in fine detail, like a slow-motion film in a movie house. He heard Necktie's anxious breath slow down, watched the squeeze of his trigger finger. He ducked into a crouch as the muzzle exploded in a burst of light and a roar of sound.

The bullet whizzed over his head and slammed into the cinderblock wall behind him, throwing small chunks of stone in all directions.

Before either adversary could get off another shot, Hunter leaped forward, capitalizing on their blind confusion. He reached out at lightning speed, grabbed Necktie's wrist and wrenched it hard. The sound of a dull crack filled the room, and the gunman let out an agonized yelp. His weapon fell to the concrete floor.

Hunter shoved Necktie aside, and the injured gunman stumbled blindly into the table. Both man and table went down simultaneously in a jumble of six legs, a broken wrist and a skull slapping against hard wood.

Once again, Suspenders aimed his gun at the sound of tumbling furniture and fired. The bullet went nowhere near Hunter, but lodged itself instead in the underside of the up-ended wooden tabletop.

Hunter stepped toward Suspenders and landed a hard, chopping blow with his fist on the big man's right wrist. No bones broke this time, but the goon let out a grunt and fumbled the gun. Hunter followed with one quick and hard right to his jaw, then another. Suspenders' eyelids fluttered. His head rocked momentarily. Hunter landed a third right, then took a step backward and watched Suspenders go down in a noisy heap.

Hunter assessed what was left of his adversaries. Both had blacked out—one from the collision with the able and the other from the blows to the face. They'd be out for a while, but there were others in the building, and they were likely to show up at any second to investigate the gunshots.

He scooped up both guns and tucked them into the pockets of his leather jacket.

Sure enough, his enhanced hearing picked up the urgent scuff of shoe leather against the concrete floor. Two sets of feet, about a hundred feet away and coming fast. He glanced in the direction of the sound and noticed a dim lantern glow getting brighter by the second. Reinforcements were headed his way from someplace at the front of the building. Along with the footsteps, he heard the click of revolver hammers.

Hunter stepped away from the two unconscious heaps on the floor and ducked into a small aisle created by two parallel rows of wooden shipping crates stacked nearly ten feet high on both sides. The first of the two henchmen came around the corner. He was tall and lanky, with a thin mustache and a head full of well-oiled silver hair. He held a lantern in his left hand and a Smith & Wesson .38 in his right.

"Hey, what's all the noise back here?" he barked. "Fallon? Artie? Mickey? What the hell's going on?"

Hunter glanced across the room at Fallon and Mickey. He didn't know which was which, but neither of them were moving. And there was no sign of Artie coming back in from his mishap out on the dock. He looked back at the newcomer and saw his partner coming up behind him—a rat-faced thug with the same combination of gun in one hand and lantern in the other.

Both gunmen were wide-eyed, apparently trying to adjust to the darkness.

"Where's the light?" Rat Face grunted. "Didn't they bring lanterns back here?"

Hair Oil ignored the question. "Hey, you mugs, quit clownin' around!" he yelled into the darkness. "What's goin' on?"

Hunter picked up the unmistakable shade of fear in the man's voice, and noticed that his lantern was rattling slightly. Hair Oil advanced further into the darkness, obviously spooked by the combination of darkness and silence, and he didn't appear to enjoy taking the lead in investigating it.

Hunter waited for Hair Oil to walk past his position amid the stacks of crates, then sprang from behind the boxes and went after him from behind. He swatted the lantern out of the gunman's hand and sent it hurling against a pile of lumber. The glass covering shattered, kerosene sprayed across the lumber and the flame went out.

But Rat Face's lantern still generated just enough light to take away some of Hunter's advantage. Hair Oil could see just well enough to turn and engage with his attacker, but the effort was rushed and clumsy. Before he could take aim in the semi-darkness, Hunter shoved him against the same stack of crates that had served as his hiding place a few seconds earlier.

Hair Oil stumbled and went down, knocking a couple of the crates down with him. He dropped his gun into a small gap amid the overturned containers. He tried to check his fall with his now empty hands, but Hunter crouched low, grabbed a handful of the man's jacket lapel with his left hand and clubbed him in the ribcage with his right. Hair Oil let out a sharp wheeze and went down the rest of the way. Hunter followed with a sharp right to the face, rocking Hair Oil's head back until he went completely limp on the floor next to the jumble of wooden boxes.

A gunshot went off, and a hot slug tore into the side of one of the crates less than two feet from Hunter's head. It came from Rat Face, the thug who'd come down the hallway right behind Hair Oil.

Hunter ducked out of the lantern glow and backed into the shadows deeper inside the room. He dropped to one knee and leaned against a stack of lumber, forcing himself to remain perfectly still and listen to his attacker's movements.

The heavy breathing was easy to isolate. Then he listened more closely and picked up the rapid heartbeat.

More fear.

But Rat Face did his best to mask it. "Awright, freak!" he barked. "Come out of there!"

Slowly, silently, Hunter rose from his one knee and crept along the backside of the lumber pile. He crouched low with each step and worked his way around to position himself behind Rat Face without giving away his movements or his location. As he crossed the space, he reached into his jacket pocket and brought out one of the guns he'd taken from Fallon and Mickey a few minutes earlier.

He didn't want to use it, but he knew it may be necessary if he wanted to get to the front of the building and get Buzz and himself out of this jam. As it was, he expected more of Diamond's men to come to the back of the building any minute to investigate Rat Face's most recent shot. If he did have to use the gun, it would be better off in his hand than his pocket.

Rat Face swept the dimly lit space with the muzzle of his gun. "I said come out, freak!" Tough talk, but Hunter heard his voice crack slightly. He'd responded to the goon's orders with silence, and the goon was clearly starting to feel unnerved.

Hunter had circled back completely and now came up behind Rat Face. When he was no more than four feet behind him, Hunter took one final leap forward and wrapped his forearm around the front of the man's neck.

Rat Face started to yelp, but it came out as a rasping, choking sound. Hunter shoved the barrel of his own gun into the man's ribcage

"Drop it," Hunter murmured, his face no more than two inches from the man's right ear.

Rat Face hesitated for a moment, but his need for a clear air passage—along with the implications of the metal cylinder pressing against his ribs—outweighed his resistance. He dropped his gun.

"Alright, talk," said Hunter, keeping his voice low. "Where's your hostage?"

"I don't...I don't know what you're..."

Hunter gave Rat Face's wrist an upward yank, and at the same time shoved the muzzle of the gun deeper into his ribcage. The gunman let out a yelp that was made up of equal parts pain and fear. "Don't play games with me," Hunter snarled, fighting the urge to raise his voice. "You know exactly who I'm talking about. Frank Hunter. The guy you took from the repair shop. I know you have him here. Where is he?"

Rat Face gasped, wincing at the pain in a shoulder that was just an inch or two from being dislocated. "He's...They've got him in the office up front."

Hunter turned the goon toward the front of the building. "Alright," he said, still close behind with the gun at his ribs. "Let's go."

CHAPTER 27
RESCUE

They'd only advanced a couple steps when they heard a voice from somewhere toward the front of the building.

"Whitey! What's goin' on back there?"

At the sound of the voice, Hunter lurched to a halt, forcing his captive to stop as well. "Are you Whitey?" he said.

Rat Face swallowed hard at the combination of physical pain and fear. With his gun and his lantern taken way, he was blind and powerless—and craven to a point that Hunter found contemptible. "No," he said. "Whitey's on the floor back there. You just knocked him out."

"Alright, listen to me," Hunter murmured. "That guy up there? You're going to tell him it's okay. Tell him there was an intruder in the back but you and the others got rid of him."

Rat Face hesitated.

Hunter gave his arm another wrench and leaned close to his right ear. "Do it!" he warned.

Rat Face raised his voice. "Yeah, it's okay!" he called out. "There was somebody prowling around the back. We took care of him."

"Somebody who?"

"Nobody," the gunman insisted. "Just an old rummy, hanging around the dock. We scared him off with a couple shots."

"Good," Hunter whispered. He gave the wrist another wrench, and Rat Face grunted. "Now, lead the way so I don't have to break your arm."

They headed toward the front of the building. Hunter had no trouble navigating through darkness, but after only a few seconds, he didn't need to. He noticed a glow up ahead, but it was a glow of a different kind this time—brighter and more consistent than the light from the lanterns he'd encountered since he entered the building a few minutes earlier.

And there was the smell too—stale and dirty. Cigarette smoke.

They turned a corner and Hunter brought Rat Face to a halt. His sense of direction had not been compromised by the skirmish in the back of the building or the walk through the dark. He looked beyond

Rat Face's shoulder and saw a doorway leading into a room built into the corner of the building where the front wall and west wall met. This smaller space looked as though it might have been a storage room or a front office at one time. The brighter light came from inside the room through the open doorway.

Hunter kept himself and Rat Face away from the light and well within the cover of shadows. Still keeping a firm grip on Rat Face's collar with one hand and holding the gun at his ribs with the other, he repositioned himself slightly to get a better look inside the smaller room.

His heightened spatial sense enabled him to calculate the dimensions with a high degree of accuracy. The room was fourteen feet wide by sixteen feet long, with one row of windows positioned high along the south wall, facing the street outside, and another row along the west wall. A wide-beam flashlight hung from a wire attached to the ceiling, creating a makeshift fixture that threw a much stronger light throughout the room and beyond the doorway than any kerosene lantern possibly could.

Inside was a hodgepodge of miscellaneous junk. Along the farthest wall was a stack of more empty wooden crates, a couple broken folding chairs and what appeared to be a dusty pile of hastily folded canvas sheets—maybe tents or protective tarps of some kind, now long out of use. Three kerosene lanterns—unlit but recently used, based on the vague traces that Hunter's heightened olfactory sense could pick up in the air—had been perched on the stack of crates.

At the center of the room was a chipped and battered wooden desk. A telephone sat on the desktop with a wire running from the base of the phone, over the side of the desk, along the floor, up the wall and out one of the windows on the west wall. Hunter couldn't see the other end of the wire, but he guessed it had been hastily rigged to a main phone line somewhere outside, probably on a utility pole along the street.

Next to the battered desk was an equally battered folding metal chair. And seated in the chair was Buzz Hunter, bound at the hands and feet, with a blindfold tied around his head.

This was obviously where Diamond had made his call earlier and put Buzz on the line.

There were other men in the room aside from Buzz, most likely around the perimeter of the inner walls. Hunter couldn't see them so much as hear them. First it was the shuffle of shoe leather, the rustle of clothing. After a moment of concentration, it was the heartbeats. Three, as near as he could tell. Maybe a fourth.

Hunter's jaw clenched at the sight of Buzz, a harmless good-natured soul bound up and dragged into harm's way. For one rage-fueled moment, he wanted to give Rat Face's arm a final sharp yank and dislocate his shoulder.

But that wouldn't help Buzz. Hunter needed to get inside the room and get him out of there. And if he could, he'd take out as many of Diamond's crew as possible.

And the only way in was through the door.

Hunter leaned in close to Rat Face and whispered in his ear. "Alright, let's go for a walk," he said. He added some pressure on the gun at the man's ribcage. "Not a word. Just walk."

Hunter steered him toward the door and gave him a firm shove, staying close behind once Rat Face started to move. The few seconds it took to cross the space to the doorway gave him enough time to triangulate on the breathing and the heartbeats inside the room and confirm his original guess. There were two other men inside besides Buzz, each of them on opposite walls.

They reached the doorway. Rat Face started to hesitate, resisting Hunter's pressure from behind.

Rat Face crossed the threshold first. Hunter kept his grip on his arm but hung back in the shadows. He was certain now of another heartbeat in the room.

But where? Two on either side of the room and Buzz in the chair made three. *Where was the fourth?*

Both men—one standing at the right hand wall, the other at the left—turned to look at who was coming through the door.

"Zig, what're you...?"

The man's voice trailed off as he and his partner on the other side of the room immediately noticed Rat Face's odd posture, his pained and anxious expression, his arm at an unnatural angle and twisted backward and up between his shoulder blades.

The goon on the right side of the room pushed away from the wall and pulled his gun. "Wait a minute," he growled. "Who's that behind—"

In a move that was swifter than a single thought, Hunter raised his gun over Zig's right shoulder and pulled the trigger. The gun roared in the small room and the hanging flashlight shattered into hundreds of fragments.

In the short flash of sparks, Hunter's finely tuned senses took in every detail in crystalline slow motion. Zig—he of the rat-like face—winced at the roar of gunfire just a few inches from his ear. Over Zig's shoulder, Hunter saw the wide-eyed, slack-jawed stare of the two thugs standing at either wall—their faces a mixture of puzzlement, surprise and a hint of fear. One reached into his coat for a gun. The other tossed a cigarette butt to the concrete floor and then reached for his weapon as well.

In the middle of the room, Buzz looked just as surprised as the gunmen surrounding him. He couldn't see anything through the blindfold, but he obviously heard the gunshot, and he twisted and squirmed against the ropes at his wrists and feet.

Hunter heard the accelerated breathing from the two gunmen, punctuated by the click from the hammers of each of their weapons. And as the last few sparks from the ruined flashlight died and the room fell into darkness, the space immediately transformed into an eerie but razor-sharp world where everyone and everything shimmered in a sea of infrared.

Then came the shots. The first one, from the left, went wide and slammed into the doorjamb just to the right of Hunter's shoulder. The second, from the right, took Zig in the right arm.

Unwilling to use Zig as a human shield, but equally unwilling to release his grip and let him move freely and gain some strategic advantage, Hunter took the barrel of the gun away from Zig's ribcage and clubbed him at the base of his skull with the butt. Zig crumpled to the ground at Hunter's feet, but Hunter wasted no time leaping over him and bounding deep enough into the room that he couldn't be seen in the blackness within.

The gunmen on either side of him each fired again, then a third time—six slugs so far, three from one side of the room and three from the other, in an attempt to hit a target somewhere in the middle.

Not the smartest idea, thought Hunter.

Most of the shots were wasted in the darkness. One came close, but Hunter saw it coming—sensed it the moment it left the barrel of the gun—and ducked away.

He worried less about his own safety. He'd learned in the last few minutes that if he focused his senses enough, he could avoid the worst of the gunplay—especially if it was from shooters who couldn't see what they were doing. His greater concern was for Buzz, who was immobilized in the center of the room and in the line of fire from all directions.

Hunter immediately went on the offensive, stuffing the gun back into his jacket. The fewer bullets flying across the room, the better. With everyone but himself blinded by the darkness, he had no trouble rushing the gunman to his left and dropping him with a hammering right cross. The gunman stumbled backward, slammed against the wall and slid to the floor.

He was still sliding as Hunter took three steps backward toward the center of the room. He spun clockwise as he moved, and met the second gunman in the middle of the floor, just a couple feet away from the desk where Buzz was bound and struggling. Still spinning, he clubbed the second gunman with a backhand to the jaw. The gunman's entire frame lurched to the left from force of the blow. His arm involuntarily snapped upward and outward from his body, clipping Buzz at his temple with the butt of his gun.

Hunter watched Buzz's head rock slightly, but his attention was drawn away by a scuffling sound behind him, near the door he'd just come through a few seconds earlier.

A third man—the extra heartbeat Hunter hadn't been able to account for—had been shielding himself from the scuffle and the gunfire by crouching alongside a file cabinet next to the door. His back was to Hunter as he crawled over a couple fallen crates blocking his path, then stumbled over Zig, who was laying in the doorway clutching his wounded arm.

Hunter recognized him, even from behind.

Diamond.

Hunter started after him as he made his way out of the room, but he stopped short at the sight of another figure—gun drawn—heading right toward him through the doorway, pushing his way over and around the same obstacles that had obstructed Diamond on the way out.

"In there!" Diamond growled, jerking head back through the

doorway in Hunter's direction. "Get 'im!"

It was Whitey, the oily-haired goon Hunter had put down just a couple minutes earlier in the back of the building. His face was bruised and puffy from beating Hunter had delivered.

"And get the ledger!"

Diamond darted to his left and was out of sight. With Whitey coming through the doorway and waving his gun around in the dark, Hunter couldn't go after Diamond. He had to protect Buzz.

Whitey swept the room and fired two blind shots into the darkness. Neither round came anywhere close to Hunter or Buzz, but slammed into a bulletin board mounted on the wall opposite the doorway, above the stack of crates.

What came next was a lethal chain reaction. The impact of the bullets jarred the board loose from its wall anchors, sending it into a vertical slide down the wall. The board stopped abruptly at the point where the crates met the wall, then toppled forward and upset the kerosene lanterns resting on top of the stack. Most of the lanterns crashed to the floor, where their glass covers shattered and a spray of kerosene spilled across the smooth concrete surface.

Within seconds, the mercurial pool of kerosene made its way to the smoldering cigarette butt on the floor, and the entire stream of liquid ignited. The flames moved in every direction, along the floor and backward up the stack of crates, until the entire back end of the storage room and everything in it—wooden crates, canvas tarps, folding chairs—erupted into a wall of flame.

CHAPTER 28
A FIERY TRAP

Backlit by the fire's demonic glow, Hunter was suddenly an easy target for Whitey. And Whitey didn't waste any time. Hunter watched the snarling grimace spread across the gunman's face as he raised his gun and drew down on him.

It was all crystal clear in the glow of the rising flames. The weapon was a .38 snub-nosed Colt, pearl handle, with a small nick in the cylinder—a random scar on the gray metal from some past criminal enterprise.

Whitey's thumb hooked the hammer and pulled it back. His snarl grew wider, more wolfish.

Whitey flexed his forefinger. Hunter crouched.

By the time the muzzle exploded, Hunter was airborne in a leap that took him upward and sideways, nearly six feet off the ground and almost parallel to the floor. Spinning in mid-air, he grabbed the closest edge of the rectangular bulletin board that was now resting on its side atop one of the crates and burning at one corner.

The bullet sliced past him, just below his arched back, and slammed into the wall beyond.

Still in the air, Hunter used the momentum of his spin to hurl the flaming wooden slab through space in a spinning motion, just as he'd fired the smaller tiles across the back room a few minutes earlier.

The large rectangular projectile connected with Whitey's outstretched arm, slapping his wrist with enough force to knock his gun loose. By the time Hunter touched back down in a three-point stance, Whitey was doubled over, clutching his forearm and cursing at the pain in his bloodied wrist and hand.

Hunter leaped forward from his crouched position and grabbed Whitey by his wounded wrist, which made him curse and wail even more loudly. Hunter twisted the arm sharply, forcing Whitey to turn completely. Hunter shoved him forward, into the file cabinet next to the doorway.

Whitey groaned as his face collided with the metal panel.

"Where'd Diamond go?"

"He…he just ran out."

Hunter glanced through the doorway, realizing that the big prize had probably slipped away and he was left to deal with underlings. He swore under his breath. "Yeah, I saw that," Hunter barked. "Probably better than you did. Where's he headed?"

"I…I don't know!" Whitey gasped, a measure of panic creeping into his voice.

"Don't lie to me!"

"I swear I don't know." The voice was rapidly deteriorating into a whimper. "He got nervous after he heard the gunshots in the back. Once you showed up and the lights went out, he scrammed."

Whitey's last couple words gave way to a racking cough as smoke began to fill the room.

In addition to the cough, Hunter's enhanced hearing picked up something else—something in the distance, outside the front of the building.. The squeal of tires, and the sound of an engine revving hard and fading into the distance.

Hunter yanked Whitey away from the file cabinet and back toward the center of the room. Whitey staggered, his face a bruised mess. The punch he'd taken from Hunter in the back room had already blossomed into a swollen patch of purple around his eye, and the more recent encounter with the filing cabinet wasn't helping things. Hunter turned him around to face him, and drove a punch into his jaw that rocked him backward and down into a crumpled heap on the floor.

He scanned the room quickly, tuning his senses for any further movement or threat. The haphazard array of crates, overturned chairs and unconscious or semiconscious bodies scattered around the room seemed to dance in the eerie, uneven glow of a fire that was growing brighter and hotter by the second. Beneath the insistent murmur of flames, he could hear the steady breathing of four unconscious gunmen sprawled on the floor—Whitey, Zig and the two who'd been waiting for him when he came in.

Much more pronounced, though, was the anxious breathing of the conscious man tied in the chair.

And there was something else, too. Something slowly creeping into the range of his hearing. Something far off in the distance, well beyond the walls of the warehouse.

The wail of police sirens.

Hunter moved quickly to the chair where Buzz was tied. He opened the desk drawer and rummaged for something—a pair of scissors, a box cutter, any leftover artifact that would help him cut the ropes. The best he could come up with was a letter opener with one side sharpened to a fine edge.

He stepped behind Buzz and yanked off the blindfold. Buzz glanced over his shoulder as far as he could in his restrained position, and continued to squirm against the ropes around his wrists and ankles. He let out a defiant grunt. "You...You stay away from me, you son of a—"

"Easy, easy," said Hunter, kneeling behind the chair and sawing at the ropes around Buzz's wrists. "It's okay. I'm not going to hurt you. Just hold still while I cut these..."

169

Buzz suddenly stopped squirming at the sound of the voice behind the mask. "Jack?" he said, stifling a cough as the smoke in the room started to thicken. "Jack, is that you?"

Hunter didn't answer. He merely grinned into the darkness and let out a short chuckle as he continued sawing at the ropes.

The sound was enough for Buzz to recognize him. "What the hell…? How did you—?"

"No time now, Buzz," he said, fighting against the deadly smoke working its way into his nostrils. "I need to get you out of here. And these other gorillas, too."

Hunter worked furiously, finally making his way through one of the turns of rope around Buzz's wrists. He unraveled the bindings just enough for Buzz to shuffle them off, then pulled the chair around with Buzz still in it and went to work on the rope around Buzz's ankles

"This is a hell of a mask you've built, Buzz."

Buzz now had more freedom to turn and look at Hunter. "Holy cow! You're wearing the—"

"It's amazing, Buzz. I'm not sure I can even describe it. I can see in the dark. I can hear everything. My reflexes are like lightning. Sometimes I feel like I'm moving faster than I can even think. I've lost track of how many times I've been shot at in the last ten minutes and I've dodged every slug that came my way."

Buzz just shook his head. "Golly," he whispered. Then he stopped suddenly as he cocked one ear. "Wait," he said. "I hear sirens."

"I know," said Hunter. "I started hearing them about thirty seconds ago." With a final thrust, he tore through one turn of rope around Buzz's ankles and instantly started unraveling.

Buzz leaned over and lent a hand. "Jack, you gotta get out of here," he said, his words coming in rapid fire. "You can't be here when they get here, especially not if you're wearing that thing."

"Not yet," he said. "I need to get you someplace safe. And like it or not, I need to get the rest of these monkeys out of here, too."

Hunter glanced around the room. He was about to grab the closest thug and start hauling him toward the door when his eyes settled on a small shelf that was close enough to the doorway to remain untouched by the flames creeping along the opposite end of the room. Resting on top of the shelf was a brown leather journal.

He remembered the command Diamond had shouted just moments earlier.

Get the ledger.

Hunter moved from behind the desk, stepped over one of the goons sprawled on the floor, and picked up the journal. He riffled through the pages for a second or two, then stuffed the journal into his jacket.

Buzz unraveled the last of the rope around his ankles and scrambled out of the chair, stumbling against the numbness in his legs and feet and retching against the smoke that was creeping into his lungs.

Hunter grabbed his arm, steering him away from the heat and toward the doorway leading out of the room to the open space of the warehouse where the air was at least a little clearer. "Get out of here!" he shouted over the flames that were now roaring. "Head through the outer room to the door that leads to the front of the building!"

Buzz glanced at the three bodies on the floor. "Let me help you with…" His words dissolved into a harsh sound that was something between a cough and a gasp.

"No!" Hunter shouted, giving Buzz a shove. "I'll take care of them! Get moving!"

Buzz stumbled toward the doorway, doubled over in an uncontrollable cough and nearly blinded by the thickening smoke. Leaning against an overturned chair to steady himself, he tried to step over the wounded thug whose crumpled form was blocking the door, but he staggered and tumbled to the floor.

Hunter was a few feet away when he saw Buzz go down. He'd been trying—with diminishing success—to fight back his own coughing fits while struggling to haul one of the goons out of the room. Although his eyes were protected by the goggles, there was nothing to stop the smoke from filling his lungs too. And the flames, fed by the numerous wooden crates around the room and whatever was inside them, were only getting closer and hotter. If he or Buzz or any of these sleeping goons sucked in any more air, they'd either die from smoke inhalation or burn to death.

And what about the three goons at the back of the building? Were they still out cold? If not, where were they and what were they doing? For all Hunter knew, they could be waiting right outside the room with their guns pointed at the doorway.

His lungs screaming against the smoke and the heat, Hunter dropped the thug he'd been dragging toward the door and headed to where Buzz was laying. By the time he got there, he was on his hands and knees, and he and Buzz were both gasping for air that was nowhere to be found.

CHAPTER 29
ESCAPE!

Hunter felt as though his chest was just seconds away from exploding. He looked through the smoky haze at Buzz's face and saw eyes that were squeezed shut and a face that was twisted into a grimace of pain and streaked with tears and grime. They were just a few feet from the doorway, but he couldn't even see the opening anymore through the smoke.

His mind raced. Just a little bit of fresh air would be all they'd…

Then it came to him.

The windows.

He couldn't see them anymore, but he remembered windows along two of the four walls in the room. He'd almost forgotten about them because they were so high on either wall.

Just a little bit of fresh air.

Hunter pulled the gun back out of his jacket. He had no idea how many rounds were left, but he pointed the weapon at a forty-five-degree angle from the floor and fired. Instantly he heard the shatter of glass.

He changed direction slightly and fired again. Another shatter. He fired one more time and heard the sound again.

Hunter felt a rush of air, and after a few seconds the smoke cleared just enough that he could see three broken windows along one wall.

He pulled the trigger a fourth time, but the gun was empty.

He reached into his other pocket for the other gun he'd confiscated at the back of the building, but the pocket was empty. He'd probably lost it in his mid-air spinning and throwing maneuver a few moments earlier.

He turned away from Buzz and groped along the floor. There had been guns everywhere just a few moments go—too many for his liking. All he needed to do now was find one that had been dropped when he took down the two thugs in the room.

In the tricky dance of light from the nearby flames, he caught sight of a lump on the floor and recognized the shape. He reached out, grabbed the gun and fired four more rounds. Four more widows shattered in a shower of glass.

The good news was that the air was clearer. Nothing close to a spring day, but enough to catch a momentary breath. The bad news was that the rush of fresh oxygen coming through the broken windows stoked the flames, and the room instantly became hotter and more deadly. Hunter could breathe a little more clearly, if only for a moment, but he had to move quickly—even more quickly than before.

Hunter gathered up a reserve of strength, snaked an arm under Buzz's armpit and around his chest, and hauled him through the doorway.

The front entrance to the warehouse was some twenty feet away, and the air between the office space and the main door was quickly filling with smoke, even with the new airways Hunter had created in the smaller room. Hunter knew Buzz wouldn't be safe until he was completely outside the building—away from the smoke and flames.

He hustled Buzz to a small entranceway near the main door and gently put him down on the concrete floor. He eyed the door and instantly replayed the last few moments in his mind. Normally, a long-vacant building like this one would be sealed up with chains and padlocks at every point of entry, but Diamond had just made a quick exit moments earlier, so it had should have been open.

Hunter shoved at the door and it gave way easily. His guess was correct. But was this the smartest way out?

The sirens were getting louder. Hunter really didn't want to step out of the building and find officers outside with revolvers and shotguns pointed at him. He poked his head through the doorway and gave a quick glance up and down the street, taking in a huge gulp of fresh air as he looked in both directions.

He paused just long enough to concentrate on the distant wail. The police were no more than two minutes away.

Hunter raced back inside to Buzz, who was still conscious but coughing uncontrollably while fighting to get up on his hands and

173

knees. Hunter wrapped an arm around his back and chest and hoisted him up all the way. He half dragged him to the door, which had swung back to the closed position, and kicked it back open.

"Come on, Buzz," he urged. "Get on your feet and get some air."

Within a couple seconds after crossing the threshold, the night air revived them both. Hunter's mouth tasted like a coal bin, but his lungs felt clearer. Buzz was still coughing violently, but he managed to get his legs under himself and start moving under his own power.

Hunter hustled Buzz a good forty feet from the entrance and sat him down on the sidewalk. He knelt down and examined Buzz's eyes and face.

"You alright?"

Buzz responded with more labored coughing, but he waved Hunter off. "Yeah," he rasped. "I'm okay."

"Stay right there."

Before Buzz could answer, Hunter headed back into the building, back into the smaller room where the fire was climbing higher and burning hotter than ever. Between the deadly flames and the rapidly approaching sirens, he only had seconds to retrieve the three incapacitated gunmen.

He grabbed Whitey first and dragged him across the floor by his wrist. Still unconscious from the hammering Hunter had given him, he was deadweight across the entire stretch of floor to the warehouse entrance. Hunter dragged him across the threshold and dumped him on the sidewalk.

Zig was more trouble. He was heavier, and although he'd been grazed in the right arm by a bullet from one of his fellow goons, he'd never really lost consciousness. Hunter could tell just by watching him that the convulsive coughing and retching from the smoke was sending waves of pain up and down his wounded arm and all through his upper body.

But Hunter had very little time and even less patience for the gentle treatment. He crouched down, grabbed Zig by the collar and hauled him out of the room and across the same stretch of floor to the warehouse entrance and the pavement beyond. Every inch of the way, the gunman's combination of moaning, wailing and smoke-infested retching sounded like the death throes of the damned.

The other two were out cold. They were smaller and lighter than

Whitey and Zig, which enabled Hunter to drag them both out at the same time, each by an arm. The room had become a furnace. A few more seconds and they would have burned alive.

He dragged them through the main door and piled them alongside the other two, glancing upward at the flames now licking outward from the broken windows facing the street. He turned rejoin Buzz, who was still sitting on the pavement several yards away from the pile of gunman and trying to suppress his racking cough with only limited success.

Hunter was about to speak, but Buzz put up a hand to stop him. His convulsing lungs prevented him from getting many words out.

They both turned their heads in the direction of rhythmic flashes of red suddenly visible to the east—four police cars and two fire trucks, all rounding the corner at the far end of the street less than a quarter mile away.

"Jack, you gotta get outta here!" Buzz choked. "If they find you here..."

Hunter was reluctant. He put his hand on Buzz's shoulder. "I know," he said quickly. "You sure you're okay?"

"I'm okay," Buzz hacked. "Just...just need to...catch my breath."

Hunter hesitated. It didn't sound that simple to him. He glanced up the street. "They'll take you to the hospital," he said. "I'll meet you there."

"Jack, go!" Hunter rasped. "Hurry!"

Hunter took one last look into Buzz's eyes, then stood up and darted away, disappearing around the building and into the shadows.

◆　◆　◆　◆

Eight minutes later, Hunter was cruising through the Administrative District at a moderate speed. He'd removed the mask and tucked it into a pocket of his jacket before leaving the River District. It was going on eleven o'clock, early enough that there was still some motor and pedestrian traffic moving through the downtown area. A masked man on a motorcycle would draw entirely too much attention at this time of night.

He turned down Newton Avenue and pulled up to a parking space at the curb, about a block away from the Third Precinct. He cut the engine and dismounted—slowly, casually, with no outward sense of urgency—pulling the ledger out from inside his jacket and tucking it under his arm like a magazine or a library book.

He strolled toward the police station entrance, scanning the sidewalk ahead for anyone who might recognize him and hoping no one would. He deliberated about how far he might get into the building before bumping into someone he knew. It wouldn't be far, even at this hour. He was the son of a Union City cop—one of the most revered officers in the city's history—and there were veteran members of the police department with long memories.

Hunter ducked into the revolving door and emerged inside the front entrance. He quickly scanned his surroundings. The night desk was off to his left, about twenty feet away, but it was vacant at the moment. Maybe the sergeant on duty had momentarily stepped away for coffee or a trip to the restroom. Whatever the reason, it was a break in his favor.

He tucked the ledger behind the base of a potted plant just inside the entrance, then turned and re-entered the revolving door. In and out of the building in no more than eight seconds, he hit the sidewalk and headed back toward the motorcycle.

Less than three minutes later he was a mile away from the precinct, slowing down and pulling up to a pay telephone booth on a side street off Newton.

CHAPTER 30
REGROUPING AND RECKONING

Diamond was back in his upstairs office at the Paramount, thanks in large part to Kowalski. Ever the efficient getaway man, Kowalski had been parked outside the Watt Building with the engine running when Diamond scrambled out of the warehouse to escape the smoke and fire—and get away from whoever the hell had stormed into that front office where he and his men had been holding Buzz Hunter.

They'd made it back to the Paramount shortly after midnight. Simone was there when they arrived, but he stepped out of the room and into the hallway shortly after they came in. Kowalski took his usual position at the door and remained silent as Diamond went into a tirade, cursing the unknown intruder who had fouled the operation.

The storm of Diamond's rage had lasted nearly a half-hour, but it eventually blew out. Now, at a few minutes before one a.m., he stood behind his desk with his arms folded, surveying the three men who'd dragged themselves all the way back from the edge of the river to the Paramount. They'd practically stumbled into the room just a few minutes earlier and launched into a jumbled explanation of what had gone on—and what had gone wrong—in the back of the Watt Building. It was a confused chorus of three voices talking over each other about an attacker who took them all by surprise and the subsequent narrow escape out of the back of the building just as the fire department and the police showed up at the curb.

As near as Diamond could decipher from the disjointed narrative, the three men—Artie Garrett, Mitch Fallon and Mickey Salerno—had apparently covered five blocks on foot just to make their way out of the River District, then hailed a cab to take them the rest of the way.

The room was dimly lit by a desk lamp, but no amount of shadows could hide the fact that each of them separately was a disheveled mess and all of them together were a goddamn embarrassment.

Garrett stood with slumped shoulders, which made him look even more portly than usual. He held one hand behind his neck and massaged a nasty looking bruise just under his hair line and near the base of his skull.

Fallon and Salerno both sat in chairs. Fallon had trouble speaking, thanks to some severe looking bruises along one side of his jaw. He appeared to be having trouble with his right wrist, and he avoided using it by keeping it limp in his lap.

Mickey was the worst of the three. He sported a large, reddish-purple bump on his temple. Like Fallon, he was having trouble with his right wrist, but his appeared to be in much worse shape. He cradled it with his left hand and tried to keep it still. His shirt was soiled and his necktie was hopelessly askew. He was breathing hard and doing his best to stifle a whimper every time he made the slightest move. Diamond didn't need a doctor to know the wrist was probably broken.

Diamond leaned forward against the desktop on fists curled into two tight balls. He shifted his gaze at each of the three men in his office. His eyes burned with a smoldering rage.

"Alright," he said. "Slowly, and one at a time. What the hell happened at the back of that building?"

Fallon was the first to speak, braving the pain it took to do it. "I don't know, Nick," he said, his words slightly distorted by the swelling on the side of his face. "We had everything under control. It was all smooth until this guy showed up at the back door and started muscling us. He was…"

Diamond was already shaking his head vigorously by the time his lieutenant got the first few words out of his mouth. He raised a hand from the desk and waved off the rest of the explanation. "Alright, stop," he barked. "Tell me again. What guy?"

"I don't *know* who he was," said Fallon. "Nobody got a good look. All I know is, Artie went out to the dock for a smoke. Me and Mickey stayed in. We had a couple lanterns lighting up the back of the warehouse, but something knocked them over and they broke. Right after that, somebody started a big ruckus in the dark. We fired a couple shots, but we couldn't see what we were shooting at."

Fallon paused to lick his lower lip, wincing at the pain, then continued. "I got a couple'a socks in the jaw," he said, then jerked a thumb at Artie and Mickey. "These two got it pretty good too."

"Somebody knocked the cigar right outta my hand when I was out on the dock," said Artie. "Then he landed a hard one on the back of my neck. I don't remember much after that."

"We all musta been out for a couple minutes," said Fallon. "By the time we woke up, we were smelling smoke and it was gettin' kinda thick. And then we heard the sirens, and we took off out the back and ducked through some alleys. Then we headed this way."

Diamond paused to think. His mind was not entirely in the moment. He was still piecing together the rapid and confused chain of events that had taken place back at the Watt Building.

"I was in that front room with the shopkeeper and everybody else," he said. "Bugs, Crane, Whitey and Zig. We all heard the shots in back, and I sent Whitey and Zig back to see what was going on."

Simone stepped quietly back into the room. Diamond looked up at him.

"I just got off the phone with Union Mercy, just now," said Simone.

"They put me on the line with the emergency room. The nurse there says they got a guy with a gunshot wound to the arm. That's gotta be Zig. I asked about who else might've came in with him. She says there were three others—one with a banged up face and hand. Said they all got too much smoke, too. That's all I could get. She started asking me questions—who am I, how do I know these guys. I just hung up."

Diamond nodded. "Someone came right to the door right behind Zig and shot out the light," he recounted. "One of our own boys—maybe Crane, but I can't say for sure because it was too dark—shot at the first thing that came through the door, which was Zig."

He shook his head, confused and frustrated at the same time. "I didn't get a good look at who came in behind Zig," he said, "but whoever he was, it sounded like he was tearing the place apart."

Simone cleared his throat nervously. "Listen, Nick," he said. "We've got four of our boys in that emergency room. I'm concerned about what they might say. After what just happened tonight, you know there's gonna be cops all over that hospital."

Diamond glanced at Simone, then looked away. "The ledger," he muttered after a moment, shaking his head. He thumped the desk with his right fist and glared at the haggard-looking trio that had crawled back from the river and dragged themselves in front of him. "What the hell happened to that ledger?"

Mickey hesitated for a moment. Even through the pain, he looked genuinely confused. "Well...How could we...?" he said, his words halting and tentative. "You were right there, Nick. You coulda—"

The gun was up off the desk before Mickey could finish the statement. Diamond was suddenly standing straight now, with the weapon aimed directly at a point between Mickey's eyes.

"Shut up!" Diamond barked.

Mickey went silent, flinching at the sound of the words and the sight of the gun barrel staring directly at him from no more than eight feet away. And just beyond the weapon were Diamond's eyes, staring straight down the barrel and into his own, wild and unpredictable, as though something behind them was not properly connected to reality.

The room went silent. An electric charge hung in the air for a long moment. Then Diamond's voice changed to something quieter, but much more deadly. Deadly as jagged steel. "Shut. Your. Trap."

The other four men in the room—Garrett, Fallon, Simone and Kowalski—shifted their eyes back and forth between Diamond and Mickey. Beyond that, no one made a move. No one made a sound. Mickey, eyes wide and mouth agape, put his good hand up in a yielding gesture. "Sure Nick," he said, his voice quiet and a little bit shaky. "Just take it easy, okay?"

Diamond lowered the gun slowly, the crazy fire in his eyes dimming.

Mickey stammered out a suggestion. "It...It might'a burned up, Nick."

Diamond turned to look at Mickey. He frowned, tilting his head slightly as though considering the suggestion. Then he raised the gun again—quickly this time—aimed it squarely at Mickey's face, and pulled the trigger.

The roar was deafening in the small room. Mickey's head jerked backward instantly—a crimson hole in his forehead, an expression frozen in a mask of surprise. The force of the gunshot rocked his limp body backward, until both he and the chair he'd been sitting in toppled in a confused heap on the floor.

Diamond lowered the gun, his eyes fixed on Mickey's lifeless body on the floor. A puff of smoke and a strong whiff of nitrous hung in the air. "It might have," he said calmly. "But maybe not."

The remaining four men in the room stood with eyes wide and mouths agape, glancing back and forth between Diamond and the lifeless body on the floor that had been Michael "Mickey" Salerno seconds before. No one said a word. No one moved a muscle.

"Get him out of here," said Diamond, staring at the body. His voice was quiet and even, yet blood-chilling at the same time. "And then find me that ledger."

He looked away from Mickey and waved at the room with his arm. "And then gather up all the files and everything else here that's important," he said. "We're clearing out of here before sunrise."

Simone had stepped forward and crouched alongside Artie to help lift Mickey's body, but he stopped suddenly and looked at Diamond. His face formed a question, but given what had transpired just seconds earlier, he was clearly apprehensive about asking it.

"Where, uh...where we going, Nick?" Simone said finally, keeping a wary eye on the gun that was still in Diamond's right hand.

Diamond tucked the gun into his belt, then turned away and

headed for the office door. "Someplace with a better view."

He pushed through the door and disappeared into the outer hallway.

CHAPTER 31
QUESTIONS AND MYSTERIES

Hunter sat in an uncomfortable wooden chair in a corner of the emergency room at Union Mercy Hospital. Just a few feet away from him, Buzz sat at the edge of a bed, stifling the occasional cough while buttoning up his shirt. They were separated from other ER beds and patients by a full-length curtain hanging from a horizontal metal rod near the ceiling.

Hunter had stopped to make an anonymous call to the Third Precinct to alert the police to the ledger he'd dropped in their entranceway. From there, he'd stopped at the Republic Building just long enough to park the motorcycle back in the garage, make a quick change into street clothes, and then head to the hospital in his car to check on Buzz. Before he'd even found Buzz, he spotted three cops walking the halls of the emergency room. And he suspected that there were at least a few more elsewhere that he didn't see. Not obtrusive, but definitely a presence. Hunter guessed that Buzz wasn't the only refugee from the burning warehouse to end up at Union Mercy.

Buzz would be okay. He'd spent a little more than an hour getting his lungs cleared with the help of a steady dose of pure oxygen pumped through a mask tied to his face. The nurses had given him a couple rounds of drops to flush the grit and the sting out of his eyes. An ER doctor had also looked at the bruise on his temple and the cut that went with it, and decided that a few stitches were in order. After about an hour-and-a half of observation to make sure he hadn't suffered a concussion, the doctors gave him the all-clear.

Beginning about thirty seconds after the oxygen mask came off, Buzz had barraged Hunter with rapid-fire questions: Did the mask suppress his fear? Did it make him physically stronger? What was it like to ride the motorcycle with his senses keyed so high? Could he actually see the bullets coming at him? How did the mask respond to the heat and the smoke? How did he feel now, after the fact, a couple hours later?

Despite his excitement, Buzz had kept his voice low all the while and spoke in a sort of familial shorthand, so as not to give anything away to the docs, nurses, orderlies, other patients, or any of the other miscellaneous traffic that moved through the ER hallways. Hunter had done his best to answer in kind, but he admitted that he was still trying to make sense of the whole episode himself.

Buzz adjusted the collar of his shirt and rolled up his sleeves. Hunter noticed that he could still smell the smoke in his cousin's clothes, and realized that he should have brought some things for him to change into for the ride home.

A young nurse stepped in. She had dark hair, and looked to be in her late twenties. She held a small cylinder in one hand and a brown paper bag in the other. "Mr. Hunter?"

Both men looked up simultaneously. "If you mean the patient," said Buzz, "that's me."

The nurse smiled. "My name is Joan," she said. "Before we send you home, the doctor wanted me to give this to you."

Buzz looked at the cylinder as Joan held it up. "A Benzedrine inhaler," he said.

"That's right," said Joan. "We usually give these to asthma patients to relieve some of their symptoms. Now, we know you're not an asthma patent, but under the circumstances, the doctor thought you should use it for a couple days."

Buzz took the cylinder. "Okay," he said. "How often?"

The nurse frowned. "Well, that's a good question," she said. "Normally we'd tell you to use it whenever you're feeling short of breath, but for reasons that no one can seem to figure out, there's been a shortage of these things over the last couple weeks."

Hunter and Buzz exchanged a glance.

"The drugstores all over town are reporting a run on the inhalers in their stock, so patients who would normally buy them from drugstores have been coming to the hospitals for their supply—which means we've been experiencing a shortage as well. So unfortunately, you'll have to conserve, because we can only give you two of these. If you can, try to limit your use of the inhaler to three or four times a day."

Buzz shrugged. "Oh, I'll be okay," he said. "If I need it at all, I'm sure that'll be enough."

Joan smiled. She took the inhaler back from Buzz and dropped it into the bag with the other one. "Very good. I'll be back in just a minute with some discharge papers for you to sign and then you can be on your way."

Hunter watched the nurse as she disappeared beyond the curtain. He listened as her footsteps on the tiled floor faded into the distance, and when he was sure she was out of earshot, he looked back at Buzz and leaned forward in his chair.

"The capsules," he said quietly.

Buzz shook his head. "Yeah, I don't get it," he said, lowering his voice to match Hunter's. "What's the big deal with those things?"

"I think I might know."

"Huh?"

"I heard a conversation," said Hunter. "Two of Diamond's goons in the back room of the warehouse. They said he's been taking a bunch of capsules that are making him crazy."

Buzz's brow furrowed for a moment. "Asthma inhalers? How would that make somebody—"

Buzz stopped and both men turned as another figure pushed the curtain aside and stepped into the small space. It was Mike Dugan, escorted by a hatchet-faced nurse who looked many years older and much harder than Joan. She made no effort to mask her annoyance at the idea of a detective disturbing her patients.

Hunter felt a sudden tightness in his chest at the sight of Dugan. If some of Diamond's men had been brought here for medical attention, and a detail of police officers had been dispatched to the hospital to keep an eye on things, he should have expected Dugan to be making the rounds as well. He'd have a lot of questions, and Buzz—who'd been at the center of the chaos—would certainly be on his list. All of which meant that the next few minutes could be dicey.

The nurse glared at Dugan. "Please be brief," she said. She closed the curtain and marched away.

Despite his apprehension, Hunter put on a friendly face and shook hands with the detective as he came through the curtain. Dugan, who'd met Buzz on a few prior occasions, turned to shake hands with the recovering patient.

"I hear you've had a hell of a night," said the detective.

Buzz shrugged. "Ah, I'm okay. Just some smoke and a bang on the head is all."

"Pretty tough talk for a guy who was kidnapped, held hostage and escaped from a burning building all in the span of a few hours." He gave Hunter a quick glance, then focused on Buzz. He reached into his coat and pulled out a notepad and a pen. "Mind if I ask a few questions?"

Hunter put up a hand in a yielding gesture. "Mike, I really don't know if this is the best—"

Buzz made a similar yielding gesture at Hunter. "No, it's okay, Jack. It's fine."

The two cousins locked eyes for a moment, and Hunter did his best to telegraph a silent message: *Just keep it simple. You know what parts to leave out.*

Dugan pulled an empty chair away from the wall and settled in. "Okay, Buzz, tell me what happened. From the beginning."

Buzz took a deep breath. "Well," he said, "I knew they were bad news the minute they walked into the shop."

"What time?"

"Around five-thirty. About a half-hour before I usually close up."

"How many?"

"There were three. Well, four altogether. Three who came into the shop, and a fourth one waiting outside, behind the wheel of the car."

"Did you catch any of their names?"

"Well, it's not like they politely removed their hats and introduced themselves. But they called the driver Johnny. And one of the guys who sat with me in the back seat was called Zig."

Dugan scribbled in his notepad. "So the three of them came in at about five-thirty, and then what?"

"They asked me if Jack was around. I didn't like the way they were asking, and like I said, I didn't like the looks of them, either. So I says, 'Who wants to know?' Then they start talking tough, telling me not to give them any backtalk. I just said, 'Listen, you want to talk to Jack? He's down at the Justice Center. Same place he is every day, along with the DA and a bunch of other lawyers and judges. And there's probably a few cops and detectives there too, so be my guest. I'm sure they'd all love to meet you.'"

184

Dugan cracked a smile. "Well, Buzz," he said, "you apparently had no trouble giving it right back to them."

Buzz let out a cough and made a dismissive wave with his hand. "Ah, they're a bunch of hoodlums."

"Okay, then what?"

"So one of them says, 'Well, if the assistant DA isn't around, I guess you'll have to do.' Next thing I know, two of them are coming behind the counter and holding my arms behind me. The third one just stood there with a gun. I could see that they all had guns, so I didn't put up a fight."

Hunter felt his knuckles tighten at the thought of Buzz being manhandled by a couple armed thugs on his own territory—in the shop were he made his living, the building that had been in their family for two generations, and the place they both called home.

"Okay," Dugan prompted.

"So they put a blindfold on me and walked me out to the curb," said Buzz. "There was a car waiting. I could hear the engine running and smell the exhaust."

But there was no way you could've known what kind of car," said Dugan, "because you had the—"

"It was a Buick."

Dugan stopped scribbling and looked up from his notepad, his expression perplexed. "But if you were blindfolded, how did you know it was a Buick?"

Buzz shrugged and glanced at Hunter, who stifled a grin. "Mike, let me explain something," said Hunter. "Buzz and I have been tinkering with engines since we were kids, all the way back to before the war, and he had a four-year head start on me. Back in the days when the rich folks were the only people in this town who were driving automobiles, Buzz was one of the only people in this town who could fix them. So trust me, if he says he was riding in a Buick—blindfolded or not—it was a Buick."

Dugan nodded and scribbled another line. Without looking up, he said, "I don't suppose you could tell me from the sound of the engine what color the car was."

Buzz shifted his weight on the edge of the bed. "Sorry," he said.

Dugan looked up from his notes. "So, assuming that your eyes were still covered when they parked the car and took you inside,

185

by what intuitive powers did you determine that you were at the Watt Building?"

Hunter didn't like the tone. "You looking for information, Mike, or just looking for a fight?" The protective edge in his voice was unmistakable.

Dugan paused to take a deep breath and rub his eyes with his thumb and forefinger. "I'm sorry," he said after a moment. "It's late." He glanced at his watch. "Actually, it's early. Whatever the case, everybody's tired. And frankly, I'm hearing things from different sources about the events of the last five or six hours that just aren't adding up."

Buzz and Hunter exchanged a quick glance, then turned their eyes back toward Dugan.

"It's okay, Lieutenant," said Buzz. "It's like this. You know that fishy smell you get down by the river this time of year?"

Dugan nodded.

"I got a whiff of that between the car and the building after the driver parked the car. And then, once they got me inside, I smelled the kerosene lanterns burning. And then a little bit later, I heard them talking about rigging up the telephone to an outside utility pole and I figured I was someplace with no phone line and no electrical power. So when I put all that together, I had a pretty good idea where I was."

Dugan's mouth turned up in a half-grin that defused some of the earlier tension. "If you ever decide to close up that shop for good, Buzz, you ought to consider detective work."

"Yeah," said Buzz, "I hear that's where all the big money is."

Dugan arched an eyebrow. "Yeah, that's what they tell me, too."

The detective flipped to a new page in his pad. "So tell me what happened after they let you talk to Jack on the phone," he said.

"Well," said Buzz, shifting his weight on the bed, "I'm afraid there's not much to say. They kept the room pretty dark, and they had me tied up in a chair for at least another half-hour. I was alone for most of the time, and of course I had the blindfold, so I couldn't see anything. But I managed to work the ropes around my wrists and loosen them up a little bit. After a while, I heard some scuffling and yelling outside the room. They must have been arguing about something, I don't know. I couldn't make it out. Next thing I know, one of the goons comes right up next to me and he sounds mad as a hornet. Not really mad at

186

me, but just mad, you know? I stopped working at the ropes, but he came around the desk and said something like, 'Alright, we're getting out of here.'"

"Did he say where they were planning to take you?"

"No, he just gave me a whack on the head with something. Really rang my bell. I know I was out for a few minutes, and when I came to, the ropes were undone and I was out on the sidewalk, propped up against a lamp post in front of the building. I could hear the sirens, and I looked around. The other four were all sprawled on the pavement near the street, and they were still unconscious. Then the police cars and firetrucks pulled up. A couple of them made sure I was okay, and the rest of them got busy putting out the fire."

Buzz gave a final shrug. "And here I am."

Dugan looked at him for a moment, then closed his notebook, as though he were finished with his questions. But there was a hint of uncertainty in his eyes, a moment of hesitation in his voice.

Hunter glanced from Dugan to Buzz, then back to Dugan again. *Here it comes.*

"Uh, listen, Buzz," said Dugan. "There are four other guys here, part of Diamond's crew. They were at the warehouse. You might even recognize them if you saw them, but we're not letting them get anywhere near you just now—if ever. They're under observation down a separate hallway, and we put some officers outside their rooms."

"I imagine they got a lot of smoke too," said Buzz.

"Well, they did. But it appears to be a little more than just smoke that landed them here."

Buzz frowned. "I don't follow you."

"Somehow in all of this, it looks like they got roughed up pretty good, but we were able to ask them a few questions…"

Dugan shifted in his chair again. He was getting to a part in the story that clearly making him uncomfortable, but he pushed ahead.

"They all said something about a guy who appeared from the back of the building, probably through the back entrance, where some of Diamond's other men were apparently guarding the back doors."

Dugan hesitated a moment. Buzz looked at him with a blank expression and didn't say a word.

"They said he…They tell me he was wearing some kind of mask."

Buzz frowned. "A mask?"

"Yeah. And some crazy goggles, they tell me. They said he dragged one of the guys from the back of the building and stormed into the room where you were being held."

Dugan looked at Buzz, apparently hoping for some glimmer of confirmation. Buzz just looked back at him, his face in a puzzled frown.

"They said he moved very fast," Dugan went on, sounding almost embarrassed at the fantastic story he was relating. "So fast they couldn't even get a clean shot at him, and that he really gave it to the guys who had you tied in that chair."

Dugan paused again, shaking his head slightly as he looked into Buzz's eyes. "Any of that sound familiar to you?"

Buzz stared into the distance, his eyebrows shifting into a puzzled expression. For a moment, the only sound was the murmur of nurses and other hospital workers moving along the outer hallway. "Golly, I'm sorry, Lieutenant," he said finally, shaking his head, "but I don't remember anything like that. Now, like I said, I think I might have been out for a couple minutes. But even so, that story sounds pretty rich to me."

Dugan scratched his chin and looked down at his notes. The tilt of his head accentuated the circles under his eyes and the tired shadows on his face. "Well, it's probably nothing," he said with a shrug. "But it's odd that they all told me similar stories in separate conversations."

The interview ended abruptly when one of the most menacing figures Hunter had encountered all night suddenly reappeared in a small opening of the curtain.

CHAPTER 32
MAD POWDER

The grim-faced nurse—the one who'd escorted Dugan into the room several minutes earlier—came back and stood in the curtain opening. She got right to the point. "Alright, Detective," she said, "I'm afraid you'll have to leave now. This patient needs to go home and get some rest."

Dugan glanced up at the nurse with an arched eyebrow. He was clearly taken aback by her demeanor, but apparently too tired to argue. He looked at Buzz and Hunter, tucking his notepad into his jacket and rising from his chair.

Hunter stifled a grin, partly amused but mostly relieved at the interruption in Dugan's line of questions.

"Jack, we can talk more in the morning," the detective said.

Hunter looked at his watch. "It *is* morning."

Dugan shrugged. "Well, after the sun comes up anyway. I'm sure your boss and mine will want a full briefing."

The detective said his goodbyes to the two men and ignored the nurse as he made his way past the curtain and down the hall.

Joan, the younger nurse, stepped into the curtained area just as Dugan stepped out. She held a clipboard and addressed Buzz.

"Mr. Hunter, can you see well enough to sign some papers?"

Buzz looked up at her and blinked twice. "Oh, sure," he said. "Still a little itchy, but I'm fine."

"Wonderful. If you can fill these out for us, you can be on your way."

"Sure thing."

She handed him the clipboard and a pen. "I'll come back for them in a few minutes."

She pushed through the curtain and Hunter followed her out. "Excuse me, miss...uh...Joan? Do you have a moment?"

The nurse stopped and turned toward him. She glanced up the hallway toward the nurse's station. "Of course," she said. She tilted her head toward the curtained space where Buzz was still sitting and smiled. "He's a doll. Is he your brother?"

"My cousin," said Hunter. "But we grew up together. He's like a brother."

Her smile broadened. "How nice." She paused for a moment, and her expression darkened slightly. "I don't know all the details, but I've heard a few things about what he's been through tonight. He seems... surprisingly calm."

"He can be tough," said Hunter. "Sometimes...he takes more guff than he deserves."

"It's nice that he has you to look out for him."

Hunter shrugged. "I wonder if I could ask you a question."

"Of course."

"The Benzedrine inhalers," he said. "The ones that seem to be in such short supply?

"Yes?"

"What can you tell me about them?"

She hesitated. "Well, I'm not a doctor, and I'm not a pharmacist. I'm not sure if I'd be the right—"

Hunter took out his wallet and handed her his card. "I understand," he said, "but if I told you it was a law enforcement matter, would you be willing to provide a little, uh, *unofficial* help?"

She read the card. "Oh," she said, her eyes slightly wider. "I didn't realize you were—"

Hunter smiled. "It's okay," he said. "I promise not to have you arrested."

"That's a relief."

"Just a couple questions?"

"Yes," she said. "Yes, of course."

"The inhalers," said Hunter.

"Yes, the inhalers. Benzedrine is a drug that helps to open up the bronchial passages." She put a hand up to her chest. "The lungs, I mean. We give them to asthma patients all the time. You can usually buy them in any drugstore, but as I said…"

"Right. For some reason, there's been a run on them lately."

"Yes. It's very odd."

"Are there any side effects to this Benzedrine?" Hunter asked.

"Well, it's interesting that you would ask."

"Interesting how?"

"It's a stimulant," said Joan. "If it's taken in large doses, it can give you extra energy."

"Like, say, if you want to stay awake for long periods."

"Yes. Like a lot of coffee, only quite a bit stronger."

"And why is that interesting?"

"Well, Benzedrine has only been available for a couple years, but there are already stories of people misusing it for that very purpose. Taking it in excessive amounts for extra energy, to keep themselves sharp."

"But too much?"

"Well, too much can make you anxious, jittery," said Joan, holding up a hand and shaking it. "It can affect your judgment."

"What if someone took an awful lot?"

"Well, as I said, I'm not a pharmacist…"

Hunter shrugged. "Sure," he said. "Just a guess, though."

"Well, the drug is in powder form. There's a strip of paper inside the cylinder and it's coated with the powder. People looking for the kick will open up the cylinder, take out the paper, crumple it into a tiny ball and swallow it like a pill."

"Which would be far more than the typical dose for an asthma patient," said Hunter.

"Yes. And if someone were to consume the drug like this several times a day for a long period of time, it could lead to extreme mental instability. High levels of anxiety, short temper, maybe even a breakdown of some sort."

Hunter pondered the information for a moment. "Hm," he said finally. "I think I'll stick to coffee."

"Probably a good idea."

They were silent for a moment. She glanced down the hall toward the nurse's station again and then back at Hunter, leaning her head toward him slightly. Her voice was suddenly quieter. "Is this about… you know…Diamond?"

"It might be," said Hunter. "I'm a lawyer, not a detective. But I hear things and I ask questions. I try to figure things out."

"A lot of people are hoping you figure it out soon. I don't know if this city can take much more of that guy."

CHAPTER 33
CRIME JOURNAL

Hunter stepped into a meeting room just down the hall from Taggert's office shortly after seven-thirty the following morning. He'd slept very little, but he felt wide awake and his guard was up. Navigating through the next half-hour could prove to be tricky.

He'd driven himself and Buzz home from the hospital at about one-thirty. All the way home and for a good hour after they got there, Buzz had peppered him with even more questions about the mask: Did the goggles help his vision in the smoke? Did the heightened and accelerated mental activity tire him out? Any side effects that he could identify? By the time Hunter was able to shut him up and get some sleep, it was three a.m.

What sleep he did get was fitful, and it had been cut short by a six-o'clock phone call from Gallagher, asking him if Buzz was okay and telling him to get to the police department early for a briefing with Taggert and Dugan.

Gallagher was already in the room, pipe in hand, and just sitting down at the long table when Hunter walked in. Taggert was standing at the head of the table, shuffling through some papers in a file folder.

Bill Ferguson, the fire chief, came in a few paces behind Hunter with a folder under his arm. Pruett walked in right behind him. Ferguson looked fatigued, but his hair was neat and his uniform was crisp and pressed as always.

Hunter turned to Ferguson and the chief held out his hand.

"Good to see you, Jack," he said. "It's been a while." His voice carried an energy that seemed inconsistent with the circles under his eyes.

"It has," said Hunter. "What've you been up to?"

Ferguson frowned and gestured at the room and everyone in it. "Same thing you and Ed and the rest of us have been up to."

Hunter shook his head. "Don't I know it."

Everyone took seats, but Taggert remained standing. "Alright, let's get started," he said. "Mike's on his way. As you can probably guess, he had a hell of a night. He's taking a couple minutes to grab some coffee and get his notes together. He should be here shortly."

He turned to Ferguson. "In the meantime, Bill, tell us what we know about last night."

Ferguson cleared his throat. "We've had a team of investigators out at the warehouse since about two-thirty this morning," he said. "They're still gathering evidence, but I can already tell you that the scorch patterns on the floor and up the wall in the office space at the front of the building are a clear sign of some form of accelerant. We found kerosene lanterns in different parts of the building—some empty, some full, some whole, some in pieces. We found a broken one in the office space, so we're fairly certain that the accelerant was the kerosene."

"So can we call this arson?" said Gallagher, relighting his pipe.

Ferguson turned to the district attorney. "Good question," he said. "We know there were people in that building last night who were up to no good, but based on what you and Dugan have already told me since we sent the trucks to respond to the call last night, they were using that room in that building as a holding cell for a kidnapping victim." He paused and glanced at Hunter. "By the way, Jack, I'm really glad to hear your cousin made it out of there alright."

Hunter nodded.

Ferguson turned back toward Taggert and everyone else in the room. "So the question, then, is whether the fire was started intentionally, or was it just a mistake by some thugs who were in the middle of committing an entirely different crime. Hard to say at this point."

Taggert nodded. "How bad is the damage?"

"For the most part, it's limited to the southeast corner of the building—at the front, where that office was located. That portion is pretty well burned out, but we got the fire under control before it could spread to the rest of..."

Ferguson's voice trailed off as Dugan walked through the doorway and closed the door behind him. All eyes turned toward the detective, who carried a small stack of loose papers, legal pads and manila folders under one arm. His eyes were red-rimmed, with circles underneath, and Hunter noted that he was wearing the same clothes he'd been wearing at the hospital several hours earlier. His tie was loose and hanging below his unbuttoned collar, and he needed a shave. Yet, for all the signs of fatigue, he looked somehow energized at the same time.

"Good morning, gentlemen," he muttered, circling around the table to take a chair next to Taggert. "Sorry I'm late. Needless to say, I've had my hands full over the past several hours." He put the stack of materials on the conference table and pulled a pen from inside his jacket.

Taggert gestured toward Ferguson. "Bill was just telling us about the extent of the damage in the fire," he said. "What's the latest at your end?"

Dugan took a couple pages of handwritten notes off the top of his stack. "Well, I have some very new information, so I'm just going to jump right in, if it's alright with everybody."

Taggert raised his eyebrows and frowned, obviously intrigued by the promise of new information. "Certainly," he said. "You take it from here."

"I spoke with the four men from Diamond's operation who were brought into the emergency room last night. One of them is Rudy Ziglauer. His closest and dearest friends call him Zig. He had a gunshot wound to the right arm. Another was Jake Whitman, also known as Whitey. His face is a mess. Two others, Jerry Crane and George 'Bugs' Bucatelli, both got banged up pretty good too."

"Banged up how?" said Gallagher.

"Well," said Dugan, "when I saw them last night, aside from the smoke inhalation, they all looked like they'd come out on the losing end of a street brawl. Whitman had a mild concussion, and a hell of a lot of bruises on the side of his face, and a banged-up wrist. Crane and Bucatelli looked as though they'd taken a few punches as well. They didn't say much, really. The doctors had given both of them some painkillers that made them a little goofy, so some things weren't making much sense. But they also knew they didn't have to tell me much without a lawyer present."

"Mike," said Ferguson, "our investigators went through the whole building, not just the front where most of the fire damage took place. They said it looked like there was some trouble in the back of the warehouse too."

"Right. It appears there was some sort of scuffle there. We found a wooden table in pieces, a broken beer bottle, some broken lanterns, some packing crates in disarray."

Gallagher drew on his pipe. "Whoever was back there, are they accounted for?"

Dugan shook his head. "Don't know," he said. "We tried to get Diamond's men to tell us who else was in the building, but they're not talking."

Dugan's back straightened in his chair, and Hunter was fairly certain he saw the detective's chest puff out a bit. "But none of that matters," he went on, a hint of triumph creeping into his voice. "They can get all the lawyers they want. We've got something much better."

And out it came from the bottom of Dugan's stack of papers and folders—a ledger with an ornately tooled brown leather cover. The same one Hunter had taken from the burning warehouse just a few hours earlier.

Taggert eyed the ledger. He hadn't seen it yet. "What the hell is that?"

"It's the place where we turn the corner on this thing," said Dugan.

"I've only had a chance to look at it for a few minutes. It's a ledger that records money and goods and services going into and out of more than a dozen nightclubs. I haven't given it a thorough look yet, but it also includes lists of personnel, including one Nick Diamond."

Taggert gave Dugan a quizzical look. This was news, even to the chief.

"It was left just inside the door at the Third Precinct late last night," said Dugan. "Then someone made an anonymous call to tell the desk sergeant it was there."

Taggert looked uneasy, but Dugan pushed forward. The detective opened the ledger to a random page and pushed it across the table in Taggert's direction. "And we're not just talking about the usual legitimate expenses for food service and entertainment," said Dugan as the police chief thumbed through a few pages. "That's in there, sure, but there's plenty more."

Dugan stood up and leaned over Taggert's shoulder. "Page over to the middle section, Chief."

Taggert did so and took a moment to scan a random page filled with columns of numbers etched in neat handwriting. He shook his head and muttered, "Good Lord."

Gallagher looked back and forth between Taggert's face and the ledger. "What is it, Sam?"

"Gambling revenues," he said slowly, flipping a few pages forward from his starting point, then a few pages backward. "At least three months' worth, as far as I can tell." He flipped another page and scanned all the way to the bottom. "Close to a million dollars."

Pruett let out a whistle. Dugan turned to the consultant and addressed him directly. "You think that's something?" he said. "Here, you'll appreciate this even more." He leaned over Taggert's shoulder again and flipped the pages in the ledger to a section closer to the back of the book. "Like I said, I haven't had a chance to look at this very closely yet, Doc, but I recognized the stuff in this section right off the bat. I'm sure you will too."

Dugan straightened up and took a step back so Pruett could lean over from his chair and get a better look at still more columns, but of a different kind this time. Pruett frowned as he scanned the information. "These are…these are some very dangerous chemicals," he said after a moment. "Ammonium nitrate…hexanite…"

"The kind of stuff that's used to make explosives," said Hunter from across the table.

Taggert tilted his head in Pruett's direction. "Dr. Pruett's the expert here, but it sure looks that way to me."

Pruett nodded an affirmation.

"From the Pharaoh inventory," Gallagher suggested.

"Most likely," said Dugan.

"Sure," said Taggert, still scanning the page. "Hell, where else in this town would you find this stuff in these quantities? Or where else in this state, for that matter?"

"That's it," said Hunter, leaning forward, almost out of his chair. He jabbed a finger in the direction of the ledger and struggled to control the edge of excitement in his voice. "That book is everything. It's all there. It's all we need to take Diamond down. We just need to—"

"Wait a minute," said Taggert. A darker edge had suddenly entered his voice. It took the entire room and everyone in it by surprise. No one said a word as Taggert flipped deeper into the back pages and scanned the contents of each.

"These are..."

All eyes were on the chief of police. Dugan took a step forward to better see over his boss' shoulder.

After a moment, Gallagher said, "What is it, Sam?"

Taggert scanned another page and shook his head. "My God..."

"What?" said Hunter.

"Shipping schedules," Taggert muttered.

Gallagher leaned forward in his chair. "What kind of shipping?"

"Rail. From the West Coast. San Francisco."

"San Francisco?" said Hunter. "What the hell is he bringing in from—?"

"He's not the one bringing it in," said the chief.

"Sam, we're not following you," said Gallagher.

Taggert flipped a page. "Opium."

Hunter was almost out of his chair. "What!"

"Coming into the West Coast," said Taggert, "all the way from the Orient."

"So who's bringing it in from the West Coast?" said Gallagher.

"It appears to be part of some kind of arrangement with the Chinese."

"You mean the Chinese here?" said Hunter.

"Yes. I'm seeing rail schedules, quantities, drop points. Diamond apparently has established some kind of distribution agreement with the Ho Sheng Brotherhood here in Union City."

Gallagher's eyes widened. "The Ho Sheng?" he said. "Good Lord. They've been quiet since the end of the tong wars. And that's been what, almost twenty years now?"

"Quiet," said Taggert, "but apparently active." The chief went silent for a moment as he flipped to the last pages in the ledger that included any writing. He stopped at one page, blinked, and quickly flipped to the next. He flipped back to the previous page and scanned it again.

He shook his head and sighed. "There's more."

Gallagher frowned. "What?"

Taggert laid the open ledger on the tabletop, turned it around to face Gallagher and slid it across the oak surface in the DA's direction. "Women," said the chief. "A list of names."

Gallagher arched an eyebrow at Taggert, then drew the book toward him and scanned a few notes on an open page. After a moment he nodded.

"Quite a few, it would seem," said the DA.

"Prostitution," said Hunter.

"Looks that way," said Taggert.

"So the gambling is just the tip of the iceberg," said Gallagher. "Nicky Diamond is building a narcotics and prostitution network in Union City."

CHAPTER 34
ANONYMOUS ALLY

Hunter leaned forward. "Ed, can I see that for a minute."

Gallagher slid the book across the table toward Hunter but turned his attention toward Dugan. "How'd you say you got hold of this?"

"Uh, that's a good question," said Dugan. "Like I said, it was delivered."

The five other men in the room looked at him with quizzical expressions.

"Delivered how?" said Taggert. "By whom?"

Hunter kept his eyes on the ledger as he flipped through a series of pages that included a list of restaurants and nightclubs. There were many.

"We don't know," said Dugan. "Brooks, the overnight dispatcher at the Third Precinct, said the phone call came in at about eleven-twenty p.m. The caller didn't identify himself and didn't stay on long. But apparently he told Brooks there was something in the vestibule of the front entrance to the precinct that we might want to see, something that could be help us get a handle on Diamond."

"This caller," said Gallagher. "He mentioned Diamond by name?"

"Yeah. Brooks said those were the guy's exact words. 'Something that could help us get a handle on Nicky Diamond.'"

Taggert shook his head. "More mysteries," he said. "Okay, go on."

"So Brooks told Stover, the sergeant on duty for the eleven-to-seven shift. Well, given the mention of Diamond, and all the talk about him in the past couple days, Stover said he thought for a minute about the possibility of a trap." Dugan tilted his head in Ferguson's direction. "He actually gave some thought to calling in some the fellas from the fire department and having them bring some protective gear, but he realized that most of the fire crew on duty was busy at the Watt Building, so he went to the entrance and checked it out himself. Said he felt better when all he saw was a book laying on the floor behind a potted plant, but even then, he was a little twitchy for a few seconds when he pulled it out. In the end, obviously, nothing unpleasant happened."

"Any prints?" said Taggert.

"I had it checked. Unfortunately, there are prints all over it, so much that nothing is clear. But there's no question that it's been in or near some kind of a fire. The thing reeks of smoke."

"And given the events of the past several hours and the contents of the ledger," said Taggert, "I don't think it's too hard to guess exactly which fire it had been in."

"So presumably," said Gallagher, "someone who'd been at the fire got a hold of the ledger and brought it to the Third Precinct."

Hunter continued flipping through the ledger and remained quiet. He wanted to avoid this path, but he knew the conversation was headed straight for it.

Taggert rubbed his chin. "I wonder," he said, "if that has anything to do with that story that Diamond's four goons were telling in the hospital."

And here it comes, thought Hunter.

"What story is that?" said Gallagher.

"Some crazy stuff about a guy with a mask who showed up at the scene and started a brawl with them just before the fire started," said Taggert. "One of them even said the guy had something to do with the lanterns catching fire."

Gallagher responded with a quizzical face. "Wait a minute. What? A guy wearing a mask?"

Dugan shook his head wearily, as though he were already growing tired of trying to explain it. "I don't know, Chief," the detective sighed, carefully dodging the district attorney's question and keeping his focus on his boss. "When Ziglauer mentioned it, I just chalked it up to some kind of hallucination. Maybe too much smoke or something. But then the other three told me a similar stories in separate conversations, which makes me wonder."

"Well, if you want some kind of a decision about arson," said Ferguson, "it would be good to have more information about whether there really was such a person at the scene when the fire started. If he was part of Diamond's operation—"

"How would he be one of Diamond's men?" said Taggert. "We have four of Diamond's men in the hospital telling us that this guy—whoever he is, if he even exists at all—roughed them up pretty good, maybe even shot them. That doesn't sound to me like a member of the gang."

Hunter closed the ledger and slid it across the table toward Dugan. "Mike mentioned all of this last night at the hospital when he stopped by to ask Buzz some questions," he said. "I wouldn't put too much stock in it. Buzz said he didn't see anything like that, and I'd take his word over any of those guys."

"Well, sure, I would too," said Dugan. "But we also know that Buzz had a blindfold on for part of the time that he was there. Then he took a lump on the head, and he said he was knocked out for a few minutes."

Hunter glanced at Gallagher sitting to his right, and then back at Taggert and Dugan across the table. "Well, you fellas are the detectives," he said. "But the way I see it, there was a fire, there was some shooting, it was dark, there was the sound of sirens coming down the street. Hell, it must've been chaos in that place for at least a few minutes, maybe longer. Who knows what these goons saw—or what they think they saw?"

Out of the corner of his eye, Hunter saw Gallagher nodding in agreement through a thin haze of pipe smoke. Emboldened by this silent gesture of concurrence, Hunter leaned forward in his chair and pressed his point further.

"I don't have any idea what happened in that warehouse last night," he said. "I don't know that any one of us does, and as far as I can tell from what we know—and what we don't know—it may take us days to sort it all out. But the fact of the matter is that four men from Diamond's operation have been handed to us somehow. We already have them on kidnapping charges at least, but I'm sure we could get a lot more out of them if we pushed them. And not only that, we have a book full of names and numbers that throws a lot of light on Diamond's operation. Whatever happened last night, I suggest we take advantage of the opportunity."

Gallagher looked at the police chief and the detective and jerked a thumb toward his assistant. "For now, at least, I have to agree with Jack," he said. "Every hour we spend trying to reconstruct exactly what happened in that warehouse last night is an hour that Diamond can plan his next move. I think we're better off combing through that ledger and seeing if there are any clues in there as to what that next move might be—and maybe, God forbid, seeing if we can get ourselves a step ahead of him for a change."

The room was silent for a moment as Taggert weighed the attorneys' input. "I agree," he said finally. He turned to Dugan and tapped a forefinger on the book. "How fast can we get the contents of this thing transcribed and made into five or six copies? I have to believe that if you and a couple of your men—and the rest of us—could all look at this information at the same time, we might start to see some patterns."

Dugan paused to consider. "Well, if we want to do it quickly, we'd need to put somebody on it full time."

Gallagher glanced at Hunter. Each knew exactly what the other was thinking: Betty Carlyle. "We have a girl here who's very good," said

Gallagher. "She's sharp and she's fast. She could type up everything in that ledger in less than two days."

Pruett cleared his throat, tilting his chin at the ledger on the table in front of Taggert. "There's probably quite a bit of chemistry in that book," he said. "I'm sure I could help her with some of the technical information that might not be clear to her."

Taggert looked at Gallagher. "Can we borrow her for a couple days?"

The district attorney nodded. "We'll get her work reassigned and then bring her over right after lunch."

"Fine," said Taggert. He gestured to Dugan and Pruett and said, "We'll put her in the same office where Dr. Pruett is set up and they can get started this afternoon."

Hunter turned the conversation in a different direction. "Alright, let me ask this again," he said. "Do we have any leads as to where the hell Diamond is right now?"

"We don't," said Dugan. "There was some evidence to suggest that he'd been using The Paramount Club—Dutch Markowitz's place—as a front for his headquarters. But if that was ever the case, it isn't now."

Hunter leaned forward in his chair. "Wait a minute," he said. "I was just..." He caught himself at the last second and exchanged a quick glance with Gallagher, who had been flipping through the ledger. "What do you mean it isn't the case now?"

Dugan looked down at his notes. "As of this morning, Markowitz has had a sign up on the entrance saying the place is closed until further notice. No activity, no traffic in or out, no lights, nothing."

"It doesn't matter," said Gallagher, his eyes fixed on a page in the ledger. "The Paramount is just one of more than twenty establishments listed in this book. Before we even start talking about transcribing the contents, I can take this to a judge and probably get a warrant before the end of the day."

The DA looked up at Dugan and Taggert. "Sam, if we play this right, you should be able to start making some arrests tonight and shut a whole bunch of places down in the process."

"As far as I'm concerned," said Dugan, "the entire Diamond case is in that book. If you can get us legal access to any or all of those places, we could be on our way."

"I'll get over to Reynolds' office as soon as possible," said Gallagher.

The meeting adjourned. For the first time in days, everyone left the room with an extra measure of energy in their stride.

CHAPTER 35
RELOCATION

Gallagher came to Hunter's door shortly after lunch. "Betty's heading over to the police department in a few minutes," said Gallagher, tilting his head toward the outer hallway. "She's filling a box with office supplies right now. It's only a couple blocks, but I don't want her lugging that stuff the whole way. Can you make sure someone calls her a cab?"

"Oh," said Hunter. "Well, I'm…I can give her a ride myself." He rose from his chair abruptly and crossed the room to the coat rack in the corner.

Gallagher arched an eyebrow and looked back at him.

"What?" said Hunter.

Gallagher shook his head. "Nothing," he said. "Not a thing."

Hunter slipped into his jacket and shot his cuffs.

"She's at her desk," said Gallagher as Hunter passed him in the doorway. "I don't think you'll have time to put on a tux."

Hunter stopped short and shot Gallagher a quick glare. Gallagher responded with a shrug as Hunter moved on and headed down the hall.

He found Betty at her desk, arranging items in a box—notebooks, stapler, paperweight and various other incidentals. "Hi, Betty," he said. He was vaguely aware of the surreptitious glances from three other secretaries seated at nearby desks.

Betty looked up. "Oh. Hello, Jack." Her hand drifted to her forehead to adjust a lock of hair.

Hunter cleared his throat. "Can I give you a ride to the police department?"

"Oh, that's…I wouldn't want to trouble you. I can call a cab."

"No, it's no trouble at all."

She smiled. She had enormous eyes. "Thank you," she said. "That's very kind of you."

Hunter shook his head. "Really, it's no trouble."

"Alright. I'm just about ready." She turned her attention back to the box and tucked a cup full of pens and pencils into the last available corner. She scanned the contents of the box for a moment and shrugged. "Well, I guess that's everything."

"Well, if you've forgotten anything, I can...I mean, I'm sure someone can bring it over to you."

"I'm sure I'll be fine."

"Here," said Hunter, lifting the box and tucking it under one arm. "Let me take it for you."

Betty turned to the other secretaries and waved. "Well, girls, I guess I'll see you all in a couple days."

All three women smiled back at her, but Hunter noticed that they were looking at him as well, as though he and Betty were the subjects of a pleasant looking photograph. He cleared his throat again and used his free hand to put on his hat. He nodded to the women. "I won't be long," he said, gesturing toward the elevator. "I'll be back in about a half hour."

Hunter turned and ushered Betty down the hallway. He was fairly certain he heard whispering behind him as they went.

At the elevator door, a man in a black uniform tipped his cap to Hunter and Betty. Hunter smiled at him. "Hello, Woodrow."

The elevator man smiled back. "Afternoon, Mister Hunter. Ma'am. Going down?"

"Yes," said Hunter. "To the lobby."

"Very good, sir."

The doors closed. Woodrow tilted the lever and the elevator car began its gentle descent.

The silence inside the elevator made Hunter uncomfortable. He turned to Betty. "My car is right at the curb," he said. "I parked it there after lunch. I can have you there in five minutes."

"Thank you. It's awfully kind of you."

Hunter shook his head and said, "It's really no trouble." He was suddenly aware that it was the third time he'd said it in the last five minutes, and he wondered if he sounded silly.

He watched her face from the corner of his eye. Her expression darkened suddenly, and she bit her lip.

"Did you forget something?"

"Oh, no. I just hope the girls can manage the work without me."

"I'm sure they'll be fine," said Hunter. "But I'll be…I mean, I'm sure they'll be glad when you're back. I really can't imagine this taking more than a couple days. Taggert and Dugan just want someone who's sharp enough to transcribe all the information from that ledger." He paused. "And we—I mean Ed and I—we think you're the best."

The remark felt clumsy. But Betty turned to him and smiled, and he felt a little less awkward.

Her smile faded quickly as she looked back at the elevator door. "Are they sure it's Diamond's ledger?" she said.

Hunter shrugged. "Really not much doubt."

"I heard it was left at the Third Precinct."

"Apparently so. I guess there was some kind of anonymous call to tell the police it had been left inside the door."

"Goodness. That sounds mysterious. Well, I hope they catch him soon. He makes me nervous."

Hunter smiled, and she looked back at him through a furrowed brow.

"Why are you smiling?" she said. "He makes a lot of people nervous."

"Oh, I know he does. He makes me nervous, too. Actually, he makes me more angry than nervous. But what you said just now…I just met a nurse last night who said something very similar."

"Oh."

The elevator car came to a gentle stop. The door opened to the lobby and main entrance to the building at the far end. Woodrow said, "Here we are, sir. Ma'am."

Hunter tipped his hat to Woodrow as he and Betty exited the elevator, and Woodrow returned the gesture to both passengers with his usual smile. Hunter and Betty crossed the lobby to the entrance, where Hunter opened the door for Betty with his free hand.

They made their way down the stone steps. Betty said, "Was she nice?"

"Beg your pardon?"

"The nurse," she said. "Was she nice?"

Hunter turned to look at Betty but her eyes were averted, apparently focused on navigating the stairs in her heels. "She was," he said. "She took good care of my cousin in the emergency room." He gestured to his car at the curb, to the left of the steps. "I'm over here."

They reached the sidewalk, and Betty headed for Hunter's car. He stepped ahead of her and opened the passenger door.

"I heard about him," she said. "Your cousin, I mean. I hope he's doing okay. That must have been a horrible time for him last night."

"He's doing fine. Buzz can be pretty tough. I had to make him promise me he'd keep his shop closed today and take the day off."

Betty folded herself into the front seat. "I can take the box in my lap."

"Oh, no," said Hunter. "You'd be uncomfortable. I'll put it in the back." He opened the back door and slid the box onto the seat, then closed the door and made his way around to the other side of the car.

Less than a minute later, Hunter was negotiating through afternoon traffic and heading west on Liberty Avenue toward the main police headquarters. It was barely three blocks, but there was a traffic light at every intersection, and the streetcars and pedestrian traffic added to the stop-and-go of the ride.

"This last week or so," said Betty, her voice tentative. "Has it been difficult?"

"How do you mean?"

"I mean all this about Diamond."

"Oh," he said with a shrug. "Well, there's a lot to chase down. Ed and I have been putting in some late hours. A lot of meetings with the police. We're trying to build a case, and up until this morning, the evidence has only been—"

"No, I mean, has it been hard to..." her voice trailed off.

"I'm not sure I follow you."

Betty paused. "I don't want to pry," she said finally. "But I remember the awful story. I was only thirteen at the time, but I remember it. The police officer who was killed in the Justice Center in the middle of the night. He had a wife and a...a son who was just eighteen, just finished with high school and getting ready to start college. I remember thinking how awful it must have been for that young man to lose his father."

"Oh."

"And now all this again. And I can't help but think how hard it must be for that...for you."

"Well..."

"I'm sorry. I don't mean to...Maybe you don't like to talk about it."

"No, it's…You're right. Sometimes I don't. But not always. I guess it just depends on who I'm talking to."

Their eyes locked for several seconds.

The moment was cut short by the blare of a horn from the car behind them. Hunter jerked in his seat and abruptly turned his attention back toward the street, where the traffic signal had turned green.

"I guess I need to watch the road," he muttered.

◆　◆　◆　◆

Five minutes later they were stepping through the front entrance to police headquarters. Hunter had his left arm wrapped around Betty's box of office supplies.

The desk sergeant looked up at Hunter through the large rectangular opening in the wall that separated the entranceway from the headquarters interior. "Well, here comes some riff-raff."

"And who would know riff-raff better than you?" said Hunter.

The officer glanced past Hunter and got a look at Betty. He immediately cleaned up his delivery. "Oh, uh, good afternoon, miss," he said, sliding off his chair and stepping around the desk. He straightened his tie and smoothed it along the front of his shirt. "I'm Tony," he said to Betty. "Tony Mancuso." He tipped his hat and jerked a thumb in Hunter's direction. "Say, this wise guy isn't harassing you, is he?"

Betty smiled. "No," she said. "Not yet, anyway."

"Cuz if he gives you any trouble, you know, we can—"

Betty laughed before Mancuso could finish the threat. Hunter rolled his eyes. "Okay, flatfoot, hold your fire," he said. "This is Betty Carlyle. She works with Gallagher and me and the rest of us in the DA's office. So obviously she's surrounded by jokers all day long. The last thing she needs is one more."

Mancuso smiled and stuck his hand out. "Pleased to meet you, Miss Carlyle. Glad to see you making your way up to a higher class joint."

"Pleased to meet you, Sergeant."

"Call me Tony. Hey, we heard you were coming and we fixed up the room for you. Follow me." He turned away from Betty and Hunter, beckoning them with a wave of his hand as he started down a long hallway that branched off into other hallways, offices, meeting rooms, interrogation rooms and cubby holes that made up the administrative area of the police department's primary headquarters. The two visitors fell in step alongside him.

"It's all the way at the end here," he said, gesturing to the far end of the corridor. "Kinda off the beaten path, so it'll be quiet." Hunter glanced down a side corridor that branched off to the left and led to the dispatch room as Mancuso kept up his narrative. "Not too many ladies here to give it the feminine touch," he said, "but we cleaned it up pretty good."

He turned to Betty as they walked. "One thing's for sure," he said. "As long as you're here, you'll be the safest dame…er, the safest lady in Union City."

"Glad to hear it," said Betty. "Somebody has to keep the wise guys away."

Mancuso looked at Hunter and smiled. He pointed a thumb in Betty's direction. "See?" he said. "She knows the score."

They reached the end of the hallway and turned right into a room that wasn't much to write home about—cinderblock walls, tiled floors and minimal furniture. There were two desks, one of which was already covered with papers and several manila folders. There were several books on the desk, one of them open to a page showing fine print and chemical diagrams.

A couple bookshelves stood along the far wall, and several boxes had been pushed to one side. Clearly, the place had been used as a storage space before Pruett had arrived few days earlier.

"Pruett's not around?" said Hunter.

"No, he's probably in that utility room he's using as his lab," said Mancuso with a shrug.

"I've seen the place," said Hunter. "Quite a setup."

Mancuso shook his head. "I'll say. I can't make heads or tails of half the stuff he's doing." He pointed to a second desk arranged opposite Pruett's. Its surface was clean and uncluttered, save for a felt blotter and a typewriter. "Miss Carlyle, this'll be your desk. Jack, you can put her things right—"

"Afternoon, Miss Carlyle." Hunter and Betty turned toward the voice coming from the doorway behind them.

"Chief Taggert," said Betty as Taggert stepped into the room and shook her hand. "How nice to see you."

"The pleasure's all mine. And please call me Sam. Thank you so much for giving up some of your time for this."

"Oh, it's no trouble."

"If you're half as efficient as they tell me you are, I'm sure we can wrap this up in just a couple days. Certainly by the end of the week."

"Well, I hope no one did any false advertising. I'll certainly do my best."

Taggert looked around the room. "Dr. Pruett's been using this room for a few days now," he said. "We rearranged some things so we could make more room for you. Not sure where he is right now, but I'm sure he'll be around. He said he'd be happy to help you with any of the technical information in the ledger. You know, the chemistry and whatnot."

He looked back at Betty and shrugged. "Probably not the fanciest room in the building," he said, "but we're a little short on space. If there's anything you need, be sure and let one of the boys know."

"Oh, I'm sure I'll be fine," said Betty.

Taggert turned to Mancuso. "Tony, make sure she gets settled in okay."

"Sure thing, Chief."

Taggert left the room as Betty started unloading the box of supplies.

"Well, Betty, I'll be on my way," said Hunter. "You be sure and let the fellas know if you need anything. Or call us. I can drive over anytime."

Betty stopped what she was doing and looked up at him. "I'll do that, Jack. Thanks so much for the ride over."

"Sure thing," he said. He jerked a thumb at Mancuso, who was still in the room and hovering a few feet away. "And watch out for the wise guys."

Less than two minutes later, Hunter was heading back out to his car under a bright blue sky. Despite the persistent weight of the Diamond case, he couldn't help but notice what a beautiful day it was.

CHAPTER 36
STONEWALL

Gallagher came to Hunter's office at a couple minutes after four o'clock and stood in the open doorway. "You got a minute?"

Hunter looked up. "Sure."

Gallagher stepped in and closed the door behind him. It wasn't quite a slam, but it was close to it. Hunter watched his face as he settled into a chair opposite the desk. Something was wrong.

"What is it?" He kept his voice even, watching Gallagher's eyes, wondering if something had unraveled in the last few hours and his involvement in the warehouse episode had been suddenly exposed.

Gallagher looked away and said nothing for a long moment. His eyes were narrowed slightly and his jaw was tight.

Hunter waited.

"Reynolds," Gallagher said finally.

"Anthony Reynolds," Hunter prompted.

"Yes."

"What about him?"

"He won't issue the warrant," said Gallagher.

"What!"

The DA frowned and shook his head. "Won't do it."

"What the hell…?"

"Says the ledger is inadmissible as evidence, because the means by which it was obtained are questionable."

"Oh, that son of a…" Hunter tossed his pen on his desk. It bounced across the blotter and came to a stop next to a short stack of papers. "That's legal pussyfooting, Ed. That's cowardice based on a technicality, and it'll set us back weeks."

Hunter bit back on what he really wanted to say—about how he had literally walked through fire, not to mention a hail of bullets, to get the ledger and deliver it to the police.

"He even went so far as to suggest that—depending on one's interpretation of the circumstances surrounding the acquisition of the ledger, and depending on one's interpretation of the laws pertaining to theft—the ledger could even be considered stolen property."

Hunter seethed. "Godammit," he rasped. "Does he not realize that

209

all the information we need to get Diamond is in that book?"

Gallagher arched an eyebrow and leveled his gaze directly at Hunter. "Well, now," he said, "that's an interesting question, isn't it?"

Hunter looked back at his boss. He inhaled deeply and sat back in his chair. Neither man spoke for a long moment as Hunter contemplated what may have been a very significant piece of a frustrating puzzle.

After nearly a full minute of silence, Hunter was the first to speak. "Anthony Reynolds," he said slowly. "How long has he been on the bench now?"

"Twenty years," said Gallagher. "Almost exactly. Twenty years next month."

"Twenty years. That takes us all the way back to the good old days."

"Yeah," Gallagher sighed in frustration. "Back to the good old days."

Hunter paused, choosing his words carefully. "I've often wondered about that guy."

"I think a lot of people have. I know I have. For years." Gallagher spoke slowly, measuring his words just as carefully. "Some of the questionable decisions from the bench, some of the lenient sentences … There've been times along the way when some of it just didn't quite add up."

The room was silent again as both men pondered the implications of what they were suggesting. For as unofficial and confidential as the conversation may have been, Hunter felt as though they'd latched onto a dangerous thread.

But Gallagher apparently wasn't afraid to follow it. "We've been speculating for a while now about who might be tipping Diamond off to police activity," he said. "Maybe we've been thinking too small. Maybe Diamond's network includes someone higher up."

Hunter picked up the pen he'd tossed and turned it in his fingers. He stared at the instrument as it turned in his hand, and the inner wheels of his mind turned with it. "Maybe someone like a judge," he said.

Gallagher frowned and stared into the distance for a moment. "Maybe someone like a judge."

CHAPTER 37
MAX GETS THE STORY

It was seven p.m. when Hunter walked into Angie's Diner. It was just a block from his apartment, and the preferred breakfast spot for him and Buzz on any given weekday morning. At this hour, Angie herself would have gone home for the day, but her younger sister, Dolores, was behind the counter for her usual evening shift.

Dolores looked up and smiled. "Hiya, Jack." She had a sort of Myrna Loy look about her, especially when she smiled.

Hunter smiled back and waved. "Hey, darling. What's new?"

"You know. Just doing what I can to feed the city." She tilted her head toward a booth along the window where Bart Maxwell was sitting in front of a plate of meatloaf and looking up at him. "Coffee?" she said.

"Sure."

Hunter moved across the diner to the booth and settled in opposite Max. Dolores was just two steps behind him with the coffee pot, and she filled Hunter's cup before he even had his hat off.

"Something to eat, Jack?" she said.

Hunter gestured at Max's plate. "I'll have what he's having."

"But he won't look half as good as me when he's having it," said Max.

Dolores turned to Max and silenced him with a withering stare. For a brief moment, Hunter thought she might pour hot coffee directly into Max's lap.

"Have that for you in a minute, Jack," she muttered, her evil eye still fixed on Max. Then she turned and headed back to the kitchen.

Max watched her walk away. "Is it me, or is it chilly in here?"

"Trust me, it's you."

Max took a gulp of coffee. "Hey, I heard about your cousin. He okay?"

Hunter shrugged. "He's fine," he said. "I think he got a little rattled, although he still won't admit it. And he scared the hell out of me. But he'll be okay."

Max nodded and went back to his meatloaf. "Nice place," he said. "I'd heard the food was good. I'd heard right."

"And more importantly, you figured I'd pay for it."

Max shrugged. "You keep calling me and looking for information, it's going to cost you."

"Right. But if I start *giving* you information, I can stop buying you lunch." Hunter glanced down at Max's plate. "And dinner." He took a sip of coffee. "Think of this as my way of balancing the scales of justice."

"Clever," said Max. "You being a lawyer and an assistant DA."

Hunter glanced around the room and lowered his voice. "Alright," he said. "Everything that gets said at this table is off the record."

Max looked at him without answering.

"And everything that gets said at this table," Hunter added, "stays under your hat for about twelve hours."

"Okay." Max's voice went up a little, as though he were agreeing to the terms with some degree of reluctance.

"That stuff about Diamond that everyone's afraid to talk about? I think I can tell you why."

Max leaned forward slightly. "I'm listening," he said.

"The gambling and the racketeering are just a part of Diamond's operation. The picture is actually much bigger—big enough to stretch from here to China. I can't say for sure, but my guess it that the racketeering is a means to generate revenue for other aspects of his operation that he's still developing."

"When you say from here to China, what do you mean?"

"I mean just what I said."

"You're talking in riddles, Jack."

"Because there's plenty I don't know," said Hunter. "But here's what I can tell you. The police and the DA's office have intercepted an extremely helpful piece of evidence—a record of transactions that include a hell of a lot more than just gambling receipts from nightclub operations."

"Okay," said Max, looking as though he had a million questions.

"Diamond has a supply line of opium coming into Union City."

Max looked back at Hunter for a silent moment, then let out a low whistle.

Hunter kept talking. "Presumably, it's coming all the way from China into San Francisco," he said. "And then from San Francisco to Union City. The point of entry here—"

"Would be Chinatown," said Max.

"Precisely."

"There's more, unfortunately. The Chinese aren't just supplying dope. They're also helping to recruit women—working girls—for a prostitution ring that Diamond is also running."

"Jesus."

"Now, from what I can gather, it's early yet," said Hunter. "But history has shown us that Diamond prefers to be in control, and he's not the kind of guy who likes to share, so this may not be a permanent arrangement. My guess is that he's working in conjunction with the Chinese because he has to. They can provide him with resources he can't get elsewhere just yet.

"The dope or the women, or both," said Max. "Do you know any customers by name? Any names I'd know?"

"There's a list, but the information is brand new. It just came in this morning, and I haven't had a good look yet. I just glanced at a few pages of something during a meeting."

"So if I'm hearing you right," said Max, "this could be enough to connect everything and put Diamond away."

Hunter snorted and shook his head. "You'd like to think so."

Max looked at him for a moment. "But?"

"It should be enough to secure search warrants at numerous establishments and arrest warrants for numerous individuals, but Anthony Reynolds won't cooperate."

Max kept searching Hunter's face, waiting for more.

"We showed him this evidence and he balked on a technicality," Hunter went on. "Said the means by which it was acquired were questionable."

"How was it acquired?"

"It was delivered anonymously to the Third Precinct."

"What?"

Hunter shrugged. "It's a long story, but it doesn't matter."

"Okay," said Max, "so Diamond is bringing dope in all the way from China, through San Francisco and into our own Chinatown neighborhood in Union City. And Chinatown is providing working girls as well for a prostitution operation. So who the hell is Diamond dealing with in Chinatown to get all this? I mean, that neighborhood's been quiet for years. There hasn't been any trouble there since..." His voice trailed off and he raised an eyebrow.

"Go on," said Hunter.

"The Ho Sheng?"

"The record of transactions certainly points to that."

"Hell, do they even exist anymore?" said Max. "I mean, I remember hearing about them when I was a kid, before the war. But that all came to an end after the tong wars."

"Remember the name Sun Lu?"

"The unofficial mayor of Chinatown," said Max. "Owns an import store just off Lotus Street."

Hunter nodded. "I know the place."

"Lives in an apartment up above the store," Max went on. "Guy's about a hundred and fifty years old, isn't he?"

Hunter nodded again. "Eighty-one," he said. "He was a high ranking member of the Ho Sheng back in the old days. He kept a low profile, even at the height of the tong wars, but I remember my father mentioning his name to my mother now and then when I was a kid."

Dolores brought Hunter's plate in one hand and a coffee pot in the other. She put the plate down in front of him and refilled his cup. She asked him if he needed anything else but he smiled and waved her off.

She turned to Max and a layer of frost formed instantly. "You?" she said.

He held out his cup. Dolores refilled it begrudgingly, then turned and walked away.

"She's crazy about me," said Max.

"Clearly."

"So you mentioned warrants," said Max. "If Reynolds had come through, where were you planning to start?"

"The Paramount. I never doubted your information. And even if other people did, the Paramount is in Diamond's book—which is the kind of hard evidence that makes your tip much more believable to the skeptics."

Max frowned and shook his head. "Doesn't make any difference now."

"I heard," said Hunter. "Whoever was there has cleared out as of this morning."

"Looks that way."

Hunter shook his head, doing his best to suppress a wave of frustration.

Max read the expression and steered the conversation in a different direction. "Anthony Reynolds," he said, looking straight at Hunter.

"Yeah," said Hunter. "Anthony Reynolds."

Max let the name hang in the air for a moment. "You think he's…"

"I wouldn't rule it out," said Hunter.

Max stared back at him, poker faced. Hunter guessed he probably had an opinion of his own about Reynolds, but he was being a smart reporter and not letting on.

"You remember the other day," said Hunter, "when we were walking from the Justice center to the plaza at lunch time?"

"Yeah."

"You remember when I saw Reynolds getting into a big black car at the curb?"

"Yeah."

"It was a Buick."

"So?"

"So the car that Diamond's men brought to the shop to pick up Buzz? It was a Buick."

Max shrugged. His expression was skeptical. "Lotta Buicks in Union City."

"You're right. There are. But the fact remains, Reynolds got picked up in a Buick the other day. Buzz got picked up in a Buick yesterday."

Max shrugged again, but Hunter saw something in his eyes. The reporter may have been skeptical, but he wasn't completely dismissing the coincidence either.

"You've been covering this town for a long time, Maxie. You know the game and you know all the players. There's a lot you've already seen and a lot you already know, so I don't have to explain it to you. And Anthony Reynolds…" His voice trailed off.

"Is Anthony Reynolds."

Hunter started eating while Max did some chewing of a different kind.

Between bites of meatloaf, Hunter walked him through the process. "Every time the police planned a search or a raid, they needed a warrant," he said. "And every time they needed a warrant, they went to Reynolds. And every time they got the warrant from Reynolds and went into a place, it was a bust. The place was either clear of any solid evidence or just completely empty. And now that the police have some very solid evidence pointing directly to specific places and people, Reynolds doesn't feel comfortable about issuing a warrant at all."

Max took it all in. He pushed his empty plate away and took a sip of coffee. For nearly a full minute, he stared silently out the window, watching the dusk settle in over the city. "I've wondered about that guy for a long time," he said finally, still staring out the window.

Hunter almost laughed. "I said pretty much the same thing to Gallagher just a few hours ago."

"I've heard speculation and whisper for years," said Max. "Nothing you can substantiate, but plenty that makes you wonder. The suggestion of bribes and kickbacks, the appearances in public with persons of less than sterling reputation."

"Trust me," said Hunter, "from where Gallagher and I sit, it doesn't look any less questionable."

"Okay, so say all this speculation is true," said Max. "Or even some of it. Say Reynolds has a long-standing association with the criminal element in this city. And then along comes Nicky Diamond, looking to regain a foothold."

"It would stand to reason that Reynolds is connected to him in some way," said Hunter. "Hell, it would be foolish to think otherwise. For all we know, he may have been cozy with Diamond back in his Prohibition days."

Hunter took a bite of meatloaf, which apparently gave Max the signal to pursue a different line of questioning. "Hey, I heard something else about that business at the Watt Building last night. What's this about a guy in a mask who may have helped the police break up the party?"

Hunter smirked and shook his head. "What, you mean those stories from Diamond's four goons in the hospital?" he said. "I heard some of that from Dugan. Sounds to me like they got too much smoke." Hunter shrugged. "I wouldn't get too caught up in it. Buzz was there, right in the middle of it, and he says he didn't see or hear anything like that. I'll take his word over anybody else's."

Hunter finished eating. He got one last refill from Dolores, along with the check.

"That talk about keeping this to myself for twelve hours," Max said. "What's that all about?"

"Consider it background for what's coming," said Hunter. "I think things are going to start breaking very soon." Despite the long day and its setbacks, Hunter felt energized, optimistic. He chalked it up to Dolores' coffee.

He started reaching for the check, but Max beat him to it.

"I got this one, Jack."

◆　◆　◆　◆

Less than ten minutes later, Hunter pulled into the garage behind the Republic Building. He took one last look into the rapidly darkening sky as he threw the switch to close the automatic door.

He entered the building through the rear passageway and immediately headed down to the basement. He was just about certain he'd find Buzz in the sub-basement, and he was right. As he reached the bottom of the basement stairs, he caught the glow from the doorway leading down to the subterranean workshop.

Hunter crossed the room and descended the second flight of stairs, moving a little faster this time, even if he wasn't sure why. He heard Buzz's voice before he even got to the bottom.

"Hiya, Jack," he said, cheery as ever.

Hunter reached the bottom step and saw Buzz at his workbench, the place where he felt the most comfortable and the most at home. The place where he was supposed to be.

"Hiya, Buzz. You feeling okay?"

"Who, me? Oh, yeah." He stood up from his chair and faced Hunter. "Hey, I kept the shop closed and took the day off like you told me to. I think it was a good idea. I was a little jumpy this morning, but I feel a lot better now."

"Good to hear it," said Hunter. But his mind was racing to other things, and his own voice sounded as if it were coming from someone else in the room.

Buzz may have been back where he belonged, but there was still plenty about his city that was out of place and headed in the wrong direction. He was tired of pussyfooting around with a case that was moving too slow. There was work to be done.

And the night was still young.

Hunter's eyes were drawn to a small table in the corner of the room. On top of the table was the mask, mounted on a post and staring back at him, its evenly spaced row of photoelectric cells bathing in the glow of a high-intensity reading lamp.

He loosened his tie and unbuttoned his collar. "Got that thing charged up?"

Buzz followed Hunter's gaze. "What, you mean the mask?" he said. "Oh, yeah. It's been charging all day."

"Get it ready," said Hunter. "I'm going back out."

CHAPTER 38
DANNY'S BOY

Hunter revved the Henderson through the back streets of the entertainment district. Nearly fifteen hours earlier, he'd spent only a minute or two flipping through Diamond's ledger during the meeting with Taggert and Dugan that morning, but it was all the time he'd needed. Sure enough, he'd found all three of the of the nightclubs Max had scratched on a piece of paper for him a couple days before—Danny's Tavern, The Caribbean Club, The Sterling Palace. There were many others in the ledger, but he chose to start with Max's three leads. Regardless of their relative size, if the word among the reporter's well-cultivated network of sources pointed to these three places, they were likely to be hot spots.

At the very least, he'd force a few rats out of their nests before the night was over. And if he happened to run into the head rat along the way, all the better.

He started small and worked his way up. His first stop was Danny's Tavern, a small joint on Clifford Boulevard, a short street that came off West Eighteenth. It was a tired-looking place owned and operated by a surly proprietor named Danny Malone. Danny had opened the place three years earlier, right after Prohibition ended.

Hunter had heard stories from the police over the years about recurring bar fights at Danny's. Even one or two all-out brawls that had spilled out of the building and onto the street. Given his history, Malone was lucky to have hung onto his liquor license and his lease as long as he had. Running a gambling operation in partnership with the most notorious criminal in the city's history would bring all that to an end. Hunter would make sure of it.

He parked the motorcycle in an alley two blocks from Malone's place and covered the rest of the distance on foot. He snaked his way through the shadows, behind buildings and beyond the reach of the streetlamps along Clifford Boulevard. In less than two minutes, he was creeping along a pair of trash dumpsters along the back wall of Malone's place.

The tavern was a freestanding building, small in comparison with most of the other establishments along the same strip. The interior glow from the ground floor windows along the sides and back of the building cut into the darkness outside, but not enough to leave Hunter completely exposed. There were still corners and recesses where he could stay covered and out of sight.

Regardless of any light or activity on the main floor, Hunter was more interested in what was happening in the basement. And given that every window had been blacked out along the wall where the building met the pavement, there obviously was something happening underground to warrant his interest.

He crept along the side wall, crouching low and taking care to avoid the light from the street. He didn't need light. He could see just fine in the dark. What he did need was sound.

Enhanced by the circuitry in the mask, his olfactory sense was already picking up a rich mix of perfume, cologne and liquor from inside. The combination of smells only grew stronger when he stopped at one of the basement windows.

He couldn't see through the blacked-out panes, but he could listen. He stopped just the right of one of the windows, flattened his back to the wall and turned his head slightly to sharpen his focus on any sound coming from inside.

Like some high-speed thresher, his mind deftly sorted and processed the jumble of incoming sounds. There was music—rhythmic but quiet, from a radio somewhere in the room. The clink of ice in glasses. The skilled, rat-a-tat shuffle of coated playing cards. The clatter of wooden chips on a hard surface. The murmur of words and short phrases:

"Hit me."

"I'll stick."

"Nineteen."

Blackjack.

He kept listening, focusing specifically on the shuffling sound. Five decks, maybe six. Nearly a half-dozen tables.

That would mean six dealers. Maybe three or four players to a table. There could be thirty people in the room. Maybe more. The best way in would be…

A different sound now. Different smells. All from a different direction.

Behind him. About twenty feet and closing in steadily. Cheap cologne and the stale odor of cigarette smoke on clothing. The crunch of shoe leather on pavement.

Hunter shifted his weight slightly, but otherwise remained motionless and kept his head turned away, feigning unawareness yet triangulating on every sound coming up behind him.

The click of a hammer, a little more than a foot away from the back of his head.

His muscles tensed.

"Alright, pal," the voice murmured. "Get up on yer feet before I blow that silly mask off yer—"

Hunter leaped from his crouch at lightning speed and spun in the direction of the voice before the figure behind him could even finish the threat. He kicked up his left leg and caught the gunman's right wrist with his boot. The thug barked in pain and the gun bounced out of his hand and hit the concrete with a metallic *thunk*.

Thankfully, the gunman hadn't had the time or the reflexes to fire before dropping the weapon. A gunshot would have drawn attention from inside the building and elsewhere on the street. Instead, he doubled over on himself, clutching his wrist and whimpering like a wounded dog.

"Okay, I'm up," said Hunter, now facing his assailant head-on, knees bent in a crouch, fists out in a defensive stance. His voice was quiet but taut. "What happens now?"

Still doubled over, the thug charged. Even without highly tuned senses, Hunter would have seen it coming a mile away—the brace of his shoulders, the clumsy shift of his feet just before the advance.

Hunter cocked his arm and his shoulder and delivered a blow that connected squarely with the thug's oncoming chin. The thug went down on one knee. He would have toppled completely if Hunter hadn't grabbed his arm and yanked him upright.

The thug's face had twisted into a mask of pain. His lower lip was puffy and bleeding.

"Come on," said Hunter, steering the thug toward the back of the building. "Let's go for a walk."

Hunter yanked him along at a brisk pace. The thug's steps were unsteady. He stumbled once, but he managed enough of a shuffle to keep up. He kept his head down and his hand at his jaw, but he managed to glance up just once.

"What's with the crazy mask?" he mumbled.

"Big world," said Hunter. "Must be Halloween somewhere." They took a few more steps. "What's your name?"

"Huh?"

"Your name. Come on."

The thug did his best to maintain the tough-guy act. "I ain't gonna—"

Hunter squeezed down on his arm like a vise.

"Charlie!" he yelped.

"Charlie what?"

"Charlie McNeil."

After a few more steps they reached the back of the building, and Hunter shoved McNeil backward into the side of one of the dumpsters. He kept a firm grip on McNeil's arm and grabbed his collar with his free hand. "What are you doing out here, Charlie?"

"I...I watch the place for Danny," said McNeil. Despite the pain in his arm and his face, despite his compromised circumstances, he grew suddenly defiant. "Who are *you*? What the hell are *you* doin' out here?"

Hunter let go of McNeil's collar. He cocked his forearm again and pointed a fist directly at McNeil's face.

McNeil winced. His feet shuffled involuntarily and his free hand went up to shield his face. "No, no!" he pleaded. "Don't hit me no more!"

"Listen to me, Charlie. You want to know who I am? I'm a guy who's sitting on half a lifetime of frustration right now, and you're at the wrong end of it. So if I ask you some questions, you need to give me some answers, and they need to be good ones."

McNeil swallowed hard. "A-Alright..."

"Tell me about Danny."

McNeil shrugged. "Whaddya wanna know? He runs the joint."

"I know that." Hunter tilted his head toward the basement window where he'd been prowling just moments before. "You got people playing cards down there?"

McNeil shrugged again. Either that or he was trying to loosen Hunter's grip on his arm. "It's...It's just small-time stuff."

"Yeah? Has Danny been reading the papers? Does he know the police are coming down hard? Even on the small-time stuff?"

"I know, I know. But they muscled in. Danny didn't want to do it but they made him."

"Who? Who muscled in?"

McNeil hesitated. "I...I don't..."

Hunter wrenched McNeil's arm and cocked his fist one more time. McNeil flinched. "Here, let me make this easy for you," Hunter growled. "It's Nicky Diamond, right?"

McNeil hesitated. "Yeah," he said finally, still flinching in anticipation of another blow to the face that could come at any minute. "Yeah, Diamond."

"Right. And what else is Danny running down there?"

"Wh-whaddya mean?" McNeil looked genuinely confused now.

"Any dope?"

"Huh? Hell, no."

"What about women?"

"What? You mean like working girls? No, nothing like that. Just cards. Just small-time stuff, I swear."

"How much?"

"Huh?"

"How much does Malone make on cards?"

"I...I dunno. Couple thousand a night, I guess. More on weekends."

Hunter opened his fist and grabbed McNeil's collar. "What do you know about the Ho Sheng Brotherhood?"

McNeil swallowed hard. "The what?" His voice was shaking. "I don't ... Jeez, I ain't heard about them guys since I was a kid. I don't know nothin' about them!"

He was telling the truth. Hunter could see it in his eyes. McNeil was brainless muscle on Malone's payroll and nothing more. Probably a bouncer inside the building when he wasn't patrolling the outside.

He was several steps removed from the Diamond operation—far enough that he couldn't be considered a member of the operation at all. On the scale of small timers, he was probably one of the smallest.

"Okay," said Hunter. "Let's walk some more."

"Huh? Where…where we goin'?"

Hunter steered him toward the steps leading up to the back door. "Let's have a seat. You look like you've had a rough night." They reached the back wall after a few strides. Hunter turned McNeil to face him and gave him a hard shove into a seated position on the top step. McNeil grunted at the impact of his backside against the concrete.

Next to McNeil as an iron railing anchored into the concrete steps and bolted at one end to the back wall of the building. Hunter positioned himself directly in front of McNeil in case he tried any quick moves to get up from the steps and dart away. "Alright," he said, "take off your belt."

"What?"

"I said take off your belt."

"Hey, what are you? Some kinda—?"

"Keep it up and I'll make you take off all your clothes. The belt. Now."

McNeil looked at him and hesitated for a moment, then started unbuckling. Hunter held out his hand, and after a minute, McNeil handed over the belt.

"Okay," said Hunter, grabbing the thug's hands. "The railing. Let's go."

"Huh?"

Hunter smacked the metal railing with his palm. "Your hands," he prompted. "Up here. Come on. I've got a busy night ahead of me."

McNeil held up his hands, one on either side of the railing, and Hunter strapped his wrists to the metal bar in several tight loops.

"Hey," McNeil barked. "That hurts!"

"You had a gun at my head a minute ago. I'd say you're getting the easy end of the deal."

Hunter threaded the end of the belt through the buckle and secured it with the brass hook. He gave the job a quick assessment by tugging on the belt and on McNeil's crossed wrists. Unless McNeil was planning to chew the belt off with his teeth, he wasn't going anywhere.

"Alright, here's what's going to happen," said Hunter. "I'm going to send some people to talk to you."

A look of terror instantly spread across McNeil's face. "What... what people?" He tugged on the leather around his wrists and winced at the pain.

"You'll find out when they get here. When they do, you need to tell them everything you've told me, and probably more. Whatever they want to know. They'll probably want to go inside and talk to Danny, too. I suggest you and he cooperate."

McNeil seemed to be missing most of what Hunter was saying. He appeared to be stuck on the first part of Hunter's instructions. "Wh-who you gonna...?"

Hunter shrugged. He took a few steps backward, toward the edge of darkness. "Gotta run, Charlie."

McNeil was tugging harder now, panic etched in his face. "Wait a minute! Wait!"

Hunter turned and disappeared into the shadows.

He moved quickly through the alleys and retrieved the motorcycle, then covered another four blocks on wheels. Along the way, he kept the bike in a low gear to avoid any excessive noise that would draw attention. He ended up at the outer edge of the business district, in the back lot of a bank at the corner of West Twenty-Third and Sloan. He dismounted and carefully made his way to the front of the building, scanning his surroundings at every turn for any dark shadow or corner that could provide cover from the random pedestrian.

He knew the block and he knew the corner. And he knew there was a telephone booth in front of the bank. The overhead light came on when he ducked inside the booth. He reached up, unscrewed the bulb and quickly dialed for an operator.

He glanced up and down the street and tapped his fingertips on the inside panel of the booth as he waited for the call to connect.

"Come on..." he muttered.

After a few seconds that seemed like days, an operator came on the line.

"I need the Union City Police," he said. His voice was quiet, controlled, but he delivered the words in rapid fire. "It's an emergency."

After a few more seconds, another female voice—a police dispatcher—came on the line. "Union City Police."

"Danny's Tavern," said Hunter, skipping any preamble. "Clifford Road, off East Eighteenth. There's a lot of money changing hands there tonight, and none of it's legal."

"Hold on," said the dispatcher. "Who is this?"

"You've got thirty or forty people sitting around a half-dozen tables in a room in the basement. They've been playing blackjack all night long, and they're not doing it for matchsticks."

"Listen, mister, you need to—"

"There's a guy named Charlie at the back door. He'll let you in, but you'll have to untie him first."

"Wait a minute. You're saying someone is tied up at the back of the—"

"Danny's Tavern is part of Nicky Diamond's operation. If you don't believe me, tell Mike Dugan to look it up in Diamond's ledger."

There was a pause. The mention of Dugan by name and Diamond's ledger had caught her off guard. Hunter immediately wondered whether being so specific would turn out to be a mistake.

"Sir, I'm going to have you speak with—"

"You're wasting time. If you get some detectives there soon, they'll probably get some people to talk."

The dispatcher was silent for a moment. Hunter heard the background murmur of her colleagues taking other calls on other phone lines. He heard something else, too. Not through the telephone line but beyond the small booth, from somewhere up the street.

Footsteps. Two sets, moving together. Leisurely, but heading in his direction.

"A-Alright," the dispatcher stammered after a couple seconds. "You said Danny's Tavern."

"Danny's Tavern. Eighteenth and Clifford."

The dispatcher started to speak again, but Hunter hung up and bolted from the booth just as a young couple came around the corner arm-in-arm. It would be up to the next caller to put the lightbulb back in.

He slipped back into the shadows and headed for the motorcycle.

CHAPTER 39
CARIBBEAN CAPER

The Caribbean Club was quite a bit larger and more upscale than Danny's Tavern. Then again, being more upscale than Danny's wasn't saying much.

The club was owned by a guy named Augustus "Gus" Horton, who also owned a bowling alley about five blocks away. Hunter had never been inside the Caribbean, but he'd heard that it had a theme that was consistent with its name—eighteenth century nautical décor, seafood entrees named after islands, waitresses in stylized pirate outfits, and various other tacky appointments. More importantly, he'd been told that the management kept a spacious room in the back for private engagements. If there was action here tonight, he suspected this back room would be where he'd find it.

But he wouldn't know for sure until he got inside.

The club was on Holloway Avenue, halfway between West Fifteenth and West Sixteenth. He approached the place in much the same way that he'd approached Danny's Tavern—parking the motorcycle in a remote spot a couple blocks away and covering the rest of the distance on foot, staying under the cover of shadows as he moved through the network of back alleys behind the buildings fronting on Holloway. The back of The Caribbean Club had better lighting than Danny's, so he needed to be more cautious as he made his way toward the rear of the building.

The rear entrance was a scarred metal door at the top of two steps with a high-wattage electric bulb over the door frame. The door had no handle, which meant that it locked from the inside. Anyone coming out the back would need a key to re-enter the building, or at least something to prop open the door—which explained the brick on the top step, off to the side of the door.

Hunter kept low in the shadows near the wall of the adjacent building and watched the back door of the Caribbean. After a few minutes it opened, and he immediately picked up a fishy smell—partly from inside the building and partly coming directly off the figure who emerged through the doorway.

The man was tall and thin, no more than twenty years old. He wore a scowl on his face that appeared to be permanent. The cook's hat on his head and the apron covering the front of his clothes from his chest to his knees suggested that he was a member of the kitchen staff.

He kicked the brick into place to prop open the door, then descended the two steps, muttering some mild profanity to himself and pulling a pack of cigarettes from under his apron.

He turned his back to Hunter's line of sight from the shadows, lighting a cigarette and stuffing the half-used pack back under his apron. After a moment, he blew a cloud of smoke into the night air with a heavy sigh that sounded like an early resignation to a lifetime of defeat.

Hunter stepped up behind him without a sound and muttered two short syllables:

"Go home."

The kid let out a gasp and jumped, and the cigarette slipped out of his fingers and dropped to the pavement. "What the hell...?"

He turned, took one look at Hunter's mostly-covered face and gasped again. His eyes went wide and he took two quick steps backward, nearly tripping on his own feet. "Jesus, what the hell...? Who...?"

"I said go home," said Hunter, keeping his voice low but forceful. "You don't want to be here." He nodded toward the door propped open at the top of the two steps. "I'm about to go inside, and you don't want to be in there when I do."

"Wh-what are you gonna do?"

The kid was shaking. His breath came in short bursts. His heart was hammering in his chest. Hunter knew because he could hear it.

"Never mind. Just beat it. Get a cab, a street car, walk home, I don't care." He took a step forward, and the kid's eyes grew even wider. "The last guy who gave me a hard time in an alley wound up regretting it, so this is the last time I'm going to tell you. Get out of here before I drag you back in there."

The kid backed up another two steps. He glanced at the back door and then back at Hunter.

"And while you're at it, start looking for a new job," Hunter said. "This place may be going out of business soon. Now go!"

Hunter barked out the last words hard enough to hit the kid like a slap, and the kid jumped again at the sound of them. He turned and bolted into the darkness—hat, apron and all—toward the front of the building and the street beyond. Hunter wondered for a moment whether he'd hail a cop, but judging from what was likely going on inside the club, he gambled on the fact that the kid would keep his mouth shut and not risk the possibility of making trouble for himself.

He turned and bounded up the steps leading to the back door of the building. Within seconds after crossing the threshold, his enhanced sensory capabilities told him plenty about the lay of the land. In some other part of the building, he heard the whisper of shuffling cards, the muted rattle of dice on felt-covered surfaces, the surge of voices with every roll, the revelry of patrons taking in games of chance and washing them down with wine and other heady spirits. He smelled seafood and liquor...and something else. Something vaguely sweet, like a combination of syrup and flowers, yet somehow sinister at the same time.

Beyond the doorway was a short, narrow hallway that ended in a T. When Hunter got to the end, he glanced left and right and spent no more than three seconds assessing the floor plan from his limited vantage point.

To the right was nothing consequential—a small storage recess where various cleaning supplies had been haphazardly stashed. To the left was a longer hallway leading to the kitchen and the private party room.

He ducked back into the entranceway and pressed his back to the left-hand wall, taking a few seconds to contemplate his options. He noticed a fuse box mounted at eye level on the opposite wall and stepped toward it. He opened the box and found a full panel of fuses for every circuit in the building. Without hesitation, he began unscrewing fuses—two at a time, with both hands.

Out went the lights. In quick succession, entire rooms and hallways fell into instant darkness. Appliances in the kitchen shut down, ceiling fans slowed, and the building gradually went silent—but only for a second or two, until the faceless voices of confusion from all corners of the restaurant began to escalate and fill the void.

Hunter quickly scanned the labels on the fuse box panel and noted that one circuit was dedicated to a specific function. He left that one alone and headed down the darkened hallway toward the banquet room.

The confusion in all parts of the building—including the public dining area toward the front—rapidly picked up momentum. The murmur of amusement was giving way to the apprehension that inevitably comes with the dark and the unknown. Anxious voices called for flashlights, demanded a word with the manager, insisted on some kind of explanation.

Hunter heard it all—every word, every exasperated breath. He knew he had very little time to act before someone would bring another source of light into the hallway and he'd lose whatever advantage he had.

The hallway leading to the kitchen and the party room was quickly filling with people—some of them patrons, some of them kitchen staff, all of them groping and stumbling in the darkness. One of them, a beefy gorilla of a man in an ill-fitting suit, appeared to be a bouncer. He emerged from the party room with a scowl on his face and a gun in his right hand. He guided himself through the darkness by running his left hand along the wall of the hallway. Along the way, he grumbled something to no one in particular about checking the fuse box.

Hunter stood near the fuse box and waited for the bouncer to make his way toward him. Just before the man nearly collided with him, Hunter reached out and swung his fist like an ax, bringing it down on the man's right forearm. The bouncer let out a grunt as the gun fell to the floor. Before he could make any other sound, Hunter dropped him with a left to the breadbasket and a hard right to the jaw.

Hunter took only a second or two to assess the heap on the floor. When he was certain the bouncer would be out of commission for the next few minutes, he stepped over him and moved down the hallway to the party room.

At the entrance to the room, he surveyed a confused tangle of patrons and employees. They were blinded by the darkness, but Hunter could see it all. Dealers and card players had abandoned their games. Some were trying to gather up their money, while others were trying to gather up other people's money. Still others were just trying to find a way out of the room. Waiters and waitresses struggled to keep their serving trays upright and secure in their hands amid the increasingly frantic swirl, but most of them failed. As a result, the floor was littered with broken glass and china, and slick with spilled cocktails.

The backdrop to all of this was the persistent, vaguely sweet smell he'd first caught when he'd entered the building less than two minutes earlier. It was much stronger here in the party room—so much stronger that he could literally follow it with his nose.

He scanned one end of the room and noticed a partition separating a small corner of the room from the rest of the dining and gambling and revelry. A smoky haze hung above and around the partition, thick enough and pungent enough for Hunter to start putting two and two together.

He pushed past a knot of patrons handicapped by a combination of darkness and inebriation and made his way toward the cloud. He circled around to the opposite side of the partition and found five people—three men and two women—sprawled across a small sofa and two easy chairs like lifeless rag dolls. Their eyes, if they were open at all, were glassy and vacant. They appeared to be in a mindless stupor, euphoric and oblivious to the darkness and pandemonium in the room beyond the partition.

The furnishings were fitted with deep cushions and luxurious upholstery, and framed in woodwork crafted with ornate and exotic oriental carvings. Alongside the sofa and chairs were similarly carved wooden side tables, and on each table was a smoldering long-stemmed clay pipe resting in an ashtray of polished jade.

Hunter took a few quick steps toward the partitioned space to rouse the hopheads and break up their party, but he stopped suddenly when he saw his own shadow spread across the floor in front of him by a sudden flood of light from behind. He turned and looked directly into a flashlight beam coming from the entrance to the party room.

There was no way to see beyond the glare, but Hunter guessed that it might be Horton, the owner. Whoever it was, he swept the room with the flashlight beam that threw hard light across the sea of confused humanity shuffling around the room.

The figure with the flashlight took two steps into the room and started barking into the darkness and chaos. "Carson! What the hell...?" The beam jerked suddenly as two patrons walked directly into him from opposite directions and nearly knocked him over. "Dammit! Somebody check the fuse box! Carson! Where the hell are you?"

Hunter was fairly certain now that the guy with the flashlight was Horton. And he was also pretty sure Horton was calling for the bouncer he'd just put down several seconds earlier near the rear entrance. He saw the beam coming in his direction. He could have ducked away in plenty of time if not for the mass of aimless patrons milling around, bumping into him and each other. The light caught his face and continued to sweep the room, then immediately swung back to his face.

Hunter quickly ducked away and lost himself in the frantic crowd, listening to more shouts from Horton:

"Hey, you! Hold still! Carson! Where the hell…?"

Hunter watched the quick sweep of the beam as Horton tried to find him again and track him. He made a wide swing around the perimeter of the room. Moving along the wall adjacent to the entrance, he glanced up and noticed a decorative fishing net mounted on the paneling. The netting had ceramic imitations of seashells in and around the folds and was strategically arranged to enhance the maritime décor.

With only a split second of thought and without slowing his movement along the wall, Hunter reached up and yanked at the netting. It came away in his hands with almost no effort. He gathered it in both hands and threw it over his shoulder, keeping his eye on Horton and working his way through the crowd to approach him from behind.

He crossed the final stretch of floor space and grabbed Horton's right arm with one hand and the back of his neck with the other. Hunter clamped down on each point of contact like a steel vise.

"Hey!" Horton grunted. "What the…?"

Hunter leaned in close behind Horton's right ear. "Let's go!" he muttered.

Horton immediately started flailing and writhing in Hunter's grip. "Hey, get your dirty hands…" His voice trailed off at first, then he turned his head suddenly and shouted. "Carson!"

"Don't bother," Hunter growled, keeping a firm grip on Horton's arm and neck. "If you're calling for your bouncer, he's taking a nap in the hallway. Now come on!"

Hunter dragged Horton backward, out of the party room and away from the rear entrance so he couldn't make any quick moves down the back hallway to get away. Horton stumbled momentarily as Hunter hauled him into the kitchen, which was now empty of staff. Hunter figured the combination of sudden darkness all over the building and the shouting and confusion in the back room had made them skittish enough to head through the dining room to the front door and out of the building.

He let go of Horton just long enough to pull the netting off his shoulder and toss it over Horton's head and wrap it around his shoulders and waist.

Horton squirmed and writhed against the layers of netting that were quickly piling up around the length of his frame. With each desperate shove of his hands or thrust of his legs and feet, he only grew more entangled. In just a couple seconds he lost his balance completely and tumbled awkwardly to the kitchen floor.

Hunter followed him down on one knee, with one hand reaching through the netting just enough to hold onto his jacket collar in an iron grip.

"Where's Diamond!" he rasped.

"What? I don't know who you're—"

Hunter jerked at Horton's coat and his entire body shook. "Don't lie to me! Is he here?"

Horton flinched. "No, no, no…I…I don't know where he is. He hardly ever comes in here. Maybe only been here once or twice."

"Where does he hang his hat?"

"I don't know, I swear! I heard he was…" his voice trailed off.

"Spill it!"

"I heard he was at the Paramount, but then I heard he had some trouble there so he had to find a new place."

"Where you getting the dope?"

"What? I don't know what you're—"

"Don't waste my time. You know exactly what I'm talking about. That big cloud in the other room. I can smell it from here, and so can you. Where do you get the dope?"

"Some…somebody delivered it."

"Who? Diamond?"

"No. He sent somebody. A couple weeks ago."

"Somebody who?"

"I don't know who the guy was. Zeiger, or Zeigler, or somethin'…"

"Ziglauer?"

"Maybe. I dunno…"

Horton continued to squirm and struggle against the netting, but he was hopelessly ensnared. "Hey, come on," he pleaded. "Lemme outta this—"

"Keep talking!"

"I don' know anything else! The guy only came the one time. We were supposed to get more of the stuff soon, but I ain't seen it yet."

Hunter didn't say a word for a moment. He watched Horton writhe and strain against the netting, but he knew the efforts were useless. When he was fairly certain that Horton had no more information to give him, he stood up and took a few steps backward.

Horton looked up at him from his helpless position on the floor, his expression a mix of indignation and fear. "Hey, where you…? Wait a minute! Come back here!"

Hunter glanced around the room. He grabbed the edge of a stainless steel table and gave it a shove with one hand. It was heavy, but not so heavy that he couldn't move it a few inches across the floor. He took hold of the edge with both hands, braced his shoulders and stepped backward, dragging the table with him. It was a struggle, but he made quick progress, dragging the table out of the kitchen, across the hallway and to the doorway leading to the party room.

Several people had already made their way out and were groping and scrambling for a way out of the building. More were coming through the doorway as he approached it. He gave the table one more yank and shoved it in front of the doorway.

A few patrons collided with the table and fell backward. A couple others stumbled but regained their footing enough to climb over the obstruction.

Among the few who made it out of the room was a tall, skinny figure. Something about him looked familiar, but he was moving quickly and his face was turned away at an angle that made him impossible to identify in the confusion. Hunter resigned himself to the fact that a few were just going to get away.

He darted back to the kitchen, where Horton was still struggling and cursing on the floor in the tangled folds of the net. He found a second table just like he first and started dragging. Horton heard the sound of metal scraping against the floor and launched into a renewed tirade that carried a lot less bluster than before and a lot more apprehension and fear.

Hunter ignored him. He dragged the table back to the party room doorway—even more quickly this time than the last—and found more patrons climbing over the table and out of the room. He crouched low and spread his arms across the full length of the second table. He gripped the edges, braced his shoulders and gave a mighty heave.

The table came up from the floor—a foot, two feet, three feet. Hunter wavered momentarily, his back and shoulders screaming against the weight. After a couple more inches and another second or two, he leaned forward with a fierce grunt and hoisted the table in his arms onto the surface of the one in the doorway. The result was a two-tiered blockade of stainless steel that spanned the width of the doorway, standing almost seven feet tall and weighing more than five-hundred pounds.

More patrons kept coming, pushing and shoving at the makeshift retaining wall. Hunter knew it wouldn't hold forever—the top table was already starting to budge from the shoving from the other side of the doorway—but it would hold them for at least a couple minutes. It might be enough.

Horton was screaming from the kitchen now. Hunter wasn't even sure he was hearing words anymore, but the tone of his voice said it all. Blinded by darkness, huddled on the floor and bound up in netting, hearing the frantic commotion from the party room across the hallway, he was overcome with panic.

Hunter headed back down the hallway toward the back door, climbing over Carson, who as just starting to stir but not posing any immediate threat. He stopped at the intersection of the two hallways, just a few feet away from the fuse box he'd nearly emptied just a couple minutes earlier. Mounted on the wall was a fire alarm box. The alarm operated on a dedicated circuit—the one circuit in the entire building that Hunter had not disconnected.

He opened the alarm box, reached inside and yanked the handle.

Instantly, the alarm launched into a piercing wail. For Hunter, whose hearing was already attuned to a much wider range of frequencies than the typical human ear, the sound was beyond painful, literally deafening. Instinctively, he ducked away from the sound and his hands went to either side of his head to cover the auditory receptors built into the mask and block out the sound. Behind the goggles, his eyes squeezed shut.

It was time to get some distance between himself and the building.

The fire department would arrive in as little as five minutes. They'd get one look at the situation and bring in the police a few minutes after that.

But Hunter would be long gone.

It was time for the main event.

CHAPTER 40
STERLING SURPRISE

Hunter had been inside the Sterling Palace before, so he knew the lay of the land before he even got there. It was a spacious two-level affair on Seneca Avenue. The street level included an ornate front lobby that led to a main dining area with a large dance floor at the center and a bar off to the side. The upper level included a separate cocktail lounge with a terrace that overlooked the stretch of Seneca along the front of the building. The upper level also included a few private gathering rooms and office space for the management. A mezzanine spanned the entire perimeter of the interior and overlooked the dining area and the dance floor below.

He approached the building from behind like he had done with the previous two. The back wall included a service entrance for kitchen staff, waiters and other employees. Also along the back was a rear entrance for the public—complete with an awning and signage.

On this particular night, though, a temporary sign near the back entrance read: CLOSED FOR PRIVATE ENGAGEMENT. Hunter hadn't seen the front entrance, but he assumed there was a similar sign posted there as well.

The back door was fitted with tinted glass, but Hunter could see well enough through it to catch a glimpse of the greeter just inside. The "greeter," of course, was nothing more than hired muscle—the collector of an entrance fee and the checker of incoming guests to make sure none of them looked like trouble or potential trouble.

Hunter had neither the time nor the patience for another confrontation at the back of another building. There was a rhythm to this one-man campaign he'd been waging over the last hour, and it had reached a speed and conviction that no longer allowed for petty distractions and delays.

Besides, his enhanced olfactory sense was picking up a heavy scent of opium, which was now very familiar since the encounter at The Caribbean Club. He was able to discern that the scent was coming primarily from the upper level.

He'd start there, the central location of the dope and the alcohol, the place where any adversaries would be the least ready for someone with heightened senses and enhanced reflexes.

He did a few seconds of quick reconnaissance, circling as close to the front of the building as possible without stepping into the glow of the lights along Seneca Avenue, and discovered that the second floor terrace was empty. There was no stairway directly from the front sidewalk to the terrace, but the fire escape along the side of the building would get him there.

He climbed the fire escape two steps at a time, taking care not to make a sound on the metal stairs. At the top, he quickly worked his way to the stone terrace, crouching low, out of site from anyone inside or on the street below.

Coming to a stop at the entranceway leading from the terrace to the cocktail lounge, Hunter closed his eyes and tuned in to the sounds coming from inside. He picked up two separate heartbeats, positioned close to each other at one end of the room. A voice for each heartbeat, and a meandering conversation between the two in slurred and vaguely disjointed speech. The clink of ice in glasses. A third heartbeat—this one by itself, fifteen or twenty feet away from the other two. The methodical, deliberate sweep of wet cloth across a smooth surface. The gentle tap of large glass bottles against wood.

Clearly there were people in the lounge, but apparently not many. Still in a crouch, Hunter hugged the shadows and inched his way across a few feet of terrace space and into the lounge.

Inside, the lounge was dimly lit by a series of lanterns consisting of candles mounted inside colored glass globes. There were four of these positioned evenly along the length of the bar, and one on each table throughout the lounge. The minimal lighting made it easier for Hunter to slip inside unnoticed.

At the far end of the room, two men sat at opposite sides of a small rectangular table, drinking cocktails on ice and talking about nothing in particular. Their eyes were glassy, their gestures and movements sloppy. Twenty feet away, a bartender swept the long horizontal surface of his workspace with a damp rag and frequently turned his back to the room to arrange and rearrange bottles on the shelving behind him.

Hanging over all this, apparently from somewhere beyond the bar, was a persistent haze of opium smoke that was not just thick but nearly overpowering—especially when one's olfactory senses were finely tuned to even the slightest air currents.

Hunter crept a few steps closer to the bar, being careful not to draw the attention of the two patrons at the table no more than twelve feet away. He took two more steps to a position about four feet from the bar, then set himself for the attack.

In a sudden explosion of energy, he pumped his legs upward and threw his weight forward in a standing jump that propelled him several feet off the ground and across the remaining distance to the bar. An instant later, he slammed down hard with both feet on the horizontal wooden surface of the bar, crushing several glasses under his boots and knocking several more in every direction.

The bartender spun instantly and staggered backward at the sight of the terrifying masked figure crouched on the bar directly in front of him. He backed up into a row of liquor bottles, knocking several of them off the shelves and onto the unforgiving tile floor where they shattered into thousands of fragments. Spirits sprayed everywhere and mixed with the crystalline shards of bottles and drinking glasses that already littered the floor.

The bartender recovered quickly, shouting over his shoulder to someone beyond the lounge. A figure appeared almost instantly to Hunter's left, in a doorway connecting the lounge to the upper hallway of the restaurant. The figure was coming fast. He was armed, and he was drawing down on Hunter.

Barely glancing at the oncoming figure and moving at lightning speed, Hunter grabbed a bottle of whiskey off the bar with his left hand and gave it a backhanded hurl. His aim was true. The bottle rocketed in a straight line across the open space and connected with the gunman's face. The tapered glass container smacked against the gunman's cheekbone and bounced away, but didn't break until it hit the floor.

The gunman howled and staggered backward, his face contorted in pain. His left hand went to his cheek just below his eye as he stumbled and fell in the doorway. On the way down, he dropped the gun and put his right hand to his face. Sprawled on his back, grunting in pain with his eyes squeezed shut and both hands on his face, he rocked back and forth in a patch of broken glass and spilled whiskey.

The bartender cowered in a corner behind the bar, curled up and practically paralyzed in a ball of fear. He posed no immediate threat. The two men seated at the table in the lounge, meanwhile, got a quick look at what was happening and scrambled out of their seats. Hunter glanced after them as they made a beeline for the terrace. He willingly let them go, listening as frantic footsteps hammered their way down the fire escape to the street. There would be bigger fish to fry in this place tonight.

His first order of business was the fallen gunman. He leaped off the bar just as quickly as he'd leaped onto it, and landed just a few feet from the doorway where the man was still rocking and moaning on the floor. Hunter quickly picked up the man's gun and pocketed it in his jacket.

The gunman propped himself up on one hand and immediately winced at the random glass shards that dug into his palm. He removed his other hand from his face to reveal coal-black eyes, a cheek bruised and bloodied by the flying whiskey bottle and craggy features set in an angry scowl. His rage lost some of its steam momentarily when he looked back at an assailant whose head, eyes and face were almost completely covered by a leather mask and goggles, but he quickly recovered.

"What," he said, "you wanna get tough with me, punk?" He did his best to look and sound menacing while trying to get up on his feet. None of it worked.

Hunter responded with a hard right to the cheek that had already been cut by the bottle. The bouncer's head rocked back. His eyes turned upward and his lids fluttered to a close.

"Yeah," said Hunter. "How'm I doing so far?"

He didn't get an answer. He didn't expect one from a guy who was back on the floor and now out cold.

Instead, he heard a gasp from about thirty feet away, behind a closed door. A woman's voice, coming from inside one of the private rooms down the hall from the lounge. Whoever she was, she sounded alarmed.

Then a man's voice. "Relax, baby. What's the matter?" The words were slurred just a little, like someone who'd had a couple and was just starting to relax but wasn't too far gone yet.

Hunter moved in the direction of the voices. The hallway was lit as dimly as the cocktail lounge, but Hunter could see it all in fine detail—every doorknob, every hinge, every inch of paneling along the walls and carpeting on the floor.

He heard the rustle of fabric, then the female voice again. "No," she protested, "let go of my arm. Something's going on out there."

"Ah, it's nothing. Come on back here and relax."

That voice...

The clink of glass against glass. The gentle murmur of liquid cascading a short distance from one container to another. "Here, let me pour you—"

"No," said the woman. "Something's happening in the hallway. Something's wrong. Go...go take a look."

"Oh, for the love of..."

An exasperated sigh. Soft footsteps—socks without shoes—across the floor inside the room.

The door opened. A soft glow from inside the room spilled into the hallway. A gray-haired figure stepped out. He wore an undershirt and trousers, with suspenders off his shoulders and hanging down by his waist.

He glanced to the far end of the hallway—his head turned away from Hunter, who came up fast from behind. Then the figure turned in Hunter's direction to scan the other end of the hall.

Anthony Reynolds.

Hunter almost stopped when he saw the face, but he recovered quickly and kept on coming. Reynolds' eyes widened at the masked figure coming at him.

"Who the hell...?" He did his best to sound indignant, but Hunter heard the pounding heartbeat, the rapid breathing. Hunter heard fear.

Hunter reached out and locked his hand onto Reynolds' upper arm like a vise. "Hiya, Judge."

Reynolds grunted at the sudden pain in his arm. "Get your hands—"

"Having a good time?" said Hunter, ignoring the protest. He made a show of assessing Reynolds' attire. "A little underdressed, no?"

Reynolds tried to shrug him off, but Hunter held on with an iron grip. "Get your goddamn hands off me, you lousy thug," the judge barked. "I swear to God, I'll—"

He never got to the end of the threat. Hunter used his free hand to grab a hunk of Reynolds' undershirt, pulling him close with a sharp jerk until their noses were no more than three inches apart. Reynolds' face slackened and his eyes grew wide. His bravado suddenly evaporated as he stared frantically into the dark goggles but found nothing that could be leveraged, negotiated, bought or bullied.

"This party's over, Judge," Hunter murmured. "It's all coming down. Get me?"

Reynolds' mouth moved for a moment, but no sound came out. Hunter held his gaze through the goggles for another second or two, then spun him toward the stairs at the end of the hallway.

"Alright," he said. "Let's go for a walk."

Reynolds started to resist, but Hunter kept his iron grip on the judge's arm. "Oh, stop it," Hunter said, his voice taut with irritation. To emphasize his impatience, he reached into his jacket pocket and came out with the gun he'd taken from the bouncer just minutes earlier. He kept it pointed away from Reynolds, but he made sure the judge saw it. "You think this is a game?"

Reynolds glanced at the gun and stopped resisting. With Hunter's hand still on his arm, the two men moved toward the stairs.

"You…you one of Diamond's men?" The tremor in Reynolds' voice was unmistakable. "I don't understand. I've been helping him for weeks now. Why would he—?"

Hunter almost laughed at the suggestion. "No," he said, half escorting and half dragging Reynolds to the stairs. "Look at me. Do I look like one of Diamond's crew?"

"I…I don't know what you look like. I can't even see your—"

"You're not supposed to. Keep moving."

They reached the mezzanine. A quick glance over the railing was all it took for Hunter to estimate more than five hundred people below.

The dining room didn't have a whole lot more lighting than the upper level, save for two small chandeliers above the dance floor. Overhead, a half-dozen banners of decorative velvet cloth—each about sixty feet long, all of them a deep shade of burgundy—hung from a central point on the ceiling and radiated outward, draping above the dining hall and ending at equidistant points along the mezzanine, where they were fastened to the railing by metal hooks.

But there were no dancers on the floor, and there was no music. Just an exclusive group of Union City's upper crust, dressed in expensive suits and gowns, hovering over and around a roulette table and two card tables positioned at the center of the polished wooden dance floor.

The tables were smeared with piles of wooden chips. There were plenty of women. Some appeared to be wives, many appeared to be there in some other capacity. All of them were adorned with extravagant jewelry and wearing dresses that cost more than what most Union City residents made in a month's time.

The space off the dance floor included more than two dozen tables and booths, nearly all of them filled with patrons who were eating, drinking, fraternizing or engaging in some combination of all three.

In a matter of seconds, Hunter picked four familiar faces out of the crowd—a city councilman, a prominent physician, a state senator, the head of one of the largest accounting firms in the city. And he was sure he'd find more if he kept looking.

But that was time he didn't want to waste. He raised the gun and leveled it at one of the chandeliers, which was only slightly above eye level, given their position on the mezzanine. He fired a single shot. Lightbulbs exploded, sparks flashed, damaged sockets sputtered, and a few shards of crystal showered onto the tables below.

The room exploded in a collective gasp. The panicked sound was still hanging in the air when Hunter shifted his aim to the other chandelier hanging twenty feet away from the first one and fired again. The second fixture sputtered and went dark just as quickly as its mate.

The room was mostly in darkness now, save for a few atmospheric lights at each corner. Hunter's goggles instantly engaged, defying the darkness, and everything and everyone in the room shimmered in his field of vision.

The anxious sounds from the crowd below surged even more. But this time the response was more than just a chorus of agitated voices. There was movement, urgency. Some patrons instinctively ducked at the sound of the two back-to-back gunshots. Others, the more brave souls, scanned the length and width of the large room to determine the source of the sound. Still others—mostly those seated at dining tables and gaming tables—wasted no time lurching out of their chairs and heading for the front and rear exits.

But they didn't move in any orderly way. They were a frightened herd, blinded by darkness, swirling and churning as a single chaotic entity.

There was no way he could see the outside of the building from his position on the mezzanine, but he was certain that the street would be a congested mess in another minute or two.

Hunter was about to drag Reynolds to the stairs and down to the main floor when he spotted two figures—one from the front entrance and one from the rear—vigorously fighting their way toward the center of the room, against the current of humanity scrambling for the exits. It only took him a few seconds to realize that the two men were armed, and they were slowly making their way toward the stairs leading up to the mezzanine where he was standing with Reynolds.

And both men had their eyes trained on him and the judge.

They weren't police officers. Hunter was sure of it. They would have been announcing themselves as such to the crowd if they had been, maybe even holding up badges. No, these two wore dark, contemptuous expressions. They moved like angry gorillas, shoving people out of their way with a belligerence that no Union City cop would ever bring to the job. These two were Diamond's men.

But the police were on their way. Hunter could hear the sirens in the distance, probably well before anyone else in the room could. They were likely responding to the crowd that was no doubt filling the street in front of the building.

The gorillas were getting closer to the stairs. Hunter was suddenly keenly aware that his time and his options were ticking down. Still holding Reynolds' arm in the iron grip of his left hand, he quickly turned his attention to the disheveled judge. He stuffed the gun into his belt, which freed his right hand to yank one of the suspenders dangling off the waistband of Reynolds' pants.

"What...what're you doing?" the judge stammered as the leather strap came away in Hunter's hand.

Without a word, Hunter grabbed Reynolds' right wrist and pulled it toward the railing. Reynolds' eyes went wide when he realized what Hunter was up to. The judge fought back, writhing and squirming against Hunter's grip.

"No..." said Reynolds, sounding somehow indignant and panicked at the same time. "No, the police will..." His voice trailed off as he jerked and writhed in a fit of resistance that was almost inhuman.

Out of patience and out of time, Hunter slammed a fist into Reynolds' mid-section. The judge barked out an enormous gasp of air and doubled over, and his arms went slack.

"The police," said Hunter, picking up where Reynolds left off, "will find you here in this shiny hell hole, half-dressed, just upstairs from an illegal gambling operation and right down the hall from a quiet little room with a smoldering opium pipe inside. My guess is they'll find your wallet and identification in that room, somewhere near the pipe. And they might even find a woman who will give some very embarrassing answers if they start asking questions.

Hunter quickly lashed Reynolds' wrist to the railing as the judge—still doubled over—coughed and wheezed against the pain in his stomach and struggled to get air back into his lungs.

Reynolds, his face red and his knees wobbling, dropped to one knee as Hunter stepped around behind him and yanked the left suspender off the other side of his pants. He grabbed the judge's left wrist and tied it to the railing less than a foot away from his right hand.

When he was sure both of Reynolds' hands were secure, he crouched down and grabbed a handful of the judge's disheveled hair. Hunter tilted Reynolds' head upward, forcing the tethered, cowering figure to look directly into the dark lenses that covered his own eyes. "And then," said Hunter, "this long association you've had with Nicky Diamond—all the way back to the days when good cops died to protect this city from bad men—will be out in the open."

Separate from the shouts and confusion below, Hunter was aware of new sounds from a different direction—the cocktail lounge some thirty feet behind him.

Footsteps. Maybe the bouncer he'd knocked out a few minutes earlier had come around and...

No. Two sets of footsteps.

Cops.

They'd come up the fire escape, just like he had.

First one came out from the back hallway. Then a second, two or three steps behind the first. Their guns were drawn, and the minute they saw Hunter, they were up and pointed directly at him.

"Police!" said the first one. "Don't move!"

CHAPTER 41
OVER AND OUT

Hunter leveled his gaze at the officers and stood completely still.

"Put your hands up slow!"

Hunter hesitated, then raised his hands slightly—no more than shoulder level. He glanced backward, down into the chaos of the ballroom for just a second—just long enough to see four cops intercept the two gunmen who'd been headed for the stairs a moment earlier.

But there were more cops—three altogether—maneuvering their way through the crowd and beating their own path to the stairs, presumably to investigate whoever had shot the lights out of the chandeliers.

Reynolds was still on his knees at the railing, but he was starting to get his breath back after the blow to his mid-section. He immediately used it to berate the two officers with their guns drawn. "You!" he barked to the one standing a few feet to the rear and off to the left of the other. "Get over here and get these goddamn things off my hands!"

Both cops appeared to recognize Reynolds, which was causing some confusion and hesitation on their part.

Hunter turned back to face the two cops directly in front of him. The only way back to the terrace and out of the building would be through them, and that wasn't an option. He may have been quicker than anything human, but he didn't have faith that he could dodge slugs delivered head-on from two well-trained shooters at close range.

"Alright, now," said the cop, his weapon still steady on its target, "since you've got your hands up, you're gonna take off the crazy mask! Nice and slow and easy!"

The stairway was cut off. The path ahead was cut off. The options for escape were just about nonexistent.

More than just a glance this time, Hunter turned the full length of his body away from the two cops, his hands still up at shoulder level.

"Hey, whaddya…? Turn around, dammit!"

Hunter wasn't listening. He was assessing the long stretches of velvet fabric suspended from the ceiling, calculating geometry and physics at a mental speed that spanned only the smallest fractions of a second.

"I said turn around!"

Hunter crouched and then leaped. Up and forward in a flawless arc that took him more than four feet into space and over the railing like an Olympic diver. He reached outward in mid-air and grabbed hold of the velvet fabric.

He barely heard the cop's voice behind him: "Hey!"

The force of his full, unsupported weight—slightly more than one-hundred-eighty-pounds—yanked hard on the hooks that held the fabric to the railing and pulled them loose from their moorings. It was exactly what he'd anticipated, exactly what he'd hoped.

But would the anchors at the other end hold fast to the ceiling? The next seconds would tell the tale.

He swept downward in a smooth pendulous arc, over the heads of the crowd, across the length of the ballroom. The air rushed against the small portion of his face not covered by the mask as he concentrated on maintaining the proper balance and trajectory.

The arc had bottomed out and was now bringing him upward again. Up ahead and coming fast was the plate-glass window above the front entrance to the building.

Thirty feet at the most. And what was waiting on the other side of the glass was anyone's guess.

He kicked his feet out in front of him and tucked the exposed portion of his face as deep into his chest as he could manage.

Twelve feet.

The glass exploded away from him in thousands of fragments and sprayed in all directions. He let go of the long velvet banner, and when he came out the other side of the window frame, he was some twenty-five feet off the ground.

The aerial view seemed to unfold below him in slow motion. It was complete chaos—more than a dozen cops trying to herd a sea of displaced patrons milling around in a nervous daze in the middle of the street. Regular traffic had ground to a halt. Horns blared and motorists shouted out their windows. A street car sat idle, its passengers with their heads out the windows and craning their necks to get a look at the mess. Bystanders along either side of the street gaped in confusion. Roof lights from a half-dozen patrol cars flooded the scene with a rhythmic splash of red and blue, and more patrol cars were approaching from up the street.

Within just a second or two, gravity took over and Hunter's outward trajectory deteriorated into a downward slope. He tucked his legs back in, grabbing his knees and curling himself into a ball. Despite his instinctive effort to keep his head up, he felt himself pitching forward.

The ground and everything on it—every person, every vehicle, every inch of pavement—was coming up fast. He'd hit something in just another couple seconds, but he couldn't say what.

He saw a man in an expensive suit and a woman in a long gown and heavy makeup walking quickly with the flow of the crowd in an effort to leave the scene before one of the cops could detain them. They both looked up in horror and froze at the sight of a human projectile hurtling in their direction. Another group of four people—none of them expecting the sudden stop—collided with them from behind.

Before any of them could recover and keep moving, Hunter slammed into all of them at once like a bowling ball from above. They all went down, Hunter included, in a symphony of grunts and shrieks. Hunter heard the scuffle of shoes, the tear of fabric. He heard a crack and hesitated to think what might have caused it.

He rolled with the fall, through and beyond the tangle of fallen bodies. Struggling against inertia, he brought himself to a stop, then rose to one knee and turned quickly to assess the collateral damage at the point of impact.

"Are you…are you alright?" he stammered.

There were six altogether—four men, two women—each of them stumbling just to get to their hands and knees, let alone their feet. One of them appeared to be in quite a bit of pain. They all looked up at him and stared mutely, apparently unable to comprehend the idea of talking to a masked man who'd just flown out of a second-story window and knocked them over like tenpins.

Others in the crowd stopped to get a look at him, their curiosity momentarily outweighing their desire to avoid the police.

"Hey!" A voice from behind him, forty feet away, accompanied by footsteps at an uneven pace—fast, slow, fast again. He turned and saw a young cop struggling to make his way through the crowd. His gun was drawn. "Hey, you! Hold it!"

At the sound of his voice, the onlookers quickly dispersed.

He won't shoot, thought Hunter. *Too many people.*

Hunter turned away, quickly scanning his surroundings for some small opening in the churning crowd that he could duck through. He found a gap and slipped through it.

"I said hold it!"

A gunshot went off, and the crowd responded with a collective shriek. Those in the immediate vicinity of the sound broke into a run.

But even with his back turned, Hunter knew he was safe. So was everyone else, whether they believed it in their panicked state or not. His highly sensitized hearing picked up the trajectory of the gunshot. The cop had fired a warning round into the air, probably hoping it would stop Hunter in his tracks.

It didn't. He kept moving, gaining even more and better cover amid the crowd that was now churning and swirling in an even higher state of panic and confusion than before.

He heard the cop call to another officer nearby. "Russ! That guy in the mask! Get him!" But Russ, the second cop, was more than twenty feet off to Hunter's left—which might as well have been a mile, given the chaotic scramble of humanity that separated them.

In a span of just eight or ten seconds, Hunter slipped through the thickest part of the mob and into the shadows of the nearest alley.

Less than two minutes later, he was back on the motorcycle and working his way through a maze of dark backstreets and access roads.

He had one last stop to make.

CHAPTER 42
LATE NIGHT IN CHINATOWN

It was almost one a.m. when Hunter rode into Chinatown. The streets were quiet and deserted, and he did his best to keep them quiet by cutting the engine and coasting most of the way. He pulled into an alley behind Sun Lu's import shop and parked the motorcycle in the shadow of a dumpster behind the adjacent building.

He stayed in the shadows for a moment to assess the back of Sun Lu's shop. There was a rear entrance on the ground floor, and a metal staircase that scaled the back wall and terminated at a small balcony on the second floor. At the balcony level was a set of wooden double doors, and on each door was a relief carving of a dragon that spanned the full length of the wood panel. Hunter figured this to be the rear entrance to Sun Lu's apartment.

He turned back to the motorcycle and opened a small metal box mounted on the frame. It was a basic maintenance and repair kit for the engine, including a few precision tools for fine tuning. Despite the darkness, the goggles gave him a clear view of each tool. He removed a metal probe—three inches long but no more than a sixteenth in diameter—and snapped the lid of the kit back into place.

He tucked the probe into his pocket as he crossed the lot to Sun Lu's shop and made his way up the back stairs.

When he reached the balcony, he put one hand on each doorknob and turned them both gently. As he'd predicted, the entrance was locked. And as he'd hoped, both doorknobs were controlled by a single lock. He took out the probe, and with one hand on one of the knobs, he went to work.

Slowly. Carefully. Not a sound.

He found the catch, felt the click.

The knob turned.

He pocketed the probe, then pulled both doors open slowly, making sure to stand off to one side to avoid any bullets, knives or other surprises from inside the room. After a few seconds, when he was fairly certain he wasn't in the line of any immediate fire, he took a tentative step into the doorway and scanned the room.

It appeared to be a bedroom, although the combination of bookshelves and furnishings also suggested a den as much as sleeping quarters. Sun Lu sat at a desk at the far end of the room, facing the doorway where Hunter stood but peering into a book directly in front of him on the desk. On the wall a few feet behind Sun Lu was a closed door, one that presumably led to a hallway and other parts of the apartment.

A hand-painted porcelain teapot and a matching cup filled with steaming tea occupied a portion of the desk, off to the side of Sun Lu's book. The glow from a small desk lamp was the only light in the room.

The old man slowly raised his eyes from the book. "I have found in my later years that sleep does not come easily to me," he said.

"Sun Lu," said Hunter.

The old man nodded. "I am he."

Hunter looked back at the man without speaking. He heard the click of a hammer from underneath the table, and then it came up—a decidedly American-looking Colt semi-automatic.

Hunter stood perfectly still, holding his hands open and slightly away from his body where Sun Lu could see them clearly. "I didn't come here to rob you or do you any harm," he said.

"And yet you hide your face."

"It's a long story, and I don't think either one of us wants to waste time."

"Indeed. Time is precious."

"I need to talk with you. I'm not armed, and I give you my word that I won't step any closer than I am right now."

Sun Lu stared back at Hunter, apparently contemplating the overture. After a long moment, he put the gun down slowly and rested both hands on the desk. Hunter noted that the old man's right hand was positioned just a couple inches from the weapon.

"Say what you have come to say," said Sun Lu.

"You've done business with Nick Diamond."

Su Lu did not speak.

"You don't have to answer," said Hunter. "I know you have. He keeps a ledger of all of his business dealings—the restaurants, the gambling, everything. Your name is in the ledger. You've provided him with goods and services—opium, women for hire."

"This ledger you speak of," said Sun Lu. "You have seen it?"

"I have. Diamond no longer has it. It's in the hands of the police now, which means that they, too, know of your association with him."

"You know these things because you represent the police? Or perhaps you represent Mister Diamond?"

Hunter hesitated. He could sense that he was being steered into a corner.

"I represent…"

Sun Lu looked at him in silence, his expression vaguely amused. He looked as though he could have waited an eternity for this masked intruder to finish his statement.

"Justice," said Hunter.

Sun Lu's eyes crinkled at the corners. His mouth turned up slightly at either end. If the resulting expression wasn't a smile, it was something close to it. "Justice," he said. "A word that can mean so many different things, depending on where one stands in relation to the world."

Hunter started to speak, but a sound from beyond the inner door stopped him.

Footsteps, bare feet, coming fast.

His muscles tensed. He instinctively dropped into a crouch. He heard a male voice from beyond the door and down the hall say something in Chinese—something like, "Yay-yeh."

Su Lu turned his head toward the door and called back. It sounded to Hunter like, "Wo hen how!"

The footsteps kept coming, and the inner door flew open. A short, stocky Oriental appeared in the doorway. He looked to be only nineteen or twenty. He wore pajama pants and nothing more, but the gun in his hand made up for any lack of protective covering.

In a split second, the young Asian glanced at Sun Lu, then turned toward Hunter and leveled the gun at his chest.

Sun Lu put a hand up and repeated the order he'd given a moment before.

The youth held his fire, but kept the gun pointed at Hunter and glared at him with cold, dark eyes.

Hunter, still in a crouch, stared back at the youth and his gun. No one said a word or moved a muscle for a full ten seconds.

The youth growled something at Hunter, but Sun Lu quieted him by repeating his order one more time.

"I won't overstay my welcome," said Hunter. "But remember this: Your association with Diamond needs to end. The opium, the women—it all needs to end. Now. Your hands are already dirty, and they'll only get dirtier if you continue down this path. The police and the district attorney want Diamond, but they'll come for you too. And I don't think you want to spend your last years in jail. You've lived a long life, especially when you consider Chinatown's history. You've had peace in this community for almost two decades. Doing business with Diamond would undo all of that."

He took a step backward but kept his eye on the youth with the gun.

"You said yourself that time is precious," Hunter said to Sun Lu. "Make the best of what you have left."

Hunter took another step backward, and the youth fired.

250

Hunter sensed it coming and dodged left. The bullet missed his ear by mere inches.

Sun Lu yelled something in Chinese. It sounded like "Ting jee!" but Hunter didn't wait around for a translation. The last thing Hunter saw before ducking back toward the shadowy staircase was Sun Lu reaching up from his chair and grabbing the youth's forearm in an effort to keep him from shooting again. The old man yelled the command a second time.

More chatter followed—obviously an argument, even if Hunter couldn't make out the words. The disagreement created enough of a distraction and a delay for Hunter to make his way down the stairs and across the back lot of the shop.

Hunter had come to issue a warning and nothing more. He'd had no intention of intimidating an old man in his home or brawling with a trigger-happy valet—or whoever the youth was—just to make some kind of point.

He kick-started the motorcycle and shot off in the darkness on a deserted back street.

He was done for the night. It was time to go home.

CHAPTER 43
THE MAN IN THE MASK

Hunter walked into police headquarters at a few minutes before seven a.m., balancing an unlikely combination of fatigue and exhilaration. He was running on less than three hours of sleep, but he felt like he'd made more progress with the Diamond case in one night than anyone else had in several days—even if his methods had been far less than orthodox.

Gallagher had called him at home an hour earlier. Hunter had been expecting the call. The DA had just got off the phone with Taggert a few minutes earlier. Taggert hadn't told him much, but Gallagher and Hunter were expected at police headquarters as soon as possible for an emergency meeting with the chief, Dugan and the mayor.

The morning chatter from all corners of the department—and the hum of excitement that came with it—hit Hunter the minute he entered the building.

"...found Horton on the floor in the kitchen, wrapped up in a bunch of netting..."

"...rounded up almost eighty people from three different locations..."

"...said Reynolds was half-dressed, on his knees, with his hands tied to the railing by his own suspenders..."

He waved to the desk sergeant, who was poring over the front page of the morning edition of the *Tribune*. Hunter had yet to read the story, but he suspected the byline would be Max's. The sergeant gave him the nod and directed him to the conference room down the main hallway.

"...twenty feet over everybody's head, swingin' across the room like Douglas Fairbanks..."

"...all kinds of dope up on the second floor. And a few dames, too. And I ain't talkin' about waitresses, either."

Hunter passed the chief's office, where the door was ajar but the room was empty.

"...looks right at them, then turns around and just jumps...right over the railing..."

"...guy comes flying out the front window, like he'd been shot out of a cannon..."

He proceeded to the conference room, where he found Gallagher and Taggert standing near the table and speaking with Bentley in quiet tones. All three men looked up when Hunter came through the door.

"Gentlemen," said Hunter. The others nodded in acknowledgement.

"Mike's on his way," said Taggert. "We'll get started as soon as he gets here."

Hunter arched an eyebrow and tilted his head back toward the hallway. "Lot of excitement out there."

Bentley shook his head and scowled. "I don't like it," he said.

Dugan walked into the room with a thick folder and a notebook stacked under his arm. His face was shadowed with fatigue. Everyone else in the room took his arrival as the cue to take a seat around the table.

Taggert remained standing to close the conference room door. "Alright, Mike, let's not waste any time," he said. He moved to the chair next to Dugan and settled in. "Everyone's heard bits and pieces. And I know the rumors are already starting to fly, so let's run through it from beginning to end for everyone's benefit."

"Alright, here's what we know," said Dugan, positioning his folder on the table in front of him. He opened his notebook and flipped through a few pages. "I'll do my best to keep it brief."

He took a moment to gather his thoughts, then launched into his account. "Last night, roughly between the hours of eleven and twelve-thirty, we were alerted to unusual activity at three establishments that we believe to be a part of Nicky Diamond's operation, based on the information in the ledger that we...that was delivered to us the other day. The first location was Danny's Tavern on Clifford, near West Eighteenth. We got an anonymous call with a tip about card games in the basement of the club. When our officers arrived, they found a man at the back door. Charlie McNeil, a guy who's been working as a bouncer for the place. McNeil's hands were tied to the railing with his own belt. The officers said he had a fat lip and he was pretty agitated, talking about a guy in a mask who'd grilled him for a few minutes and then tied him up."

Bentley raised an eyebrow at the mention of the masked man and exchanged glances with Taggert and Gallagher.

"The officers entered the building and arrested a room full of card dealers and several patrons," Dugan continued. "Twenty-two in all."

"This anonymous caller," said Bentley. "Did he give away any clues as to who he was?"

"We don't have an exact transcript of the call," said Dugan, "but the dispatcher said he specifically referred to Diamond's ledger, and that he knew Danny's Tavern was listed in the ledger."

"Think the caller might have been the masked guy?" said Gallagher.

Dugan shook his head. "No way to know for sure," he said, "but I certainly wouldn't rule it out."

The detective flipped to another page in his notebook and shifted in his chair. "By the time our officers were bringing the bunch from Danny's into the Fifth Precinct for booking," he said, "Fire Station Three was responding to an alarm at The Caribbean Club on Holloway. They sent two trucks, but there was no fire when they arrived. No threat of fire, for that matter. They did find the place in complete darkness. Apparently someone had removed all the fuses from the fuse box, except for the one that controlled the fire alarm circuit."

"What was happening there?" said Hunter. *Ask,* he thought, *because you're not supposed to know any of this.*

"Well, for starters, a lot of confusion," said Dugan.

"Big crowd?" said Gallagher.

"Big enough. Nearly two-hundred when you total up the patrons and the restaurant staff. Many of them had been penned into the party room at the back of the building by two stainless steel utility tables from the kitchen—one stacked on top of the other in the doorway. They were just starting to push their way through the barricade when the firemen arrived."

"I'm going to assume," said Hunter, "that the people in this party room had been doing more than just eating and drinking."

"That would be a correct assumption," said Dugan. "The place was a mess by the time the firemen got there, but they found a roulette wheel and an over-and-under table. Both had been overturned and knocked onto the floor. And there were at least six decks of cards and a couple hundred chips all over the floor as well. When they found all that, they called us."

"All these people and all this confusion," said Gallagher. "Any injuries?"

"Fortunately, no. Could've been a lot, though. There were a hell of a lot of people stumbling around in the dark when the fire crew arrived. And the tables stacked in the doorway were pretty heavy. The gambling-related items weren't the only thing that prompted them to call us."

"What else?" said Gallagher.

"We sent four officers, and then four more when we realized how big the crowd was," said Dugan. "For starters, they found the bouncer—guy named Larry Carson—at one end of a short hallway coming off the rear entrance. He'd been banged up pretty good, but he didn't want to say much after one of the officers found his gun on the floor a few feet away."

"Did you bring him in?" said Hunter.

"Yeah," said Dugan. "We brought a lot of people in from that place. A lot of them have posted bail, but we still have Carson. He's not giving us much. Says he didn't see anything, partly because of the darkness, and partly because—as he tells it—somebody grabbed him and knocked him out after the lights went out."

"What's his story?" said Gallagher.

"Oh, he's got one. A list of prior offenses that goes back several years. Burglary, assault, auto theft. Enough to warrant us holding him for a while. He's part of a much bigger picture in this incident that's matching up with the information in Diamond's ledger."

"How so?" said Gallagher.

"The officers also found some people in a corner of the room who'd been smoking quite a bit of opium. They also found the owner of the place, Gus Horton, in the kitchen. He was tangled up in a bunch of netting."

Hunter frowned. His eyebrows furrowed. "Netting?"

"Yeah. It had been hanging on the wall. Part of the décor. Somebody took it down and wrapped him up in it."

"Somebody who?" said Gallagher.

Dugan shifted in his chair. "Well, we asked him that."

"Let me guess…" said Gallagher.

"He said it was a guy in a mask."

The DA rolled his eyes and shook his head. "Jesus. Okay, go on."

Dugan took a deep breath and turned a page. "Yeah, well, it gets even stranger," he said. "At approximately twelve-fifteen, four officers responded to a call about a disturbance at a private engagement at The Sterling Palace on Seneca Avenue. A large group of patrons—a few hundred, actually—were emptying out of the building and running into the street, which caused a pretty big traffic jam. A couple people in the street said something about a shooting inside. Two of the officers entered the building though the front entrance at ground level. The other two went up the fire escape and came in through the terrace on the second floor."

The detective paused, as though he were unsure of where to take the story next. He looked up from his notes.

"Okay, for starters," he said, "all four of the officers said they could smell opium the minute they walked into the place. Especially the two on the second floor."

"What about the shooting?" said Hunter.

"The officers said the place was pretty dark. Apparently, someone on the mezzanine level put a bullet through both of the chandeliers over the ground floor."

"Gambling?" said Gallagher.

"Yeah. And then some."

"Obviously drugs," said Hunter, "based on the officers' account of the smell."

"Right," said Dugan. "They found plenty of evidence up on the second floor to corroborate the smell."

A pause hung in the air.

"And…?" prompted Gallagher.

"Some trafficking as well."

No one spoke for a moment. Gallagher leaned back in his chair and folded his arms. "Gambling, drugs and prostitution," he said. "Sounds like a hell of a party."

Dugan shrugged and scratched his head. "What's even more interesting is who was *at* the party."

Again, no one spoke. Everyone waited for Dugan's big reveal, although Dugan looked less than eager to deliver it.

"Based on some hearsay the officers picked up from the crowd, State Senator Richard Vance was on hand. So was Ben Cooper, head of Cooper, Hellman & Drake."

"The accounting firm," said Gallagher.

Dugan nodded.

"Hearsay," said Hunter.

"Right. None of the officers can confirm that."

Hunter saw the hesitation in Dugan's face. He knew from first-hand experience the night before that there was one other high-profile actor in this play, and he wanted the detective to hurry up and get to the point.

He leveled his gaze at Dugan and arched an eyebrow. "Who *can* they confirm?"

Dugan paused. "The two officers on the second floor also found Judge Anthony Reynolds on the mezzanine."

Hunter sat back. The room as silent. Bentley shook his head, his face locked in a grimace. Hunter knew the mayor had been briefed before the meeting, but he apparently was still struggling to make sense of it all.

"Wait a minute," said Gallagher, doing his best to plow through the confusion and come up with the next appropriate question. "Wait a minute. I don't understand. If Reynolds was on the mezzanine, was he the shooter?"

"Not likely," said Dugan. "If you're going to shoot a gun, you need a free hand and a clear eye. Reynolds didn't have either."

The DA frowned. "I don't follow you."

"The officers said he was on his knees," said Dugan, "only partially dressed in an undershirt and trousers. His hands were tied to the mezzanine railing, and he clearly had some liquor or drugs in his system—maybe both."

Gallagher's mouth turned downward in an expression of distaste. "Tied to the railing? Half dressed? Jesus, what the hell kind of depraved operation are we talking about here?"

"No, nothing like that," said Dugan. "There was someone at the railing with Reynolds when the officers found him."

Everyone looked at Dugan.

The detective took a deep breath. "The man in the mask."

"For God's sake," Gallagher murmured. "What the hell...?"

"He was the one who apparently tied Reynolds up. The officers attempted to apprehend him. They drew their weapons, but he, uh... he jumped over the railing."

The DA's eyes narrowed. "He what?"

"He grabbed a banner that was hanging from the ceiling and swung overhead, across the room to the opposite side."

"He...He what?" Gallagher sputtered. "He swung across the...? But the dining room in that place, along with the dance floor...That has to be a hundred feet long."

A hundred and ten, thought Hunter, recalling how the mask had heightened his vision and spatial sense to a point where he could calculate precise distances and vectors at a mere glance.

"He went through the window at the opposite end of the room," said Dugan. "Crashed right through the glass and landed on the street below."

"What?" said Gallagher. "And he walked away?"

"His fall was broken by a group of people standing in the street. One of them was treated for a broken arm."

Hunter winced involuntarily.

Gallagher went silent, apparently baffled about where to go next in his line of questioning.

"Alright," he said finally. "Where's Reynolds now?"

"He's at home," said Bentley. "Don Weller, the law director, is planning to meet him there this afternoon. He's going to advise

Reynolds to take a voluntary leave of absence from the bench."

Hunter leaned forward suddenly in his chair. "Wait a minute," he said, glancing briefly at Gallagher and then back at Bentley. "He's going to *advise* him? Hell, why don't we just send him a bottle of scotch and take him out to lunch? Maybe buy him a new suit and get him a haircut and a shave?"

Bentley put a hand up. "Now, hold on just a minute, Jack…"

But Hunter didn't hold on. He was tired, and running short of patience. And while he couldn't say it out loud, he'd literally stared down the barrel of nearly a dozen guns in the last several hours to tear the lid off a few rats' nests in the Diamond operation. "No, let me get this straight," he said. "He was found half-dressed in a funhouse full of illegal activity, which suggests that he was likely taking advantage of any or all of the services and amenities that were readily available in that establishment last night."

He had a head of steam building, and he raised an index finger to drive home his point. "And all of this comes just a few hours after Reynolds conveniently decides not to issue any arrest warrants in a high-profile, high-priority case," he said. "Why? Because based on a questionable technicality, he considers a critical piece of evidence to be inadmissible. Seems to me we should be holding him for questioning, not advising him to take time off."

Bentley leaned back in his chair and folded his arms. "Jack, I don't like the tone you're—"

Gallagher cut in. "Hold on, Steve," he said. He turned to address Hunter. "Jack, this was partly my decision. I spoke with Weller at about four o'clock this morning, and we agreed that giving Reynolds some room is the smartest thing we could do."

"How?" said Hunter.

"We need to ask ourselves what's the greater objective here. If Reynolds is implicated in any kind of illegal activity, then he should be arrested and prosecuted. But if we know the laws he's broken are connected to the biggest game in town, then we need to give him some room to maneuver. If he feels like he has that, he'll be more likely to cooperate with us by giving up some information about Diamond."

Hunter was silent. His jaw clenched as he took in a deep breath of air through his nose and let it out slowly. Frustrating as the logic was, it was also hard to refute.

"I have no doubt that Reynolds is dirty," Gallagher went on. "Up to his neck and maybe farther. I'd stake my career on it. Hell, I'll probably have to before this is all over. What's more, I know everyone in this room believes it too. But Reynolds knows the law inside and out. He knows how to use it to his advantage, and if we go after him with guns blazing, he'll surround himself with the most seasoned and high-powered attorneys in this state. And if it comes to that, he won't give us anything. He'll fight like a cornered animal, and that'll just create a distraction from the bigger prize."

"Okay, but let's be clear," said Hunter. "We've been speculating for days now whether someone—either in this building, or the Justice Center, or City Hall, or who knows where—might be tipping Diamond off to police strategy. And now we have a very clear indication that Reynolds is cozy with Diamond and taking part in recreational activities associated with his operation. There shouldn't be much doubt left about who's been funneling information to the enemy."

Taggert cleared his throat and Hunter and Gallagher both turned in unison to look at him. The chief looked more than a little annoyed.

"Look, with all due respect to everyone here in the room," said Taggert, "we can talk all day about the obvious connection between Reynolds and Diamond and how we can play it to our advantage. I want to bring Diamond down as much as the rest of you. Probably even more. And if that means maneuvering Reynolds, I'm all for it. But last time I checked, I was still a cop. And last time I checked, law enforcement was the job of the police. Not some clown in a mask. I want to know who this guy is."

Dugan shook his head slowly. "I'll second that," he muttered under his breath.

Taggert turned his attention to Gallagher, his voice growing more taut and his delivery more forceful with every sentence. "Ed, you said something about 'the biggest game in town' a minute ago. Let me be as clear as I can about this. I don't know who the hell this guy is, but we have no tolerance in this city for vigilantes. As far as I'm concerned, apprehending him needs to be just as high on the list as bringing down Diamond. Hell, for all anyone knows, this guy might be part of Diamond's operation, and if that's the case, accomplishing one of those objectives might take care of the other."

A tense silence hung in the room. The meeting was on Taggert's turf, a place where he could be very clear about his priorities and his expectations.

Dugan's jaw clenched. Hard lines etched his tired face. The chief of police had just ratcheted up the pressure on his chief of detectives, and he'd done it in front of the two highest ranking members of the city's criminal justice system.

Hunter felt a pang of empathy. Dugan wasn't the head of the detective bureau by accident. He was the best investigator in town, maybe the best in the county. No one in the room—or on the police force, or in the DA's office—would have disputed that. But recent events had put him squarely on the hot seat, in large part because of Hunter's highly unorthodox late-night adventures.

He also felt a pang of apprehension. It dawned on him—even more so than before—that he'd been playing with fire over the last couple nights. Any resulting burns could be severe enough to not only end his career but probably land him in jail—maybe right next to the cell where Anthony Reynolds belonged.

Dugan gathered his papers. "Alright," he said in a clipped voice, "assuming we're just about done here, we still have a lot of arrests to process. I want to see how many of these people I can question personally before the defense lawyers step in and everybody clams up."

After a few words from Taggert about the police and DA's office keeping in touch about developments, the meeting adjourned.

Hunter left the room with an uneasy feeling.

CHAPTER 44
A FALLEN JUDGE, A BROKEN DEAL

Nicky Diamond sat at a smaller desk than the one he'd grown accustomed to, tapping his fingers on the wooden desk top just a few inches away from his gun. He found himself in much more modest surroundings than those he'd enjoyed in the upstairs office of the Paramount Club. Gone were the oak desk, the ornate furniture and the Tiffany lamps. Gone, too, was the private adjoining room set up for leisurely diversions. Events of recent days had forced him to make do in a more utilitarian environment.

The new location was an office in Union Tower, in a section of the building that was virtually empty after several businesses had folded in recent years and vacated the space. Although the surroundings may have been less luxurious, the room had a large bank of windows along one wall that allowed a wide view of the downtown area, especially the Administrative District seven blocks to the northeast

All in all, Diamond made do. If he had to enter the lobby at all, he did so during the quieter, low-traffic hours of the day. He kept his collar up, his hat on, and avoided eye contact with the public. More often than not, thanks to an arrangement with one of Sparks' connections who worked as a guard in the south parking garage, he bypassed the lobby altogether and accessed the office by way of the service elevator at the back of the building.

Despite the change in location and the inconveniences that came with it, Diamond was able to stay sharp and take care of the business at hand. It helped that Simone had gotten his hands on a substantial new supply of the cylinders. Diamond had arranged about a half-dozen of them on the desk top. He picked one up and cracked it open, then pulled out the strip of coated paper and swallowed it whole. It was his second in less than an hour.

His hands trembled throughout the ritual. The tremor was partly due to the stimulating effects of the white powder he was now pushing through his system on a constant basis, and partly the result of the frustration stemming from his current circumstances. Indeed, each fueled the other.

He swallowed and leaned back in his chair, assessing the damage as he waited for the wave to hit him.

Hunter, the assistant DA who'd visited the Paramount the other night, had made it clear that he was wise to the club being Diamond's base of operations. So Diamond had had to take his base of operations elsewhere—to a place that was more high-profile, and hence more risky.

On top of that, the police had arrested several people the night before who'd been directly or indirectly affiliated with his organization at some level or another, including two of his lieutenants at The Sterling Palace. And then there was Malone, Horton, the Sterling staff. There was the low-level hired muscle at each location—McNeil, Carson, whatever imbeciles the Sterling had watching their room. And there were the card dealers and the other attendants who ran the tables. And of course, the ladies at the Sterling.

And that didn't include the four others—Whitey, Zig, Crane and Bugs—who let themselves get caught in the mess at the Watt Building barely forty-eight hours earlier. They'd all been released from the hospital and taken directly into police custody.

How soon before one of these people—or any number of them—started singing? How soon until the whole organization was completely compromised before he could even finish setting it up?

Twenty-four hours ago, Diamond could have relied on Anthony Reynolds to manage the situation from his position on the bench in order to avert or minimize any damage—or potential damage—from their arrest and detention. But a lot had changed in twenty-four hours. Now the judge was in hot water after some idiot with a mask delivered him to the police under highly compromised circumstances. Reynolds' leverage had been neutralized, at least indefinitely and maybe even permanently. That same masked idiot—whoever the hell he was—had taken down three of Diamond's businesses and punched a good-sized hole in his entire operation in a single night.

Worst of all, the police and the DA's office also had Diamond's ledger—a detailed record of the operation, including the gambling revenues and expenses from the nightclubs, the opium clientele and distribution channels, and all of the employees and contacts in the prostitution ring. It was a highly incriminating piece of evidence that Reynolds had managed to suppress, but now that Reynolds' ethics and affiliations had been called into question, how long would the ledger remain inadmissible in court?

He knew all of this could easily put him away if various loose ends didn't get tied up, and he wasn't entirely sure how he'd do that.

But then the powder kicked in and the wave swept over him, and for a brief moment at least, his concerns went away and everything was clear. The burst of energy gave him a renewed sense of control over the situation. He would come up with a plan, and everything would work out.

In the midst of his introspection punctuated by a chemically-induced jolt of new optimism, he'd nearly forgotten the five other men in the room. Vince Marshall sat cross-legged in a folding chair directly across the desk from Diamond. The consigliere regarded Diamond with a neutral expression, and his only movement was the barely perceptible tap of his right index finger on his knee.

Further back in the room were Sparks and Wireless, seated at either end of a small sofa. Sparks had been part of Diamond's inner circle since he'd returned to Union City, so his presence in the room was not uncommon. But Diamond had also told Sparks to bring Wireless with him, although he didn't say why.

Farthest away, in a dimly lit corner, sat Anthony Reynolds, his eyes red with fatigue and his face twisted into a scowl. He sat motionless, but he radiated anxiety and agitation like heat from a stove. He looked as though he were trying to hold onto some sliver of dignity in the wake of all that had transpired the night before, but exhaustion and anxiety appeared to be getting in the way. His reputation and his career had been completely compromised, and he clearly wasn't happy about it.

Louie Simone sat in a chair a few feet away from Reynolds. Given Reynolds' circumstances, Diamond had taken Simone aside privately and instructed him to stick close to the judge to ensure that he didn't go anywhere or do anything that could further complicate the situation.

Kowalski was in the hallway right outside the closed office door, assuming his usual role as the silent sentry. So if Reynolds did try anything stupid, he wouldn't get far.

If Reynolds was as miserable as he looked, Diamond wasn't happy either, but for reasons that had nothing to do with the judge's precious reputation. Reynolds had been in Diamond's pocket for years. Any power the judge had acquired had largely come from him. Reynolds had managed to hold onto it for the dozen years Diamond was out of the picture, and he'd been more than willing to pick up where he'd left off when Diamond made his way back to Union City.

Reynolds had just become one more liability in a series of frustrating setbacks in Diamond's much larger plan. This, more than any concern about Reynold's precious reputation, was what frustrated Diamond at the moment.

Diamond looked at Marshall. He rubbed his face and his chin in an effort to keep his jittery hands busy. He was about to speak when Kowalski stepped into the room from the hallway.

Diamond immediately read tension on Kowalski's face. He glanced down and saw that he had his gun out and down at his side.

"What's going on?" said Diamond.

Kowalski raised an eyebrow. "Apparently," he said, "Sun Lu wants to talk to you."

Diamond's brow furrowed in confusion. "Sun Lu," he said. "What do you mean?"

Kowalski shrugged. "Just what I said. Sun Lu wants a meeting."

"I don't understand," said Diamond. "Who told you this?" He gestured across the room at Marshall and Simone. "If he wants to set up a meeting, his people need to come to Vinnie or Louie. That's how we've always—"

Kowalski interrupted with another shake of his head. He put up his free hand in a yielding gesture. "Nick, I'm not talking about setting anything up," he said. "He and three of his men are in the hallway. He wants to talk to you right now."

The tension in the room escalated instantly. Diamond glanced at Marshall and Simone with wary eyes. "What the hell...?" he murmured, rising from his chair and picking his gun up off the desk. Marshall and Simone stood up instantly, without a word, and moved toward the door. Simone had his gun out before he was even halfway across the room.

Diamond glanced at Sparks, Wireless and Reynolds. "You three stay here," he said.

Kowalski pulled the hammer back on his gun but kept it at his side. He re-opened the door and went through first. Simone followed immediately behind him with his gun in the same state of readiness. Marshall came next, followed by Diamond.

Kowalski led them all down a short stretch of hallway, then turned right toward the elevators, where three Asians—each with a contemptuous scowl on his face, each with a gun in his hand and down at his side—stood in formation around the compact form of Sun Lu. Diamond recognized two of the bodyguards as the grandsons whom they'd encountered previously in the back room of Sun Lu's shop. He didn't know whether the third was another grandson, nor did he care.

Mounted on the wall opposite the elevator doors was a long mirror, four feet high by seven feet wide, in an ornate bronze frame. The mirror and all the men reflected in it created the illusion of a larger space filled with twice the number of people. Beyond the mirror and the elevators, the main hallway ended at a wall that consisted almost entirely of a large, multi-paned window overlooking the city.

But the view of the city couldn't have been further from Diamond's mind at the moment. His face twisted into a scowl as he locked eyes with Sun Lu's bodyguards and then Sun Lu himself. Standing with the aid of a cane, the old man looked back at Diamond with a hint of defiance in his dark eyes.

"What the hell are you doing here?" he said directly to Sun Lu. "How did you even know where we—"

"I am a businessman. A good businessman makes sure he understands his customers."

"Listen, Fortune Cookie, you can't just come up here and—"

Marshall took two steps forward, and all three of Sun Lu's bodyguards immediately raised their guns and pointed them at Marshall. Kowalski and Simone raised theirs in response. The hallway was suddenly electric with weapons and targets and hard faces.

Marshall stopped dead in his tracks and held his hands out at his side in a conciliatory gesture. "I'm not armed," he said, looking at all three of Sun Lu's men. Then, with his hands still held out, he turned back slightly to look at Kowalski and Simone. "Let's everybody relax for a minute, alright?" Despite the guns and the tension, his voice was surprisingly calm.

After a silent moment, all five guns in the room went back down slowly, but no one made any move to put their weapons away. No one appeared to relax.

Marshall turned back to Sun Lu. He folded his hands in front of him and bowed. "Sun Lu," he said. "Your visit is an honor. Tell me what we can do for you."

Sun Lu raised an eyebrow. "I will not waste time or words," he said to Marshall, with an occasional glance toward Diamond. "I have come to inform you that our association is ended. There will be no further shipments, no more services." His voice was even and carefully modulated, but forceful.

Marshall's brow furrowed. "I'm not sure I understa—"

"I am told of a ledger. A record of your business."

Marshall didn't respond immediately. Diamond saw an opening and stepped forward.

"Yeah, so what's it to you?" he growled.

Sun Lu turned to Diamond, unintimidated by his surly tone. "I am told that it is no longer in your possession," he said. "I am told it is now in the hands of the police."

"Let me assure you," said Marshall, "that we have matters in order, and there's no need for concern over—"

"There is a man in a mask," Sun Lu went on. "He moves quickly in the darkness. So quickly that he is difficult to stop."

Marshall shook his head and attempted a reassuring gesture with his hands. "Sun Lu, those are rumors and nothing more," he said. "We know of no such—"

"Do not insult me. I do not speak of some phantom or trick of the mind. I have seen this man myself."

"That's crazy talk," Diamond muttered.

Marshall turned to Diamond and put his hand up in a yielding gesture. "Nick, wait just a minute," he said. He turned back to Sun Lu. "You've seen him where?"

"In my home. We have spoken."

Both Diamond and Marshall were visibly taken aback.

"In your…" Marshall stammered. "How did…what did he say to you?"

"Our conversation was short. I was not pleased with what he had to tell me, but I do know this." He turned and looked directly at Diamond again. "I know that I trust his words more than any I have heard spoken by you."

"Why you slanty…"

Diamond raised his gun quickly. The Asians responded in kind. Kowalski and Simone put their guns up. Hammers thumbed back on both sides of the room.

Marshall quickly reached for Diamond's arm and eased it back down to his side. "Easy, Nick," he muttered. "Easy. Easy." He glanced at Kowalski and Simone and raised his other hand in a calming gesture. "Fellas, please."

At the same time, Sun Lu spoke in short Chinese syllables to his own men: "Ting-jee. Ting-jee." And the guns came down. He turned to one of his men and issued a quiet command. The man immediately turned to the wall and pushed the button to summon the elevator.

Sun Lu turned to face Marshall again. "Our association is ended," he said. "It would be wise of you to regain control of your records and put your affairs in order. You may be comfortable with your own negligence, but I assure you that I am not—and I will not be a casualty of it."

Diamond and Marshall stared silently back at Sun Lu. The old man and his three bodyguards stared back at them, as though they might hold their gaze for the remainder of the afternoon and well into the evening.

The elevator door opened, and the spell was broken. One of the bodyguards turned and ushered Sun Lu into the rectangular space of the elevator car. The other two followed, backing in to maintain continuous eye contact with Diamond and his men.

The door closed behind them, and Diamond stared at the elevator door for a long moment before turning back down the hallway.

"Come on," he said to the other three men, retracing his steps toward the office. "I have a plan."

CHAPTER 45
BIG PLANS

Diamond was the first one through the door leading back into the office. With a fiery scowl etched on his face, he crossed the room to the desk, picked up a ceramic coffee cup and hurled it against the far wall, where it shattered on impact.

The fact that the cup came close to hitting Reynolds on the way to its target was no accident. The judge flinched and ducked, shielding his face from any flying debris. Wireless and Sparks, though not as much in the line of fire, reacted the same way.

Diamond paced the room as an idea that had been taking shape in the back of his mind for a long time—at least a few weeks—quickly made its way to the forefront.

Marshall said, "Nick," in a quiet voice, as though he might bring him down from his agitated state. Diamond responded with a fierce glare, and Marshall said no more.

Diamond made a few more passes across the length of the room without speaking. "We need to shake this thing up," he said finally.

Marshall arched an eyebrow and shook his head slightly. "I don't follow you."

Diamond didn't bother to explain. He turned his attention instead to Sparks and Wireless.

"I want to do something big," he said to both of them.

The two men glanced at each other and then back at Diamond. Sparks shrugged. "Sure," he said, trying to sound casual but not sounding casual at all. "What are you thinking?"

"Something that'll send a message. A big message, to everybody. I'm sick and tired of cops and DAs and judges getting in my way. I got no time for sneaky little Chinamen and half-brained club owners making things complicated. And I sure as hell don't have time for some crazy guy in a mask mucking up my business."

Sparks and Wireless looked back at him, apparently waiting to see where the preamble was going.

"I want to put all of them on notice—everyone from the mayor to the cops to the cab drivers to the palooka on the street corner. I want to make it clear that I'm taking charge again and I'm not going anyplace this time and I'm not playing any games with anybody."

Sparks nodded slowly, apparently just trying to follow along. "Okay, so what do you want to—"

"Every building," said Diamond. "Every place where the power is—city hall, the police department, the justice center, the county administration building—I want to take it away. I want to send it all up in a blaze."

Marshall leaned forward in his chair and made a yielding gesture with his hand. "Hold on, Nick," he said. "I'm not exactly sure what you're getting at, but I think you might need to—"

"No, I mean it," said Diamond, growing more animated with every word. "I been thinking about this for a while. The only way to take control of this city is to take away the buildings where all the power is."

"Yeah, but Nick, you're talking about mass destruct—"

"I know exactly what the hell I'm talking about," said Diamond. His eyes were fiery and his nostrils flared. "I'm talking about something big. Something that's gonna make it clear that stealing my books and arresting my boys and declaring some kind of screwy war on crime ain't gonna stop me."

He turned to Sparks and Wireless. "Can you two wire it up?"

Wireless looked uncertain. "How many buildings are we talking about altogether?"

Diamond paused to consider. "We'll say ten, all around downtown. All the ones I just said, and a few more."

"It'd take a couple days," said Wireless.

"I want to shut down the city first," said Diamond. "Cut all the power so we can take all the attention away from everything else and make this the main event."

Wireless furrowed his brow and cocked his head to one side, as though he were trying to fully grasp what Diamond was asking. "You mean the electric power?" he said. "The whole city?

"Yeah, that's what I'm talking about."

"Jeez, that'd take..." his voice trailed off as he shrugged and looked toward the ceiling, apparently trying to estimate a strategy and a time frame in his head.

Still pacing, Diamond slowed as he approached the edge of his desk where his gun was resting. The fingertips of his right hand swept the desktop and lightly brushed the handle of the gun. He raised his left wrist and glanced at his watch.

"It's nine o'clock now," he said. His voice was casual on the surface, but there was something going on just underneath, something vaguely but unmistakably menacing. "I want the power out by sundown. That's about twelve hours away, maybe a little more. I want all the buildings wired and ready to go up at midnight."

It wasn't a question at all, and Sparks and Wireless both knew it. Their backs stiffened and they sat upright in their chairs. Wireless' eyes widened slightly. He and Sparks glanced at each other and then looked back across the room at Diamond.

"Yeah, I...we can wire it up," said Wireless. "I'll need some supplies, and some help setting it up." He tilted his head to one side, toward the man sitting next to him. "But I can't take Sparks with me. He needs to be—"

"I know," said Diamond. "Tell Artie and Fallon to give you whatever help you need."

Marshall cleared his throat. "Uh, Nick," he said, "I don't know if this is—"

It was Reynolds who cut him off this time. The judge was out of his chair and full of bluster. "This is insane," he barked, approaching Diamond's desk with clenched fists. "I don't want any part of some crazy plan to blow up half the—"

He stopped short when Kowalski stepped away from the doorway and reached inside his jacket. At the same time, Simone was out of his chair and falling in step behind Reynolds while reaching into his own jacket.

Diamond glanced at Kowalski and Simone. He shook his head and waved them off without saying a word to either man.

"It's alright, Tony," he said to Reynolds in a calm voice. "Just relax. You've had a long night." He motioned to an empty chair just a few feet away from where Marshall was seated. "Have a seat. You want a drink? Louie, why don't you pour Anthony a—"

"I don't want a damned drink, and I don't need to relax!" Reynolds' expression was fierce, and eyes that looked so tired just moments earlier now blazed with new energy. He jerked a thumb toward Sparks and Wireless. "What you're planning, that's madness. I won't have any part of that. None whatsoever. It's bad enough that the cops have connected me to you and your filthy operation, all because of some thug in a mask, but I will not have my name further dragged through the mud because of some plan to blow up a bunch of buildings."

Diamond looked back at him, his face inert and expressionless. He shifted his glance to Marshall momentarily, then looked back at Reynolds. The judge ignored whatever silent communication was taking place between Diamond and Marshall and kept venting.

"I've done a hell of a lot for you, Diamond. A hell of a lot of favors from the bench, including that pretty big one about the ledger just the other day." He gestured toward the door again. "If you start doing crazy stunts like that—even crazier than your usual style—those favors will come to an end and I'll blow the whistle on every one of your operations. I will have no part of—"

"Alright, alright, come on, Tony," said Diamond, putting a hand up to slow him down. His lips had turned up in a smile, but his eyes suggested something else. "Come on. We're not going to make threats at each other, are we? That's not the way you and I talk to each other. Not after all these years."

Reynolds stopped, his storm apparently blown out.

"The truth is," said Diamond, "you're absolutely right."

Reynolds took in a deep breath of air. His back straightened and shoulders went back slightly. His bearing suggested a hint of triumph, as though he'd won the round.

Diamond continued, his voice calm and even. "It looks as though those favors *will* come to an end. From what I understand, the law director will be meeting with you later today and advising you to step down, maybe permanently."

Reynolds' confident expression melted away.

"See, you may have thought I didn't know about that appointment, but I do. Now, as you know, that ledger is a detailed record of our various businesses—not just the nightclubs, but also the opium and the girls. It includes information about all of our expenses, our revenues, and of course, all of our customers and clients."

Reynolds shuffled his feet. He avoided Diamond's gaze and nervously scratched the back of his neck.

"All of our clients but one," said Diamond. He paused, letting his words hang in the air for an extra moment. "You see, Tony, up until last night, nobody but a very small group of people knew you were a part of my filthy operation. I agreed to keep your name out of that ledger in exchange for the assistance you've provided from the bench. But if you're not on the bench anymore, that would mean you'd be of no use to me."

Reynolds' face went white. His left eye seemed to twitch at Diamond's suggestion that he was no longer of use to him. "Well, now...wait, Nick," he said. "There's no need to—"

"Now, I suggest you go on home," Diamond went on. "Maybe get a little rest. And after you meet with the law director, you and I can talk some more and decide whether you can still be of any use to my filthy operation."

The judge started to speak, but he appeared to be at a loss for what to say. At the entrance to the room, Kowalski turned and opened the door. He looked back at Reynolds with a blank expression.

Reynolds turned to Diamond, and the two men looked at each other for a long moment. Diamond finally tilted his chin toward the open door without a word.

The judge retraced his steps to his chair and picked up his hat. He turned and crossed the room silently, shoulders sagging, and shuffled out.

Kowalski closed the door behind him, and Diamond immediately looked across the room at Simone. "Give him a minute," said Diamond, tilting his head toward the door, "and then follow him."

Simone nodded.

"He's probably going home, but just make sure," Diamond went on. "When he gets there—or when he gets wherever he's going to go—get it done. He may be planning on doing it himself. I don't care. Just make sure it gets done."

Simone nodded again. He put on his hat and checked his watch, making sure to give Reynolds a brief head start as instructed.

Diamond turned his attention to Sparks and Wireless. "Alright," he said. "Wait out in the hall. I'll give you a list of buildings in a minute." He was no longer operating from any pretense of request. This was the mission and these were commands. "Sparks, you put together the devices, then get where you need to be." He turned to Wireless. "You get the buildings rigged, and then turn out the lights at sundown. Like I said, get Artie and Fallon, and anyone else you might need to help you. This is the big show, and I want everyone to see it clearly. No distractions."

Both technicians nodded, then headed past Kowalski and out the door. Marshall started to speak, but his words were buried under the force of Diamond's rapidly coalescing plan.

Diamond glanced at his watch and then looked across the room and nodded at Simone. "Alright, Louie, get going," he said. "Get it done before the law director gets to his house."

Simone nodded and started heading out. He was almost across the threshold when Diamond added, "And then we need to get that ledger back from the cops."

Simone stopped, nodded to Diamond one last time, then went out.

Marshall watched Simone disappear down the hallway, then looked back at Diamond for a moment without saying a word. Diamond saw the hesitation in his eyes. "Is there a problem?" he said.

Marshall shook his head. "No, Nick," he said. "Not a problem at all."

CHAPTER 46
KIDNAPPED!

Hunter came through the main entrance to police headquarters at eight p.m. with a thick book under his arm. Betty had called Gallagher late that afternoon. She said she'd be working late with Pruett in hopes of having a finished transcript of the entire ledger by noon the next day. She wondered whether there was someone in the office who could bring her desk edition of Webster's dictionary to her on their way home. Hunter had gotten wind of the request, and Gallagher didn't seem too surprised when he offered to make the delivery himself.

Hunter stepped up to the evening desk sergeant—a short, curly-haired fireplug named Arnie Blake whom Jack had met a few years earlier, shortly after he'd started at the DA's office. Blake looked up from a folded page of newspaper on the desk in front of him and his eyebrows went up. He tucked a pencil behind his ear.

"Say, Jack," he said. "What brings you here so late in the day?"

Hunter took the sergeant's hand and shook it. "Hiya, Arnie," he said. "I'm here to see Betty...Miss Carlyle. I brought a book she asked for. It's a dictionary. Maybe you've heard of it. Can I take a walk back there?"

"Yeah, sure," said Blake. "You know the way back, right?"

"Sure do," said Hunter. "I was just back there a couple days ago."

"Good," said Blake, "because I sure wouldn't want to miss any of the excitement here at the desk with the crossword puzzle from today's *Tribune*."

"Wouldn't dream of taking you away from it," said Hunter. He headed down the hallway. "Thanks, Arnie."

"Sure thing, Jack." He raised his voice as Hunter headed down the main hall. "And if you think of a six-letter word for 'undoing' by the time you come back, let me know."

"Demise," Hunter said over his shoulder.

"Ah, you lawyers are always showin' off."

"It's what happens when you carry a dictionary around." Hunter grinned and threaded his way through the main administrative area toward the long hallway that led to the temporary office set up for Betty and Pruett. Along the way, he waved or nodded to a few people

273

in the department whom he knew, and a few people whom he didn't.

At the start of the hallway, he turned his head to the right to look inside a small kitchen where coffee was brewing in a pot. A plump, middle-aged woman stood at the sink, stirring a steaming cup. She looked up at Hunter and gave him a friendly smile.

"Hi, Jack!" she chimed. "How are you?"

Hunter smiled back. "Hello, Margie," he said. "I'm fine. How are you?"

"I'm just about to start my shift," she said, looking at her watch.

Margie Crump had been working the switchboard in the Union City Police Department for nearly twenty-five years. The last five were spent on the overnight shift. She'd made the switch to nights shortly after her husband had died, in the hopes of filling up the quiet and lonely hours with some kind activity that would be distracting and meaningful at the same time. To what degree her plan worked wasn't clear to Jack. She maintained a cheerful and bubbly exterior, but he wondered sometimes whether she still grieved.

If she did, she had the support of many friends. Every employee in the police department—including all six precincts—knew her, and every one of them loved her.

Margie tilted her head and gave him a puzzled expression. "What brings you here?"

"Oh, I...I have a book that Miss Carlyle requested," said Hunter, gesturing down the hallway. "It's a dictionary. I thought I'd bring it to her on my way home. She said she'd be working late. I hope she's still here."

"I bet she is. She's been working hard on finishing that ledger. Golly, she's a sharp gal. And pretty, too. Want some coffee?"

"No, none for me, thanks. But I wondered if...I thought I might bring some to Betty...Miss Carlyle, I mean."

Margie looked back at Hunter for an extra beat, and a momentary glimmer of some universal feminine wisdom appeared in her eyes. "Ah," she said. And suddenly her friendly smile was even wider, and a new level of enthusiasm made its way into her voice and her movements as she hummed around the small space. "Well, sure," she said, reaching into an overhead cupboard. "There's plenty of cups here, and I don't know how she likes hers, but there's cream in the icebox and sugar on the counter.

Hunter nodded and cleared his throat. "Okay," he said. "Thanks, Margie."

"Sure, Jack." She picked up her cup and patted his arm with her free hand. "I have to start my shift, but it's so nice to see you here. Come again soon, okay?" She glanced down the hall, and the same glimmer returned to her eyes one last time, along with that smile—the one that made Hunter sad for Bob Crump, who was gone too soon and no longer around to appreciate all of its radiance and warmth.

Hunter took a cup and filled it with a combination of coffee, cream and sugar, based on his best recollection of how he'd seen Betty fix hers. With the cup in one hand and the book in the other, he headed down the hallway toward the spare office at the end.

Call it a lawman's sixth sense, but he was still about thirty feet from the door to the office when something he couldn't explain made the back of his neck tingle. Maybe it was the sound of nothing when he should have been hearing the clatter of a typewriter or the murmur of conversation between Betty and Pruett. Or maybe it was the faint but unmistakable whiff of something he couldn't quite define—a smell that might have made sense in a hospital, but seemed completely wrong here.

And it grew stronger with each step.

He reached the office door and turned to look into the room.

The place had been ransacked. Betty's desk was overturned and the usual array of office items—pens, pencils, paperclips, stapler, and the like—was everywhere on the floor. Her typewriter was tipped on its side with a sheet of paper still in the roller. Loose sheets of paper—some blank, some filled with typewritten text—were scattered in all directions. Pruett's desk was askew from its original location in the room, but still upright. A bookshelf had been knocked at an angle and several volumes had fallen in and among the papers and other items. A corkboard that had been mounted on the wall near Pruett's desk hung at an odd angle, and several pushpins and small notes once mounted on the board now littered the top of the desk and mixed with the rest of the chaos on the floor.

Hunter forced himself to remain calm and think clearly, which wasn't easy, given the presence in the air of what he now clearly recognized as chloroform. It was thick and sinister in the confines of the room, and he made a conscious effort to limit his intake to short

275

breaths—or if possible, hold his breath altogether.

He scanned the room until his gaze settled on the door on the opposite wall that led to the parking lot behind the building. The door didn't appear to be damaged. There was no sign of forced entry.

If Betty and Pruett were taken by force, how did their abductors get in? And why the hell would anyone break into a wing of police headquarters in the first place?

None of it made any sense.

Hunter quickly set the coffee cup down on a ledge by the entrance to the room and stepped inside. Some part of him said the room was full of evidence that shouldn't be touched or tampered with, but his legs ignored the warning and kept moving.

He focused on the top of Pruett's desk, still standing on four legs. No ledger. He scanned the floor and its spill of papers, notes, books, pushpins, pens and pencils, scattered papers and other items. He took a quick look around Betty's up-ended desk. No ledger that he could see.

His eyes stopped at two objects on the floor, nearly obscured by the hard shadow underneath the overturned desk. He stepped closer and crouched down to pick up both items.

One was a pink scarf, presumably something that Betty had been wearing around her neck. The other was a narrow strip of plaid fabric that had been stretched and twisted into a hard knot at one end and a tear at the other. Hunter raised the strip closer to his face to examine it more carefully. It was Pruett's bow tie, looking as though it might have been yanked and torn from around his neck in some kind of struggle.

All of it together painted a picture that wasn't pretty. Betty and Pruett gone, apparently taken against their will. And unless his nose was deceiving him, it's likely that they were doped in the process. And on top of all that, the ledger was gone.

He was vaguely aware of commotion down the hall, the murmur of raised voices at a distance, but given the unsettling discovery right in front of him, the sound was barely at the edge of his consciousness.

He stood quickly and scanned the room one more time, momentarily considering the possibility of looking around more—maybe examining some of the typewritten sheets or checking the drawers of both desks. In the end he chose not to. He was already bending the rules by being in the room at all. It was time for a cop.

He moved quickly back to the doorway, cupped a hand to the side of his mouth gave a shout up the hallway for some help. He heard more of the excited murmur he'd noticed before from the front of the building, but didn't get anyone's attention. He shouted a second time, and a young lieutenant stopped at the opposite end of the hallway and turned his head in Hunter's direction.

Hunter beckoned with a wave of his arm. "Got trouble back here!" he shouted.

The cop looked distracted, but headed toward Hunter at a trot. He looked to be in good shape—too good for the strained look on his face—and Hunter sensed that the tension had to do with something other than the relatively short jog down the hallway.

Hunter was now completely out of the office and standing in the hallway. The cop slowed to a fast walk as he approached him and said, "What's going on?" Without waiting for an answer, he moved past Hunter to the entrance to the office. He turned the corner, took one look into the room and let out an exasperated sigh. "Oh, Jesus…"

He took only one step into the room and then stopped himself and turned to Hunter. "Have you touched anything?" he said quickly.

Hunter shrugged. "No," he said, telling only a partial truth. He jerked a thumb at the cup on the ledge by the door. "I came in here to bring her some coffee," he said. "I took one look and I started making noise to get somebody in here."

The lieutenant swore under his breath and stepped back into the hallway.

"You might want to get Dugan down here," Hunter said.

The cop shook his head. "Not anytime soon," he said. "Dugan's got his hands full right now."

Hunter waved a hand at the room. "I don't see the ledger anywhere. If it's gone, he's going to want to know about—"

"We just got a homicide call less than two minutes ago," said the lieutenant, his words coming in rapid fire.

Hunter locked on the young cop's gaze, waiting for the rest.

"You know Reynolds?" said the lieutenant. "The judge?"

Hunter felt the hair on the back of his neck stand up again. "Yeah?"

"He's dead."

"What!"

"In his house, this afternoon. Housekeeper knocked on the door of his study to tell him the law director was there to see him. Didn't get an answer, so he walked in and found him dead in his chair."

Now Hunter understood the excited voices in the hallway a few minutes earlier. "Why do I get the feeling you're going to tell me it wasn't a heart attack or some other natural cause?" he said.

"Hardly. Piano wire around his neck."

Hunter let out a burst of air through his teeth.

The cop started back up the hallway at a brisk trot. "Wait here," he said "I'll get the sergeant and one of the detectives to come down. Don't touch anything in there."

Hunter watched the cop head back up the hallway and turn down a side corridor.

This is it, he thought. *Diamond's big play.* He had a feeling Reynolds' murder and the kidnapping of two civilians while retrieving the ledger was just the beginning—the setup for something dramatic that would unfold in the next few hours. Diamond was all about the dramatic.

Despite the cop's instructions to wait, Hunter slipped back into the room and crossed to the exit door, examining it more closely this time but still not seeing any signs of damage. He pushed through the door and headed out to the parking lot, where he quickly covered the full length of the building until he reached his car.

Before he got in, he glanced in several directions to make sure no one was around, then reached into his jacket pocket and pulled out Betty's scarf and Pruett's bow tie—both of which he'd pocketed before he called for the cop in the hallway. He held one item in each hand and raised one to his face and then the other, sniffing both for traces of chloroform.

He stared into the distance. His eyes narrowed as gears meshed and turned slowly in his head, and suddenly his veins turned to ice as a huge piece of the puzzle fell into place.

In a single explosive burst, he climbed into the car, gunned the engine and tore out of the parking lot in a squeal of rubber.

CHAPTER 47
POWER GRAB

Diamond sat in the spacious back seat of a 1933 Packard Eight, watching the evening traffic as he devoured the powdered-paper contents of not one but two more cylinders. He tossed the spent inhaler capsules on the floor of the car and leaned back in the leather seats, waiting for the kick. He rested his hands on his lap, struggling to keep them from trembling. He couldn't remember the last time he'd slept more than two hours at a time.

Kowalski sat up front and drove nearly to the end of Warehouse Row in the River District. He pulled up in front of the Harper Warehouse, a forty-thousand-square-foot storage center that was the next-to-last stop on the half-mile strip. A twelve-foot-high barbed-wire fence marked the building's eastern property line. On the other side of the fence lay eight acres of municipal property that was home to Union Power and Light, the city's primary power station. Better known among local residents as simply Union Power, the facility's vast combination of transformers, power lines, service terminals and operations offices spanned a two-block stretch and towered fifty feet above the ground at its highest point. It was the very last piece of property on Warehouse Row.

Kowalski had almost brought the car to a complete stop when Diamond leaned forward and said, "Pull around the back."

Kowalski obeyed silently, maneuvering the car down a service driveway that ran along the west wall of the building. At the end of the driveway was a back parking lot whose surface was an uneven and untended combination of gravel, dirt and patches of weed.

A delivery truck, the one Diamond's crew had used for the Pharaoh heist a few days earlier—along with various other operations—was parked in the lot.

The Packard was still moving when Diamond saw Wireless, Artie Garrett and Mitch Fallon hovering around an array of large electrical equipment along the back wall of the building. The arrangement included several bulky rectangular objects—each the size of an icebox, more or less—along with various other components, all strung together in a network of heavy-gauge cable. An additional set of cables extended from one end of the assembly, snaking along the ground and into the distance toward the power station on the adjacent lot.

"There they are," said Diamond. He started opening the back door of the car while it was still slowing down. Kowalski brought the car to a stop.

Diamond stepped out, leaving the car door open behind him, and approached Wireless and the two other men. Kowalski turned off the engine and stepped out as well. He moved in the opposite direction, taking a position on the driveway at the back corner of the building and fixing his gaze on the stretch of road in front of the warehouse. He absent-mindedly pushed his jacket aside with his right hand and hooked his thumb on his belt, just a few inches from where he'd tucked his gun.

Wireless was finishing the last of the connections and examining the mystifying tangle of circuitry running through and around the bulky hardware. His face was drawn and pale, and heavy shadows underscored his eyes. His hands shook slightly as he secured a few final circuits.

He'd been running hard for eleven hours. He'd spent the morning with Sparks, Garrett and Fallon assembling ten explosive devices. By noon, Sparks had left to take care of other business, leaving Wireless, Garrett and Fallon to spend the early part of the afternoon smuggling the devices into various public buildings around town as dictated by Diamond. It had been nerve-racking work, dodging the attention of security guards, elevator operators, washroom attendants and the like in an effort to plant the devices in restrooms, maintenance closets, ventilation ducts and other remote corners.

Once the devices were in place, Wireless had made his way to the Harper Warehouse, where he'd wired up an array of ten-thousand-watt radio transmitting equipment—most of it stolen—in the back room of the building. It had taken him, Garrett and Fallon more than two hours to haul the framework and cable for a twenty-five-foot multi-directional antenna—also stolen—onto the warehouse roof and hoist it into operating position.

But the real excitement had started at around seven-thirty, barely an hour ago, when he and the other two men—each of them armed with Thompson automatic machine guns—stormed the power station and quickly subdued the security guards and the night-shift operations crew. Wireless had hijacked the power from one of the station's twelve transformers and re-routed it to the rectangular units that he and Garrett and Fallon were now assembling.

Diamond eyed the units arranged along the back wall of the warehouse. Each of them was much smaller than their monolithic counterparts at the neighboring power station, but still formidable looking in their own right. Wireless had tried to explain to him earlier that these were just smaller transformers—something called step-down transformers—but beyond that, none of it made any sense to Diamond. He had absolutely no understanding of electricity or electrical circuits.

He turned and looked at Wireless. "This gonna be ready in a few minutes?"

Wireless had been twisting a wrench to bolt down a final series of connections. "Yes," he said. His voice was taut, as though he were trying to work through a wall of fatigue and suppress jangled nerves at the same time. Gone was the sly and mischievous tinkerer of previous days. In his place was someone who'd come to the bitter realization that he was caught up in something not just illegal but evil, and he was in too deep to get out.

Diamond sensed the anxiety in the engineer's voice. His eyebrow arched. "I want to go on in a few minutes," he said, a sudden edge in his voice. "It needs to work."

Wireless stopped turning the wrench and looked back at Diamond, but only momentarily before his eyes flicked away. Diamond's underlying message was clear. Wireless nodded, mumbling an affirmation, and then turned his attention back to his work.

Kowalski, still standing lookout near the driveway at the corner of the building, turned suddenly toward Diamond. "Here they come," he said.

Diamond nodded. "Alright," he said. "Bring them back here. Not out front."

Kowalski headed back down the access driveway on foot at a brisk pace. Diamond moved to the corner of the building where Kowalski had been standing. He watched as Kowalski reached the front of the building and stepped far enough out toward the road to wave down an oncoming car—the black Buick—and guide the driver up the access driveway.

Less than thirty seconds later, the Buick was pulling into the back lot and coming to a stop alongside Kowalski's Packard.

Kowalski looked inside the car and frowned. "He's alone," he said.

The driver's side door of the Buick opened and Simone emerged. Diamond felt a considerable weight lift when he saw the ledger in Simone's hand.

Diamond looked inside the car. "Where the hell's Sparks?"

Simone shrugged as he stepped around the car to where Diamond was standing. "He helped me get the girl in the car, then he said he was going to meet up with Marshall at his office," he said.

Diamond frowned. His eyebrows furrowed. "What for?"

Simone shrugged again. "I dunno," he said. "Sparks said Marshall called him and told him to come to his office. Said they'd meet up with us before midnight."

Diamond waved it away. "She in the back seat?"

Simone nodded. "Yeah. She's still out."

"Any trouble?"

"She fought us pretty good," said Simone. "Made a mess. But we put her out and got her in the car." He turned toward the three men wiring up the equipment and pointed at one of them. "Fallon," he said, poking his thumb over his shoulder and toward the car. "Come on over here and get this dame out of the car."

Fallon stepped away from the transformers and walked across the lot to the car, adjusting his trademark suspenders along the way. Simone opened the back seat door. Fallon bent at the waist and hunched himself halfway into the car. After contorting his shoulders and upper body for a few seconds, he re-emerged with the limp form of Betty Carlyle in his arms.

Eyes closed, face pale in the rapidly falling darkness, she was clearly unconscious. Her head rested against Fallon's chest. Her right arm rested in the small space created by the bend of her narrow waist, while her left arm hung loose from her shoulder.

Fallon looked expectantly at Diamond. "What do you want me to do with her?" he huffed. Despite his sizable frame, Fallon was apparently out of shape.

Diamond cocked his head in the direction of the building some forty feet behind him. "Take her inside."

Fallon headed for the rear entrance to the building.

Diamond turned to Simone. "Take the Packard. Get over to Marshall's office and pick up him and Sparks," he said. "Wait a little bit, then after everything goes dark, come and meet us at the new location. You know where. Go in through the south parking garage."

"There's gonna be a guard at the garage gate," said Simone. "There always is."

"I know it. His name is Huffman. He'll get you into the building. Sparks knows him. That's why you'll want to have Sparks with you when you get there."

Simone nodded. "Alright," he said, turning back toward the Packard.

Diamond clapped him on the shoulder. "Like I said, wait a bit. A half hour, maybe forty minutes, then come over. It'll be good and dark by then. Darker than usual. And the cops'll be out watching the streets, so if you take any main streets, be careful."

"Alright," Simone said again. He climbed back into the car, started the engine. Kowalski waved as Simone headed back up the access drive and toward the street.

Diamond turned and walked back to where Wireless was standing and surveying the last several hours of work—the transformers, the wiring, the antenna assembly mounted on the roof—with an apprehensive eye.

"Alright," said Diamond. "You know how I want this to go. I go on, I do the spiel, and then when I'm done, we shut it all down." He glanced to the east, at the enormous power station on the next lot over. "All of it."

Wireless looked at Diamond and then back at his network of wiring. He paused for a moment, his mouth turning downward into a frown, then nodded. "Right," he said.

"Alright," said Diamond. "Let's go inside."

CHAPTER 48
TERROR ON THE AIR

Hunter headed east and gunned the engine to a speed well past the legal limit. Horns blared as he wove in and out of the early-evening traffic, but he didn't worry much about drawing the attention of a random patrol car. As of the past fifteen minutes, the police likely had their hands full with more important matters than an assistant district attorney in a hurry to get home.

He flipped on the car radio and immediately heard the urgent voice of a local announcer.

"...to bring you details about two stories developing here in Union City at this hour. We have reports that two city employees have been kidnapped, following a break-in at the main headquarters of the Union City Police Department. Information is still coming in at this time, but we are told that unknown assailants broke into a remote section of the south wing of police headquarters on Liberty Avenue and abducted a secretary and a hired consultant who were working in an office at the time."

The announcer paused briefly, apparently trying to make sense of what was most likely a flurry of information coming into the station in the span of just a few minutes.

"We, uh...In addition to the kidnapping, WRUC has also learned of the death of Municipal Court Judge Anthony Reynolds, who was apparently murdered in his home at some time in the past few hours by an intruder whose identity and current whereabouts are not known. We cannot confirm at this time whether the two stories are related in any way, but we will continue to..."

The news announcer's voice was suddenly buried in a piercing screech of static. Hunter glanced away from the road and frowned at the radio on his dashboard. He took one hand off the wheel and tapped the console a few times, hoping to re-align a poorly connected wire or a loose tube, but the static kept coming.

Then it cleared, and the next sound he heard was a voice that turned his blood to ice.

"Attention, Union City. This is Nicky Diamond..."

The voice paused just long enough for Hunter to sense the same familiar knot tightening and growing in the pit of his stomach—the same one that formed every time he thought about Diamond, let alone heard his voice. Then the message went on:

"You might remember me from the old days. I ran some businesses here that provided services to a lot of people in this city and the surrounding area. Unfortunately, some people insisted on breaking up the party and I had to leave town for a few years."

The signal was distorted, unrefined, no doubt generated by bootleg transmitting equipment with enough power to bury every other signal in a wide radius. What's more, Diamond was delivering his message with a contrived cadence in his voice, as though he were reaching for some measure of eloquence and showmanship, but the effort fell short. All of his underworld power and charisma couldn't hide the fact that he was still an uneducated street thug, reading clumsily from some melodramatic script. If he hadn't been so crazed and dangerous, he would have sounded like an idiot.

"At this hour," Diamond continued, "I have taken control of City Hall. I have several associates who have locked down the building."

"Dammit!" Hunter hissed, slamming his palm on the steering wheel and gunning the engine. The voice went on:

"Now, to me, public safety has always been important, so we made sure everyone had a chance to clear out. Well, almost everyone. The ones who did get out will thank me, because they'll have a much better view from outside the building, or anywhere downtown for that matter. However, the mayor is still at his desk. Maybe he's tied up with the business of running the city. Maybe he's tied up with this war on crime he just announced the other day. Whatever he's working on, one thing's for sure. He's tied up."

Hunter swore again as he sped through a red light and barely veered away from two oncoming cars. He was vaguely aware of the blaring of more horns in his wake as he focused on the voice coming from the radio.

"But some of you may remember that I'm the kind of guy who likes to do things with a bang. I like a good show. Anybody can keep a guy in a chair with a lot of rope, but I used some wire too."

The knot in Hunter's stomach tightened as he thought of the piano wire that had squeezed the life out of Reynolds. *No*, he thought. *He's talking about a good view, a good show. He's got something else in mind.*

"Listen carefully," Diamond went on. But something had changed. His voice was cold now, jagged as raw steel. Any attempts at showmanship were over. "Your mayor is wired to a bomb, and the bomb is wired to the door of his office and every other door leading into and out of the building. Any cops want to come in and rescue him, the building goes up and anybody inside goes up with it."

Hunter took a hard right off the main road and onto the last stretch of blocks leading to the Republic Building. Tires squealed, and for just a moment the car felt as though it might have been up on two wheels.

"Now, here's the best part," Diamond went on. "Even if no one tampers with the bomb at City Hall, or any of the entrances to the building, it'll go off at midnight."

Hunter glanced at his watch and swore. Eight-forty.

"And that's just the beginning. You can count on plenty more fireworks. I'd say more, but I don't want to spoil any surprises."

Diamond paused momentarily, presumably for some dramatic effect. For a moment, the only sound from Hunter's radio was the distorted ambient hum of the bootlegged transmission. Hunter shot through an intersection, swerving around an oncoming car and inviting the angry blare of more horns.

Then the message resumed. "Maybe you're thinking all of what I'm saying is impossible," Diamond's voice droned. "Maybe you can't believe I have the resources to engineer a plan like this and pull it off. If you have doubts, ask yourself how I took control of the air waves all over the city."

Despite his reckless speed, Hunter's vision was sharp enough to catch a glance at either side of the street, where drivers huddled in cars parked along the curb—every one of them leaning close to their radios, expressions darkened by the ominous voice emanating from their dashboards.

"Whatever you believe or don't believe," said the faceless voice, "the sun is going down and the city will be in darkness soon. So be sure to get a good seat. The good people of this town are in for a show like nothing they've ever seen before. And when the sun comes up again, it'll be a new day for Union City."

The voice went silent. Then the piercing screech of static returned for about three seconds, followed by what sounded like a cleaner broadcast signal devoid of hum or distortion. A confused murmur of voices came through Hunter's radio, then a single voice—professional yet tentative at the same time—cut through the others. The same news announcer who'd been on the air before Diamond cut in.

"We…We are aware of a transmission that has interrupted our broadcast, apparently from Nicky Diamond, the infamous crime boss who terrorized this city more than a decade ago…We have very little information at this time about the source of the transmission or how it broke into the WRUC signal, but...we assume the message comes as some sort of response to the war on crime announced by Union City Mayor Stephen Bentley, the Union City Police Department and the district attorney's office just a couple days ago."

The newsman's voice was halting, struggling to make sense of the confusion that had erupted. The shuffle of papers underscored his voice as he pushed onward.

"I'm...I'm just now getting word that police have closed off several streets around City Hall and have assembled on all sides of the building," he said. "Several city employees had been reportedly forced out of the building by gunmen earlier this evening. To the best of our knowledge, no one has been hurt, but based on what information we're receiving—and certainly based on the transmission that just interrupted our broadcast moments ago—Mayor Bentley is reportedly still inside City Hall."

Another pause, then the announcer continued.

"We're...we're being told that some sort of electrical wiring has been attached to all points of entrance and exit around City Hall. For the time being, at least, police are making no attempts to touch any of the doors leading into or out of the building. Police are advising residents to avoid the downtown area until further—"

Once again, the voice gave way to static. Hunter glanced at the radio, half expecting Diamond's voice to return, but there was nothing more to be heard.

He looked back at the road. And in that instant, every light on the street—every traffic signal, every streetlamp, every glow from every store front window—blinked out.

In seconds, Union City was in darkness.

CHAPTER 49
DEATH AND DARKNESS

Diamond heard a sharp pop and crackle from outside the Harper Building, followed by the severe flicker of lights inside and the sudden swell of excited voices outside. Seconds later, he was aware of a burning smell, and although he couldn't make out specific words, the anxious voices persisted.

Wireless had just stepped out a minute earlier—just after Diamond finished his broadcast—to shut down the power grid. Diamond wasn't sure what that process was supposed to look like or sound like, but he was pretty sure something wasn't right.

Flashlight in his left hand and gun in his right, he moved down the short passage to the rear door. As soon as he pushed through the door into the night air, the smell hit him square in the face: not just smoke, but something more deadly.

Burnt flesh.

"What the hell...?" he muttered.

He immediately saw Wireless, Kowalski and Fallon standing in a semicircle, their flashlights trained on a crumpled form on the ground. It was Artie Garrett, arms and legs contorted at strange angles, face frozen in a ghastly, wide-eyed mask of agony. His hands and arms—even his shirt sleeves—were darkened to near blackness, his hair partially burned away.

Diamond stepped toward the cluster of spectators, adding his own light to the beams dancing over and around the charred corpse. "What the hell happened?" he prompted.

Wireless had begun pacing nervously, just a few feet from the body. "Godammit," he rasped. "I told him to keep his hands away from the main feed line. There's gotta be two-thousand..." He shook his head and rubbed a shaky hand across his ashen face. "Godammit!"

Diamond flashed his light on Wireless' face. "Alright, calm down," he barked. He peered through the darkness at the adjacent lot beyond the fence and nearly a hundred yards away. The power station was a dark, lifeless silhouette against a moonlit sky.

He tilted his head toward the towering structure. "It's shut down?" he said, confirming the obvious.

Wireless squinted into the beam from Diamond's flashlight. He was either straining his eyes against the light, or annoyed at the question, or both. "What?" he said. "Yeah, we shut it down." He gestured at the charred body near his feet. "But come on. Artie's...I mean..."

"Alright, get inside."

"What?"

"I said get inside. There's more to do."

Fallon looked down at Garrett's remains and then back at Diamond. "What, are we just going to leave him out here?"

"In a few minutes, we're going to be done here. And once we're done, I want this place and everything in it to go up."

Wireless and Fallon looked at him uneasily. Fallon glanced toward the door leading back into the building, then looked back at Diamond.

"The girl," said Fallon.

Diamond's voice didn't waver. "I said everything."

His gun was still at his side in his left hand. He thumbed back the hammer. He never raised the weapon, but the sound was not lost on any of the men standing in the darkness.

Diamond focused his attention on Wireless. "Sparks built the bomb this afternoon, and now you need to wire it up," he said. He turned to Fallon. "And you need to help him."

Kowalski looked at Wireless and Fallon with an arched eyebrow and waved toward the door. "Alright, you heard the man," he said. "Let's get inside."

CHAPTER 50
TRACKING THE WAVE

Hunter roared into the back lot of the Republic Building and stopped with a screech in front of the garage door. Without any power, the door opener wouldn't work. He killed the engine, leaped out of the car, and raced to the door leading into the building's back stairway.

Slamming the door behind him, he turned to head down the stairs leading to the basement. He noticed light coming from below, and guessed that Buzz had engaged the generator that he'd rigged up for electrical emergencies.

Before Hunter hit the third step on the way down, Buzz was coming up the same way.

"Jack, have you heard the—?"

"Yeah, I had it on in the car."

"Jeez, they got Judge Reynolds."

Hunter started down the stairs at high speed. "He had it coming," he said.

"Huh?"

"There's more," he said. "Diamond's men kidnapped Betty Carlyle, one of our secretaries."

"What!"

"You heard me. No more than forty minutes ago, but that's already too long." The two men met in the middle of the stairway and stopped. "Did you hear Diamond's message?"

"I sure did," said Buzz. "It sounds bad, Jack."

"Trust me, it is." Hunter put a hand on his cousin's shoulder and steered him back in the direction of the basement. "Buzz, listen, you know more about radio than anybody else in this city. What can you tell me about that transmission?"

Despite the grim situation that was rapidly unfolding, Buzz's eyes and face spread into a sly grin. "Plenty" he said, turning away and heading back down the stairs. "Follow me."

They moved quickly into the basement, then crossed the basement to the stairs leading to the sub-basement. "I knew something was up after the first couple seconds," said Buzz as the two men headed for the lower chamber. "The signal sounded too distorted. Too much hum."

Hunter nodded. "Right. No licensed broadcast station in this city—or any other city—would generate a signal that dirty."

They reached the landing. "Over here," said Buzz, gesturing toward the adjacent wall. Both men crossed to a workbench where Buzz kept his shortwave equipment—a transmitting and receiving rig that he'd built himself and used to communicate with other shortwave operators around the city, the continent and half the globe.

"Okay," he said, "We've got the omnidirectional antenna up on the roof, right?"

"Sure," said Hunter. "We put it up together, about a year ago."

"Right," said Buzz, tapping an index finger on a small control box on the workbench. "I use this directional control to turn it a full three-hundred-sixty degrees. That way, I can radiate my signal in as many directions as possible."

"But it also works the opposite way, right?"

"Yep. I can use the same directional control to triangulate on the source of an incoming signal. It helps give me an idea of where some of the shortwave operators out there are calling from."

"But this would have been a lot stronger than your typical amateur

290

radio signal," said Hunter. "Even stronger than a local one. Nobody has that kind of wattage in their attic or their basement."

Buzz nodded. "Right," he said. "So I was able to able to think fast enough to turn on the directional control and track the signal for about forty or fifty seconds. It wasn't much. I could have done better if the transmission had been longer and I'd had more time. But I was able to narrow the source down to a general geographic area."

He reached up and pointed to the northern edge of a city map hanging on the wall over the workbench. "Right around here," he said, touching his index finger to the map and tracing a wide circular pattern around the river district. "Maybe about four to six miles northwest of where we are right now."

Hunter touched a finger to the same area of the map. He zeroed in on the river and traced his finger along the waterline and the area just south of it. "Exactly," he muttered, almost to himself.

"Exactly what?"

"A hunch more than anything else, but based on what you're saying, it's adding up to what I had suspected."

Buzz looked at the map, then at Hunter, then at the map again. He scratched his head.

"Okay," said Hunter, still looking at the map where his finger was still pointing. He was keenly aware of the seconds ticking by, and the sense of urgency that ratcheted up with each one of them. "Okay. As long as we're in this neighborhood, would you say the Harper Warehouse is fair game?"

Buzz shrugged. "Sure, I guess. But that's just one spot. The signal could have come from anywhere in that general area."

"Alright," said Hunter, smacking the side of his fist against the map. "That's where I'm headed." He instantly peeled off his jacket and tie and tossed them on a nearby chair.

"What, you're going to go looking for him? Yourself?" A pattern of worried lines etched themselves on Buzz's forehead. "Jack, I know you're a lawman, but come on. Isn't this up to the police right now?"

Hunter shook his head. "You heard the radio," he said, moving across the room to a metal cabinet secured with a combination lock. "The police are all over City Hall, trying to figure out how to rescue the mayor. Nobody in the police department had the equipment or the time or the know-how to trace that signal the way you just did. But if we're right about the source of Diamond's transmission, then I think it'll lead me to Betty. And if I can find Betty, chances are good that I'll find Diamond as well—or at least someone or something that can lead me to him."

Hunter spun the dial on the lock as he spoke, stopping at the proper left-right-left combination of numbers. In seconds, the cabinet door was open.

"But what makes you so sure about the Harper building?" said Buzz.

Hunter pulled the leather jacket and the pair of heavy boots out of the cabinet. "I'm not sure of anything," he said, kicking off his shoes and stepping into the boots, "but if your equipment is right, and my hunch is right, it all adds up."

He lifted the mask from the pedestal where it rested underneath the glow of the lamp and held it carefully in both hands for a moment. Staring back at him from the goggles that Buzz had sewn directly into the leather were dual reflections of his own face, distorted somewhat by the smoky tint and the contoured surface of each lens, yet a completely recognizable alternate version of himself.

"Okay, but it's dangerous, Jack," said Buzz, his voice almost pleading. "What if we told the police—?"

"No!" Hunter barked, slamming the cabinet shut. "This is mine! I'm going to get him, Buzz. He killed my father. He killed your uncle. I've been living with that for nearly fifteen years, and now I have the chance to make it right. The police can come along if they want, but I'm going to finish this."

He positioned the mask over his head and strapped it down. The mental rush was intoxicating, just as it had been when he'd put it on before. He flexed his neck and shoulder muscles. Every sound in the room, every image in his field of vision, every surface he touched, the air itself—all of it was suddenly electrified. Any frustration he'd felt just seconds earlier at Buzz's protests instantly dissolved, and in its place was a razor-sharp focus on the task at hand.

Hunter looked at Buzz through the goggles. Knowing that Buzz could no longer see his eyes, Hunter grinned and gave him the thumb-up with his right hand.

Buzz hesitated. "Alright, listen," he said. "Wait a minute..."

"Buzz, I mean it. I can't waste any more—"

But Buzz had turned away and moved to a corner of the room. "No," he said. "Forget it. I'm not going to stop you. But wait just a minute." He reached for an old leather jacket hanging from a hook on the wall.

It was part of Jim Hunter's service uniform. The police department had given it to Hunter's mother fourteen years earlier, just a few days after her husband's funeral. It had hung on the wall since Virginia Hunter passed away six years later.

Lieutenant James M. Hunter's badge was still pinned to the lapel. Buzz removed the badge and walked back to where Hunter was standing.

"Take this," he said. "Uncle Jim…I mean, your dad…He'd want you to have it with you." He tucked the badge into a pocket in the lining of Hunter's jacket.

"Buzz…"

"Just be careful, okay?"

They looked at each other silently for a few seconds.

"You're the smartest guy I know, Buzz."

"Somebody has to be. Because you're just full of dumb ideas."

Hunter grinned, and after a moment, Buzz grinned back at him.

"Alright, Jack," said Buzz, smacking his cousin on the shoulder. "Go get that son of a bitch."

Hunter turned away and bolted up the stairs.

CHAPTER 51
DANGER AT THE RIVER

Hunter was still three blocks from the Harper Warehouse when he throttled back on the motorcycle engine and relied mostly on the bike's momentum to cover the remaining stretch. He sacrificed some speed in the process, but he knew he'd draw less attention if the engine wasn't revving right up to the front door of the building.

He cut the engine completely and coasted into the back lot of the building just west of the Harper Warehouse—two lots away from the Union Power station at the end of the street. He quickly dismounted and parked the motorcycle behind a pile of cinderblocks and railroad ties. With the entire River District devoid of a single functioning street lamp, and with nothing more than the glow of the moon to cut through the resulting darkness, he knew the two-wheeled vehicle would be well hidden.

Crouching low and staying close to the back wall, Hunter concentrated his enhanced hearing and vision in an effort to pick up any unusual sound or movement in his immediate surroundings. There were no voices, no scuff of shoes on gravel, not even the sound of breathing or a single heartbeat. What he did catch was a hum, quiet and steady, coming from the direction of the warehouse.

Still hanging close to the wall, he crept toward the opposite end of the building. When he reached the far corner, he found an access driveway separating the lot where he was standing from the adjacent Harper Warehouse lot about a hundred feet away.

He saw two vehicles parked in the Harper back lot. One was an unmarked delivery truck, and the other a black Buick.

Not just any black Buick. *The* black Buick. The one that had seemed to be following him around town in recent days. The one he'd watched Anthony Reynolds climb into on a downtown street corner when he was walking with Bart Maxwell a couple days earlier. The one that Diamond's goons had driven when they pulled up to Buzz's shop and took Buzz to the Watt Building. The one that left clear enough tire tracks at the police department barely an hour ago before driving away with Betty and Pruett inside.

He scanned the Harper Warehouse lot from his limited vantage point for just a few more seconds. When he was sure there was no one in or around the two vehicles—or anywhere else outside the building—he took a chance and stepped away from the wall to get a better look at the lay of the land.

Suddenly the hum he'd been hearing made sense. The warehouse looked as though it had been turned into a makeshift electrical substation all its own—a much smaller, cobbled-together version of the full-scale municipal power station on the next property over. Four large transformers—each about the size of an icebox, each probably generating 500 volts—stood along the back wall of the warehouse, not far from the back door. Two cables extended from the back of each transformer and snaked along the ground into the distance, siphoning energy from the monolithic Union Power looming in the darkness nearly two-hundred yards off.

Hunter's eyes followed a second set of wires that emerged from the transformer array and crawled up the back of the Harper Warehouse, all the way to the flat roof forty feet up. Mounted at the top of the building and stabbing the night sky was a twenty-five-foot-tall vertical antenna. Given its position on the roof, the highest point of the antenna had to be nearly sixty feet above ground.

So far, his hunch about where to find Diamond appeared to be panning out. This was clearly the source of the pirate broadcast that had blanketed the city, and the wattage necessary to get on the air—and bury every other radio signal in town in the process—had been stolen from the power station right next door. And judging from the car and the truck parked in the back lot, some combination of Diamond, his goons, Betty and Pruett were inside. What's more, someone among Diamond's ranks, probably the same person who'd rigged the transmission—and Hunter was fairly certain he knew who—had found a way to shut down whatever municipal circuits they weren't using and bury the rest of the city in darkness.

But there was even more to Hunter's hunch that brought him to this dark place. He needed to get inside the warehouse, where he knew he'd find not only Betty Carlyle, but also more evidence about the extent of Diamond's sinister network.

He crossed the access drive silently and made his way around the parked car and truck. The closer he got to the hulking transformers, the more aware he became of the electric energy pulsing through them. Their collective hum—once distant but now at the forefront of his consciousness—was a vibration as much as a sound, a sensation made all the more pronounced by the auditory enhancers in Hunter's mask.

He moved past the enormous setup, wondering whether the ambient electrical field around the four large units was strong enough to create some kind of interference with the circuits woven into his mask. He couldn't be sure, but it was likely. He did his best to filter out the hum and focus his hearing on whatever was on the other side of the rear entrance to the building. Hearing nothing, he grabbed the door handle and opened it slowly, just a few inches.

At a glance, the coast appeared to be clear. Beyond the door was a short hallway that led to two storage rooms before the space opened up to something much larger. The interior was shrouded in nearly complete darkness, save for a glow from a half-open door at the opposite end of the hallway. Whatever the source of the glow, it occurred to him that he was standing in what was probably the only building in town with the luxury of electric power at the moment.

He moved further into the entrance to create some distance between himself and the hulking electrical units. He made sure to leave the rear door ajar in case he needed to back out quickly. Back pressed to the wall, he stepped sideways to a point just short of the half-open inner door.

Within a few seconds, he heard voices on the other side.

"Where's the girl?" It was Diamond, his voice edgy, his heart rate accelerated.

"I put her on the cot in the other room." Hunter recognized this second voice, but from where? He thought for a moment and it came to him: one of the two gunman in the back room at the Watt Building. One of the two men sitting at the table playing cards. The one with the suspenders. "I think she's starting to come around," he went on, "but we got her hands and feet tied up."

"Give her another dose," said Diamond.

"You sure about that? We gave her a pretty strong hit of the stuff back at the office. If we give her too much, she could—"

"Give her another dose."

"Okay."

Hunter heard footsteps moving out of the room on the other side of the door and toward some other place in the building.

There was a momentary pause, then Diamond's voice again. "This gonna work?" It sounded like a threat as much as a question.

"What? Yeah, it'll work." This voice sounded hoarse, more than a little anxious, but Hunter recognized it. His jaw tightened into a grimace. It was Willis Gray, the radio engineer from WRUC.

My friends call me Wireless.

Gray had been on his knees when Hunter bumped into him at Bentley's press conference. But he wasn't admiring the woodwork as he had claimed at the time. He was examining the design and the hardware of the front entrance to get an idea of how to wire it up. Apparently this plan to rig the building had been percolating for days if not weeks.

Hunter remembered the familiar looking figure he'd seen at The

Caribbean Club just a couple nights after the press conference—the one whose (use em dash) face he couldn't quite make out, slipping out of the chaos with the rest of the churning crowd.

Willis Gray, whose friends called him Wireless.

"I designed the system myself," Wireless told Diamond. "I took Sparks' devices and wired each one at every location. There's a transmitter and a receiver. Each one runs on a battery. It has to, because we cut the power to the buildings. The tone from the transmitter on one unit sets off the timer for the next one in the—"

"Alright, alright," Diamond barked. "I don't need the whole goddamn story."

Hunter's mind raced. *What system? Multiple locations. One transmitter setting off a timer for another.*

He was getting a bad feeling.

He took a slow, silent step closer to the doorway, turning his head slightly to zero in on whatever voice he might hear next. The voices were only part of a more elaborate symphony. He heard the rustle of clothing, the scuff of shoes against the concrete floor, the breathing of at least three sets of lungs and possibly a fourth. The ability to separate and monitor each individual sound enabled him to map the room and the position of each man in it.

Hunter stood no more than five feet from the doorway, just beyond the edge of the glow from within the room. He crouched slightly, his muscles tightening as he prepared to make his move into the room.

But he never got that far. His focus on the sounds in the next room drew his attention away from shuffle of feet coming up behind him. By the time he was aware of it, it was too late.

The back of his head exploded in a sudden burst of sharp pain, and he felt his legs crumple underneath him.

The rest was darkness.

CHAPTER 52
SURPRISE DELIVERY

Kowalski stepped into the room with an unconscious figure hoisted over his shoulder in a fireman's carry. Diamond had been pacing in front of the radio equipment while keeping one eye on Wireless and Fallon, both of whom stood hunched over a work table in a corner of the room, wiring a timer to the bomb Sparks had assembled earlier in the day.

All three men stopped suddenly when they saw Kowalski just inside the doorway. Diamond took one look at the load on the big man's shoulder and his brow furrowed in confusion. "What the hell…?" he said, even before he could get a look at the limp figure's face. "Who…?"

"He's heavy," said Kowalski. "Where do you want me to put him down?"

Diamond quickly crossed the room to a metal folding chair near a corner and turned it to face the center of the room. "Here," he said. "Here in the chair. Who the hell…?"

Kowalski shifted his weight and hefted his broad shoulders. "Get a load of this, Nick," he grunted, dropping the load squarely on the chair. The unconscious figure's head lolled to one side, and suddenly Diamond saw the whole picture.

The man in the mask.

Diamond glanced wide-eyed at Kowalski. He was speechless.

"Caught him out in the hallway," said Kowalski, "snooping around by the door."

"You've gotta be kidding me," said Diamond, his voice almost a whisper.

Kowalski knelt next to the slouched figure and put a hand on each shoulder to keep him from slumping too far and falling out of the chair.

Diamond turned to the two men at the work table. "You," he said, pointing at Fallon. "Find some rope. Or some wire. Anything. Make it quick. We need to keep this guy upright in the chair."

Fallon stepped away from the table and disappeared into an adjacent storage room.

Diamond looked back at the figure in the chair and shook his head. "You have got to be kidding me," he said again. He kept staring, and gears turned in his agitated mind. A plan began to take shape.

Fallon emerged from the storage room with a coil of rope and a box cutter and crossed to where Kowalski was kneeling next to the chair. Diamond stepped back as the other two men began cutting lengths of rope and tying the masked man's hands and feet.

When they had finished, they stood up and took a few steps back to assess the unconscious figure that was now securely anchored into the chair.

"Alright," said Diamond with a measure of triumph in his voice. "It's time to see who this clown is." He turned to Kowalski and tilted his head toward the rear entrance. "Johnny, go back outside and wait by the back door."

Kowalski looked back at him through a furrowed brow. "Huh? Go outside? Wait a minute, Nick. If you're gonna take off that mask, I wanna know who—"

"Don't argue with me. We've just killed all the power to the entire city. We broke into that power plant and locked the overnight crew in a storage room. For all we know, we may have cops here soon. Now go outside and watch that door and make sure the car's ready in case we need to make a quick move."

Kowalski turned and headed for the back entrance, making little effort to hide his resentment at being denied the chance to finally see who was behind the mask that had been unravelling their plans for the past few days.

But Diamond didn't waste time thinking about it. He turned quickly toward Wireless, who was making a few minor adjustments to the bomb assembly.

"You," he said to Wireless. "Come here."

The radio technician did as he was told.

Diamond tilted his chin toward the bomb on the table across the room. "You ready to activate that thing?"

Wireless nodded. "Yeah. It's ready to go."

"Alright," said Diamond. "Here's what I want you to do…"

CHAPTER 53
WIRED FOR DEATH

The smell was the first thing to come back to him. Hot breath near his face, laced with a stale combination of nicotine and liquor. The breath had a voice. Two voices. They both came at him in an edgy murmur that was somehow very close and yet miles away at the same time:

"This one's dead, but don't touch."

"Why not?"

"Never mind. It's too hard to explain. Just don't touch."

Hunter thought he should know the voices. He thought he'd figured them all out earlier. But now his head just swam.

He blinked several times, and the world slowly came back into focus. He was aware of a dull, throbbing ache at the back of his skull.

Somewhere, not far off, he heard the tick of a clock.

After a moment, he realized that he was sitting upright in a hard chair, his head and shoulders slumped forward. The only thing that kept him from falling completely forward was something around his wrists, holding them together behind the chair.

But no. There was something else holding him upright. Something—he didn't know what—heavy and constricting around his chest.

After a moment he heard footsteps recede into the distance, and with them went the voices and the foul breath. In its place came a whiff of something far more sterile. Something faint but persistent. Something that reminded him of laundry, or a swimming pool.

Chlorine. Soap.

He tried to bring a hand up to cradle his aching head, but the restraints on his wrists—they felt like rope—kept him from doing it. His fingers were partly numb and partly tingly, but he could still wiggle them.

He tried to move his feet, but they were immobilized as well, each tied to one of the front legs of the chair.

He was completely bound in the chair, hand and foot.

His head continued to throb as he blinked a few more times. Still in a slumped position, his field of vision consisted of his lap, and a concrete floor just a couple feet beyond that. His thoughts churned and swirled like a cloud of puzzle pieces that just wouldn't connect. Slowly, even without the ability to touch his face, he became aware of something that was missing.

The mask.

It had been taken off, and his face was exposed.

What the hell is happening?

Despite what he'd heard, despite the pain and the disorientation, he was fairly certain he wasn't dead. His splitting headache may have made him wish otherwise, but he was very much alive. And even if he were dead, why would someone caution against touching him?

Hunter heard another set of footsteps—just one person, coming toward him this time rather than moving away.

He mustered the energy to raise his head and look around, and the dull ache in his skull instantly blossomed into an intense pain that filled his field of vision with stars and made him wince.

He fought through the pain, blinking a few times and scanning the room. It was a drab rectangle of unpainted concrete and cinderblock, lined with industrial-sized barrels made of dull gray steel. Along with the barrels were dozens of wooden crates stacked five or six high in some places. Words like CHLORINE BLEACH and AMMONIA were stenciled on the sides of the barrels and crates, which explained the persistent smell in the room.

To his left, about twelve feet away, was the sleeping form of Betty Carlyle, sprawled on a cot made of canvas stretched across a wooden frame. He stared at her long enough to confirm the steady rise and fall of her chest. She was in a drug-induced sleep, but apparently unharmed.

A cone of hard light covered him from above. Its source was a single bare bulb at the end of a wire hanging low from the ceiling. Everything beyond that was darkness. It didn't make sense to him at first. The power had gone out all over the city. How could there be…

Then he remembered.

The array of transformers outside, wired up at the back of the building to siphon electricity away from the power station next door.

He was inside the Harper Warehouse, probably one of the only buildings in town—maybe the only one—that was still tapped into the city-wide power grid.

He looked back down at himself, and suddenly felt as though all the air had gone out of the room.

Strapped to his chest was a vest made of dynamite sticks woven together in a network of electrical wire. Mounted onto the whole contraption was a timer, ticking away the seconds.

He was wired to a timed device that was set to explode.

A human bomb.

Hunter stared at the apparatus for a moment, then closed his eyes. He made a conscious effort to control his breathing, ignore the throbbing in his head and think as clearly as he could.

He opened his eyes and scanned the room. The light from the ceiling filled only a part of the space, leaving plenty of dark corners created by the barrels and stacked crates. But he'd heard the footsteps just a moment before. He knew someone was still there, and he was pretty sure he knew who it was.

"Come on out, you snake," Hunter growled, ignoring the intense pain that accompanied the mere act of speaking. "Come out of the dark and show me your face."

Hunter heard a dark, guttural sound that might have been a laugh. After a moment, there were more footsteps from behind a stack of crates. He tracked the sound with his eyes and watched as a lean figure emerged from the shadows.

Nicky Diamond.

He looked older than Hunter remembered. It had been fourteen years since his trial, and he'd served a twelve-year prison sentence, so the years had taken more than their usual toll. But Hunter could never forget him. His once-black hair had gone a little bit gray, but his eyes were still black and shiny. His hands were at his sides—a gun in his right, Hunter's mask in his left—and his face was twisted into a wolfish grin.

The two men locked eyes and stared at each other in silence. Hunter watched as Diamond took a couple more steps away from the crates and toward the chair where he was bound hand and foot.

Hunter noticed something about Diamond's movements. Something deliberate yet agitated at the same time. His breath came fast, and he tapped the barrel of the gun against the side of his right thigh. His eyes were bloodshot, his pupils enormous. Hunter could only guess at the amount of Benzedrine he'd consumed over the past few hours—and over the past several days, for that matter.

Diamond tore his gaze away from Hunter. He held up the mask and frowned at the mysterious configuration of leather, opaque goggles and photoelectric cells, all stitched together into a single piece of headgear.

He looked back at Hunter. "You're not carrying any identification," he said, "So who the hell are you?"

Hunter glared back at him. "You really don't know, do you?"

"What do you mean?"

"Last time I saw you was in a courtroom, when I was nineteen years old. The DA threw a mountain of evidence at you and you walked out in chains."

"What the hell are you talking about?"

"You had control of this city, but the DA and the few cops who weren't in your pocket in those days managed to build a solid case. It was so solid that you had to send your goons into the Justice Center one night to steal the files and the evidence. But they couldn't do it. One good cop stopped them."

Diamond's eyes flashed recognition. "Hunter," he said.

"That's right. Jim Hunter. My father. He was the last thing standing between you and a ruined city, and he stopped you. He died doing it, but he stopped you, you sick son of a bitch. And the only reason you didn't get the chair is because two important witnesses never took the stand. One killed himself and the other disappeared under mysterious circumstances—although I'm betting you could probably shed some light on the mystery."

Diamond chuckled. It was an evil sound that settled Hunter's bet.

He held up the mask and regarded the intricate combination of leather, photo cells and dark lenses. Hunter counted on the fact that Diamond wasn't smart enough to fully understand what he was looking at.

"So Union City's dynamic young legal crusader is also Union City's masked vigilante," said Diamond.

Hunter shook his head. "Doesn't matter who or what I am," he said.

Diamond tossed the mask halfway across the room, and Hunter watched it arc through empty space and land on the cot next to Betty, who didn't stir. Diamond punctuated the landing with a shake of his head and a dismissive chuckle. "You can hide your face, but it doesn't matter," he said, his voice suddenly turning dark. "I'll tell you exactly who and what you are. You're the same chump your old man was."

Don't react, thought Hunter. *He's trying to push you. Don't react.*

"You have caused me a hell of a lot of trouble," he said. "That business in the Watt building with your egghead cousin. And then my three nightclubs a couple nights later. And then you got into my business with the Chinese."

"Glad I could make your life interesting."

"Maybe," said Diamond, appraising Hunter from head to toe. "But from where I'm standing, I'd say yours is looking pretty interesting right now."

Hunter didn't answer. Diamond did have a point.

Diamond glanced at his watch. It was a quick, reflexive movement, but the tremor in his hand was unmistakable.

"So here's how it goes," he said, looking up from his watch and gesturing at the device strapped to Hunter's chest. "It's five after eleven right now, which means that thing's gonna go off in twenty-five minutes."

He kept his eyes on Hunter but tilted his head toward the unconscious woman lying on the cot at the opposite end of the room. "It's going to finish you and the girl, for sure. And it's also going to bring this whole building down."

Hunter felt something well up in him—more rage than fear. His jaw flexed as he stared back at the sneering figure standing no more than five feet away, directly in front of him. He wanted Diamond to keep talking—long enough to see what kind of information he might give up, but not so long that he'd have no time left to figure some way out.

If some way out even existed at this point.

"Think of it as an opening act," said Diamond.

Hunter looked back at him. He didn't understand, but he wasn't about to give him the satisfaction of asking for an explanation. But Diamond was more than ready to fill him in.

"You see, Hunter, the best fireworks show is the one that keeps people guessing about what's coming next, and from where. It appears that there's been quite a blackout—city-wide, as a matter of fact."

"I know all about it," Hunter snarled.

"Yeah, well, I'd like to say it was one of those accidents that sometimes happen with the municipal power system, but that just wouldn't be true. See, I have a friend who's good with electricity. He set it up."

"Willis Gray. The same friend who set up the radio transmission a couple hours ago."

Diamond snapped his finger. "Yeah, that's the name," he said, suddenly remembering. "Everybody calls him Wireless."

"So I've heard," said Hunter. "And you've got another guy, don't you? Somebody who knows all about explosives and building bombs."

Diamond shrugged, and his face twisted into a smirk. "In my line of work, it's good to have specialists on the payroll."

He licked his lips. His breath hitched slightly in his chest. Now he was getting to the good part.

"Okay. So, first, you and the lady here—and this entire building—all go up in a roaring ball of flame that people are going to see and hear all the way to the next county over. Then the main event moves downtown, and the mayor meets a similar fate at City Hall. You probably heard that part in the broadcast."

Diamond began to pace. He was visibly aroused by the picture he was painting.

"But here's the part I didn't tell the good people," he said. "And it's the best part." He licked his lips. His voice grew huskier. "Wireless set it up, so he knows how it works better than I do, but the bomb at City Hall is rigged through some kind of shortwave system—some crazy radio business that transmits tones or some damn thing. Hell, I don't know."

A signal generator, thought Hunter. Transmitting a tone by shortwave to activate an electrical circuit at another location. Detonating a bomb by remote control.

"The important thing is, the bomb at City Hall is connected to similar devices in ten other locations around the city. The whole thing is set up to create a chain reaction of explosions—every ten minutes for about an hour and a half."

Hunter's jaw clenched as he stared up at Diamond. He tugged reflexively at the ropes cutting into his wrists, ignoring the sting and the ache that immediately followed. Diamond's face was ghastly white, his red-rimmed eyes slightly out of focus. He was a sickening picture, but not nearly as horrifying as the image in Hunter's mind of downtown Union City in ruins.

"The bomb at City Hall goes off at midnight," Diamond went on. "If it isn't deactivated, your mayor will die a very messy death. And for the next hour or so, a hell of a lot of important downtown real estate will be leveled."

Hunter stared back at him silently, taking it all in.

"You're out of your mind," he said finally.

"This is my city, Hunter. All the cops and the detectives and the DA and the G-men—they all tried to take it from me almost fifteen years ago. Your old man died in a pool of blood thinking he could stop me. But he couldn't. He could slow me down, maybe, but he couldn't stop me. None of them could. This is my city, and now I'm taking it back, even if I have to tear it down and rebuild it myself. The gambling is just the beginning, just a way to regain a handle on things. You know it, the cops know it, we all know it. Anyone can get booze now, so it's time to move on to the bigger stuff—drugs, dames, all the things that people really want but can't talk about. I'll be in control of all of it."

"All of what?" Hunter shot back. "If what you're telling me is true, this town'll be a pile of rubble by tomorrow morning. And you know that if things start blowing up in the next couple hours, the feds will be all over this in the morning. Hell, they're probably here already. And they'll look in every hole and under every rock until they find you."

Diamond was already taking a quick step forward before Hunter had finished speaking. He shifted his weight and set his shoulders. "Shut up!" he roared, swinging a back-handed blow across Hunter face.

Hunter did his best to roll his head and shoulders with the momentum of the blow, but the rope that held him to the chair limited his movement. Within seconds, the throbbing in his head was now accompanied by a similar throbbing in his jaw. He tasted blood in his mouth.

Diamond bent at the waist and grabbed Hunter's chin with the hand he'd just used to slap him. He leaned forward until his nose was no more than six or eight inches away from Hunter's. "It doesn't matter," he hissed, his eyes glowing with a rage that danced at the edge of sanity. "It's mine. And I'm taking it back."

He was sick, unhinged, a child in the throes of a raging tantrum. His toys had been taken away, and he wanted them back. But none of it was going the way it was supposed to go. His plan was unraveling more and more with each passing minute, and it was more than he could stand. If he couldn't have what he wanted, he'd destroy it all in the one way that would give him the most twisted, perverted satisfaction.

"Alright," said Diamond, taking another look at his watch. "It's ten after eleven. I have a front-row seat for this show." He pointed his chin at the apparatus on Hunter's chest. "And I sure as hell don't want to be here when that thing goes off."

He glanced across the room at Betty, lying still on the cot. "Give the dame a kiss for me when she wakes up," he said, and his eyes did a lurid dance across every inch of her frame. "Seems a shame," he said, "but when you and the cops declared war, you knew there'd be casualties. You probably just didn't plan on being one of them, and I'm sure she didn't either."

He turned and walk away.

Hunter shouted, "Burn in hell, Diamond!"

But Diamond didn't look back. "No," he said. "I think that's your job this evening."

Even without the mask, Hunter could follow the sound of his footsteps to the back door and out of the building.

Then the room was silent. He couldn't raise his wrist to check his watch, but he could read the timer strapped to his chest.

It was twelve minutes after eleven.

CHAPTER 54
DEPARTURE IN THE DARK

Cutting through the darkness with his flashlight, Diamond walked across the back lot of the Harper building toward the Buick, where he found Kowalski smoking a Chesterfield and standing next to the car on the driver's side. Mitch Fallon stood on the opposite side of the car from Kowalski. The operative better known in Diamond's circle as Wireless—whose real name, as Hunter had reminded him, was Willis Gray—stood a few feet away from Fallon, shuffling his feet nervously and taking long drags on a cigarette of his own. On the ground near Wireless' feet was a leather bag he used to carry his tools and electrical gear.

"Alright, let's go," said Diamond.

Kowalski took a drag on the cigarette. "Who is he, Nick?"

"Huh?"

"The guy in the mask. Who is he?"

"Never mind," said Diamond, feeling more than a little irritated that the young assistant DA had made a fool of him. And the fact that he was the son of the one cop who'd stood in his way so many years ago didn't help. "You wouldn't believe me if I told you."

Kowalski was silent. His expression was hard to make out in the darkness, but his resentment was almost palpable. "Okay," he said finally, tossing the last of the cigarette. "Where to?"

"We'll head downtown. I'll explain where we're going on the way."

Kowalski glanced at the delivery truck parked about thirty feet from the car. "What about that thing?"

Diamond glanced at the truck and looked back at Kowalski. "What about it?"

"Seems like a big piece of evidence to leave behind if the police are going to come looking. And they will come looking."

"Once this place goes up," said Diamond, "everything in it and everything around it is going to burn. Including the truck." He pointed at the remains of Artie Garrett, still lying on the ground near the transformers. "And that, too."

"But even if some parts are left after the blast, don't you think they can be identified?"

Diamond tilted his head toward the rear entrance. "That guy in there has enough stuff wrapped around him to take out the whole building," he said. "And even if any part of the truck is still in one piece afterward, there's nothing in it that they can pin on us. It's empty. And the plates are bogus. Believe me, starting in the next hour, and for the next several days, this place is going to be the least of their concerns."

Kowalski shrugged. He looked a little skeptical. "Alright," he said after a moment. He opened the driver's side door. "Let's go."

Diamond turned to the other two men and pointed to the glowing cigarette in Wireless' fingers. "Put that out," he said. "You get in back. Fallon, up front."

Wireless took a final drag on the cigarette and tossed it into the darkness. All four men climbed into the car. Sixty seconds later they were heading south.

Toward the city.

CHAPTER 55
FINDING THE EDGE

Hunter scanned the room, trying to ignore the maddening tick of the timer on his chest. He glanced at Betty, lying motionless on the cot. He stared at her ribcage long enough to make certain it was still rising and falling with some regularity. She'd been given a lot of dope over the last few hours, but as long as she was breathing steadily, Hunter could only assume she was okay.

He forced himself to take a deep breath of his own and think clearly. This was no easy task, given the tick of the timer mixed with the persistent throbbing in his skull from the blow in the back hallway. He looked down and tried to examine the assembly strapped around his upper torso. Fourteen sticks of dynamite, all of them wired to a detonating device positioned more or less at the center of his chest, roughly parallel to his sternum. From the detonator, two taut wires—each no more than four inches long—ran in a horizontal straight line along the underside of the dynamite to the timer.

Diamond was right. He was wearing enough firepower to take out most of the building if not all of it.

He stared at the two wires, piecing together the conversation he'd just heard a few minutes earlier when his head was still swimming back to consciousness.

This guy here is dead, but don't touch.

He remembered a conversation he'd had with Buzz a couple days earlier. It seemed like a lifetime ago.

The alarm system on the door to Mrs. Dooley's garage.

Two wires.

This guy here is dead...

And then it all fell into place.

He wasn't talking about me, Hunter thought. *He was talking about the damn wires.*

Just like the alarm system. One wire carried the charge, and the other one was the trip wire, the "dead guy."

And in this case, they were identical. So which was which?

The answer wasn't going to make any difference if he couldn't free himself from the chair.

His hands were tied together at the wrists behind the chair, but they weren't tied to the chair itself. Both hands were partially numb from the pressure of the ropes, but he still had some feeling in each of them. Using what minimal range of movement he had, he slowly ran the tips of the first and second fingers of his right hand along the rear edge of the seat.

He closed his eyes and concentrated. The chair was an old, battered thing. Maybe there'd be…

Yes…

His fingers stopped on a jagged edge.

He couldn't see it but he could feel it. The original construction of the chair was such that, on all four sides of the seat, the metal edges had been folded down and then welded to a smooth seam at each corner. But years of weight and use and misuse had opened a seam at one of the back corners, leaving a quarter-inch gap between two edges of exposed jagged metal.

Not exactly an ideal cutting knife, but it was the best he could hope for under the circumstances.

The ropes holding his ankles to the front legs of the chair limited his maneuverability, and he wasn't about to disturb the bulky dynamite vest wrapped around his torso, but he shifted himself in the chair as much as possible. He positioned his wrists along the bent and jagged edge at the back of his seat.

He took a deep breath. Slowly at first, and then with more speed and pressure, he began rubbing the rope across the metal edge.

The timer on his chest read eleven-seventeen, and it kept ticking.

CHAPTER 56
DARK STREETS

Diamond sat in the back seat of the Buick and watched the downtown streets through his window. With everything on the street in darkness—every traffic signal, every streetlamp, every office light snuffed out by the city-wide blackout that he himself had engineered— there wasn't much to see.

But the space overhead was a different story. Police searchlights, no doubt powered by gasoline generators, swept the sky in steady and continuous back-and-forth patterns. Judging from the lights in the sky, he imagined the police also had searchlights trained directly on the walls of City Hall.

More than just dark, the streets were also deserted. The few pedestrians who would normally be on the streets in the downtown area at this hour had gone indoors. The police had asked the population to avoid the downtown area once they'd determined that City Hall had been wired to explode, and it was a potential disaster that few citizens felt brave enough to flirt with.

The result was an eerie stillness in a sea of stygian darkness. The hum of the slow-moving Buick was the only thing to cut through it all.

Johnny Kowalski sat in the front seat behind the wheel and Fallon sat in the passenger seat next to him. Wireless sat in back, next to Diamond. At the start of the ride, Diamond had told Kowalski to work his way south, toward Union Square at the center of town, but to stay off Union Boulevard. He'd been no more specific than that.

"Stay on the side streets," he muttered. "Away from City Hall. The cops are watching City Hall and the main roads, so steer clear of all that."

Kowalski tilted his beefy face upward slightly and met Diamond's eyes in the rearview mirror. He nodded and shifted his gaze back to the road.

"Not too fast, either," Diamond added. "Just nice and easy."

Fallon leaned forward and switched on the radio. "Lemme see if I can get some news."

Kowalski frowned and shook his head slightly. "Not if the power's out all over town," he said. "Won't be any radio stations on the air."

"I know, but how far out of town does the blackout go?" said Wireless. He'd been silent since they'd left the warehouse, and now he sounded sullen and resigned. "Maybe you can pick up that station in Bridgewood."

Fallon spun the dial for a couple more turns, and the radio responded with a chatter made up of signals from distant cities or empty static where local stations had been broadcasting an hour earlier. After a few seconds, he zeroed in on the urgent voice of a news announcer:

"…this program to bring you a news bulletin. We have reports that Union City is in darkness at this hour as police officers and

311

federal agents are responding to a bomb threat at the Union City Administrative Building on the city's Liberty Avenue. Officials at the Union City Police Department confirm that a powerful explosive device has been planted within the building in the office of Union City Mayor Stephen Bentley. We are told that the bomb may in fact be attached to Bentley's person."

Fallon craned his head toward Diamond in the back seat and started to speak, but Diamond put a hand up to silence him. The announcer's voice continued:

"A threat was issued city-wide earlier this evening by way of a high-powered and unauthorized radio transmission from an unknown source. The voice issuing the threat claimed to be that of mobster and racketeer Nick Diamond, whose operation has apparently resurfaced in the area following the end of his twelve-year incarceration for murder, illegal alcohol trafficking, destruction of government property and numerous other offenses."

The announcer paused momentarily, apparently attempting to process incoming information before continuing with his report.

"Union City police have confirmed that every point of entry at City Hall is also wired directly to some sort of explosive device," he went on, "and that the devices are set to explode if any police officer or anyone else enters the building in an attempt to rescue the mayor. It is not known at this time whether any other city officials or employees are inside the—"

Kowalski interjected, keeping his eyes on the dark streets in front of him. "He said federal agents, Nick. I don't think I like this."

"Never mind that," Diamond murmured. "Just stay off the main streets, like I said, and head for Union Tower."

Diamond watched as both men in the seat in front of him reacted with a start. Even from behind, he recognized the quizzical tilt of both of their heads.

"Union Tower," said Kowalski. "You mean the office?"

"Yeah," said Diamond. "That's what I said. I told Sparks we'd meet him there."

Fallon let out a whistle and shook his head. "With no electricity to take the elevator? Thirty floors up? That's gonna take some time on the stairs. And some wind."

"Never mind that," said Kowalski. "Are you sure we should be doing this, Nick? The train station in the basement of that place is one of the only ways in and out of the city, so you know the cops are gonna be all over the terminal and all over the rest of the building."

"Don't be too sure," said Diamond. "The cops and the feds are covering at least a three-block radius around City Hall right now. The few cops the department can spare are gonna have their hands full at Union Tower. With the power out, the terminal in the lower level will be shut down and no trains will be coming in or out. The place will be a crazy house for the next couple hours, maybe all night. In all that kind of confusion, we won't have any trouble getting into the building by the back way."

He turned to Fallon and scowled. "That's assuming the stairs won't be too much for your delicate little gams."

Fallon shrugged. "Well, no, I was just sayin'…"

Kowalski still sounded skeptical. "Yeah, but if there aren't enough cops to keep the place under control, that's all the more reason why they'd just shut the whole building down."

Diamond reached forward from the back seat and grabbed Kowalski by the shoulder with a wiry grip. "We're going to Union Tower," he snarled. "Go to the south parking garage," he said. "There's a guard there who knows we're coming. One of Sparks' connections. Guy named Huffman. He'll get us in."

Kowalski went silent. He glanced at Diamond in the rearview mirror, then looked back at the road.

CHAPTER 57
TIES THAT BIND

Hunter swung his shoulders back and forth in a small but consistent arc, forcing himself to concentrate, forcing himself to maintain a steady, rhythmic motion. At the same time, he maintained as much tension as he could in the tiny space between one wrist and the other—which wasn't much, considering how tightly they were bound together. He couldn't turn his head far enough around to see what, if anything, was happening to the rope. The best he could hope for would be some fraying—enough that the tension might eventually snap a few coils and loosen the whole thing enough to free his hands.

The timer read eleven-twenty-two.

What little feeling he had left in his hands suggested that something wet and warm was oozing around his wrists and into his palms. Unable to see his hands, he could only imagine the level of chafing and bleeding at this point.

Don't panic, he thought, pacing his thoughts and his breathing in time with the movement of his shoulders. *Keep moving. Keep it steady. Back and forth.*

After another minute, he felt something pop loose. Suddenly the tension on his hands was less severe. He fought the urge to twist his hands and wrestle his way out of the rope.

Don't rush. Just keep moving. Back and forth.

Another pop. More space between his wrists, more flexibility.

It was working.

Back and forth. Back and forth.

Another pop. He twisted his wrists and tugged them in opposite directions, and the last of the rope uncoiled and spilled on the floor behind the chair.

He let his shoulders and arms sag for a moment, barking out a guttural noise that came from a mix of pain, fatigue and relief.

He was free!

He brought both hands out from behind him and held them in front of his face, wiggling his fingers and opening and closing his fists. As he suspected, each wrist was a bruised and bloody mess, but he'd never been so happy to see his hands in his life.

But the sense of triumph and relief was short-lived.

The timer read eleven-twenty-three.

CHAPTER 58
INTO THE TOWER

Diamond leaned forward in the back seat and stared into the darkness beyond the front windshield as Kowalski turned the car into the short access drive to Union Tower's south parking garage. The glow from the searchlights sweeping the skies was now completely obliterated by the monolithic fifty-five-story building looming directly in front of them. Slowing the car to a crawl, Kowalski leaned forward and bored his eyes into the darkness to see the way in front of him and keep from veering off the driveway and into the iron gate.

Halfway up the driveway, just beyond the gate, a square of shifting light suddenly appeared, seemingly in mid-air. It took Diamond and the two men in the front seat a moment to recognize the glow as the sweep of a flashlight beam from inside the window of the small guardhouse at the entrance to the garage.

Diamond tapped Kowalski's shoulder. "Stop the car."

The light in the guardhouse window went dim, and then reappeared as a long vertical sliver as the flashlight beam emerged from a doorway on the side of the small wooden structure.

"That's him," said Diamond. "That's Huffman."

The figure holding the flashlight stepped down from the guardhouse door and moved toward the car. He wore a long coat and a hat that appeared to be part of whatever uniform the tower parking attendants wore, but that was all Diamond could make out in the darkness.

The guard fixed the beam directly on Kowalski's face. Kowalski turned his head slightly, squinting and holding up a hand to shield his eyes from at least some of the intense glare.

"Roll down the window," said Diamond. Kowalski obeyed.

The guard stopped at the side of the car and ducked his head slightly to get a look inside the window. Diamond noticed that he was holding a gun at his side in his left hand while sweeping the four faces inside the car with the beam from the flashlight in his right. He wondered whether the gun was standard issue for Union Tower parking attendants. He suspected it wasn't.

"Got Nick Diamond in there?" His voice was hushed, as though forced into a whisper by the blanket of darkness and the grip of fear that had taken hold of the city.

Diamond snorted impatiently, wondering how one of Sparks' connections couldn't know who he was. "Yeah, I'm Diamond," he said, leaning forward to address the guard through Kowalski's window. "You Huffman?" he said.

"Yeah."

"We need to get inside and upstairs."

The beam stopped on Diamond's face for a moment. Like Kowalski,

Diamond also squinted into the shaft of intense light. "And you can point that goddamn thing somewhere else," he added.

Huffman waved the beam away from the car and toward a place beyond the gate. He stepped slightly to one side of the driveway and glanced over his shoulder at the rows of cars in the garage. He turned back and looked down at Kowalski in the driver's seat. "Alright, pull in," he said. "Slowly. No lights. And don't rev it. Put it anywhere you see a spot."

Kowalski rubbed his eyes, trying to readjust to the darkness after the glare of the flashlight. "Hell, I can't see *anything* now, let alone a parking spot."

Diamond settled back into his place in the back seat. "Just drive," he said.

In less than a minute, Kowalski had pulled the car into a spot not far from the guardhouse. Huffman had followed them to the spot on foot, and with his flashlight pointed at the ground, he stood near the car as Kowalski cut the engine and the four occupants emerged from the vehicle.

Huffman produced two additional flashlights from the pocket of his coat. "Here," he said. "You'll need these, especially when we get inside."

Kowalski took one of the lamps and Fallon took the other. All four men turned as one and headed for the south entrance to the tower a little more than fifty yards away. Kowalski and Fallon kept the beams short, pointing them at the ground near their feet.

They walked in silence for part of the way. The only sound was the scrape of eight leather soles against concrete. About halfway to the entrance, Fallon turned to Huffman and spoke up. "You sure this is a good idea?" he said. "Gotta be some cops inside, no?"

Huffman shrugged. "There's a couple at the main entrances," he said. "That's really all they can spare. The rest are a long way from here, either standing around in front of City Hall or patrolling the entire area around it. The couple cops who are here aren't letting anybody in or out until the business in front of City Hall is settled one way or another."

Diamond turned to Kowalski. "See? What'd I tell you in the car?"

Kowalski's only response was a shrug and a nervous tap of his flashlight against his leg.

Huffman gestured toward the wide sliding metal door as they approached. "This is a service entrance I'm taking you to," he said. "It leads into a part of the building that isn't open to the public. Won't be any traffic there, and no cops either. I checked it myself after I heard from Sparks and he told me you were coming. It's clear."

He unclipped a ring of keys chained to his belt as the group came to a stop at the south service entrance. He picked a key from the ring and unlocked the door, then reached down and slid it upward. He put a hand up in a yielding gesture intended for the three other men, and put an index finger to his lip.

He looked directly at Diamond. "Wait here," Huffman said quietly. "I'll take a quick look inside."

Diamond fingered the gun at his belt. He felt an edge of irritation at being told what to do by a simple parking garage guard—even if the guard was indirectly connected to Diamond's network—but he merely nodded.

Huffman stepped through the doorway and into a spacious shipping area that resembled a yawning black cave in the absence of any electric lighting. He kept his gun raised to waist level and pointed into the darkness. Diamond and his two men watched him from the threshold of the sliding door, the beam from his flashlight dancing just a few feet ahead of him.

Diamond, Kowalski, Fallon and Wireless watched as Huffman—his gun still at waist level—turned and flashed his beam down a connecting hallway to the right. He stepped out of their line of sight for a moment, then returned, his gun at his side.

He turned toward the four men waiting in the doorway and beckoned them with the beam of his flashlight. "Okay," he said in a low voice. "The stairway looks clear."

Diamond glanced at Fallon and saw that he already had his gun out. He motioned for him to go through the doorway first. Diamond fell in line behind Fallon, and Wireless and Kowalski brought up the rear. Wireless was unarmed, but Kowalski had his piece at the ready. All three men moved in single file toward the guard's flashlight glow at the end of the short hallway.

They reached Huffman, who gestured down the side hallway he'd just investigated. He threw his beam at a door at the end of the hallway. "The stairs are just beyond that door," he said. "It's gonna be a hike, but it should be clear all the way up. I'll leave the service door unlocked so you can get out on your own."

Diamond and his three men moved passed Huffman and headed for the door. The guard brought up the rear, then stepped around them to open up the door at the end of the hallway.

The space at the foot of the stairs just beyond the door was a yawning sea of blackness, save for the pool of light from the combined flashlights. Diamond had his own gun out now. He could hear Fallon's rapid breathing and his tentative steps across the threshold, and he sensed a similar measure of apprehension behind him from Wireless—the only one of the four without a weapon. He nudged Fallon's arm with his elbow. "Let's go," he said. "We got a lot of stairs to climb." He glanced over his shoulder and told Kowalski, "Stay close."

By the time they were halfway up the first flight of stairs, they heard the door at the bottom close behind them. Wireless sucked in a quick gulp of air and hesitated as the sharp sound echoed up the cinderblock stairwell.

"Keep moving," Diamond growled.

Guided by the uneven dance of two flashlight beams, they made their way up the stairs.

CHAPTER 59
DISMANTLING DEATH

Once the feeling had returned to his fingers, Hunter had had no trouble untying the ropes at his ankles. The hardest part had been making sure not to jar the apparatus strapped to his chest. In the end, it took less than a minute.

It was the next task at hand—the most delicate of all—that concerned him the most.

The pounding from the blow to the back of his head had subsided somewhat, but the dull throb was still distracting.

If I could just think more clearly.

It didn't matter. It was eleven-twenty-four. There was no more time. He had to move.

Slowly, carefully, he rose from the chair, holding his upper body as steady as possible as he did so. He stood still for a moment, trying to will the circulation back into his numb and aching legs and feet.

His first steps were wobbly. He forced himself to stop and give his lower extremities a few seconds to adjust. The good news was that his circulation was returning. The bad news was that his ankles and feet screamed with the pain of a thousand needles as his blood made its way back into his lower limbs. The extra weight around his chest—ten or twelve pounds, as near as he could figure—didn't help at all. A trickle of sweat at each temple slid down the sides of his face as he fought to ignore the pain.

He clenched his jaw and took a deep breath. He slid his right foot forward. Then his left.

Go slow.

He was still wobbly, but he allowed himself a measure of optimism as he noted the feeling coming back to his feet.

He pointed himself toward the cot where Betty lay and took two more steps, moving more quickly this time. A few more, and he was standing over the cot, holding his left hand against the wall to steady himself.

Betty's face was pale, except for the dark circles under her eyes, but she was breathing evenly. She didn't appear to be in any immediate danger. Hunter knew he had to help himself before he could help her.

Bending at the knees rather than the waist to avoid jostling the device on his chest, he reached down and picked up the mask with his right hand. He took his left hand away from the wall and carefully raised the mask over his head.

Would it even work? Had Diamond or any of his men damaged the circuitry in any way?

He slipped it into position over his head, and the effect was almost instantaneous.

The room looked clearer in his field of vision, brighter somehow. The hum of the transformers just outside the building was more pronounced. In only a second or two, the pain at the back of his head practically disappeared. And most importantly, his thinking was suddenly clearer. Sharper. Faster.

Hunter stepped away from the cot, away from the wall, and focused his mind—which was a lot easier to do now.

He took a deep breath and concentrated.

The bomb couldn't go off without a detonator, and the detonator would be part of a circuit. The circuit couldn't work without a power source—probably a small dry-cell battery tucked somewhere within the explosive vest.

What did Buzz tell him about the alarm he'd built for Mrs. Dooley's garage? A hot wire and a trip wire. The hot wire was part of the alarm circuit itself. The trip wire was not, but any change in the tension of the trip wire would close the circuit and set off the alarm.

Or in this case, set off the detonator.

So the trick was to leave the trip wire alone and disconnect the circuit wire.

But which was which?

He looked closely at both wires. Even with the enhanced vision of his goggles, they looked virtually the same. Same gauge, same coloring, same markings on the insulation.

So which was which?

Carefully, with almost no pressure whatsoever, he ran a finger across one of the wires. Then he shifted his finger barely a quarter-inch and did the same thing with the other wire.

He repeated the process. First one, then the other.

He closed his eyes and concentrated.

Again. One, then the other.

My God...

He could feel it. The faintest whisper of a vibration in one wire, but not in the other.

He could actually *feel* the electric current running through the hot wire.

But could he really? Or was it just some trick of an anxious mind facing the very real and very imminent possibility of oblivion?

There was only one way to know for sure.

He gently took hold of the vibrating wire with his thumb and forefinger. He glanced down at Betty's face, held his breath and sent up a prayer.

He yanked at the wire, and it came loose in his fingertips.

A second later, he was still breathing. The room was silent, save for the hum of the transformers. The cinderblock walls surrounding him were still intact. The Harper Warehouse was still standing.

And he and Betty were still alive.

Hunter exhaled, and his head nearly spun from the wave of relief that swept over him. He put his hand to the wall again and took a few deep breaths. He was fairly certain that he was out of immediate danger, but this was no time to get sloppy. Betty needed a doctor.

He very carefully detached a few of the wires that held the dynamite vest together. After a few seconds, the entire assembly went slack. In a few seconds more, he had it completely off. Rather than take any chances, he moved to a far corner of the room and laid it gently on the floor where it would remain undisturbed.

He crossed quickly back to the cot and wasted no time picking Betty up in both arms and heading out of the room. He moved down the hallway toward the rear entrance and stopped momentarily to check her breathing. Steady, but shallow.

She might be alright just sleeping it off, but she'd had two heavy doses of chloroform in just a few hours and he wasn't about to take any chances. He needed to get her to the hospital, but he'd need something with more seats than a motorcycle to get both of them there.

He pushed through the back door and stepped out into a sea of darkness, with nothing more than the eerie glow of a half moon and a few stars cutting through an otherwise black void. In the aftermath of Diamond shutting down Union Power, every streetlamp on the block—and every other block in the River District—had gone dark.

But Hunter could see. The back lot was completely empty, save for the delivery truck. It was no ambulance, but it would have to do.

He hefted Betty in his arms and stepped toward the passenger side of the truck. When he got there, he lowered her feet to the ground and propped her against his shoulder just long enough to test the passenger door and find that it was unlocked. There were no keys in the ignition or anywhere else inside the vehicle, but for a guy who'd tinkered with engines and carburetors and alternators ever since he was twelve—ever since the first automobiles arrived in his town more than twenty years earlier—a truck without keys was no obstacle at all.

He got his arm back under Betty's legs, lifted her high and gently folded her into the front seat. He closed her door and made his way around the front of the truck to the driver's side, where he ducked down on the floor under the dashboard and found the ignition wires.

Twelve seconds later, the engine was running.

CHAPTER 60
CITY VIEW

It took them almost thirty minutes to make their way up to the office. All four men were breathing hard when they reached the landing. Kowalski stepped to the front of the group and pushed open the doors leading to the main hallway. Fallon seemed more than happy to give up his lead position in the ominous march. Wireless quickened his pace from behind, as though he wanted to be sure not to be left in the dark.

Kowalski held the door as everyone else stepped through, then closed it quietly behind them. He turned and guided Diamond and the other two men down the hallway. In addition to their flashlight beams cutting through the dark passage, some additional illumination from the eerie combination of soft moon glow and sweeping searchlights filtered into the hallway through the large multi-paned window on the end wall.

Moving as one, all four men headed to the right, down one of the side hallways to the office. Kowalski produced a set of keys and unlocked the door. They stepped inside quickly and Kowalski left the door slightly ajar behind him.

Just as in the hallway, the moon and the distant searchlights threw a small amount of light into the room through the row of windows spanning the north wall of the office, but the room was still murky with shadows and dark corners.

Diamond muttered a curse about the stuffy air, yanking off his jacket and hanging it on a coat tree standing just a couple feet from the door. He crossed the room to a storage cabinet and brought out a kerosene lantern, then retraced his steps and positioned the lantern on a small table next to a desk to the right of the door. He turned to Wireless, then tilted his chin at the lantern.

"Get us some light," he said.

Wireless nodded and dug into his pocket for matches. When he brought a pack back out, his hands were trembling. He managed to get a match lit, but fumbled with the lantern on the table.

Kowalski noticed the struggle and stepped toward Wireless. "Here, give it to me," he said. He lit the lantern, and a dim, soft glow immediately pushed at the darkness, but still left hard shadows in various corners of the room.

Kowalski blew out the match and tossed it in an ashtray on the desk. "Listen, Nick," he said. "What about the rest of the guys? I mean Whitey and Zig and Crane and Bugs."

Diamond had staked out a small stretch of the office floor and started pacing. At the mention of the names, he stopped and gave Kowalski a quizzical look. "What about them?"

Kowalski shrugged. "They're out of the hospital but they're all still in custody," he said. "At some point, especially after tonight, it's a good bet they're going to start talking. With Reynolds out of the picture, there's no one in the system to cover for them, and there's no one to protect us from whatever they might tell the cops. And now with the feds involved, it's only going to get—"

"No!" said Diamond. His expression was fierce now, his eyes red-rimmed and dilated. He glanced at his watch. "In a little more than a half hour, everything is going to change. We're going to end this!"

"I don't know if that's...I mean, I'm just saying maybe we should talk to Vin before we go any further with this. We may be in a corner here, and he may know—"

"I'd like to know where the hell he is right now," Diamond growled, trying to ignore a vague sense of suspicion that had been nagging at him since Simone told him at the warehouse that Sparks was meeting with Marshall at his law office. "And Sparks, too."

Diamond moved to the desk and fished two more cylinders out of his pocket. He cracked them both open with shaky hands and stuffed the powder-coated paper strip from each into his mouth.

He opened a side drawer of the desk and pulled out a metal flask. He unscrewed the cap, took a quick gulp and closed the container back up again. Jaws flexing and eyes wide, he tossed the flask back into the drawer, then pulled a pair of binoculars out of the same drawer before slamming it shut.

Kowalski took his usual position by the door, apparently choosing to keep any further reservations to himself. Fallon leaned against a bookshelf. He struck a pose in an effort to appear nonchalant, but his shiny, darting eyes gave him away.

Wireless had long since given up any pretense. His eyes looked far away, as though he were still staring at Artie Garrett's charred remains. His feet shuffled. He tried leaning against the wall but he couldn't be still and he couldn't get comfortable. His face was pallid and strained, and he had to fight a persistent tremor in his hands just to light a cigarette.

Diamond looked at his watch. Eleven-thirty.

He scanned the streets below through the binoculars. Even at this high vantage point, the taller buildings obstructed some of his view, but City Hall wasn't hard to find. It was the only knot of light and activity in an otherwise dark and deserted cityscape. The flash of lights from the fleet of police cars clogging Liberty Avenue illuminated a three-block radius.

He kept scanning, searching for the other targets: the Justice Center, the County Court House, the County Records Building, all the rest.

He looked at his watch again. Twenty-nine minutes.

God, he thought, *this is going to be beautiful.*

CHAPTER 61
HUNTER AT GUNPOINT

Hunter pulled into the driveway leading to the emergency room entrance at Union Mercy. He immediately noticed an electric glow from inside the building, and his highly sensitized hearing picked up the hum of emergency generators from somewhere along the outer perimeter of the building.

The generators would obviously be powering the lights and medical equipment inside. The parking lot lights were out, which he considered a stroke of good fortune.

He brought the truck to a quick stop in a section of pavement close to the entrance. Hunter's plan was to get Betty in, get himself out, get back in the truck and get away as fast as possible—preferably before anyone stopped him to ask questions.

He jumped out of the truck with the engine still running and circled to the passenger side, where he opened the door and lifted Betty in his arms, making sure her head was cradled against his shoulder. As he turned away from the car and took a few quick steps toward the building, her head rolled slightly from side to side. Her eyes remained closed, but something low and distressed emerged from her throat—a moan at first, but then something more focused. A single word. Hunter turned his head and tilted it toward her face to try and make it out.

"Pru…" she mumbled. "Pruett." It was all she could manage. Her head rolled back against his shoulder and was still. Her deep breathing resumed and she was silent again.

Hunter frowned. "I wouldn't worry about Pruett," he muttered.

Aided by the cover of darkness, he circled around to a side wing of the building and slipped through the glass door, hoping the less traveled entranceway would have fewer hospital personnel moving through it—or better yet, none at all. Inside, he stood at the end of a short hallway that led to a longer main corridor. The hallway was empty, and the emergency lighting was minimal, but he heard the murmur of voices and activity coming from the main corridor.

He glanced left and right, looking for a gurney, a table, an empty examining room, anyplace where he could set Betty down in a comfortable position without drawing a lot of attention to himself. He found nothing. Against his better judgment, he moved toward the main corridor.

Just around the corner he found an empty gurney pushed against the left hand wall. Further along the wall, a pair of swinging doors led to another part of the emergency unit. The sight of the doors made him hesitate, but he stepped around the corner and carefully laid Betty down on the gurney mattress. He was just about to slip a pillow under her head when the swinging doors opened and an orderly came through, walking backwards and pulling a wheeled cart loaded with bandages, syringes and other miscellaneous supplies.

Hunter froze. The orderly turned and looked back at him and lurched himself and his cart to a halt, his face a mask of surprise and fear. For a split second, the young man glanced down at the woman on the gurney, then back at the goggles of Hunter's mask. After a moment, the orderly found his voice.

"Hey, what the hell…?"

Hunter put a hand up. "It's okay," he said. "This woman needs help."

The orderly's eyes narrowed. "I'll bet she does."

"Listen to me. She's been drugged. Chloroform."

The orderly kept his eyes on Hunter but turned his head slightly in the direction of the corridor and raised his voice. "Security!"

Hunter glanced down the hall and back at the orderly. "No…"

The orderly had shifted into a crouch—ready to fight, or at least try some kind of restraining maneuver. He kept his eyes on Hunter and shouted again. "Hey! Security! We got trouble here!"

"No, dammit, this woman is…" Hunter's voice trailed off. He was looking at the orderly, but he was keenly aware of what was starting behind him at the end of the corridor—the voices turned in his direction and choked off in surprised gasps, the urgent footsteps, the heightened tension.

"What's going on?" A male voice from behind him, some twenty or thirty yards down the hall. He turned and saw a security guard heading in his direction at a brisk pace. The guard took one look at Hunter's mask and stopped suddenly, his expression suspended in a moment of confusion and disbelief.

"What the hell…?" he muttered. Just like the orderly a couple seconds earlier.

Hunter put his hands up in a yielding gesture. "It's alright," he said, trying to keep his voice steady and even. "This woman needs help. There's no time to—"

The guard's hand was at his hip, pulling his weapon. "Alright, pal," he interrupted, "hold it right there."

He won't shoot, Hunter thought, although not with any certainty. *Too many people around. An unconscious woman on a gurney right next to me. You don't shoot at people in a hospital.*

His eyes were fixed on the security guard now, but he sensed movement just beyond his peripheral vision as the orderly ducked away, out of the line of any potential gunfire.

The guard drew down on Hunter, his gun pointed directly at his chest. "Step away from that gurney." His voice was even, but very firm.

Hunter didn't move. "This woman's been drugged. She needs—"

The guard pulled back the hammer. "Step. Away. From the gurney."

Hunter was cornered. His only way out was in front of the gurney and around the turn in the hallway—a maneuver that would take him directly into the guard's line of fire.

But would the guard shoot?

You don't shoot at people in a hospital.

326

Hunter crouched, bracing his legs. He tuned out the swirl of random noises from all over the hallway and the adjoining rooms and zeroed in on the guard's heartbeat. It was already accelerated and getting faster.

Head down, he broke into an instant sprint—directly at the guard for the first two or three steps, then a sharp turn to the right, down the same hallway through which he'd entered the building.

Somewhere in the turn, Hunter heard the guard fill his lungs and hold it.

Getting ready to pull the trigger.

Hunter ducked as he ran, tracing a quick dodge-and-weave pattern along the corridor.

He expected the bark of the gun after the first step or two, but he didn't hear it.

The guard was breathing again. Unevenly.

He's hesitating.

Then it came. A deafening crack in the narrow hallway. The bullet sang past Hunter's ear and slammed into the wall. Chunks of green ceramic tile exploded from the vertical surface, just inches from where his head had been a split second before.

The hallway filled with gasps and shrieks. Hunter thought he heard the guard yell, "Stop!" but he realized it was actually a different man's voice yelling, "Stop it!"

He opened up the throttle down the straight stretch of hallway, bobbing and weaving with each hammering stride toward the exit. The guard fired a second time, and again the slug missed its mark and tore more fragments of green tile out of the wall.

Less than two seconds later, he pushed through the glass door and darted toward the truck, which was still running—and thankfully, still where he'd left it. He looked over his shoulder just once, and saw to his relief that no one was following him into the parking lot.

The last sounds his heightened hearing could pick up from inside the building were two excited voices—the security guard and another man—arguing in the corridor where he'd been standing at gunpoint just moments earlier.

"What the hell are you doing? Put that away!" An older voice. Authoritative, no-nonsense.

"Huh?" The guard.

"I said put that damned gun away, and help me get this girl into one of these rooms."

327

"Doc, the guy was…he was wearing some kinda crazy mask! For all we know, he coulda—"

"I don't care if he was wearing a dress! You don't shoot at people inside a hospital, for God's sake!"

Hunter scrambled into the driver's seat and checked his watch. Eleven-thirty-five.

"Yeah, Doc," he muttered, lurching the truck into gear. "My thoughts exactly."

In a squeal of rubber, he sped off into the night.

CHAPTER 62
SIMONE'S REPORT

Simone walked into the dimly lit office alone, clearly winded from climbing the stairs, but Diamond sensed that the tension on his face had to do with more than just fatigue.

"What's going on?" said Diamond, glancing at the half-open door and expecting two more men to come through it. He looked back at Simone. "Where's Vinnie? Where's Sparks?"

"I don't know," said Simone. "I went to Vin's office like you told me. I couldn't buzz his office because there was no power, so I went up and knocked. But there was no one there. I looked up at his window— you know, on the second floor, facing the street—but it was dark. No signs of any flashlights or anything. I waited outside for a while— almost a half hour—but neither one of them showed."

Diamond scowled. He looked away, into the distance, through narrowed eyes. He couldn't make sense of it, and his suspicion deepened. "I don't like this," he said, shaking his head slowly.

"There's more," Simone said tentatively.

Diamond looked up, his eyebrow arched and his expression wary. "What?"

"I just came from the River District," said Simone. He paused, choosing his next words carefully. "I think…I think something went wrong at the Harper place."

"What do you mean? What happened?"

"Nothing."

"What do you mean nothing?"

"That's just it. Nothing happened. No explosion."

"What!"

"I was just there a few minutes ago. The place is still standing."

Diamond and Kowalski exchanged a glance. Simone knew nothing about the events that transpired after he left the Harper Building to pick up Marshall and Sparks. He knew nothing about Hunter showing up, nothing about strapping the bomb to him and leaving him in the warehouse. But it didn't matter. Hunter or not, the place was supposed to have gone up at eleven-thirty, but it was still standing.

Diamond tried to gather his thoughts, but his mind raced and frustration crept up on him quickly. He seethed for a moment, then erupted, kicking a chair across the room, where it missed Wireless by inches and slammed into the wall, tearing out a sizable chunk of plaster at the point of contact.

"Sonofabitch!" Diamond roared, nearly in unison with the chair slamming into the wall. As the chair was still toppling onto its side, he lifted a brass paperweight off the desk and hurled it at the same wall, taking out another chunk of plaster at a spot not far from the gash left by the chair. Everyone in the room ducked, instinctively shielding their faces with their hands. Powered by the velocity and force of the projectile, chunks of plaster rocketed in all directions.

Diamond ignored the noise and the flying debris. He stepped around the desk and crossed the room to where Wireless was standing and grabbed the younger man's shirt. He leaned in until the two men's faces were just inches apart.

Wireless averted his eyes. His face was ashen and sweaty under the white-hot intensity of Diamond's stare.

"What did you do?" said Diamond. His voice was quiet at first, not much more than a whisper, but there was no mistaking the savage undercurrent. Then the lid came off and he exploded into a roar. *What the hell did you do!*

Wireless was shaking uncontrollably now. "I...we...me and Fallon, we just took the rig that Sparks put together," he stammered. "We wired it up and strapped it on that guy when he was out cold."

"What?" Simone interjected in a confused voice from the other end of the room. "Strapped it on who? Nick, what the hell's he talking about?"

"The guy in the mask," said Diamond. "It's Hunter, the assistant DA. Kowalski found him prowling around the back of the warehouse."

Kowalski and Simone both went wide-eyed. Both erupted into a nervous chatter at the same time.

"Wait a minute. You mean to tell me…"

"What the hell…? You're saying the assistant DA is…"

Diamond nodded grimly. "That's exactly what I'm saying."

Kowalski shook his head, his expression a mix of shock and disbelief. "Oh, for the love of God…"

Simone was nearly dumbstruck. "I can't…" he stammered. "I can't believe…You gotta be kid—"

"Alright, save it! Both of you!" Diamond barked. He turned his attention back to Wireless, whose shirt he was still holding in an iron grip. "Now, I'm gonna ask you one more time. What the hell did you do?"

"I…I tested the circuit," Wireless went on. "I tested the timer. It all worked when I tested it. It shoulda—"

Diamond shoved him away and turned back toward the center of the room. Wireless slid down the wall. He curled into a seated position on the floor, his back still to the wall and his knees to his chest. He rocked slowly, his breathing rapid and anxious.

Diamond paced like a caged animal, his eyes glowing like hot coals planted deep in his skull.

"And there's something else I don't get," said Simone, who seemed as though he was still trying to collect himself after the revelation about Hunter.

Diamond huffed, still pacing. "Jesus Christ, Louie, what? What now?"

"The truck," Simone began, but his voice trailed off. He shook his head, as though he had no idea how to explain the puzzle, let alone come up with an answer to it.

"What about the truck?" said Diamond.

"Did you move it?"

"What? No, we didn't move it. Why the hell would—?"

"Well, somebody moved it."

Diamond stopped pacing. His face twisted into a frustrated grimace. "Louie, what are you talking about?"

"When I left the warehouse, it was parked behind the building."

Diamond shrugged. "Yeah."

"And you didn't move it. You didn't have Kowalski move it."

"No."

"Well, somebody moved it. I drove the car close enough to check the back lot, but the truck was gone. I drove around the block and I found it in an alley, about two buildings away."

Diamond looked back at him. "You sure it was our truck you saw? It's dark as hell out there."

"Yeah, I'm sure," said Simone. "Same phony plates. I even got out of my own car and got inside the truck to check it out. It was ours, alright. No keys, but get this. It'd been hot-wired."

"What the hell...?" Diamond growled. "You're telling me somebody hot-wired our truck and then drove it a block away and then parked it in an alley."

"I guess. I don't know how else to explain it."

Diamond went back to pacing, trying to conjure some kind of scenario to explain Simone's account. After a moment or two he gave up and switched gears.

"Alright, so if the bomb didn't go off, where is he? Where's Hunter?"

"I don't know."

Diamond suddenly stopped pacing again and turned his white-hot gaze on Simone. "You what?" His voice cut through the silence in the room like jagged steel.

"I...I said I don't know."

"You didn't go inside and look?"

Simone shuffled his feet. "Well, no," he mumbled. "I mean, I didn't wanna go in there if—"

"Did you just tell me there was no explosion and the building was still standing?"

"Yeah."

"Then why the hell didn't you—?"

"There was a bomb in there, Nick. I didn't know if maybe it was still gonna—"

Diamond raised his gun and put a bullet in Simone's forehead.

The sound was deafening in the small room. When it finally died away, no one made a move. No one drew a breath.

In the roar of a gun and the blink of an eye, Louie Simone—Diamond's underboss, his second in command—was a corpse.

Diamond scanned the room and locked eyes with everyone in it. "Where the hell is Sparks?"

CHAPTER 63
THE PRESS LENDS A HAND

Hunter was back on the motorcycle, heading southeast toward City Hall along dark side streets at something close to seventy-five miles an hour. It was no more than a five-mile stretch from the River District to the center of town, but he was keenly aware of the precious minutes ticking away.

He had thought about just keeping the truck and driving it all the way in, but he'd driven back to the River District instead and picked up the bike in the alley near the Harper Warehouse where he'd left it. It was the right move. The motorcycle afforded him far better speed and maneuverability than the truck ever could. He'd need both if he was going to drive directly into the heart of the madness.

He banked hard around the back corner of a vacant office building, then revved the engine on the straightaway. Without taking either hand off the bars, he glanced at his watch. Eleven-forty-one. He had to get to City Hall, get inside the building without blowing it up and triggering a series of explosions all over town, get the mayor out in one piece, and somehow do it all without drawing the attention of the police, who would be all over the street once he got downtown.

And he had exactly nineteen minutes to do it.

And then, at the end of all that, came the even bigger job. Assuming he could do it all in that time, he still had to find Diamond.

He jaw flexed and his face tightened into a grimace.

He *had* to find Diamond.

The sweeping glow of searchlights in the sky intensified as Hunter made his way toward City Hall. They were the only functioning lights in the downtown area—no doubt operating on gasoline-powered generators—which made them that much more intense against the pitch-black sky.

Hunter was still four blocks away from City Hall when he caught his first glimpse of the front of the building. The searchlight beams flooded the facade and the rows of windows stretching from the west corner to the east. The lights were his cue to cut the motorcycle engine completely and make a quick right turn down a side street.

After less than fifty yards, he turned off the side street and moved down a narrow alley behind two buildings on nothing more than momentum. He noticed a metal storage unit behind one of the buildings along the alley. The structure was big enough and dark enough to create a hiding place of sorts for the motorcycle. With a slam of his boot on the pavement, he brought the bike to a stop, hopped off and tucked the vehicle behind the storage unit.

Staying close to the shadows, he covered the remaining distance to City Hall on foot—about two-hundred yards of zig-zagging pavement that included brick-lined back alley and concrete public thoroughfare.

He was still a full building's length away from the back wall of City Hall, taking cover in the shadows of the County Courthouse, when his heightened auditory sense picked up a mechanical sound—the chug of an automobile engine in an adjoining alley. He concentrated for a moment and surmised that the car was perhaps forty yards away but headed in his direction.

He turned in the direction of the sound. There were no lights, at least not yet, but there was no mistaking that the sound was coming from a car—an older one, with a tired engine.

Hunter found an emergency exit on the side wall of the building. The door was framed in a small inset on the wall. He stepped off the pavement and pressed himself into the inset, but allowed himself the proper angle to watch for the oncoming vehicle.

The car came around the corner in the alley and headed directly toward Hunter's hiding place in the doorway. Definitely no lights, but Hunter's enhanced vision allowed him a clear enough view of the car—silhouette first, then more of the details.

It was Bart Maxwell, chugging through the backstreets in his Model T Roadster. Lights or no lights, Hunter was amazed that the police hadn't stopped him yet and ordered him to turn back. Then again, it was Max. He had a way of gaining access where few others could.

Hunter stepped out of the doorway and into the center of the narrow alleyway, directly in front of the oncoming car.

Max kept coming, but at a minimal speed—less than ten miles an hour. Hunter figured he was having a hard time navigating the narrow space in the dark. The front bumper of the car was less than four feet away from Hunter when Max suddenly saw him and slammed down hard on the brakes, bringing the car to a lurching halt.

Max's eyes went wide, and he swore at the near miss. "Who the hell…?"

Hunter stepped around the front of the car to the driver's side door, and Max squinted back at him through the open window. His expression was a mix of irritation and apprehension as he tried to make out the figure in the darkness.

After a moment, Max realized who—or what—he was looking at. His eyes went wide. His jaw went slack.

"You…" It was barely a whisper, the only sound he could manage.

"Open the storage compartment," said Hunter.

"What?"

"You've got a coil of rope, and some tools."

Maxwell's eyes narrowed. "How do you…?" he stammered. "What, you can see through metal?"

"I need to get into that building."

Maxwell snorted. "You kidding, pal? You go into that building and they're going to be picking up pieces of you all over the block for the next week. Besides, how do I know you're not—?"

"Look," Hunter barked, his words coming now in a rapid-fire staccato, "that building is just the beginning. In about seventeen minutes, half of this city is going to burn, starting with that building and the guy trapped inside. Do you want that to happen, or do you want to help me?"

Maxwell deliberated for a final second, then jumped out of the car.

CHAPTER 64
WINDOW OF OPPORTUNITY

Less than two minutes later, Hunter was making his way up the fire escape along the back wall of City Hall with twenty feet of rope coiled up and slung over his shoulder. Most of the police were in the street in front of the building, but there were three or four officers in the back lot, scanning the rear wall with flashlights. He fought the urge to clamber up the fire escape at a reckless pace, knowing that he'd make too much noise on the metal stairs and draw attention to himself in the process.

In the end, it didn't matter. One of the flashlight beams caught him about halfway to the top of the building, and the voices followed the light by only a second or two.

"Who the hell...?"

"Hey! You up there! Hold it!"

Hunter ignored the command and kept climbing. The flashlight beam followed his hasty ascent.

"I said hold it!"

A shot rang out, slamming into the brick wall of the building about three feet behind him. He figured he wasn't an easy target on the back side of a brick building with no illumination save for a few flashlight beams.

Hunter heard one of the officers shout, "Hold your fire!" There were no more shots, but the chatter from below grew more animated.

"Who is that guy?"

"...some kinda mask..."

"...heading for the roof!"

"...the hell's he doing up there?"

Hunter was, in fact, heading for the roof. And after one more flight of fire escape stairs, he reached the top of the building. With just a short hop, he swung himself over the uppermost stone ledge and onto the tarred rooftop.

He scanned the wide stretch of flat space. A few air vents, an access door to the elevator shaft, a short wooden pole at the far end of the roof that served as a hub for utility wires stretching in every direction.

The skylight, Hunter thought. He remembered Bentley and his assistant standing together in the lobby of City Hall after the press conference a few days earlier. They had talked about repair work that was planned for Bentley's office.

They'd talked about the skylight.

Hunter's heightened sense of direction in relation to the interior of the building enabled him to locate the glass panel in a matter of seconds. It was roughly at the center of the roof, slightly toward the front of the building.

He crouched down at the edge of the metal frame around the window and peered into the office below. Bentley's desk was directly below the skylight, and seated at the desk with his wrists and ankles tied to his chair was Bentley himself.

With a very familiar looking assembly of dynamite and electrical wire strapped to his chest.

Hunter watched for a moment as Bentley squirmed in the chair and tugged at the ropes around his wrists and ankles. The mayor's head darted in all directions, as though he were looking for something in the room that he might somehow use to his advantage.

Hunter noticed something else, a shortwave transmitter sitting on top of the desk, less than two feet from where Bentley was sitting. It puzzled him at first, but it made sense once he thought about it for a second or two.

With any luck, the bomb attached to Bentley was assembled just like the one Hunter had disconnected from himself at the Harper Warehouse. If so, it wouldn't be hard to dismantle. And the transmitter would be even easier to shut down.

But he had to get inside before he could do anything. And he couldn't get inside until he was sure the skylight was a safe point of entry that Diamond's crew hadn't wired like they'd wired the entrances.

He shrugged the rope off his shoulder and examined the frame, but saw no suspicious looking wires. Chipped and crumbling mortar in several places, but no wires. He closed his eyes for a moment and concentrated, running his hand slowly along the full perimeter of the frame. No electric current that he could sense. It was only a guess, but the skylight appeared to be the safe way in.

There was only one way to know for sure.

He found an eight-inch gap amid the broken mortar around the frame and brushed away some of the debris and dirt. Crouching squarely in front of the gap, he worked the fingers of both of his hands into the space. When he was sure he had the best grip he could manage, he straightened his back and braced his shoulders.

Still in a crouched position, he took a deep breath. He flexed his shoulders and arms and pushed upward with his back and his legs.

Rusty metal groaned. Dry wood splintered and cracked. He felt the skylight frame pull away from its mounting, but only by a couple inches.

He relaxed his arms and shoulders and pushed the air out of his lungs. Though loosened slightly, the frame returned to its original position.

Hunter heard Bentley shout from below. "Who's there! Who's up there!" The mayor tried to look straight up, but the restraints on his wrists and the strain on his shoulders caused by the extension of his arms behind the back of the chair prevented him from getting a clear view of the skylight.

Hunter didn't answer. He knew he had to focus every ounce of strength on the task at hand. He took a few seconds to establish a firmer grip on the frame and refill his lungs, then reset himself.

He flexed again and pulled upward. The opening between the frame and the mounting grew wider this time. His back and shoulders protested mightily. His wrists, still cut and bruised from the rope binding in the warehouse, sent screams of pain halfway up his arms. A low, involuntary growl emerged from some primal place within him. But he kept pulling upward.

He felt the pop of a bolt, then another. One of the glass panes shattered as the metal frame slowly bent under the force of his strength and his will. A second pane shattered, spilling small glass shards into the office below.

Another bolt popped, and Hunter felt the tide turn. He gave his arms and shoulders a final jerk and barked out a grunt that signaled pain and triumph at the same time. With very little left to hold it in place, the entire window frame tore away from the mounting, leaving a gaping rectangular portal leading directly into Bentley's office below.

No blinding flash. No roaring explosion.

But Hunter's work here was just beginning. There was still a vest full of dynamite strapped around Bentley's chest. And a bomb ticking away at every entrance to the building.

He checked his watch.

Eleven-forty-nine.

CHAPTER 65
HELP FROM ABOVE

Bentley squirmed in his chair, and kept trying to get a glimpse of what was happening above him. "Who...who's there!" he shouted. He sounded confused, disoriented by the combination of darkness and fatigue—and probably a healthy measure of fear. "Be careful! I've got a...there's a bomb!"

Hunter ducked his head and listened closely to Bentley's labored breathing and the hammering of his heart in his chest. He remembered the feeling all too well.

"It's alright!" he shouted down through the broken skylight. "I'm going to get you out!"

He grabbed an end of the rope and tied it fast to a rusty but secure stub of rebar protruding a few inches from the mortar frame. He grabbed the rest of the rope, still coiled, and took just a couple seconds to set himself on the edge of the mortar before starting his descent. As he did so, a fist-sized chunk of mortar broke away under his leg and fell straight down. He sucked in a gulp of air as his enhanced vision tracked the chunk's vertical trajectory into the darkness. It connected with Bentley's temple on the way down, then broke into smaller fragments as it hit the floor.

Bentley's head rocked to one side, then the other, then came to rest on his left shoulder. Hunter looked down for a moment at the mayor's unconscious form in the chair and hoped like hell that his rescue efforts hadn't resulted in any serious damage. He'd know soon enough.

Hunter slid off the edge of the mortar frame and slipped quickly down the length of rope, thankful for the protection of his leather driving gloves against friction and cuts. All told, the descent from the skylight to the office floor was fourteen feet—not too deep, but deep enough to warrant the rope. He landed feet-first on Bentley's desk and instantly jumped off.

Bentley had a cut on his temple, but it didn't look too severe and his breathing appeared to be steady. If anything, the mishap would make the next moments easier.

Hunter stepped quickly around the desk and knelt down in front of

Bentley's chair to inspect the bomb. He breathed a quick sigh of relief. The design was virtually identical to the one that had been strapped to his own chest earlier. Two wires—one live and the other a trip.

He reached up and rubbed the tip of his forefinger along one of the wires, then stopped and did the same with the other. And just like before, he felt the vibration in one but not the other.

He held his breath and yanked the live wire. It came away in his hand. He tossed at away and ran his fingertips along the full surface of the dynamite vest wrapped around Bentley's chest.

His blood froze.

He still felt a vibration. An electrical current still running through the wiring.

But where did it...?

Hunter glanced at the desk, where the shortwave transmitter was sitting on the desk top. It was a simple Hartley oscillator. Two coils, a capacitor, a vacuum tube and a handful of other small parts—all of it wired together on a slab of wood no bigger than a kitchen breadboard, with a wire antenna stretching to the nearest window sill. Probably no more than five watts, but more than enough power to send a signal to another building just a few blocks away. He looked down and noticed another pair of wires. This pair ran from the dynamite vest to the transmitter.

Of course. The detonator in Bentley's vest had been connected to a power source, just like the setup strapped to Hunter's chest at the warehouse. And Hunter had disconnected Bentley's power source, just as he had previously.

He gave the transmitter a quick once-over. No power source that he could see. So the power to the transmitter had to be coming from the same source as the one that powered the detonator before he disconnected it. While Hunter may have deactivated the bomb on Bentley's chest, some secondary circuit still active inside the vest was powering the transmitter. And that circuit was about to send a tone through the transmitter. And a receiver at the next location in the chain—some other downtown building—would pick up that tone and trigger the next explosion. And there was no telling how many buildings, and for how long.

He had to stop the chain reaction before it started.

Hunter yanked at the wires running from the vest to the transmitter, and they tore away from the assembly mounted on the wooden block. Just to be certain, he pulled the tube from its socket and ripped the other parts from their mountings. He tossed the wooden board and all the loose components into a corner of the room. Tubes shattered against the wall and induction coils and splintered wood fell to the floor in a ruined heap.

He stepped around the desk and knelt down next to Bentley's chair. The dynamite vest had been strapped onto the mayor's torso the same way Hunter's own vest had been strapped onto him in the warehouse. It took him less than thirty seconds to loosen the straps and pull it off.

Still on one knee, Hunter gave Bentley's head a quick inspection. Despite a dark bruise and some swelling around the cut at his temple, he looked as though he'd be okay. He leaned forward and hoisted the mayor over his right shoulder in a fireman's carry, then raised himself to a standing position.

Moving as quickly as possible with at least a hundred-seventy pounds of deadweight over his shoulder, he made his way out of the office and headed for the stairs. Balancing the extra weight got a little more tricky on the three flights of steps, but he made it down to the lobby in less than a minute.

He propped Bentley up against the wall in a half-seated position on the floor at the foot of the stairs. Bentley's limp body sagged and his head lolled to one side, but he remained more or less in an upright position.

Hunter stood and checked his watch. Seven minutes to twelve. He glanced down at Bentley one last time, then turned and sprinted down the hallway leading to the west wing of the building.

It was easy now. He knew the setup. He understood the circuit. He dismantled the bomb rigged to the west entrance, yanked the wires off the door frame and left the conduit in a loose tangle on the floor. He did it all in about forty seconds.

He turned and headed back up the hallway, past Bentley in the lobby—still slumped on the floor and unconscious—and down the opposite hallway leading to the east-wing entrance, where he repeated the same process with the bomb mounted there.

Barely a minute later, he was at the rear entrance, dismantling connections and ripping the guts out of another one of Diamond's custom-made death boxes.

But the trickiest step—the main entrance at the front of the building—was still ahead of him. The device mounted on the front door wouldn't be the challenge. What waited just beyond the door would be an altogether different matter.

Hunter headed back to the lobby and approached the main door. Bentley was starting to stir. His eyes were still closed, and it would be a while before he could stand and walk, but he gingerly touched the gash at his temple and winced.

Through the door, Hunter could hear the tense murmur of voices outside the building—some of them no further than twelve or fifteen feet from the entrance. There were too many voices to estimate the exact number of officers watching the door, but Hunter guessed dozens. Further away from the building, he heard more voices, along with a symphony of engines from what sounded like a fleet of patrol cars and firetrucks.

Judging from the proximity of the voices, he guessed that at least some of the cops were positioned on the stone steps leading up to the entrance. More on the sidewalk and spilling into the street.

Hunter found the bomb on the floor of the lobby, just to the right of the door at the base of the carved woodwork that made up the door frame. He found the circuit wire and ripped it out, rendering the trip wire useless.

From outside, he heard two anxious voices rise above the others.

"Alright, we're at less than two minutes to twelve." It sounded like Hank Crenshaw, the fire department captain. "I just don't think... Mike, there's nothing more we can do here."

"But Bentley's still..." Mike Dugan's voice.

"I know. I know. There's..." Crenshaw lowered his voice. "Mike, I'm sorry. You know we have to get these men away from this building. If this thing blows, a lot of people are going to get hurt badly. Or worse."

"God dammit." Dugan's voice, barely a whisper. "Alright," he said aloud, but quietly at first. Hunter could picture the detective's face, etched with the burden that came with failing to save Stephen Bentley's life.

And then Dugan raised his voice, presumably to address the ranks. "Alright," he said. "We're out of time. The clock is ticking and there's nothing we can do. We need to fall back! Off the steps!"

341

The murmur of voices surged. Hunter heard the scuffle of footsteps on stone—downward, backward, away from the building.

"Back to the street!" Dugan ordered. "Find some cover behind the cars or one of the trucks!"

Hunter reached up and yanked away the wiring that ran along the perimeter of the door, from the hinges to the handle.

"Mike, wait a minute!" Crenshaw's voice again, still near the other side of the door and suddenly more animated.

Hunter yanked the last of the wire off the door.

"There's..." Crenshaw stammered, "I'm hearing...There's something happening on the other side of this door!"

"What?"

The scuffle on the steps stopped abruptly.

"Hey!" It was Dugan's voice, followed by the click of a hammer at the back end of a service revolver. Hunter triangulated on the sound of the detective's voice. He could tell Dugan's shoulders were squared to the front of the building now and he was shouting directly at the door. "Hey! What's going on in there! Open the door slow, and come out with your hands in the air!"

Inside the lobby, Hunter backed away from the door frame and positioned himself at the center of the doorway, less than four feet from the threshold. He set himself and counted to three.

He kicked open the door and immediately ducked back into the shadows and positioned himself off to one side of the doorway, flattening his back to the wall. A gust of fresh air entered the lobby, but with it came a whiff of exhaust fumes from the various police and fire vehicles idling in the street. Hunter heard the sound of at least fifteen hammers pulling back from fifteen barrels of fifteen service revolvers.

"All clear!" he shouted. "Bentley's inside!"

That was all the help he could afford to give them. He knew they'd come through the doorway any second. But he also knew there would be some hesitation before they actually came across the threshold, and they wouldn't start shooting until they were certain that Bentley was nowhere in the line of fire. He would need to make the best use of those few extra seconds to fall back and find some way out of the building other than the front door.

He heard a single voice above the murmur. "Alright, step out of there with your hands up!"

Dugan.

Hunter took one last look at Bentley—who had opened his eyes and was squinting into the darkness—and pushed away from the wall. Keeping out of the line of sight through the gaping doorway, he crossed the lobby and headed back up the stairs.

Nearly a half-mile away, St. Michael's struck twelve.

CHAPTER 66
MIDNIGHT SILENCE

Diamond stood at the window with his binoculars trained on City Hall as the bells of St. Michael's rang in the midnight hour. Fallon and Kowalski stood a few feet behind him, also watching out the window at the city below.

As the twelfth and final bell faded into the night, the room fell silent. Diamond kept staring through the binoculars.

It must be just a few seconds off, he thought. *The timer must not be synchronized to the exact second. It'll just be a few more seconds.*

And after a few more seconds came and went, he took the binoculars away from his face and checked his watch. Nearly a minute after twelve.

He raised the binoculars to his face again and scanned Liberty Avenue. At least a half-dozen police cars with lights flashing. Three fire trucks that he could see, maybe more.

Another full minute passed. Fallon broke the silence. "It's not..." he began, shaking his head. "There isn't any—"

He was cut off by Diamond's voice, a low growl that quickly escalated to a roar. In a single motion, Diamond hurled the binoculars at the far wall, turned away from the window and crossed the room to where Wireless was still huddled on the floor. The young radio engineer was now shaking uncontrollably and nearly hyperventilating—all of which made for a pathetic sight and sound that only made Diamond more incensed.

Diamond pulled his gun out of his belt and bent over Wireless' trembling form. He grabbed Wireless by the collar and yanked him upright.

"Get up," he roared. "Get up, you stupid little…"

Wireless rose clumsily to his feet, partly of his own will and partly at the mercy of Diamond's rage-fueled strength.

Diamond pinned Wireless against the wall and leaned his full weight against him, shoving the barrel of his gun into the man's rib cage. Wireless flinched. His hands went up in an instinctive shielding gesture.

"Don't…don't…" he whimpered, his eyes squeezed shut.

Although Wireless usually stood a good three or four inches taller than Diamond, it was hard to tell at the moment by his cowering slouch.

"Nothing's happening out there," Diamond growled, shoving the gun deeper into Wireless' ribcage. "What the hell went wrong?"

Wireless flinched at the pressure in his ribs and shook his head vigorously. His tremulous voice delivered little more than a meaningless babble. "I don't know. I don't know. I don't know…"

Diamond was close to pulling the trigger. Fallon and Kowalski were so preoccupied with the confrontation unfolding in the room that neither one of them noticed Sparks in the doorway.

"What's going on?" he said.

Four heads turned at the sound of the voice.

Diamond took his gun away from Wireless' ribs and immediately turned toward Sparks before he could get too far into the room. Wireless leaned back against the wall and sucked in an enormous gulp of air, like a drowning man coming to the surface at the last possible second.

"Where the hell have you been?" Diamond barked.

Sparks glanced down at Diamond's right hand, which was now down at his side. Sparks' expression was suddenly wary of the gun in Diamond's hand and the agitated look in his eye. He kept silent for a moment.

"I didn't have a car," he said finally, keeping his voice even. "I had to walk all the way from Marshall's office, down the backstreets and the alleys to steer clear of the police. I couldn't see a thing. Then I had to find Huffman in the dark behind the building without drawing any attention."

"Wait a minute," said Diamond. "What are you talking about? Vin has a car."

"He's…He's not coming."

"What do you mean he's not coming?"

"Just like I said. He's not coming. He skipped out."

"Wait a minute. What the hell are you saying?"

"He said he didn't like the way things were happening. Said everything was coming apart. He said some other things too. Things you probably wouldn't want to hear. He told me I should try to get out too." Sparks paused. "But I didn't. I came here."

The room was suddenly silent. Sparks glanced at everyone in the dark space. Kowalski rubbed his face, his expression uneasy. The news Sparks had just conveyed was clearly not sitting well with him.

"Vinnie," said Diamond. His voice was small, and a little bit far away. He fought to harden himself against the sting of betrayal and the wave of sadness that came with it. The situation at hand allowed no time for such things.

Another silent moment passed. Sparks checked his watch and looked across the room at the panorama of the downtown cityscape outside the window. "It's after midnight," he said.

"You're goddamn right it is," said Diamond, the dangerous edge quickly returning to his voice. "And the warehouse in the River District is still standing. And so is City Hall."

Sparks' eyes widened. "What? What do you mean?"

"Just what I said."

Sparks' eyes narrowed. His head cocked on an angle and his face twisted in confusion. "No," he said. "That can't be. Are you sure?"

"Louie was there. He saw for himself."

Sparks shook his head in denial. "That can't be," he repeated. "He doesn't know what he's talking about. Where is he now?"

Diamond gestured to the floor in the corner. Sparks turned and saw the body that had been Louie Simone just a few minutes earlier. Diamond had ordered the other men in the room to move him into the corner, but the lifeless face was still a ghastly white mask with a hole in the forehead and blank eyes frozen in a final moment of terror.

Sparks was still staring into the dead eyes when Diamond said, "Ask him yourself."

Sparks shuddered, clearly shaken by the sight of Diamond's second-in-command lying dead on the floor from a bullet to the head. Sparks was no dummy. He could have surmised who and where the bullet came from.

"I've built everything we've ever used," he said. "I've built them all myself. They've never failed."

"Well, your batting average so far tonight is pretty damn bad," said Diamond. "And let me tell you, the one at that warehouse was pretty important. More so than any of us thought it would be."

"What do you mean?"

"That freak in the mask showed up. And get this. He's Jack Hunter."

"What!"

"You heard me," said Diamond.

"But…But that can't be," Sparks stammered. "The assistant DA?"

Diamond turned away and seethed for a second or two. "I am getting tired of hearing you tell me what can't be," he said. "It can be. And it is. And he's made a hell of a lot of trouble. So when Kowalski found him hanging around the back of the warehouse, he knocked him out and brought him inside. It wasn't part of the plan, but it all came together nicely. I had Fallon and Wireless tie him into a chair and then strap the thing to his chest. That way, I could not only get rid of any evidence in the building, but get rid of him and the girl too."

Sparks was still shaking his head, apparently still trying to comprehend the idea that the masked man was Jack Hunter.

Diamond didn't give him much time to think. He grabbed Sparks by the lapel with his left hand. "But your bomb didn't go off!" he roared, waving his gun toward the window. "And the one at City Hall didn't go off either!"

"I…I don't know!" Sparks shot back defensively. "I wasn't there when they were wired up." He glanced past Diamond at Fallon, who was leaning against the wall with his arms folded, then settled his gaze on Wireless, who had regained some of his composure but still leaned against the opposite wall looking anything but relaxed.

Wireless glared back at Sparks. "What are you saying?" he snapped. "I wired them up right!" His voice escalated quickly, to something near hysteria. "I wired up every goddamn bomb in the city! I wired up every doorway at City Hall! I shut down a power station and built a transmitter in just a few hours! I know how to do this stuff better than anybody! Don't try to tell me—"

"Alright, that's enough!' said Diamond. He let go of Sparks' jacket and immediately turned to Kowalski. "Johnny, I need you to go back to the warehouse and make sure Hunter and the girl are taken care of."

Kowalski's eyes went wide. "What?" he said, clearly surprised by the order. "Nick, I don't know if…I mean, the police are all over the—"

"Do it!"

Kowalski looked back at Diamond. Neither said another word for a moment, but something subtle happened in Kowalski's face—something fleeting that Diamond couldn't quite identify.

Kowalski reached inside his jacket and pulled his gun from his belt. "Okay," he said.

He checked the cylinder quickly, then clicked it back into place. "Okay."

He turned to Fallon and said, "Watch the door."

Then he pulled his flashlight from his pocket with his free hand, turned toward the door and walked out of the room.

CHAPTER 67
ROOFTOP GETAWAY

Hunter could already hear the police storming through the front entrance to City Hall by the time he reached the second floor. None of the exits on the ground level would have been an option. His only way out was the same way he'd come in. He pounded his way up to the third floor and retraced his steps back down the hallway to the Bentley's office.

He stopped suddenly before he crossed through the office doorway. The police had spotted him on his way up the fire escape a few minutes ago. How soon before they'd make their way to the roof and come through the broken skylight? Was it already too late?

He didn't have much choice.

He stood with his back against the wall just next to Bentley's door and focused his hearing. No footsteps, no whispered commands, no heartbeats. He ducked his head and rolled his shoulders away from the wall to take a quick glance inside.

All clear.

He barreled into the room, taking only two long steps beyond the threshold before leaping onto Bentley's desk and using it as a platform to jump straight up and grab the rope that was still dangling from the skylight.

His jump was high enough that he was able to grab the rope only a foot and a half shy of the mortar ledge on the roof from which it hung. After just a few seconds of shimmying up the rope and climbing over the ledge, he was back on the rooftop under the open sky.

Hunter did a quick scan of his surroundings, then crouched down and unhooked the rope from the rebar lodged in the mortar. He gathered the rope into a quick coil and broke into a hard sprint toward the west end of the building. He was halfway to the edge of the rooftop when he caught sight of stray flashlight beams and heard sounds coming from two directions—the north wall about fifty feet to his right and the skylight opening about sixty feet behind him.

The police were on their way up the fire escape and through the mayor's ceiling. Word had obviously traveled around the perimeter of the building that it was now safe to move in.

He was still sprinting for the edge of the roof when he glanced to his right and saw two cops, then a third, cresting the edge of the rooftop. And there were more. Without looking back, he counted two sets of footsteps now on the rooftop by way of the skylight and coming up fast behind him.

Flashlight beams darted in all directions as the officers tried to get a bead on him in the dark. Without slowing down, he established a tight zig-zag pattern in hopes of making it a little harder for them and buying himself a couple extra seconds.

He headed for the short utility pole mounted on the roof. The pole was a connecting hub for four parallel power lines that stretched in a downward, diagonal slope across a thirty-foot-wide alley and connected to the County Courthouse, the next building over on Liberty Avenue.

His plan was still taking shape in his mind when his feet skidded to a stop at the edge of the roof, just a few feet from the pole.

His mind raced. Swinging from power lines couldn't be a good idea. The possibility of touching something live would...

Wait. No.

There was no power in these lines. Every power line, every transformer on every utility pole in the city, had been dead for a few hours.

He tossed one end of the rope over the lowest wire with his right hand and caught it on the other side with his left, essentially creating a loop of rope over the wire. He tugged hard on the loop to test the strength of the wire. Would it suspend his weight long enough and far enough to get him across the alley to the next building?

He listened without turning. Footsteps pounding hard on the rooftop. Two officers coming up behind him. Thirty yards away. Slowing down and flanking him from two sides. Guns drawn and hammers back.

"Hold it! Let go of the rope and step away from the ledge!"

Hunter ignored the command.

"Turn around and step away from the ledge!"

He didn't turn around, but otherwise he did what he was told. He braced his arms and shoulders and stepped off the ledge, pointing his feet outward and downward into open space.

Gravity did the rest, taking him on a diagonal descent over the alley. He heard shouting and swearing from the officers as he cleared the roof, followed by the crack of one gunshot, then another. Both slugs sang past him and slammed into the side of the courthouse just ahead of him.

And just ahead of him was coming up fast, but not so fast that his heightened senses couldn't process the combination of mass and acceleration that was propelling him through space and enable him to anticipate his jumping off point.

In the end, his dismount and landing were a matter of instinct as much as calculation. He let go of the rope ends at the precise moment and stumbled onto the second-floor landing of the fire escape, putting up one hand to grab the railing and holding up the other to keep from slamming into the side of the building.

He immediately got his feet under him and headed down the stairs.

He heard the cops on the City Hall rooftop above and behind him, shouting to their fellow officers on the ground.

"He swung over to the courthouse!"

"He's coming down the fire escape!"

But if he was last seen on the City Hall rooftop just seconds ago, how could he be at the courthouse now? The cops on the ground couldn't figure it out fast enough to respond and make their way across the alley.

The extra three or four seconds of confusion were all Hunter needed to reach ground level, slip into the shadows and head for his motorcycle parked less than a block away.

CHAPTER 68
HUNTER AT THE TOWER

It was almost twelve-fifteen when Hunter pulled the motorcycle around to the parking garage along the south side of Union Tower. It would be his best chance of getting into the building. The other more common entrances were more likely to be heavily guarded by police.

It had been a short ride—barely a quarter mile—from the alley on Liberty Avenue where he'd parked the bike to the rear entrance to the tower. He'd covered the distance on back roads and side streets, with his lights out and his engine in a lower gear to avoid any attention from the police.

He'd fought the urge at every block to open it up and take it to top speed. With Bentley and City Hall secured—and hopefully no other buildings in immediate danger—he was fairly certain he was no longer racing against the clock. But even so, he didn't want to waste any time finding Diamond.

He pulled into the garage entrance. He didn't expect to see anyone on duty in the guardhouse, but he was mistaken. A guard stepped out of the small building. He had a flashlight in his left hand and, more importantly, a revolver in his right.

Hunter had used this garage several times in the past month alone. He knew for a fact that the guards here were considered convenience attendants more than security officers, and they were not supposed to be armed.

The flashlight came up first, and the beam hit him square in the face. The guard took one look at the dark goggles staring back at him from the other end of the beam and muttered, "What the hell...?"

Hunter watched the gun come up, as if in slow motion. Before the guard could level the weapon, Hunter steered the bike directly at him and gunned the engine. A sudden look of horror spread across the guard's face as the growling motorcycle closed in on him like a two-wheeled monster.

The guard fired without taking proper aim and the slug flew somewhere into the darkness.

By the time the guard could hope to squeeze off another shot, the front wheel of the oncoming machine slammed into his mid-section and knocked him backward and off his feet. The gun and the flashlight bounced out of his hands and clattered in opposite directions across the concrete garage floor and into the shadows.

Dazed and winded from the fall, the guard was slow to get up—which gave Hunter enough extra seconds to kill his engine and prop the bike up against the guard house.

The guard had just got his legs under him and was barely upright when Hunter was upon him. He grabbed the guard's leather jacket with his left hand and cocked his right fist back until it as even with his shoulder.

"You're going to get me inside that building," said Hunter, his jagged voice echoing in the cavernous garage. "Thirtieth floor, right? That's where the party is, isn't it?"

"I don't know what you're—"

Hunter clamped down harder on the guard's jacket and jerked his fist back without actually delivering a punch. The guard flinched and let out a small yelp, dropping to one knee.

"Stop it!" Hunter barked, leaning over him. "I don't have the time, and I don't have the patience." He glanced across the dark garage and got a glimpse of the service entrance leading into the tower. "You're going to get me inside that service entrance."

The guard hesitated. He'd lost his leverage, physical and otherwise, and he knew it. It had disappeared into the darkness with his gun. "I don't have...I need a flashlight," he stammered. "I can't see where I'm going."

"I can," said Hunter, "and that's all you need to worry about. Forget the flashlight." He yanked the guard back onto his feet and turned him in the direction of the building with a shove. "Get your keys out and let's get going."

"I...I don't need the keys. The door's unlocked."

Hunter paused, wondering if the guard was pulling some kind of trick. "Alright," he said after a moment. "But you're sticking with me. You're going to show me the way inside."

He grabbed the guard's collar with one hand and his right arm with the other and turned him toward the service entrance. After only a couple steps, the guard started to squirm, as though he might be trying to position himself to break away. Hunter saw the maneuver coming long before the guard could hope to make a move. He planted his feet and delivered a moderate blow to the guard's ribcage.

The guard doubled over and coughed hard.

"Knock it off," said Hunter. "And don't think about making a run."

The guard shook his head. "Okay," he rasped, barely able to get any sound out.

"Okay," said Hunter. "Let's go inside."

Hunter opened the metal door and slid it upward on its tracks. "You first," he said, pushing the guard in front of him.

They stepped into a service area that was pitch-black, but Hunter could see the lay of the land just fine. A wide entranceway—big enough for large boxes and crates, forklifts, and just about any other goods or equipment—extended for about twenty feet, then ended in a T.

"Okay, where to?"

The guard gestured with his free arm. "The stairway's up and to the right."

"Alright, let's—"

Hunter froze. Footsteps just around the corner. Muffled, as though they were on the other side of a wall or a door.

One person. Big. Heavy. Coming from above and working his way down. Coming down the stairs.

The guard glanced at Hunter. Now he heard it too. Hunter looked back at him, squeezing him at both points of contact—his arm and his collar. "Not a sound," he whispered.

A door opening. And now the footsteps were louder, clearer. A flashlight beam bounced around the perpendicular hallway ahead of them.

Four seconds later, the tall figure came around the corner from the right. The flashlight beam hit Hunter and the guard squarely in the face and the footsteps stopped abruptly.

Hunter heard the voice. "What the hell...?" Then the click of the hammer.

It all happened in a crystal-clear dance. The right arm came up. Slowly, it seemed, but maybe just in Hunter's mind. Hunter shoved the guard away, toward the left wall, then ducked to the right.

The gun went off.

The next sound he heard was the guard's voice. "Godammit! You... You shot me, you sonofa..."

Hunter turned and saw the guard clutching his shoulder and small rivers of blood running between his fingers. Twelve feet away, the tall figure with the gun swore, his voice signaling his confusion. Even with the flashlight, he couldn't get a clear sense of what was happening in the darkness.

Hunter rushed him. Another shot went off. He knew it would be wide before the slug left the barrel. It slammed into the wall to his right, not even close. He kept moving forward.

In two steps, he was upon him. He grabbed the gunman's right hand and wrenched it hard. The gunman cried out and his weapon fell to the ground. Hunter kicked it away.

The gunman went down on one knee, then the other, grunting from the vise-like pain at his wrist. Hunter slammed his right fist into the gunman's jaw, and his head rocked back. Hunter landed another blow, and the man crumpled to the floor.

Hunter stood up straight. He glanced back at the guard, who was laying on the ground and holding his shoulder. There was blood, but the wound looked like a graze and nothing more.

He turned away and headed for the stairs.

CHAPTER 69
SPARKS BY ANY OTHER NAME

Despite his ability to see clearly in the darkness, the thirty floors were more challenging than Hunter had expected. The absence of light wasn't the problem, and he was in good enough shape to take the stairs quickly. It was the sound that concerned him, especially with his senses keenly tuned to every rustle of his own clothing, every scuff of boot leather that accompanied every move he made in the otherwise silent stairway. Was he as loud as he seemed? In a building powered down to silence, would he give himself away?

He checked his steps more carefully with each flight of stairs, taking care to keep his footfalls as quiet as possible so as not to be heard by anyone on the floors above him.

At the thirtieth floor landing, he slipped quietly through the double doors that led to the main hallway. He instantly took in the layout—two elevators along one wall, a long mirror mounted on the other. On the wall at the opposite end of the hallway was a large, multi-paned window that spanned eight feet by six feet—most of the height and width of the wall itself.

His heightened olfactory sense immediately picked up a vague smell of burning kerosene. From a side passage coming off to the right of the main hallway, he noticed a soft glow from a half-open door about midway down the corridor. The glow threw a straight edge of diffused golden light along the tiled hallway floor. With no electricity in the entire building, Diamond and his crew were illuminating the room with lantern light.

But the kerosene smell was only part of what Hunter picked up. There were voices, too. One angry voice in particular.

Diamond.

Hunter glanced at his watch and almost smiled. It was nearly twenty minutes after twelve, and things weren't going well for poor Nicky Dynamite.

"What about the other bombs in the other buildings?" he heard Diamond say, his voice dripping with derision. "Are they all going to fail?"

"I…I don't know. They're all tied to the first one, the one at City Hall. The transmitter was supposed to send a tone to a receiver in the next building—the County Records building—to trigger the bomb there. And then it's supposed to go down the line."

Hunter heard it all from the hallway, where he hung back in the shadows, a few feet from the door with his back pressed against the wall. He leaned forward slightly, just enough to peer through the four-inch crack between the door and the door frame, and got a visual confirmation of what he already knew.

Willis Gray. Working for Diamond, wiring up explosives.

"Maybe it…Maybe it didn't have anything to do with the circuit," said Gray, his words coming fast and laced with panic, as though something deadly was creeping up on him and he was ready to gnaw off a limb to escape it. "Maybe it's something about the way Sparks built the bomb. Maybe the chemical balance was wrong. Maybe—"

A second voice interrupted indignantly. "No. I'm not going to listen to any of that. Everything I've built has performed just as designed. Are you suggesting that I just suddenly started making faulty explosives this morning?"

And there it is, thought Hunter, who had no trouble recognizing the second voice. It was the same voice he'd been hearing for days—in meetings with the police, in long-winded explanations about chemical properties and combustive compounds, in conversations about the family cleaning supply business.

The other "technical consultant" in Nicky Diamond's inner circle—a man known simply as Sparks—was one Oliver Pruett, chemical engineer and former manager of the Pharaoh Chemical plant.

Hunter's hunch had panned out from start to finish. When he'd discovered the ransacked office in the police department earlier that evening, Betty's scarf reeked of chloroform but Pruett's bowtie didn't—which suggested that she'd been drugged but he hadn't. A few minutes later, in the sub-cellar of the Republic Building, when Buzz had given Hunter his best estimate about the geographic area where Diamond's pirate broadcast had most likely originated, Hunter had guessed at the Harper Warehouse because Pruett had told him days ago that his family business used a building at the end of Warehouse Row as a storage center for cleaning materials. And cleaning agents were exactly what he'd smelled the minute after he woke up after the blow to the back of his head.

What's more, after Hunter had escaped from the warehouse and rescued Bentley, Hunter knew where he'd likely find Diamond because Pruett had told him about his family's office space on the thirtieth floor of Union Tower—which also happened to be an ideal vantage point for the city-wide fireworks that Pruett and Gray had engineered.

Hunter was fairly confident that he'd pulled the plug on the entire chain of explosions. It was time for him to launch some fireworks of his own.

CHAPTER 70
THE WIRELESS OPTION

Wireless squeezed his eyes shut and ran both hands across his ashen, sweaty face. "Look, wait a minute!" he said, nearly pleading. "I can…There's another way to do this!"

"What do you mean?" said Diamond. He felt a tightness in his chest that came not only from frustration and rage, but also a measure of desperation.

"The remote control box," said Wireless. "I can calibrate it to the same frequency that the transmitters and receivers all over town are set to." He crossed the room, brushing Sparks out of his way as he did so, and knelt down at his tool bag resting in the corner.

"What do you mean?" said Diamond. "Are you saying I can—"

"Yeah, yeah," said Gray, rummaging through the bag. "You can use the box to trigger the next bomb in the sequence. The one at County Records." He pulled out the same remote control box he and Diamond had used before.

"Yeah, it should work," said Wireless, as though he were talking himself off the ledge of a tall building and doing his best to suppress the panic that came with it. "Just let me…"

His voice trailed off as he continued to rummage. His hands trembled as he pulled out a screwdriver and began loosening the bolts holding the protective metal plate onto the back of the box. He had the plate off the box in less than thirty seconds.

"I can just…" he muttered, but his words devolved into a quiet mumble as he dug into the box with the screwdriver.

Diamond watched as Wireless made some kind of adjustments to the remote control device, thinking aloud in disjointed words and phrases as he worked.

"Yeah, I can just…" Wireless went on. "It's set to the same frequency as the transmitter. Just like I set it up for Hirschfeld's place. And the Stor-All joint. It…it'll work."

"You sure?" said Diamond.

"Yeah, I'm sure." Wireless put the plate back into place and screwed the bolts back down. He tossed the screwdriver back into the bag, stood up and crossed the room again. "Okay, here it is."

Diamond reached out with a trembling hand and took the box.

"But listen," said Wireless, "it may not—"

Oblivious to Wireless' voice, Diamond pushed the button. He looked out the window, waiting.

Nothing.

He pushed again, twice this time. Then three times in quick succession.

Nothing.

"Sonofabitch!" he barked, turning toward Wireless with a fiery glare. Without hesitation, he pulled his gun and drew down on Wireless.

Wireless flinched again. "No, wait!" he yelped. "See, that's what I was trying to tell you." He spoke in rapid fire now, as though his life depended on his next few words—and he knew it did. "County Records is nearly a quarter mile away. That remote control device doesn't have the signal strength the reach the receiver connected to the bomb we planted there—at least not from here, not inside this building."

"What do you mean?" Diamond growled "What the hell are you talking about?"

"There isn't enough power and range in that little thing to send a signal strong enough to get beyond this tower all the way to County Records." He glanced around the room. "It doesn't help that we're standing inside a tower of concrete and steel. It's hard to get a signal past all that without hundreds of watts and an antenna somewhere outside the building."

"So how the hell are we supposed to—?"

"You...You have to get outside the building," said Wireless. He gestured at the box in Diamond's hand. "And you have to...You have to get that antenna up so you can send a strong enough signal to reach the receiver and activate the detonator."

Diamond scowled, not at all satisfied by Wireless' solution. "How the hell...?" he snarled. "We're thirty floors up. How the hell would I—?"

Diamond's query was cut short by a sudden and deafening crash as the office door exploded inward, tearing completely off its hinges and knocking over the coat tree as it tumbled into the room. Fallon, who'd been standing at the door since Kowalski went downstairs, staggered forward as the large wooden panel struck him from behind. He barely kept from hitting the floor face-first.

The doorway was now a gaping rectangular opening, with splintered wood where the hinges had been anchored just seconds before.

And within that broken rectangular space stood the masked figure of Jack Hunter, braced for his first attacker.

CHAPTER 71
SHOTS IN THE DARK

Diamond spun to face the damaged doorway, peering into the darkness of the outer hallway. "What the hell...?" he growled.

And then his eyes grew wide as he stared into two clouded lenses hiding Hunter's eyes. "You!"

In a split second, Diamond's gun was up and leveled at Hunter's chest. Hunter was acutely aware of Diamond's every move, his every breath.

Barely a second later, another figure immediately to Diamond's left was stumbling out from under the unhinged door and pointing his gun in the same general direction. Hunter instantly took note of his suspenders and recognized him as one of the men he'd encountered in the back room of the Watt Building a couple nights earlier.

Hunter was keenly aware of two other figures in the room—not just their location but their breathing and their heartbeat. Pruett and Gray—otherwise known as Sparks and Wireless—stood near the wall opposite Diamond. Either they were unarmed or they were too stunned at the sight of him to draw whatever weapons they had.

And there was a fifth body—one with no heartbeat at all, on the floor in the corner at the back of the room.

Four muted voices grunted in a mix of surprise and disbelief. Two hammers on two revolvers clicked back. It all happened in a razor-sharp slow motion that lasted no more than two or three seconds.

Hunter glanced at the two muzzles pointed at him from slightly different directions. Diamond and Fallon, neither one more than twelve feet away from him, both of them aiming somewhere between his head and his chest.

Too close. He'd already learned enough about the limits of his reflexes and agility to know that multiple shots at such close range would be too much to dodge.

Too much to dodge, maybe, but he could give both shooters a handicap.

With lightning speed, Hunter ducked into a crouch and grabbed Diamond's jacket that had fallen to the floor when the coat tree toppled. He immediately pumped his legs upward and forward, leaping headlong across the room and toward the table near the desk several feet away. A gun went off, but Hunter's sudden launch through the space of the room created enough confusion for the shot to go wide.

Hunter crashed into the table, splintering two of its legs and breaking the flat tabletop into two pieces. Another shot rang out, but it was a hasty one as Diamond and the three other men in the room scattered to the far corners to avoid the human projectile moving through it. The lantern that had been on the table spiraled into the air, end over end, until gravity pulled it back toward the floor. Hunter, still moving from the momentum of his leap, snared the lantern in the folds of the jacket like an offensive lineman on the gridiron scooping a forward pass out of thin air.

The jacket had snuffed the lantern and left the room in darkness by the time Hunter hit the floor. He grunted at the jolt of pain that shot through his shoulder and ribs, but he was able to roll with the fall enough to avoid any serious injury.

More gunfire, from more than one weapon this time, but these were desperate shots in response to the sudden blackness of the room. Hunter was back on his feet and having no trouble maneuvering away from the crossfire and coming at the trigger men from behind and all sides.

He was a whirlwind in the darkness, weaving his way through and around the tangle of blind confusion and stray bullets, delivering rapid-fire combinations in all directions—a sharp left to the jaw of one, a solid body blow to another, a hard uppercut to a third. And for Diamond, a made-to-order roundhouse right that sent him stumbling backward. Already staggered by Hunter's punishing barrage, the four men stumbled and went down easily amid the fallen coat tree and the chunks of broken table that littered the floor.

They were sprawled helplessly on the floor, arms and legs in every direction. Diamond looked dazed, but Fallon looked far worse. His hands were at his mid-section, which was bleeding severely. He'd apparently taken one of the bullets in the blind crossfire.

Hunter turned to Gray, the sniveling radio engineer. He'd obviously taken another one of the wild shots. He lay on his side, eyes in a blank stare and head bleeding at the temple. Hunter leaned toward him slightly and focused, listening for a heartbeat. He caught the vibration, but it was fading quickly.

His concentration was interrupted by a scuffling sound on the floor a few feet behind him. He spun just in time to see Pruett—the man otherwise known as Sparks—scrambling in a half crawl to follow the sliver of dim light coming through the slim opening of the door. He was making a break for the hallway, and probably the stairs.

It only took Hunter four long strides to catch up with Pruett, who had reached the threshold of the door and used the doorknob as a hand-hold to get himself to his feet. Hunter grabbed Pruett by the collar and twisted his arm around his back with the other.

Even with his hold on Pruett, Hunter kept one eye on Diamond, who was still on the office floor, just a few feet away from the door and getting himself back on his feet. Diamond still had his gun in is hand. He made a half-hearted attempt to sweep the room, even though he couldn't see anything.

Hunter looked away from Diamond and shoved Pruett into the hallway, where the only light was the faintest glow from faraway searchlights streaming through the large window on the wall. Another shove, and Pruett half stumbled, but Hunter kept him more or less upright.

Even with his arm pinned behind his back, Pruett put up enough resistance to keep Hunter from gaining the necessary leverage to deliver a blow that would subdue him. Pruett reached into his belt and actually got hold of a gun tucked there. But rather than give him the chance to take aim, Hunter lurched Pruett forward—into the main hallway, where he slammed Pruett against the wall face-first, just to the right of the elevator doors. Pruett, his face pressed against the paneling, grunted out a burst of air as his glasses came loose and fell to the floor. His free hand fumbled and the gun landed on the floor near his and Hunter's feet.

Hunter had to finish this and go after Diamond before he could have a chance to make a run for the stairs. Still holding Pruett against the wall, he removed his vise grip from the man's collar and arm and spun him around to face him. He pinned Pruett's shoulders against the wall with a powerful left forearm and cocked his right fist back to deliver the blow that would put him down.

It was then that he heard movement in the office doorway several feet behind him, along with the heavy breathing.

Followed by the click of a revolver hammer.

CHAPTER 72
PUTTING OUT SPARKS

Diamond's mind churned in a swirl of natural adrenalin, chemical stimulant and blind rage. His jaw flexed involuntarily and his eyes widened in the darkness. His breath came in short bursts through flaring nostrils.

So dark...So hard to see...Barely enough light to...

He raised the gun and fought to keep his hand steady.

Christ, that guy's fast. He's working Sparks over at an impossible speed...

Diamond fired, but Hunter—although a good twenty-five feet away—seemed to be somehow aware of the squeeze of his finger on the trigger, ducking away before the slug left the chamber.

Diamond knew the instant he fired that he'd missed.

Sonofabitch! How can he...how can anyone move like that?

With the shot still echoing in the hallway, Hunter disappeared into a dark corner and out of sight. Diamond, his gun still raised, suddenly had a clear view of Sparks, whose jacket was soaked with a stain of blood that hadn't been there seconds before. The stain rapidly blossomed on his shirt and the front of his jacket.

Sparks put a hand up to his chest and looked down at his bloody fingers. Even in the darkness, Diamond could see the curious and confused look on his face. Sparks turned his head in Diamond's direction, as though he might ask him a question, but no words came. Instead, he slid down the wall to a squatting position, smearing blood on the paneling as he did it, then tumbled sideways onto the floor.

He was still looking at Diamond when his eyes went vacant and he gave up his last breath.

The momentary echo of the gunshot died away, and silence hung in the dark hallway for a suspended moment.

Diamond blinked.

He stared back at the crumpled body, aided by just enough searchlight glow coming through the large window to cast a reflective glint on Sparks' lifeless eyes.

He shook his head. Slowly at first, and then faster, his breath coming in short bursts through his nose.

No. This isn't...no.

Diamond tore his eyes away from Sparks and looked down at the gun in his hand. Both of his hands were trembling.

Something flooded his mind, something he couldn't control, like an enormous ocean wave rushing up and over a rocky cliff in a gathering storm.

Was it remorse? Anger?

No.

Fear.

It came in a cold sweat, and a primal shiver than ran down the length of his spine and struck his stomach with a dull, sickening jolt. The same kind of jolt that strikes a desperate, two-bit junkie who learns that his supplier has just skipped town.

And so it was. Sparks was the one, the only one, who knew how to give Diamond the fix. The only one who knew the chemistry. Sparks was the one who brought the beautiful flash and the swirl of bright light and the savage, heart-thumping roar that came with it.

And now that was all gone.

Diamond doubled over, folding in on himself. He raised his hands—still holding the gun in one and squeezing the other into a fist—and pressed them against his temples. Somewhere in the distance, he heard the beginnings of a scream—a whimper at first that became a wail.

In some corner of his mind where a tenuous shred of reason still existed, he realized the voice he was hearing was his own.

CHAPTER 73
DYNAMITE EXPLODES

Hunter watched from a corner of darkness just beyond the shaft of moonlight coming through the window. Diamond was losing control. He stood hunched over himself in the middle of the hallway, barely ten feet from the lifeless heap that had been Oliver Pruett. His hands were at his temples—right hand holding his gun, left hand curled into a fist—and Hunter thought for a moment that he might be getting ready to put a bullet in his own head.

Then the screaming started.

Hunter didn't know exactly what it meant, or where it came from, but it started with a whimper and blossomed into a sickening wave of raw anguish that filled the black hallway like the tortured howl of the damned.

Hunter stared in fascination, aware of a feeling in the pit of his stomach that was vaguely sick yet somehow satisfying at the same time. He was watching a murderer—a vile and ruthless animal that had taken so much from him—lose his mind right before his eyes.

Still wailing in the darkness, Diamond turned to his right, away from Pruett. He raised his gun and fired randomly, putting a bullet into the paneling on the far wall. He staggered, shuffled to his left and fired again, shattering the mirror on the opposite wall.

Hunter watched the crazy dance unfold, looking for some shred of a pattern but seeing none. Diamond was more dangerous than ever, and Hunter knew that if he was going to make a move against this madman, he would have to do it now.

How many bullets did Diamond still have in his gun? One? Four? Had he reloaded in the darkness of the office when Hunter was busy with Pruett out in the hallway? He couldn't begin to guess.

It didn't matter. At the moment, nothing about Nicky Diamond was remotely predictable. His wail had subsided to a low growl, punctuated by breaths that came in quick, ragged bursts. He meandered up and down the hallway, his eyes shifting and darting crazily in the darkness, as though he were trying to formulate some simple plan in his scrambled mind as to what his next move should be. His jaw flexed spastically, and a sheen of perspiration shone on his face in the moonlight. He had lowered his right arm to a forty-five-degree angle, but his finger was still on the trigger, and Hunter was keenly aware at every moment where the barrel was pointed.

Diamond's erratic circuit was gradually taking him toward the double doors at the end of the hallway. Consciously or otherwise, he was heading for the stairs.

Hunter moved along the wall in a half-crouch, just beyond the edge of moon glow, doing his best to position himself between Diamond and the double doors. He came to a stop and held his breath.

Diamond stepped toward him, not seeing him but rather staring into the darkness at nothing, then veered to his left and turned away.

Hunter stepped out of the shadows and into the shaft of moon glow, keeping silent and positioning himself to grip Hunter from behind in the same way he'd gripped Pruett. He planted his feet and reached out with both arms—one to grab Diamond's collar and the other to immobilize his right wrist.

Hunter was still positioning himself when Diamond suddenly turned, raised the gun and fired in his direction—once, then again—his lungs belching an unholy sound that was part laughter and part roar. The edges of his cavernous jaws twisted into a demonic grin and his wide eyes blazed almost as brightly as the flaming muzzle of his gun.

But even at point-blank range, Diamond was firing in the dark with a hand that trembled with artificial stimulants and natural adrenalin. Hunter sensed the bullets coming before they came. He had little trouble ducking and dodging away from the oncoming assault.

Diamond fired a third time, then turned quickly and bolted toward the door at the end of the hallway that led to the stairs. He moved quickly, his shoes crunching over fragments of shattered mirror glass.

Hunter emerged from the shadows and sprinted after him, counting on Diamond's inability to sprint in one direction and shoot accurately at a pursuer coming up from behind. When he'd closed the gap to within eight or ten feet, he pushed off in a forward leap—gaining just enough ground to get his right forearm around Diamond's neck.

Hunter planted his feet and brought Diamond's sprint to a halt, putting pressure against his windpipe and forcing him to arch backward. Diamond struggled against him, his strength and his resolve fueled by a mix of chemicals, rage and insanity.

Diamond spun, still waving the gun in his right hand and clawing against Hunter's arm with his left. He grunted and cursed, a stream of spittle spraying across his chin as he struggled to get his fingers around Hunter's powerful forearm—or at least get a hold of the leather sleeve of Hunter's jacket.

They shuffled across the floor as one, demon and avenger locked together in a rage-driven dance and nearly stumbling more than once in a tangle of arms and legs.

In a dozen years, Hunter had never stood in such close proximity to his father's killer. The effect was palpable, even in the midst of the physical struggle. The combination of Diamond's raspy growl and wiry resistance, the fetid miasma of cheap cologne and stale breath and foul sweat, sent a jolt of energy through every muscle, every fiber, every cell of Hunter's body.

Bearing down on Diamond's windpipe with his forearm, Hunter felt something dark and demonic surge up from some unspeakable place within himself. A primal voice within him drowned out the rasping, gurgling noises emerging from Diamond's throat.

If I could hold him still for just...

If I could get my hands into position around his...just a quick jerk of his head and I could...

I could...

But in the midst of the clawing and the straining and the struggle, some other inner voice told him *no*.

He'd do this the right way.

He'd bring him in alive. He'd drag him into the light, in front of the whole city. In front of the law.

Just like his father would have done.

And then when the time came, after the process was exhausted, he'd watch him burn.

Diamond made a desperate attempt to jerk his head back, apparently hoping to land a head butt against Hunter's face. But the effort only threw him off balance, enabling Hunter to get a hold of Diamond's right arm and immobilize his gun hand with a vise-like clamp on his wrist.

Hunter had Diamond in a firm enough hold to lean in close to his ear. "Listen to me, you son of a bitch," Hunter growled, his voice filling the dark hallway like a buzz saw. "I can see you. I can see what you do in the dark. You and the rest of the maggots you run with. I can see it all."

As if in response, Diamond clawed even more viciously with his free hand at Hunter's arm around his neck. He squirmed and thrashed with renewed vigor in an attempt to free himself, but Hunter had all the leverage.

Diamond flexed his shoulders in a mighty effort, pushing his weight backward with enough of a sudden force to throw Hunter off balance. Hunter back-stepped quickly to keep himself from tripping under Diamond's sudden momentum. Diamond must have sensed Hunter's maneuver, and he used it to his advantage by pushing backward even harder.

Now both men were moving backward as one—Diamond pushing against Hunter and Hunter moving his feet to keep himself from stumbling under Diamond's weight and drive. Hunter kept his left forearm around Diamond's neck and his right hand on his flailing wrist, but these were about the only things he had a firm handle on.

They moved across eight or ten feet of the hallway, their feet doing a clumsy dance as one tried to build momentum while the other tried to stop it. Aided by his enhanced auditory sense, Hunter listened to the noises they were both making—stumbling feet, heavy breathing, rapid heartbeats—and was suddenly aware that something about the sound was changing. It was bouncing back at them from a nearby surface that hadn't been there before.

As they scuffled and stumbled backward down the length of the hallway, Hunter sensed the wall at the end of the corridor coming up fast behind them.

No. Not the wall.

The window.

The large window that made up more than half the wall and overlooked the expansive plaza in front of Union Tower.

Hunter struggled to plant his feet and put the brakes on their combined momentum, but Diamond thrashed and squirmed like a man possessed, clawing with his free hand at the arm wrapped around his neck and shoulders and shoving his way backwards.

Diamond jerked his head backward again, and this time he connected with Hunter's face. Hunter felt a flash of pain in his lower lip and immediately tasted blood. The impact caught him off guard, and he lost even more of what leverage he'd had, which enabled Diamond to increase his backward momentum.

Their dance accelerated. Hunter could hear their tangled footsteps echoing off the large pane of glass that was now just a couple feet behind them. He struggled mightily to push back against Diamond's rage-fueled advance, to turn them both in another direction. But Diamond moved like something not human.

Diamond bent at the knees. Hunter could sense what was coming but couldn't maneuver himself or his adversary to stop it from happening. In a final superhuman burst, Diamond pushed upward with his legs and shoulders, rearing backward at the same time.

The maneuver brought Hunter's feet up off the floor. His back slammed against the window, and the glass immediately gave way with a wicked crash and a shimmering spray of fragments that blew outward, into the night air.

In the midst of the spray were Hunter and Diamond—airborne, still locked in their adversarial embrace, just a few feet beyond the gaping window frame and the outer brick wall of Union Tower.

With nothing underneath them but a yawning, three-hundred-foot drop.

CHAPTER 74
FREE FALL

It all unfolded in slow motion for Diamond—the chiming of shattered glass, the rush of night air on his face, the kaleidoscopic swirl of a million crystalline fragments, each one catching the glow of moon and stars and the shimmer of far-off searchlights. He felt suspended in time and space in the open air, momentarily unaware of the arm still wrapped around him or the hand still locked on his wrist, experiencing the dazzling moment like some kind of transcendental encounter with the divine.

And then the weightless euphoria surrendered to the inevitable surge of gravity, the pull toward earth that started slow but picked up speed, the arm around his neck that hung on and would not let go. They plummeted as one, a tangle of flailing limbs, a counterpoint of labored breathing and guttural sounds. He felt the surge of acceleration, the rush of wind against his face. Despite his thrashing and twisting, even in free fall, Hunter would not let go of him.

They spun together in their descent. Diamond squeezed involuntarily at the trigger of the gun still in his right hand, still held away from him in Hunter's iron grip. The weapon fired at nothing but open sky and rushing air.

From somewhere, a pattern of recurring colors caught Diamond's eye: Red. Blue. Red. Blue.

He was aware of something coming up fast below them.

Pavement.

No. Not pavement.

Flat, yes, but tilted at an angle. Moving. Fluttering, like a flag.

They hit it hard—the first canvas awning stretched over the row of windows at the fourth floor. He felt a sudden, searing pain in his torso and let out a bark as the wind rushed out of his lungs. He heard a similar noise from Hunter.

He heard the rending metal and the tear of canvas as the frame that anchored the awning to the outer brick surface of the building bent and tore loose under their combined weight and speed. They rolled forward clumsily as the tangle of canvas and framework tilted away from the masonry and dropped them another twelve feet to the next awning on the floor below.

With their speed severely checked by the first awning, the impact with the second wasn't nearly as violent. But the second frame did give way, forcing the canvas to sag and tip them forward to the next floor down.

They were wrapped and tangled in canvas from two awnings when they hit the third. Diamond's neck and right arm were finally free of Hunter's grip, but now his maneuverability was severely hampered by the folds of thick fabric that had worked their way around his chest and waist and legs. What's more, the sharp pain in his midsection made it impossible for him to reach for anything that might give him purchase.

Somewhere in this same tangle of canvas was Hunter, but the billowing folds obstructed Diamond's vision. There was no way to make out where Hunter began or ended.

They fell forward, much more slowly this time, and landed on the final row of awnings, the one that hung over the ground floor windows. A metal support arm from an awning on one of the higher floors, twisted and bent to an odd angle, protruded from tangle of canvas wrapped around them. The momentum from their fall had stopped, but their combined thrashing against the shroud sent them pitching forward. They rolled off the awning and hit the pavement in a clumsy tangle of bodies, canvas and bent metal.

The impact with the hard ground sent another agonizing flash across Diamond's chest. His body instinctively folded up on itself in response to the pain, at least as much as the thick layers of canvas would allow. Although completely blinded by the canvas that surrounded his head and entire body, he could hear two voices from someplace not far off. One sounded bewildered, the other authoritative.

"What the hell...?"

"Who...?"

Diamond struggled mightily—against the canvas, against Hunter's unrelenting grip, against the pain in his chest.

The voices were closer now.

"Jesus, somebody fell out of a window!"

"Looks like more than one!"

Diamond heard rapid footsteps. He pushed and shoved his way out of the canvas, enough to smell the exhaust from a nearby automobile and glimpse the recurring, intermittent flash of blue and red light police lights flooding the otherwise dark plaza.

He turned in the direction of the voices and saw two cops—one tall, one shorter—coming up fast on foot. Both were waving flashlights directly in his eyes, which made them hard to see from where he was half laying and half kneeling on the pavement.

Diamond held up a hand to shield his eyes from the glare, wincing at the wave of pain that came with the movement. As near as he could tell, the shorter cop was reaching for his holster and the other already had his gun drawn. By the time they both stopped about ten or twelve feet from where Diamond and Hunter had landed, two guns were pointed directly at him, the polished metal of each weapon catching the flash of blue and red light.

"Alright!" the taller cop barked. "You and whoever else is in that mess! Hold it right there!"

CHAPTER 75
CONFUSION IN CANVAS

Hunter pushed a heavy fold of cloth away from his head with his forearm and emerged from the canvas just a second or two after Diamond did. His night-vision goggles were able to make sense of the confusion of flashlight beams and police lights against a backdrop of pitch blackness better than human eyes ever could, but the resulting picture was far from ideal.

Two officers. One gun pointed at him and the other at Diamond.

One of the officers, a stocky, thick-necked youth with wavy dark hair, went wide-eyed at the sight of Diamond. "Holy smokes," he muttered, with the slightest hint of a tremor in his voice. "Is that...? Jesus, it's Nicky Diamond!"

But the taller one was looking at Hunter, obviously caught off guard and confused by the mask but not willing to admit it. He kept his gun trained on him and kept his voice steady.

"Alright," he said, his words coming in short bursts. "Both of you. Just stay on the ground, right where you are!"

Hunter ignored the order. He propped himself on one knee and started to rise.

"Hold it! You, with the mask! What the hell did I just—?"

Faster than the officer could react, Hunter grabbed an edge of canvas and snapped it like an enormous whip. The fabric flew up in a wave and caught the air, billowing like a parachute.

The confusion was instantaneous. Hunter heard shouts of "Hey!" and "What the hell...?" from both officers as they suddenly lost their clear shot in the churning mass of canvas. He lost track of Diamond as well, but he was aware of movement off to one side that couldn't have been either officer. More importantly, he heard huffing and grunting that sounded like pain more than exertion. It was Diamond, and he sounded like he'd taken some kind of hit in the fall.

Hunter used the moment of confusion to his advantage. He darted in a diagonal pattern—backward and to the right—keeping the billowing canvas between himself and the two cops, and also tracking Diamond by locking on the sound of his labored breathing.

Hunter made his way into the shadows, outside the wash of the police lights and invisible to the cops, whose weapons and attention were still fixed on the heap of limp canvas on the pavement immediately in front of them. He continued to triangulate on Diamond's breathing, scanning the darkness with his goggles.

There. Off to the right, ducking low and moving along a row of bowl-shaped cement planters. Holding the gun with his right hand and wrapping his left forearm around his abdomen. His face locked in a grimace of pain.

Broken rib, thought Hunter. He considered it pure luck that he didn't have one of his own—or worse.

Hunter heard the anxious shout from one of the police officers: "Where the hell…?"

And the tentative reply: "I…I dunno!"

He looked away from Diamond momentarily and saw the taller cop sweep the area of the plaza around the heap of canvas with his flashlight. Hunter instantly ducked behind a free-standing wooden newsstand, boarded up and locked down for the night.

The beam caught Diamond out in the open, pressed against one of the planters. Shoulders hunched, he scuttled around to the dark side of the large bowl.

The tall cop fired a single shot, but the bullet slammed against the planter where Diamond had been crouched just a second before. The shot tore out a chip of concrete and threw up a small cloud of dust.

From Hunter's vantage point behind the newsstand, he could follow Diamond's movements along the row of planters. There were only five more before the end of the row, and then he'd be in the open.

It didn't make sense. Diamond was making his way *toward* the police car, where the flashing lights would just make it that much easier for the cops to get a clear shot and then haul him into the vehicle. Why would…?

He glanced beyond the car and into the distance at the ornate concrete and steel structure towering over the plaza.

Then he understood.

Diamond was going to take the police car.

Gray had told him he needed to get outside the building and get to a high enough elevation. Someplace in the clear where the remote control device could get a radio signal out to the detonator in the initial bomb in the chain.

A high elevation.

Union Arch.

Hunter knew Diamond was in no shape to run, and even if he was, he couldn't outrun slugs from the cops' service revolvers. But if he could make it to the car, he could make it to the arch.

Hunter crept along the back side of the newsstand, shielded from the flashlight beam that continued to sweep back and forth across the plaza. It was a good thirty yards of open space between the newsstand and the closest planter in the row where Diamond was hiding. He could make a run for the planters in hopes of catching Diamond by surprise and taking him down, but thirty yards was a lot of open ground to cover when two police revolvers were pointed directly at you.

He had a line of sight to Diamond's position, and a line of sight to the two officers out in the open plaza, but none of them could see him. But that momentary advantage wouldn't last long. He needed to make some kind of move.

CHAPTER 76
OFFICERS UNDER FIRE

Diamond huddled behind the planter, one knee on the pavement, and forced himself to be still. Every breath sent a wave of pain across his chest and abdomen, and he was certain he'd broken a rib in the fall. He felt the sheen of sweat on his face but fought the urge to wipe it off. The movement would just create more pain.

If he could just be still, slow his breathing, maybe he could make it stop.

He could still get out of this. He could do what needed to be done here. He could bring them all to their knees tonight and have them eating out of his hand by morning. This was his city once, and it would be his again.

He'd need help, and he'd get it. He still had a crew left that he could regroup and reorganize. Fallon and Wireless were still up on the thirtieth floor, but they looked pretty bad last time he saw them. He'd sent Kowalski back to Warehouse Row in the River District, but he'd find a way to rendezvous with him later. There were plenty of others—lieutenants and hired guns all over town who were carefully placed in positions that no one could possibly imagine. And when he was in control, more would come. And Vinnie would come back, too. He'd have it all back, just like before. And no one was going to stop him. No cop, no DA, no judge...and certainly no freak with a mask.

The whole city would answer to him. It would be his again.

Just like before.

But first he had to do what needed to be done here.

His concentration was broken by the voice of one of the cops. "Alright, Diamond. Come on out of there slow!"

He thought of yelling something back, but he saved his breath and spared himself the pain. Instead, he turned his body slowly and peered over the top edge of the planter. Wincing against the pain, he raised his gun and steadied his hand on the concrete rim, taking careful aim down the barrel and across the plaza to where the two cops were standing.

He paused for a second, then another. The cops must not have seen him in the shadows, because neither of them made a countermove.

He held his breath and squeezed the trigger.

The gun barked in his hand, sending a jolt up his forearm and into his shoulder that brought another wave of pain. The shorter of the two cops jerked and grunted, suddenly grabbing his right arm with his left hand. He dropped to one knee and lost his grip on his gun. The weapon clattered to the brick pavement.

Diamond watched as the taller cop turned and knelt down to help his wounded partner, but there was little the senior officer could do.

Diamond's face twisted into a maniacal grin. The taller cop's body language said it all: he was exposed now, forced to cover himself and a partner who was no longer able to shoot and whose mobility was suddenly compromised. They had no backup coming anytime soon, and no immediate place to run for cover in the wide-open plaza.

The tall cop looked up from his wounded partner just long enough to fire another shot, but Diamond saw it coming and had plenty of time to duck back behind the bowl. The slug tore off another chunk of concrete and ricocheted into the darkness.

Diamond counted three, then raised his head and fired again. The shot went wide, taking out the front window of a small flower shop. The tall cop ducked instinctively at the sound of shattering glass behind him. Now he and his partner were huddled together and shuffling to their left.

Diamond took in a slow breath and peered over the planter one more time. Like before, he steadied his hand on the edge of the concrete bowl and centered himself for the money shot—the one that would put the second cop out of commission and give him a clear path to the car.

"Alright, you son of a bitch," he whispered. "Here's where you get yours."

He held his breath and started to squeeze the trigger, but a sudden sound to his left distracted him.

Footsteps running hard and coming closer, and a voice like a jagged knife cutting through the shadows.

"Hey!"

CHAPTER 77
HUNTER IN PURSUIT

Hunter emerged from behind the newsstand at top speed and bolted toward the row of planters, well aware that Diamond was armed and he himself was not. He yelled, "Hey!" as a distraction, and it apparently worked. Diamond turned quickly in the direction of his voice.

He did his best to stay outside the flood of colored light from the police car as he sprinted forward, darting and weaving at irregular angles to keep Diamond from getting a bead on him. Diamond fired, but his aim was way off the mark. From Hunter's vantage point, Diamond looked shaky, unsteady, unable to take proper aim with his right arm.

Hunter was closing the distance between himself and Diamond, but his serpentine pattern made his advance slower than it would have been otherwise. Diamond looked as though he might fire again, but he appeared to change his mind at the last second.

Instead he turned away, toward the flashing red and blue lights. With his gun down at his side in his right hand and his left arm spread across his ribs, he stood up and broke into a labored but steady shuffle and headed for the car.

Just as Hunter had figured.

Hunter heard a yell from the taller police office. "Hold it right there!" He had no idea whether the order was directed at Diamond or himself, and realized it was probably intended for both. It didn't matter. He couldn't let Diamond get to the car. He kept running.

A shot rang out from the same direction as the officer's warning, and Hunter immediately felt a sharp sting in his left arm. He knew instantly that he'd been hit, but he didn't stop. He didn't even slow down.

374

Diamond was no more than sixty feet away from him and moving clumsily, but he'd reached the car. He turned back toward Hunter and fired a shot that should have been easy, but Hunter saw it coming. Even as he bore down on him with the speed of a seasoned athlete, galloping hard and covering a huge stretch of pavement in mere seconds, he was acutely aware of every movement, every sound, every flicker of light in his immediate surroundings—all of it happening in an otherworldly slow motion and crystal clarity. He dodged the oncoming slug—and the one that followed it—and kept coming.

In the distance, off to his left, he picked up the voice of the cop, muttering quietly to himself this time. "Jesus, who...?" he stammered. "How the hell did he...?"

He saw Diamond yank the car door open and climb into the driver's seat. Almost instantly, tires squealed and the vehicle lurched forward in a stink and smoke of burning rubber.

The cop fired again, this time taking out the car's back seat window on the driver's side in an explosion of glass fragments.

Legs and arms pumping like pistons, Hunter tapped into a final reserve of strength and came within four or five feet of the car's rear bumper. Before the vehicle could make any distance, Hunter aimed himself squarely at the trunk of the moving car and launched the full length and weight of his six-foot frame into the air with a herculean leap.

CHAPTER 78
SERPENTINE RIDE

Diamond heard a loud thump and felt a bounce in the rear wheels of the car, followed by an immediate drag in the engine's acceleration. Even before he glanced in the rearview mirror, he knew what was happening.

"Dammit!" he growled through clenched jaws, fighting against the combination of frustration, ragged nerves and relentless physical pain. "How the hell can he keep...?" But his words became nothing more than a frustrated growl.

He looked away from the mirror and back at the pavement directly in front of him. Up ahead was the towering Union Arch, still a good four-hundred yards in the distance.

He pushed the accelerator to the floor and at the same time turned the wheel hard to the left, and then quickly to the right. He glanced back up to the mirror, only to see Hunter clinging to the back of the car like a rock climber on a steep cliff.

The speedometer was at forty miles an hour and climbing rapidly. He steered with his left arm and kept his right arm immobilized in his lap—gun still in hand—to prevent any flashes of pain in his ribs. The strategy was only marginally successful, and each breath felt like a knife in his chest.

He swerved again with the same left-right combination, but Hunter held on. "What the hell…?" Diamond muttered. It was as if Hunter was anticipating the hard turns before he jerked the wheel.

Diamond watched the rearview mirror and realized that Hunter was slowly moving out of frame and inching his way toward the rear fender on the passenger's side. He turned his head and stole a quick glance. As near as he could tell, Hunter appeared to be straddling the distance between the edge of the rear bumper and the running board along the passenger side of the car. His only hand-hold was the handle of the rear door.

The speedometer climbed to fifty. Diamond started to raise his right arm to point the gun over the back of the front seat at Hunter's chest on the other side of the rear door window, but the movement sent a searing lance of pain through his torso. He cried out in agony and his right arm went limp on the seat of the car without firing a single shot.

Diamond struggled to catch his breath. He couldn't shoot and drive at the same time. His only weapon was the steering wheel, and the only way to lose him would be a combination of speed and erratic turns.

Union Arch was less than three-hundred yards ahead now, and halfway between him and the arch were wooden barricades posting a warning in large black lettering:

CONSTRUCTION
DO NOT ENTER

At fifty-five miles an hour, Diamond swerved into a sickening left-right-left combination. Tires squealed. For a second, he thought he might lose control and roll the car, but he stabilized his course before the momentum could get the best of him.

He heard a scuffling sound just outside the rear door. He stole a quick glance over his right shoulder, and a maniacal grin spread across his sweating, ashen face.

Hunter was gone.

CHAPTER 79
HANGING ON

Hunter had momentarily anchored himself to the car at three points—right foot on the running board, left foot still on the rear bumper and his right hand gripping the door handle. He glanced down at the pavement moving underneath him at an ever-increasing speed, then looked back at the stretch of the plaza ahead. They'd be at the barricade in less than thirty seconds, and he was pretty certain Diamond had no intention of stopping there.

He spidered a few more inches to his right along the rear fender and tentatively lifted his left foot off the bumper.

Just as he made the move, the car went into a sickening left-right-left swerve that was so hard and so sudden that even his finely tuned senses couldn't anticipate it. Tires squealed, and his mass in relation to the car shifted suddenly.

Unable to gain purchase with his left foot, his boot scuffed against the pavement at more than fifty miles an hour. He was almost thrown from the car. As it was, his head and shoulders slid down and away from the passenger window from the momentum of the swerve, and he fought to keep his upper body from skidding along the rushing pavement. His right foot securely planted on the running board and his stubborn right-hand grip on the door handle were the only things keeping him connected to the runaway car.

With a mighty effort, he fought the centrifugal force that pulled him away from the body of the car and pulled himself back to an upright position alongside the rear door of the vehicle. Once he had righted himself, he wasted no time inching further along the passenger side of the car until both of his feet were firmly planted on the running board and he had a grip on the front and rear door handles.

Hunter peered through the window of the rear door just in time to see Diamond's hand come up, just as it did before. Now on more solid footing, it was much easier for Hunter to duck away just as the muzzle flashed and the window glass blew outward.

He popped his head back up and saw Diamond staring ahead at the rapidly approaching barricades, his right arm limp in the seat next to him. Diamond stole a glance over his right shoulder and scowled at Hunter through the shattered glass window. Even with the roar of the engine and the wind rushing past his head, Hunter could hear Diamond's labored breathing and see the strain in his face.

Hunter sized up the situation and took his chance.

He yanked open the front passenger door and leaped into the car.

CHAPTER 80
FIGHT FOR THE WHEEL

Diamond glanced away from the rapidly approaching barricades and saw Hunter leaping into the car from the passenger side.

He had no time to react. In less than a second, Hunter was upon him, grabbing at his right arm and the steering wheel at the same time. Diamond tried to swing at his face with the butt of his gun, but the pain in his ribs prevented him from landing a decisive blow.

In the scuffling at close quarters inside the car, Diamond momentarily lost control of the wheel and the police car swerved wildly, forcing Hunter back toward the door that was still gaping open. Diamond grinned through the pain in his upper body, thinking he might finally shake him for good, but Hunter clung to the dashboard and narrowly avoided falling backward out of the car.

The sudden stretch of space between the two men gave Diamond a chance to take aim and squeeze the trigger. Hunter ducked away, and the slug went through the windshield, creating a shower of glass on the dashboard.

Less than a second later, Diamond adjusted his aim and squeezed again. Hunter dodged, but the only report from the gun this time was a dull click.

Empty.

The car continued to swerve at impossible angles and impossible speeds as both men fought savagely for the wheel. Hunter shoved his left forearm against Diamond's neck, which sent a stab of pain from the bullet wound in his bicep all the way up to his shoulder and neck. Diamond responded with an agonized grunt but held fast to the wheel.

The barricades were no more than fifty yards ahead and coming up fast. Hunter caught sight of the thousands of bits of broken glass scattered across the dashboard. He reached over with his right arm, grabbed a handful of fragments and tossed them in Diamond's face.

Instinctively shielding his eyes, Diamond let go of the steering wheel with his left hand, leaving control of the car to Hunter's full weight against the wheel. The car swerved into a hard left turn at nearly sixty miles an hour—hard enough and fast enough to go up on two wheels.

Up, and then over.

CHAPTER 81
ROLLING DEATH

Hunter saw it coming, sensing the momentum the instant it started. With his body still shoved up against Diamond in the driver's seat, he used his legs and shoulders to brace himself between the dashboard and the front seat of the patrol car as the vehicle went into a sickening roll and smashed through the barricade. The crash was a deafening mix of wooden barricade panels exploding in a blast of splinters and two tons of steel slamming and twisting against unforgiving pavement.

The few glass panels on the car that weren't already shattered by bullets exploded as the entire frame buckled under the force of the impact. Added to the crystalline spray was the glass from the fixtures mounted on the outside of the car—the headlights and taillights at either end, as well as the red and blue lights on the roof.

Through it all, Hunter heard grunting and jagged breathing, and couldn't be sure how much of it came from Diamond and how much was his own. He hung on as the car did a complete roll and then somehow landed upright.

He held his breath as the ruined pile that had once been a Union City patrol car finally rocked to a merciful stop.

Diamond's body had twisted away from Hunter in the roll, and Hunter no longer had a clear view of his face. He looked down and saw Diamond's left hand resting on the door handle. His right hand— the one that had been holding the gun just seconds earlier—was empty and cradled in his lap. Hunter had no idea where the gun was. Diamond was breathing but not moving, and Hunter thought for a moment that he'd finally been subdued.

Hunter gathered his breath. "Alright, you sick son of a—"

The victory was an illusion, and a short-lived one. It lasted no more than a second or two. In a sudden burst of energy, Diamond pushed the mangled driver's side door away from its frame and shoved his way out of the car, half stepping and half stumbling onto the pavement.

Hunter swore at Diamond's seemingly endless reserve of strength and tenacity that seemed to defy the pain he was obviously enduring. He chalked it up to the combination of drugs and adrenaline. He reached up and tried to grab a fold of Diamond's coat before he could clear the doorway, but the crash had left his body at a clumsy angle in the seat that prevented any opportunity for reach or leverage.

He swore again as Diamond darted away from the crumpled heap in an injured shuffle, across the fifty-yard stretch of broken glass, wood fragments and construction debris—all of it leading to the stairs of Union Arch.

Hunter climbed across the seat, clumsily shoved past the steering wheel and scrambled after him.

CHAPTER 82
TREACHEROUS CLIMB

Hunched at the shoulders and clutching his ribcage with his right arm, Diamond limped and shuffled along the fifty-yard stretch of the construction site leading up to the fifty-foot-tall structure known as Union Arch. Every footfall on the pavement sent a jolt of pain throughout his torso and forced an agonized grunt from his lungs.

The powder from the cylinders had all but worn off, which forced him to pay more attention to the pain. He no longer had any doubt that he'd broken a rib in the fall from the tower. On top of that, he'd battered his left knee and lower leg in the car crash, enough to tear at his pant leg and stain the tattered fabric with blood.

But he kept moving. All things considered, he was covering the distance fairly quickly and efficiently.

He could still get out of this.

Still clutching at his chest, he brushed his hand against the bulge in the inside breast pocket of his jacket.

The radio-powered remote control unit.

He could do what needed to be done here.

This was his city once, and it would be his again.

He slowed for just a second or two and glanced back at the crumpled police car just long enough to see Hunter some thirty yards behind him, emerging from the driver's side door. Hunter looked pretty winded himself, but he appeared to have full use of his arms and legs, and after a few tentative steps out of the car, he broke into a labored run.

Diamond clenched his jaws and swore. Driven by a rage that helped offset the pain and physical limitations, he turned away and picked up his own pace as he made a beeline toward the west end of the arch, eyeing the crumbling stairway that stretched up toward the observation deck at the very top of the structure.

Just as he reached the foot of the stone stairway, he heard the distant wail of sirens. Of course. With no explosion at City Hall at the midnight hour, the police would have been fooled into thinking his broadcast warning was a hoax. City Hall was no longer their priority. Maybe the two cops in front of the tower called for backup after the brief gun battle at the plaza. Maybe an ambulance was coming to help the one whose arm he'd clipped.

He grabbed the handrail with his left arm and took the first steps, each one cluttered with the rubble of crumbling stone and the occasional masonry tool. The rush to sidestep it all, combined with the agony of the injuries in his chest and leg, made his steps uncertain. On top of it all, the fight against gravity as he climbed the steps taxed his aching lungs.

He stumbled once, then again. The handrail, loosened by crumbling masonry, wobbled in his grip, but he held on and kept moving.

Or maybe the police were abandoning their posts at City Hall and elsewhere around town and coming from all over to see the lights. His climb to the top of the arch would be the new point of origin for this… this beautiful revelation. This beautiful, seductive miracle of bright light and glorious fire, followed by the intoxicating reverberation that rolled across a filthy city like the thunder of a purifying storm.

Let them come. He would finish what he'd started, and they'd all be here to see it. He'd do what needed to be done, and then they'd have no choice but to give the city back to him.

He stumbled again, and quickly grabbed the rail to steady himself. It wasn't debris that tripped him up this time, nor was it the scatter of tools, nor anything else on the steps. It was the combination of pain, exhaustion, rage…and something else.

A heady sense of dislocation, of disconnection.

Everything swirled in his mind's eye—the gunfight in the dark office, the deadly fall from the tower, the violent car ride. It had all happened just a few minutes earlier, and yet it was all a jumbled fever dream, illuminated by a shimmer of colored lights that emanated from someplace below him and grew brighter by the second.

He fought to hold on. In the end, he had the key to unlock the awesome truth. He had the magic box. He reached inside his jacket and slowly pulled out the remote control unit. Felt the smooth metal in his hand.

He stood up and willed himself to move forward, to keep climbing. He needed to get to the high place.

He looked over his shoulder.

Hunter was only fifteen or twenty steps below him, and coming fast.

CHAPTER 83
MADNESS AT THE TOP

Hunter worked his way up the steps, keeping his eyes glued to Diamond's every move. The chaos and exertion of the past five or six minutes—including the graze wound along his left arm from the cop's gunshot, and more than a few bumps and bruises from the roll in the car—had taken their toll, and Hunter moved slower than he would have preferred. Diamond was maybe fifteen or twenty steps ahead and above him along the side of the arch, but the good news, if there was any, was that he was in far worse shape than Hunter. He knew if he stayed focused and kept a steady pace, he'd catch up with Diamond.

But would he reach him in time?

Hunter could hear Diamond muttering to himself, something about finishing what he'd started. He was clearly unhinged. Between the countless hits of Benzedrine, the shooting of Pruett on the thirtieth floor of the tower, the three-hundred-foot fall and the injury that came with it, the death-defying car ride and everything else, he was sure Diamond's mind had been utterly scrambled.

And in case things weren't complicated and treacherous enough already, three police cars had gathered below. One had darted across the plaza to where the two cops were huddled. The other two cars stopped at the foot of the arch with their roof lights flashing. The occupants of both cars at the foot of the arch—four officers in all—had emerged from their vehicles with guns drawn, and the searchlights mounted on the side of each car had been turned upward.

Hunter tuned his highly sensitive hearing to the wail of additional sirens from the northeast. With the mayor safe and no explosion at City Hall, more cars were being sent where they were needed. And they were coming fast.

He had to catch up with Diamond. All he needed to do was…

Hunter froze. His stomach climbed to his throat when he saw the glint of metal in the moonlight as Diamond pulled the remote control unit out of his jacket.

"No!" Hunter barked. It was partly a warning, partly a prayer. He propelled himself upward, two steps at a time, now three, his boots scraping and slipping on loose mortar as he climbed frantically, steadying himself on the stone steps with his hands as he barely navigated his way through the debris.

Both men were just a couple steps shy of the observation deck at the top of the arch when Diamond stopped suddenly and turned. Hunter, unable to check his momentum from his sudden burst of speed and energy, stepped directly into the path of Diamond's fist as it slammed into his jaw. He lurched backward and stumbled for a moment, but grabbed the handrail to keep from stumbling.

Hunter regained his footing and immediately took the offensive, launching himself at Diamond—who was now at the top step—and driving a right cross to his face. Diamond staggered. Hunter saw the opening and moved in, grabbing Diamond by the lapel of his jacket with his right fist and reaching for his right arm with his left hand in the hopes of wrenching the remote control out of his grip.

But Diamond, even in his injured state, summoned enough strength and speed to spin away from Hunter, who was still one step shy of the observation deck. Unhindered by the rending of his jacket, Diamond raised his leg high enough to land a glancing blow on Hunter's right shoulder, knocking him off balance and sending him backward off the top step.

Hunter checked his fall with the help of the railing, but it was only a momentary save. Under his full weight, along with the momentum from Diamond's kick, the entire section of railing—four feet in all— tore loose from the staircase mortar and plummeted to the pavement below, where it met the concrete with a hollow *clang*. Hunter grabbed an adjacent section with his other hand just in time to regain his balance and avoid going down with the first piece of iron.

Hunter looked up. Diamond was now fully on the observation deck, facing him but backing away, his face twisted into a hellish grin. The remote control unit was in his right hand, although he hadn't yet extended the collapsible antenna.

Hunter understood. It had become some kind of twisted performance, and the top of the arch would be his stage. He would wait until he was in the ideal position, probably the exact center of the observation deck. It was now an exercise in some weird ritualistic destiny fulfillment—something for the police and the entire city to witness.

Hunter stepped onto the observation deck with both feet. He moved slowly, so as not to trigger any sudden moves by Diamond. He fixed his eyes and ears on Diamond's every move with a razor-sharp focus, paying special attention to every motion—every twitch, however slight—of his right hand.

Hunter glanced at the police cars below. There were four of them parked at the foot of the arch now, engines running. Two more raced up to meet them, and the distant wail of sirens signaled the imminent arrival of more.

There were two black cars as well—unmarked, with doors open and men in dark business suits and shoulder holsters standing alongside their vehicles. Their eyes were turned upward at the unfolding drama, and their firearms were ready at their sides.

Federal agents, thought Hunter.

Searchlight beams reached skyward, cutting through the sea of blue and red flashes at ground level and throwing a hard white light on the confrontation on high between Diamond and Hunter.

A stage indeed.

Hunter gestured at the vehicles on the ground. "There's no place to go, Diamond," he said. He listened to his own voice as though it were coming from somewhere in the distance. It was surprisingly calm. "No matter what you do in the next few seconds, they'll be waiting for you down there."

"What I do in the next few seconds will change everything," said Diamond. His eyes were wide and his pale face shimmered with sweat. Hunter held his breath as Diamond waved the remote control unit like some kind of deadly magic wand. "I can make the lights. And a noise that'll shake the whole town. It's gonna be a hell of a show. Just like the Fourth of July. I'm gonna finish what I started, and it's gonna be beautiful. This was my city, and it's gonna be mine again."

Diamond took another step backward, toward the center of the platform, his eyes still fixed on Hunter. He flashed a demented grin. Something rumbled from some deep place in his throat, until it finally emerged as the chilling laugh of a madman.

And then he reached for the end of the collapsible antenna and started pulling.

Slowly. Just a few inches.

A madman on a stage.

Hunter's heart skipped a beat. He took a step forward.

Keep him talking.

"What's going to be yours, Diamond?" he said. "Eight or ten piles of rubble from here to midtown? What are you going to do with that? Are you really trying to build some kind of empire of your own? Because it sounds to me like you're just going to make a mess."

From the crowd of cops and cars below, a voice aided by a

megaphone cut straight up through the night air like the hard beams from the searchlights: "Alright. Both of you. Stay right where you are and put your hands in the air!"

Hunter glanced over the side of the observation deck at the cops below, then back at Diamond. If Diamond had heard it at all, it didn't register in his face.

They don't know what he's holding, Hunter thought. *If they knew what it was or what he could do with it, they'd have shot him by now.*

Slowly, cautiously, Hunter took another step forward. "So you take out a couple police precincts," he shrugged. "You think it ends there? The feds will be all over this in the morning."

Again, the voice from below: "I said hold it right there!" Given his step forward, Hunter was sure the command was directed at him this time.

Diamond turned away from him and looked over the railing, defiantly waving the remote control device at the cops below. "Any of you shoot at me and I blow this thing! Y'hear me?" He waved his free hand at the panorama of downtown city blocks that stretched out before him from his high vantage point. "I'll blow this whole goddamn city!"

Hunter heard the voice below, quieter this time: "Hold it! Hold your fire! What the hell does he…?"

Diamond was still looking over the side—at the police, at the lights from their cars, at the rest of the city covered in darkness.

Hunter saw the opportunity and grabbed it.

CHAPTER 84
BATTLE FOR THE BOX

The sweep of the searchlights against the black sky, the shimmer of blue and red from the cars below. It was all so beautiful, so…seductive. And in just a minute, there'd be more lights, all over the city. And the throbbing roar of…

He never finished the thought. He was struck from behind, slightly off to the right, with a force that came at him like a battering ram and sent a new level of screaming pain throughout his entire torso. His feet went out from under him, and as he tumbled to the concrete surface of the observation deck, the pain in his left leg shot up to his hip and merged with the agony in his upper body.

Hunter was on top of him, his weight bearing down mercilessly on his chest and shoulders. Diamond heard a wail of agony and realized it was his own voice.

Hunter clamped onto his left wrist, but Diamond clung stubbornly to the metal box and fought against Hunter's weight to reach with his right hand for the end of the antenna.

Diamond grunted. He stared up at the faceless juggernaut bearing down on his chest and snarling back at him. He swore violently, and flecks of saliva spilled across his chin as he gasped at the blinding pain tearing through his body.

But he held on.

If he could…if he could just extend it. Just push the button. He could finish what he'd started.

He jerked his right leg, the only part of his body that was not already racked with pain, and drove his knee into Hunter's side, somewhere near his hip. It was far from a decisive blow, but it was enough to throw Hunter off balance for just a second—long enough to give himself a small degree of momentary leverage.

Diamond rolled quickly, forcing some of Hunter's weight to the side and creating enough momentum to get out from under him. With another thrust, he drove his right foot into Hunter's abdomen and cackled at the sound of Hunter's breath rushing out of his lungs.

Diamond was near enough to the railing to grab hold of it and use it to get his knees back under himself. He hoisted himself up with his good leg, then positioned his wounded leg for whatever extra support he could manage.

A shot rang out from below, but the slug plowed into a wide stone pillar about a foot from Diamond's shoulder. Diamond shuffled to his left and positioned himself behind the pillar to protect himself from any further gunfire.

He looked at Hunter, a dozen feet away on his hands and knees, struggling to get air back into his lungs. With the back of his right hand, he wiped a stream of blood from his lower lip and flashed a demonic grin at his masked adversary.

And then he extended the antenna on the remote control device to its full length.

CHAPTER 85
OVER THE EDGE

Hunter struggled to focus. Even with the help of the mask, his senses were dulled by the hard kick to his mid-section and the struggle for air that followed. If he could just inhale…

He looked up and locked eyes with Diamond, who grinned back at him with the scratched and bloodied face of a mad jackal fresh from a fight.

His vision was fuzzy with stars as he shifted his gaze to Diamond's hands—the left hand holding the metal box, the right hand pulling on the last couple inches of the antenna.

Hunter concentrated, willing his abdominal muscles to relax, and brought a merciful gulp of air into his lungs.

His head cleared, and his senses quickly sharpened to a razor's edge.

He slipped his hand inside his jacket.

It had to be…

He hoped to God it was still…

Yes…

Diamond pulled the antenna to its full extension.

"Now," he said, his voice filled with a grim edge of sinister victory. "Watch this, Mister Mask."

Diamond pushed himself away from the pillar. He turned away from Hunter and turned toward the sweeping panorama.

It was time for his grand performance.

Hunter felt the night air on his face. Heard the chatter of anxious police officers, the murmur of patrol car engines. He caught the rhythm of the blue and red flashes from below, and the sweeping columns of white light slicing straight up through the darkness.

He felt the heft of the shield-shaped slab of metal in his right hand.

His father's badge.

Hunter took it all in—measuring, triangulating, calculating, all in the thinnest fraction of time. His senses razor sharp, crystal clear. Reflexes fast as light.

He leaned backward, cocked his arm and fired.

His sense of time slowed. The badge seemed to float, as if weightless. But he knew it was an illusion, the paradox created by the hardware strapped to his head. In reality, the projectile spun across space in a straight line, with the speed and accuracy of a bullet.

The badge struck Diamond's left hand. His wicked grin dissolved into a flinch. His wrist jerked suddenly, his fingers opened, and the remote control box came loose and tumbled end over end in the darkness.

The box bounced against the railing with a metallic tap, went airborne once more, then made its final descent into the confused sea of lights and cars and police officers.

Diamond let out a scream. He threw himself against the railing in a desperate reach. Hunter thought for a moment that the metalwork might give way, but it held.

But Diamond's momentum was too great, his reach too far. His delusion too profound.

His feet left the ground and his body teetered momentarily across the top of the railing. He screamed again, not in desperation this time but in terror. His legs kicked instinctively, as though seeking purchase for his feet, but the movement only shifted him further off balance.

Hunter was on his feet, half darting and half stumbling toward Diamond's teetering frame.

Not this way, he thought. *He'd bring him in alive.*

Diamond's arms flailed. His hands groped frantically for any part of the railing that would hold him, but they only found empty air.

He went over, and his sickening scream went over with him.

All the way down.

CHAPTER 86
A CLOUD OF DUST

Hunter was too far from the edge of the observation deck to see Diamond complete his fall, but the sickening crash—part metal, part glass and part human flesh—told the unmistakable story.

The voices of the police officers instantly escalated to anxious shouts. Hunter stumbled to the railing that Diamond had just gone over and looked down. His guess was confirmed. A mangled figure that had been Nicky Diamond just seconds before lay sprawled across the crumpled roof of a police patrol car. The arms, legs and neck were twisted at impossible angles. Fragments of broken windshield and window glass littered the pavement around the car and shimmered like jewels in the combination of blue and red flashing police lights and stark white searchlights.

Hunter did some quick math in his head, allowing for body mass, vertical distance and acceleration. He concluded that Diamond had collided with the top of the patrol car—a hunk of cold steel far less forgiving than a canvas awning—at about forty miles an hour. He was dead on impact.

Hunter focused his hearing in the direction of the dozen or so police officers shuffling around the periphery of the carnage. He heard one cop on a radio, calling for an ambulance. The rest spoke in a confused tangle:

"…Jesus, it's Diamond…"

"…neck's gotta be broken…"

"…gonna need a tow truck…"

"…fifty feet, straight down…"

The ambulance would be a formality. Diamond was way beyond that. And it was only a matter of seconds before the police shifted their focus to their next order of business. Hunter ducked away from the railing as one voice yelled: "The other one's still up there!"

Then another voice, directed at him this time: "Alright, you with the mask! Hold it!" The same voice that had warned him and Diamond to hold still and put up their hands a couple minutes earlier. "Move back to the stairs and come down! I don't care which side, just come down nice and slow!"

He watched as officers moved across the red brick pavement in opposite directions—some to the west stairway and others to the east. He glanced to either side and saw six or eight men taking positions at the bottom of each stairway, legs spread, weapons drawn.

He saw an alley to the east that might make a good getaway route, assuming he could get past the police gauntlet—which was an ambitious assumption. He was fast, sure, but there was no way he'd be able to dodge slugs coming straight at him from a half-dozen or more guns in the hands of trained marksmen as he made his way down the stairs.

His eyes darted left and right, searching for something…anything…

There on the deck, about a dozen feet from where he was standing. A forty-pound canvas sack, about two-thirds full of cement mix.

He crossed the deck to the sack, hoisted it into the crook of his right arm, and headed toward the east stairway. The searchlight beams tracked his movements and followed him to the edge of the observation deck. He stopped at the top of the stairs and instantly heard the click of hammers.

He held his left hand straight out to his side in a sort of surrendering gesture and started down the stairs.

"Okay, fellas," he said to the small crowd of cops at the bottom of the steps. "Nice and slow! Just like you asked."

Immediately, there were more voices:

"..the hell does he got in his...?"

"Wait a minute..."

"...some kinda bag or someth..."

He was ten steps into his descent when the voice in the megaphone cut through the chatter: "Whatever you've got in your arm, drop it!"

Hunter kept coming, another eight or ten steps, as though he hadn't heard the warning.

"I said drop it! Now!"

Hunter stopped his descent, braced his shoulders.

Now.

In a flash, he hoisted the sack and swung the open end out in front of him, waving it back and forth in a sweeping motion and spilling the contents into the night air. In seconds, the space along the stairway was filled with a billowing cloud of cement powder.

The beams from the searchlights collided with the cloud, creating a thick haze that Hunter instantly used to his advantage. He darted down another four or five steps, directly into the wall of dust he'd created.

The police voices rose in a murmur of confusion and curses. Unable to track him in the cloud, they fired a few tentative shots that went way off the mark.

When he was about ten feet from the pavement below, he grabbed the right-hand rail and vaulted over it. He landed on two feet with enough spring in his knees and hips to absorb the shock, and touched down within the cover of the cloud that was quickly giving way to gravity and settling toward the pavement.

Another shot rang out, and then another, but he was moving fast in a haze that even the searchlights couldn't penetrate. He was a good thirty feet from the bottom of the stairway, which gave him plenty of room to cut sharply to the left and sidestep the detail of confused cops who were waiting for him there.

He darted away from the searchlights and sprinted for one of the alleys. He heard one more shot, and instantly heard it slam into the side of a brick building at least fifteen feet in his wake—a blind, last-ditch attempt by a shooter who couldn't even see him.

Five seconds later, he plunged into the pitch-black alley and was home free, safe in the shadows of a city still covered in darkness.

◆　◆　◆　◆

Fifteen minutes later, the sounds of a half-hearted search had died away. The big prize, Nicky Diamond, was in the back of a truck on his way to the morgue. On a night like this one, some loose ends could wait for another time.

Hunter sat on the back steps of a vacant brick building with the mask in his lap. He squeezed his eyes shut, fighting the sting of tears. A lot of running and climbing and falling in the last few hours. Not to mention a bullet wound to his left arm, several punches to the face, and some blows to the head and gut. And a cloud of cement mix, too. And not a whole lot of sleep.

Or maybe his eyes burned from the dust and grime and stink that clung to the dark corners of this damn city, despite the efforts of many good people—including some who'd given their lives to protect it.

His shoulders sagged and his head bowed. He balled his fists and held them to his forehead. His breath was coming fast, but he fought to control it. After a moment, he opened his eyes and looked up through a watery haze at the moon and stars peeking through the narrow space between adjacent rooftops.

"I got him, Pop," he said aloud, his voice shaky but defiant at the same time. "I got him."

EPILOGUE

The power was back on a little after four-thirty a.m. Angie had a pot of coffee brewing and her diner open for business by six.

At seven-twenty, Hunter and Buzz were sitting at a table next to the window. All around them was the excited chatter of customers and waitresses, all of them reconstructing the frightening events of the night before.

Buzz took his last bite of toast and wiped his fingers on a napkin. "You doing alright?"

Hunter took a sip of coffee from his cup. His own plate was already empty. "Yeah," he said. "Got some bruises—a big one on the back of my head—but I'm okay." He put the cup down for a moment and rubbed his face. "Tired, though. I didn't sleep much, and when I did, I dreamed I was falling."

"How's the wing?"

Hunter flexed his left arm slowly, then rested his elbow on the table. "Not bad," he said. "Luckily, I have a roommate and a fellow conspirator who was an army field medic in the war."

"It was a graze, but you don't want to mess around with that kind of thing. I made ten stitches to keep it closed."

"It'll be okay."

Buzz frowned back at him. "Can you take a day off?" he said. "You look a little rough."

"After what happened last night? The assistant DA can't take a day off. At least this one can't." He shrugged and took another sip of coffee. "I'll be alright."

Buzz dropped his napkin in his plate and pushed the plate aside. He reached for his coffee, his eyes drifting back to the morning edition of the *Tribune* on the table in front of him. He'd already worked his way through the big page-one story and was into the second or third page of the front section.

Hunter had glanced at the front page and nothing more before handing it to Buzz before their food arrived. He was actually surprised there were any papers to be had this morning, seeing as no presses were running until almost dawn. A small sidebar below the fold on the front page of the *Tribune* explained how a crew of reporters, editors and typesetters had worked through the night with nothing more than flashlights, lanterns and even candles to hammer out an account of the night's events. And they did it all with the full knowledge that there might not be any electric power to fire up the presses in time for a morning edition.

But the lights came back on before dawn, allowing just enough time to get it all down on the page and get it out to the streets. Both papers hit the high points—the pirate radio broadcast, the break-in at Union Power, the blackout, the standoff at City Hall, Nicky Diamond's twisted corpse on the roof of a police car at the foot of Union Arch. There were a few holes in the story—places where things just didn't add up—partly because there hadn't been enough time for more thorough coverage, and partly because there were things the police just weren't telling the press.

"Funny thing," said Buzz.

"What's that?"

"The police are going to spend months wiping the egg off their face."

"How do you mean?"

"The explosives expert they hired for technical assistance to work the Diamond case was actually part of Diamond's inner circle."

Hunter sighed. "Well, there's plenty of egg to go around. Gallagher and I sat in on several meetings with him ourselves. And all the while, we all kept asking ourselves how Diamond seemed to be a step ahead of us all the time." He folded up the paper and put it aside. He took a sip of coffee and lowered his voice. "I'm just glad there was no mention of a guy in a mask."

Buzz was still looking down at his paper. "Don't be so sure," he said. He folded back a page from inside the front section and handed it across the table to Hunter.

It was Bart Maxwell's regular column, "Take It from Max."

Hunter eyed Buzz warily, then glanced down at the page:

UNION CITY'S AVENGING ANGEL?

As always, we tip our hats to the hard-working men and women of the Union City Police Department, especially given their success in bringing the curtain down on racketeer Nicky Diamond and ending his recent reign of terror. However, we also hear talk of a different kind of do-gooder patrolling the streets of Union City in the wee hours. A few tavern owners, late-shift workers and other night owls have reported a mysterious masked man who seems to step in when danger lurks in the late hours.

A shopkeeper in the retail district reported his nick-of-time arrival and quick dispatch of an armed robber who was just getting ready to empty the till. An orderly at Union Mercy Hospital swears he marched right into the emergency room carrying a woman who'd been drugged against her will and kidnapped. Some rumors even suggest that this mysterious fellow had a hand in rescuing the mayor and keeping Diamond and his gang from blowing up half the town.

Details about this midnight guardian in our fair city are scarce. And that's assuming he exists at all—although yours truly has it on good authority that he does, and that's all that can be said for now. Whatever the case, rest assured that Max will be on the lookout.

In other news around town, we hear that the Building Commission is considering a proposal that would...

Hunter folded the paper and set it on the table. He looked up and saw Buzz staring back at him, studying his face as though searching for some kind of reaction.

Hunter was silent at first, his face inert, but the slight turn of one corner of his mouth gave him away. "'This midnight guardian...'" he said finally.

"Catchy, huh?"

"Yeah," said Hunter. "Catchy."

"Think he'll be back?"

Hunter's brow furrowed. "Who? Diamond? Not likely. He's dead."

Buzz leaned forward and looked his cousin square in the eye. "No, not Diamond," he said, lowering his voice. "That's not who I meant and you know it."

Hunter shrugged. "It's a big town," he said. "A lot of little messes to clean up."

Buzz nodded at the front-page headline on the folded newspaper staring up at them from the corner of the table. "Some not so little."

"There's only so much an assistant DA can do."

"But a guy like that..." Buzz nodded at the paper again, and Hunter knew he wasn't referring to the front-page story this time. He was more intrigued by the inside story—the one about a different kind of justice, the swift kind that happens in the shadows, under the cover of darkness, but means just as much to a city as all the fanfare on page one.

Hunter finished his cousin's thought. "A guy like that could do more."

Buzz was silent for a moment, trying to read his cousin's face. "So?"

Hunter's gaze had drifted to the window, watching the teeming city on the other side of it.

He looked back at Buzz, that same corner of his mouth turning up again as he scooped up the newspaper and rose from his chair.

"Gotta run, Buzz."

"What? Hold on, Jack. You didn't answer my—"

"Gotta go. The city's waiting." Hunter dropped a five on the table. "This should cover us both."

He grabbed his hat and jacket and tapped Buzz's arm with the folded newspaper. "Fix some radios today," he said over his shoulder, heading for the door. "Invent something amazing." He smiled and tipped his hat to the waitress on the way out, pushing through the door and disappearing into the hum of a new day.

◆　◆　◆　◆

Mike Dugan met with Hunter and Gallagher in the DA's office just before lunch. The detective brought a notebook and a manila folder stuffed with papers and settled into a chair across from Gallagher's desk.

"First things first," said Dugan. "Miss Carlyle okay?"

Gallagher glanced at Hunter.

"Uh, yeah," said Hunter. "I called Union Mercy earlier this morning and spoke to one of the nurses. She said they're going to keep her there for another day or so. She had a lot of dope in her system, but she'll be okay eventually."

Dugan nodded. "Good," he said. "Must've been a hell of a scare."

Gallagher lit his pipe. "I'd like to know how she even got to the hospital in the first place," he said, tossing his dead match into an ashtray on his desk.

"That's a good question," said Dugan. "It's part of a much bigger story that we're still trying to piece together."

"I've read the papers," said Gallagher.

"There's plenty we didn't tell the papers."

Gallagher glanced at Hunter and then back at Dugan. "We're not the papers."

"Well," said Dugan, "if your question is about Miss Carlyle, I have a security guard at the hospital telling me the, uh, the guy in the mask brought her in."

Gallagher looked back at him, his face inert. "The guy in the mask," he said.

"Yeah. The guard says he just walked into the emergency room with her in his arms and put her on a gurney."

"Nobody tried to stop him?"

"The guard said he tried to. Said he even fired a couple shots, but the guy got away. Said he never saw a guy move like this guy did."

"Anybody get a good look?" said Gallagher.

"The guard, an orderly and a couple others," said Dugan. "They all said pretty much the same thing. Leather mask and dark goggles.

Leather jacket. They said he was in and out too fast to notice much else. And they were on emergency power at the time, so the lighting in the building wasn't as good as it usually is."

Dugan flipped a page in his notebook. "The orderly did give us a description of the vehicle he drove away in," he said. "And get this. It was a delivery truck."

"Huh," said Gallagher. "Not your typical getaway vehicle."

"No, but it matches the description of the vehicle that made off with the goods from Pharaoh Chemical the other day. And early this morning, at about four a.m., we found a truck matching that description parked just a couple buildings away from the Harper Warehouse."

Gallagher's lips frowned around the stem of his pipe, and his brow furrowed at the disjointed puzzle. He blew a puff of smoke but said nothing.

"What about Bentley?" said Hunter. "How's he doing?"

"He's still at Union Mercy, too. Taggert's with him right now. Bentley's status sounds a lot like Miss Carlyle's. They're keeping him there for observation for a day or two, but he still insisted on getting a full report from the chief about what happened last night."

"Bentley needs to take a vacation," Gallagher muttered.

"He doing okay?" said Hunter.

"He has a gash on his head and a mild concussion." Dugan shrugged and gestured at the small bandage covering what was left of the wound on his own temple. "A lot of that going around, I guess. But other than that, they're saying he'll be okay."

"How'd he get the gash?" said Gallagher.

"Not sure. It was the first thing I noticed when we came through the entrance to City Hall. He couldn't tell us much at the time, he was barely conscious. And he doesn't remember much now."

"Who took out the bombs in all the doors?" said Hunter.

"You really need to ask? It was just a minute or two before midnight when the doors flew open and somebody inside the lobby gave the signal that Bentley was inside and it was okay to come in. A minute later, a few of our boys were on the roof, chasing the mask. They almost cornered him at the ledge, but he swung over the alley by riding across the power lines between City Hall and the court house."

Gallagher shook his head. "So you think he was the one who

defused the bombs at the building entrances?"

Dugan shrugged. "He may have been," he said. "And if he was, much as I hate to admit it, he may have defused the bombs in more than just one building."

Gallagher took a puff. His brow furrowed. "How do you mean?"

"We found bits and pieces of radio transmitting equipment in Bentley's office," said Dugan. "Whatever it was, it had been smashed all to hell. One of our detectives, our guy named Jarrett, got a look at the mess and remembered something Diamond said in his broadcast—something about City Hall being just the beginning of more fireworks. So he suggested that the transmitter might have been part of a bigger system."

"You mean something that might set off bombs elsewhere?" said Gallagher.

"Right. So we've spent the past several hours doing a full sweep of every other public building in a five-mile radius of City Hall."

"And?" Gallagher prompted.

"So far, we've found bombs in seven other buildings. All the bombs were hidden in the walls or unused spaces. All of them were rigged with similar transmitting devices."

The DA's eyes went wide. "Good Lord," he muttered.

"And the sweep isn't finished yet."

"So whoever the mask is," said Hunter, "if he kept City Hall from blowing up—and possibly several other buildings from a similar scenario—we can assume that he wasn't in with Diamond, right?"

"But he was driving a truck that may have been the same as the one Diamond's crew used in the Pharaoh heist," said Dugan.

"What about Diamond's crew," said Hunter, attempting to redirect the conversation.

"We rounded up a couple last night," said Dugan. "Guy named John Kowalski was in the service entrance on the south end of Union Tower. I wasn't there when the officers found him, but they said he'd been roughed up pretty good."

Gallagher frowned. "Roughed up by whom?"

"Kowalski says it was the guy in the mask."

Gallagher shook his head. "Jesus," he said. "If half these stories are true, that guy was everywhere last night."

"We have Kowalski in custody right now," said Dugan. "He seems to have a lot he wants to get off his chest this morning. He may be looking for leniency, but I almost get the idea he's just relieved to be rid of Diamond."

"How do you figure?" said Hunter.

"He was singing like a canary the minute we collared him. The arresting officer said he felt like a priest in the confessional. The sun wasn't even up yet and he was already confirming Jarrett's theory about the bombs in the other buildings."

Dugan paused for a moment, his tired face momentarily cracking a mild grin. "I'm starting to think maybe Kowalski was sampling some of Sun Lu's dope himself."

"How do you mean?" said Gallagher.

"Well, one part of his story is especially crazy."

"What part?" said the DA.

"He…" Dugan's voice broke into a small chuckle as he pointed a thumb in Hunter's direction. "He's saying he thinks the assistant DA here could be the masked man."

Hunter's brow furrowed. "What!"

Gallagher pulled the pipe from his teeth and guffawed loudly through a thin cloud of smoke.

"The guy doesn't even know me," said Hunter.

"How about it, Jack?" said Gallagher, catching his breath after the big laugh. "Are you pursuing a career in vigilante justice?"

Hunter shrugged. "Well, you know, I hear the pay's good," he said. "Times are hard. I could use the extra money." He turned to Dugan. "Who else?"

Dugan glanced at his notes. "There was a parking garage attendant in the same service entrance where we found Kowalski," he said. "Guy named Huffman. He's at Union Mercy with a bullet wound in his shoulder."

"Place is getting crowded," said Gallagher.

"No kidding," said Dugan. "Kowalski says Huffman was in on Diamond's operation."

"I suppose you're going to tell me this masked man shot Huffman?" said Gallagher.

"Not exactly, no," said Dugan. "Huffman says it was actually a stray slug from Kowalski's gun. Said he got hit when he was scuffling with the masked man."

Gallagher's face twisted in frustration. "Jesus," he said. "Who the hell is this guy?"

"Who else, Mike?" said Hunter.

"Well, when our boys picked up Kowalski, he told them there were some up guys on the thirtieth floor. Four of our guys put Kowalski and Huffman in the back of a car and stayed with them in the garage. The rest went up."

"And?" Gallagher prompted.

"Well, they found Oliver Pruett in the hallway, near the elevators. Slumped on the floor, up against the wall, with a bullet in his chest. And quite dead."

Gallagher shook his head. "Guy was right under our noses the whole time."

"Kowalski says Pruett had been Diamond's explosives expert ever since the beginning," said Dugan. "I'm talking about the *very* beginning, back when he was head of Pharaoh Chemical fourteen or fifteen years ago."

"We started thinking Reynolds was the one leaking information to Diamond," said Hunter. "And he probably was. And it's obvious now that he was pulling strings from the bench. But Pruett was the main connection. Every meeting we had with him in the room—every discussion about raids and strategy—all of it went back to Diamond."

"There were a few others in that office on the thirtieth floor," said Dugan, his voice turning grim. He flipped to a new page in his notebook. "Mitch Fallon. Kowalski says Fallon was at the Watt Building on the night of the fire, but he took off out the back when we were coming through the front door."

"This Fallon—he giving you any information?" said Gallagher.

"No. He's dead. Took a bullet in the stomach."

"You said 'a few others' on the thirtieth floor," said Hunter. "How many others besides Fallon?"

"Two. And they won't be telling us much either, for the same reason as Fallon. One was Willis Gray. He was the operations engineer at WRUC, but he apparently had a hell of a side job. Kowalski says Gray was responsible for wiring up all the explosives that Pruett made for Diamond's various operations."

Gallagher drew on his pipe. "Gray's dead?"

Dugan nodded. "Bullet to the head," he said. "One of my detectives dug a few slugs out of the walls too, so at some point there must've been a lot of bullets flying in that room."

"And the other?" said Hunter.

"Louis Simone," said Dugan. "Diamond's second in command, what mob types like to call the underboss. We found him on the floor in the corner of the room with a bullet in his forehead."

Dugan rubbed his chin. "Kowalski can't tell us anything about Fallon and Gray," he said. "Says those two must've been shot after he left the room and went down to the garage. But he says he did see Diamond shoot Simone. Apparently he went into a rage over something that happened—or didn't happen—at the Harper Warehouse and he shot Simone at point-blank range in the head."

"What did happen in the River District?" said Gallagher. "The stories about that are sketchy."

Dugan sighed. "Here's what we know. A couple of Diamond's men, including Simone, came into the office at the police department to grab the ledger. While they were at it, they grabbed Miss Carlyle, too. It wasn't hard, because they had Pruett helping them from the inside. They put her out with chloroform and took her to the Harper Warehouse."

"And this was right around the time they went into Union Power right next door with guns," said Gallagher.

"Right," said Dugan. "They rounded up the overnight crew at the power plant and locked them into a storage room. Gray showed Diamond's crew how to tap into a substantial amount of electric power to run the radio broadcast from the warehouse."

"And then they cut the power to the whole city right after the broadcast," said Hunter, remembering the lights going out up and down every street in the Merchant District the night before as he rocketed his car back to the Republic Building.

"Right," said Dugan. "Gray says the plan was to blow up the warehouse after the power went out, but…" He hesitated momentarily. "This is one of the parts we're trying to keep out of the papers."

"What?" said Gallagher.

"Kowalski says the mask showed up, so they strapped the bomb onto him, figuring they'd get rid of him, Miss Carlyle and any other evidence in the warehouse. He says it was supposed to be the first part of what Diamond called 'the big show.'"

Gallagher shook his head. "Crazy son of a bitch."

"Crazy but dead," Hunter muttered.

"But obviously this...this masked guy got free," said Gallagher.

"Obviously, because he showed up at City Hall just before midnight, and then he tracked Diamond back to Union Tower." Dugan shook his head, apparently still trying to come to terms with some of the more outrageous aspects of the story. "We had two cops stationed in front of the tower. They said they saw Diamond and this guy fall out of a high window—I mean a very high window—and crash through the awnings near the ground level. We know it was the thirtieth floor, because the window up there is broken. And it so happens that the office space for Pruett's family business in cleaning supplies is on the thirtieth floor."

Dugan paused for a moment, then started to say more, but exasperation appeared to get the best of him.

Gallagher took a draw on his pipe. "You could use some rest, Mike," he said. "There's time to sort this out."

Dugan seemed to ignore the suggestion. "There are a couple other loose ends we're following up on. There's an attorney by the name of Vincent Marshall. Keeps a low profile here in town, but apparently he's been a close friend of Diamond since childhood. We think he may be connected to all this—sort of a shadow figure working in an advisory capacity to Diamond—but he's nowhere to be found this morning. His offices are locked up and we're—"

The intercom on Gallagher's desk buzzed.

"Yes?" said Gallagher.

A tinny female voice came through the box on the desk: "I'm sorry to interrupt, Mr. Gallagher..."

"It's alright, Jenny. What is it?"

"I have a call from the police department. It's for Lieutenant Dugan."

Gallagher frowned at the intercom. All three men in the room glanced at each other.

"Go ahead and put it through, Jenny," said Gallagher.

Dugan rose from his chair as the phone rang. He stepped closer to the desk and picked up the call.

"This is Dugan."

For the next minute, the detective was mostly silent, save for a few short responses to whatever he was hearing on the other end of the line:

"What time?...Uh-huh...Any trouble?...Livingston still there?"

One final pause. "Alright," he said finally. "I'm leaving here shortly. I can be there in about a half-hour."

Dugan cradled the headpiece and sighed. He stared at the far wall for a moment without saying a word. Hunter felt the hair on his neck stand up.

"What is it?" said Gallagher.

"We sent two cars to Chinatown an hour ago to pick up Sun Lu and bring him in."

"Trouble?" said Hunter.

"Not anymore," said Dugan. "He's dead."

Hunter and Gallagher didn't speak.

"Suicide," said Dugan. "They found him in his bed, with a tea set on the night stand. Livingston, the medical examiner, took a sample from the bottom of the tea cup. Says he has to run some tests, but he's pretty sure it's laced with cyanide."

The detective tucked his notebook inside his jacket and put his hat on. "Gentlemen, we'll have to resume this conversation at a later time," he said. "As you can see, there are pieces of the story that we're still putting together."

Hunter held up a hand. "Mike, before you go," he said. "What about the feds?"

"Oh, they're around," said Dugan. "They sent a couple field agents last night, not long after we found Reynolds' body, and then they sent a few more when the lights went out. They're asking a lot of questions this morning. They want to know what we have on Diamond, what's left of his crew, Pruett, the Chinese, the whole thing."

"They asking about the mask?" said Hunter.

"Yeah. Taggert's trying to keep them at a distance, but they like to take charge, so I'm not sure how much longer we can do that. If I were either one of you, I'd be ready. They may want to come and talk to you about all this at some point."

The detective hesitated before walking out, his eyes clouded by fatigue and his expression distracted. Gallagher took his pipe from between his teeth and looked up at him.

"Who do you think he is, Mike?" said the DA.

Dugan took in a deep breath and let it out slowly. "I don't know," he said, shaking his head. His tired eyes narrowed as he turned to look out the large window on the south wall of Gallagher's office, the one that looked down at Liberty Avenue and the traffic that swept across it in every direction. "But if we ever see him or hear about him after this, we're going to get him."

◆　◆　◆　◆

The nurse gave him five minutes and no more.

Hunter tapped quietly on the door and stepped into the room. Betty lay in the bed with her eyes closed and her face turned toward the window. Hunter looked at her for a long moment. He was about to turn and walk out when her eyes opened.

She turned her head in his direction and smiled. "Jack," she said.

"Sorry. I didn't mean to wake you."

"Oh, you didn't, really. I was just resting my eyes for a…oh, those are beautiful!"

"What? Oh, these." Hunter held up the flowers so she could see them better. "We all pitched in at the office. The nurse said she'd bring a vase."

"That's so nice. They're lovely."

"Glad you like them."

"I, on the other hand, must look like—"

Hunter shook his head. "No," he said. "You look fine."

She smiled a little and averted her eyes. "Thank you."

"Are you feeling okay?"

"Yes. Just tired. They told me I'd be tired for a couple days. Maybe some headaches. But they said I'll be okay after that."

Hunter nodded. "That's good," he said. He paused for a moment, struggling for the right words. "Listen, Betty, I'm sorry you had to go through such an awful thing. We had no idea Pruett—"

"It's okay, Jack. It was frightening, but I'm okay now. And Diamond—"

"Diamond's gone. He's finished."

"The nurses told me what happened. I guess I missed most of it. But I remember…"

Hunter looked at her.

"It's all very hazy, but I remember a face. Or part of a face, like it was…covered. But there were these big black eyes."

"Huh," said Hunter.

"Anyway, whoever it was—or whatever it was—maybe I should have been afraid, but somehow I wasn't."

"The doctors said there was a lot of chloroform in your system. There's no telling what kinds of tricks your mind was playing."

She looked away and stared at the ceiling for a moment. "Maybe," she said.

From out in the hallway came the quiet murmur of doctors and nurses and other medical professionals going about their business.

Betty turned to face Hunter. "I heard Steve Bentley was hurt."

"He'll be alright." Hunter tilted his head toward the door. "He's actually right down the hall. Got a good bang on the head, but he'll be okay." His mouth turned into a lopsided grin. "Heck, he had Sam Taggert in his room this morning, giving him a full report."

Right on schedule, the nurse stepped into the room with a vase and told Hunter his time was up.

Hunter nodded to the nurse and turned back to Betty. "Well," he said, "I guess I'll be heading back. You be sure to get some rest."

"Everyone's okay at the office? Tell the girls I'll be—"

"Everybody's fine, Betty," said Hunter. "Everyone in town is okay."

◆ ◆ ◆ ◆

Several hours later, as the sun dipped low in the western sky, Hunter parked his car on the side of the quiet road that wound through Brightview Cemetery. He stepped out of the car and scanned the rolling hills peppered with headstones of every shape, size and sentiment. He flexed his shoulders and took in a deep breath of air that hinted of fresh grass and honeysuckle.

No dark clouds this time. No ominous wind or gathering storm.

For the first time in nearly fifteen years, the place felt peaceful.

He made his way up a small hill, past a series of stones etched with names he knew by heart, and came to a stop in the same familiar place.

LT. JAMES M. "JIMMY" HUNTER

1880 - 1922

LOVING HUSBAND AND FATHER

DEVOTED PUBLIC SERVANT

PROTECTOR OF THE CITY IN THE HOUR OF DARKNESS

There's only so much an assistant DA can do.

He took the folded newspaper from under his arm—the same one he'd taken from the diner several hours earlier—and crouched low. He unfolded the paper to the front page and laid it face-up in the grass just next to the stone.

But a guy like that could do more.

Hunter rose and squared his shoulders, his eyes shifting back and forth between the engraving on the stone and the newspaper headline that shouted to the sky.

"The Midnight Guardian," he said finally, his voice reaching across the void to a place that was not of this world but as real as the ground under his feet.

Think he'll be back?

Time would tell.

THE END

ABOUT THE AUTHOR

John Bruening has been a professional writer since the 1980s in a range of disciplines that include journalism, editing and publishing, marketing, advertising and corporate communications. For as long as he can remember, he's been a fan of every form of storytelling imaginable: fiction, film, theater, comics, old-time radio drama and more. He likes his heroes bigger than life and his villains dastardly, which is precisely why he's written his first novel in the classic pulp fiction style. He lives in a suburb of Cleveland, Ohio, with his wife and two teenage children.

COME ONE, COME ALL!

GET YOUR STRANGE ON!

From the minds of comics' most gonzo Golden Age creator and modern adventure fiction's most talented writers come ten tales of scintillating strangeness!

From 1939 to 1941, writer-artist Fletcher Hanks toiled in obscurity to create comic book characters who often acted as gods among men, raining cruel justice down upon evildoers in luxuriant measure and exotic grotesquery. These characters get the full treatment by a cadre of modern-day writers playing in the wild and wonderful Fletcher Hanks handbook.

Something Strange is Going On! offers brand-new tales of Stardust, Fantomah, Nabu the Jungle Wizard, Moe M. Downe, Whirlwind Carter, and Big Red McLane, among others. In breathtaking pulpy prose, the stories in this volume cover many genres: science fiction, horror, fantasy, spy thriller, sports, and the great outdoors.

Something Strange is Going On! is your portal to the weird, the wild, the insane universe of Fletcher Hanks.